ANGEL UNSEEN

J BREE

Angel Unseen
A Mounts Bay Saga Novel

Angel Unseen/J Bree – 1st ed.
ISBN-9798691860379

Unseen MC - Coldstone Original Charter

Rogan Callaghan - Unseen MC founding President (deceased)

Kingston 'King' Callaghan - President & Rogan's son

Memphis 'Hawk' Callaghan - Vice President & Rogan's son

Reece 'Hellion' Callaghan - Enforcer & Rogan's son

Thomas 'Tomi' Callaghan - Hawk & Keely's son

Ruin 'Rue' Callaghan - King's son

Reece 'Speck' Callaghan - Prospect & Hellion's son

Keely Callaghan - Hawk's wife

Katrina 'Trink' Callaghan - Hawk & Keely's daughter

Lawson Frazier - Harbin's son

Lyndon Frazier - Harbin's son

Briar 'Thorn' Johnson - Poe's brother/guardian

Alby 'Pops' Johnson - Thorn's maternal grandfather

Posey 'Poe' Graves - Trink's best friend

Prologue

The Callaghan curse.

Sounds like some old fucking fairytale, nothing that a man in one of the most powerful MCs in the country would have to deal with but there's never been a doubt in my mind that someday I'd be 'struck. My grandfather and his brothers built this MC from the ground up, started in the gun trade, and opened up a pipeline through the South until the Unseen became a fucking legend.

Didn't stop them all from losing their heads to women that only ever fucking lost them everything.

Cuntstruck.

Infatuated with the pussy attached to an even bigger cunt, leads to nothing but fucking trouble. They didn't even know there was another option there until my pops met my mom and felt the same fucking lightning bolt from the heavens and knew he was lovestruck.

The only Callaghan to not lose everything to a cunt, he's proof that maybe you can get lucky.

One out of eight aren't great odds though.

I've never fucking wanted to be 'struck. Not once.

I've watched my cousin follow his little flower child around, desperate for her to grow the hell up and be his, the whole time I've watched and I've hated the thought of it happening to me.

Strippers and biker sluts are all I fucking need.

And all is right in the world.

Until it's not.

Three

Chapter One

Angel

Coldstone, Mississippi.

Not exactly the type of place I thought I'd be running away to but the last six months in the city were fucking hard. Like, terrifying and cold and hungry at night types of hard. My trauma means finding a job is fucking impossible because everywhere I try people can't stop touching me.

I'm like a fucking magnet or something.

They just can't stop.

I can hide my shit from people just so long as they don't try to grab me or hug me or something. As long as they keep their distance, I'm good.

They never keep their fucking distance.

So now, I'm in this tiny rural town. The population size alone should be something keeping me the hell away from it, but Coldstone is famous for one thing. The Unseen MC was started here, the original charter still has a compound here and owns a helluva lot of businesses here and in the surrounding towns.

The strip club they own is one of the best in the country.

Men drive in from fucking everywhere to see the girls who dance and they're known for taking care of their assets. I'm sure half the stories are total bullshit, I mean there's no way they got into a shootout with the local cops and skinned one of them alive without the whole club being shut down, but even if some of the rumors are true then this is the place for me.

Years of dance classes have brought me here to this moment but I'm not sure my dad would be thrilled knowing what the tuition he'd paid for was getting me now.

There's a lot of shit about my life after his death he wouldn't be too fucking happy with.

I can't think about any of it.

I took my last real shower last night right before I bailed on the shitty, crackhead hotel. I feel like the whole country is full of them now, full of desperate people who are looking for their next high and really… I don't blame them. That's the real reason I stay the hell away from even the slightest high, too aware that I'd slip so far and fast into that kind of oblivion to get away from the demons in my head.

I've wanted an escape for as long as I can remember.

The town is small enough that I find the strip club without even really trying.

The Boulevard.

I park up and ignore the sputtering sort of sound the old Chevy makes. If I knew anything about cars I might be worried but I don't have money for anything maintenance related. Fuck, I'm almost out of money for fuel and food, only a couple of hundred dollar bills left that I stash in my bra at all times so I know where they are. Two hundred dollars isn't going to get me far and the outfit I bought last night on the way over here is still stinging me but if I'm really going to dance then… I gotta fucking look the part.

I lock the Chevy and hitch my bag up on my shoulder a little higher. Deep breath, gotta make this shit happen now. This is a do or die situation, Angel. Do or fucking die. I look up at the building, painted black and freaking huge, but it's not exactly what I was expecting. I step up to the door and the half look I get inside just confirms it.

The Boulevard is really nice.

Clean and neat, it looks like a super exclusive sex club or something, nothing sleazy or shady about it at all. The bouncer is already at the door and although he's freaking huge he's also clean-cut and respectful as he looks over my ID. Not once does he make a dirty comment or check me out, just looks over my license and hands it back, careful not to touch me.

Shit, this place might actually work.

"You here for a job?"

I force a smile on my face and nod. "I heard you're looking

for girls."

He nods and keeps his eyes off of me. "Diamond takes care of the hiring and firing, she's in the back. Speck can take you, he's helping out here today."

Speck.

That's a weird name but I don't mention it at all, I just nod and thank him quietly while he talks into an earpiece. It's so… formal and official. Nothing like what I expect from a biker-owned club, even with the rumors of this place.

The bouncer, his name tag says Mike, shows me to a booth and leaves a sealed bottle of water with me to drink. I wait until he's gone before I check the seal, run my fingers over the whole thing to make sure it hasn't been tampered with in some other way, but I don't find anything.

I don't drink it.

I'm too cautious, too scared about even being here to risk it, but I relax just enough into the plush cushions of the booth that I don't feel as though I'm going to vomit on my own feet.

It's already busy here, even so early in the night. Men are everywhere but they're respectful of the women, even while they're having lap dances they don't attempt to touch the women or make any terrible comments. There's no way I want to be getting that close but it's another mark in the 'yes' column for me. The longer I'm here the more I'm finding that this place might be right for me. I keep waiting to find some sign to say there's people trafficking or drug dealing going on, but the longer I sit in the booth the more comfortable I get.

"Hey, gorgeous! You must be from outta town because I'd remember that face if I'd seen it before."

I freeze and glance up to find a guy leaning against the booth table. He's grinning down at me and he has dimples. Honest to God dimples. The leather vest over his shoulders that's covered in grinning skulls and patches looks entirely out of place with his freaking dimples. He leans down to hold out a hand for me and though I'm sure he's cute enough to other people, I cringe away from him a little before I can stop myself.

His eyes take it in but the smile barely falters on his face. "It's all good, gorgeous, I'm just trying to talk to ya. We don't let girls dance here unless we like 'em."

Oh God.

There it is.

There's the warning sign, the bikers try out the girls before they dance because this guy is wearing one of those leather vests so there's no mistaking he's in the MC.

"I'm probably not cut out for this… I'm not exactly likable," I mumble and stand up.

He laughs at me and shrugs. "That face is definitely likable. What's your name?"

It's still weird to use the new one I've chosen, so I roll it around on my tongue to taste it. "Angel. Angel Valetti."

He motions for me to follow him and this time he doesn't try to touch me at all, just waits until he's sure I'm close behind him before walking me across the club and out behind the bar. There's a lot of back rooms here, a locker room and a full set of showers. There aren't any bedrooms that I can see so there's another positive. I don't wanna find myself being pimped out, that's for sure. I just wanna dance.

We pass some other girls, all of them topless and giggling at him as they pass him. He grins at them but when they move past us both he turns his body just a little like he's shielding me from their view.

It feels protective.

I don't know what to do with that.

"Diamond will check you out, make you dance for her to see if you got the goods. Did you bring something to dance in? 'Cause I mean, those shorts are hot and all but you got something a little smaller?"

I scoff at him without meaning to and slap a hand over my mouth. Jesus. Just because he looks like some hot, flirty guy, one I would've crushed after back before my life went to hell, he's still a freaking biker.

He stops outside a door and leans against the wall there. "Look. You're hot but you gotta be able to dance. Can you do that?"

I hitch the bag back up on my shoulder a little higher. "Yeah. I can dance better than the girls you got out there now."

He quirks an eyebrow. "Is that right? Well… can't wait for the show. I'm guessing you don't wanna grind on anyone though?"

My stomach drops. "I just plain won't. If it's a requirement

I'll find another club to dance at, pure and simple."

He looks at me and then glances over his shoulder but when I look behind him there's nothing there. Nothing I can see anyway.

"Tell Diamond I'm backing you."

I blow out a breath and straighten up. "Doesn't that mean I've got the job? Don't… doesn't your club own this place?"

He scrubs a hand through his dirty blond hair and out come those dimples again. "The MC owns it yeah but I'm only a prospect. I get a little more leeway around here though, being a Callaghan so I'll throw that into the ring for you. Diamond has a thing for bagging herself an Original. She's been shit outta luck so far."

None of the words coming out of his mouth make a huge amount of sense to me but all that matters is that he's open to helping me out. "Thanks. I appreciate it."

He chuckles and knocks on the door. "I'm doing it because I wanna see your ass on the stage so you probably shouldn't thank me. It's purely selfish."

I work freaking hard at keeping the flinch in, at not cringing away from him hard but his eyes are intense on my face. I wait for him to call me out on it but he doesn't say a word, just opens the door and pokes his head in.

"Gotta new girl for you. She has my vote so don't be an ass about it."

I swallow and force my back a little straighter. Even if I'm not feeling all that sunshine and rainbows about doing this… it's kind of my only option.

Strip or starve.

Starve or go home and honestly, I'd rather fucking starve than ever go back to the hell I left.

"Well, get her ass in here then. I've got paperwork comin' outta my ass today. Fucking taxes due and suppliers wanting payment for shit they didn't even send to us yet… fucking bullshit."

Her voice is a little rough, but when I step past Speck and get an eyeful of her I want the ground to just open up and swallow me.

She's naked.

She's naked and tattooed and there's a cigarette hanging

out of her mouth as she shuffles papers and sits there with a calculator. It's fucking weird as all hell but I keep my face blank.

Well, as blank as I can get it.

"I'm between bartending shifts so excuse my tits. Honestly, if they're worrying you then this place ain't for you."

I duck down onto the seat. "I'm not worried. I was just caught off guard. I've seen a lot of accountants in my time and none of them had a rack like yours."

She scoffs at my joke but the frown eases off a little. "I'm no fucking accountant, sugar, no way I'd die that slow death. I'm just handy with paperwork and been around long enough to know the score. You wanna dance here? You're pretty enough. Might make a little money."

I nod and slide my bag to the ground at my feet, rummaging around until I find my ID. "I can start tonight. Or anytime really."

She shrugs. "Hold your horses, a pretty face ain't all you need. Can you dance? Swing on a pole, ride a man's cock so good he'll throw money around this place like he don't care his rent is due?"

I swallow. "I can dance. I won't do lap dances or let anyone touch me though. That's my line, but I can get on a stage and have a man forgetting he's a man of God."

She huffs and leans back in the seat, linking her hands over her pierced belly button like this is all business as usual. "I don't take on girls who don't give men extra. Dancers are just foreplay, lap dances and extra work on the side is where the green is really made here."

She looks over me again and I try not to squirm. I need to be nothing but confident, let that shit ooze out of my pores at her until she believes what I'm saying.

I was so careful in how I dressed myself for the interview. A low cut shirt, tiny jean shorts, and the biggest heels I could find on short notice. It's not enough for her, she doesn't seem impressed.

It's fine.

The second I get on stage I can change her mind.

"You ever stripped before? You look… fresh. We don't have time to be training newbies."

I clear my throat. "I haven't but I won't need training. I have routines already and I have what it takes. I won't get in anyone's way, I'll always be here on time, and I know how to keep my mouth shut. I'll be a great addition, even without the extra duties."

I force confidence into my voice, confidence I definitely don't have. I know I can dance and the routines are sexy, something any club would want to have, I'm just not sure I can do it without puking my guts up in terror and shame.

I guess we'll see.

My hands shake as I change into the thong and the pasties.

The laws here mean I have to keep those on while I'm dancing and that's another reason this place is the right fit for me. I can't fuck this up, not even a fucking little. I triple check the mirror before I step out of the locker room and find Speck waiting for me.

His eyes do a full sweep of my body and then he starts muttering under his breath to himself.

I pitch my voice low so he doesn't hear the nerves as I ask him, "What? Do I not look like the other girls?"

He shakes his head and then motions for me to follow him. "You look a whole lot fucking better. If Diamond doesn't hire you on the fucking spot I'm calling Tomi down here to get an eyeful of you. He'd put you on the books in a fucking heartbeat."

Tomi.

That's a weird sort of biker name.

"Does he control what happens around here?"

He walks me down the hall and over to the bar. Thankfully we don't pass anyone and I get an extra minute to get my head straight.

"He's patched in already and takes care of this place. Well, him and Rue but Rue would rather stick a fucking fork in his eyeballs then walk his ass in here. Coupla the girls are after him, makes it hard to come here without being fucking mauled."

We stop at the bar to finish watching one of the other girls finish her dance. She's really good at grinding and twirling around but she's not a dancer. You can tell by the way she holds herself and that she's just a little unsure on the platform stilettos covered in glitter and feathers.

My routine is going to wipe the floor with her.

Her ass is better than mine though.

"Is she one of them? I can't imagine a guy saying no to her… not unless she's an asshole."

Speck grins and leans against the wall. "Is that your thing? You're into girls and don't want men getting close to you?"

Fuck.

Maybe I should say yes just to have that extra layer of security, but that feels so fucking wrong. "I'm just not interested. I want to dance, put food on my table, and do it all without some asshole trying to get something I don't wanna give him."

He nods and turns his attention back to the stage. "Rue doesn't fuck strippers. Or biker bitches. If he comes down here you should just stay clear of him, he's not the type. Fuck Tomi instead. He's more than happy to try out the goods."

Right.

So stay the fuck away from Tomi, got it.

"Like I said, I'm not interested."

Speck shrugs like it doesn't bother him either way, but then he pauses. "Whatever money the guys throw at you, leave it on the stage. Leave it for Diamond for tonight so she signs you on. Give her this one dance so she gives you a regular gig."

I nod and let out a breath. If he thinks I can do this then I guess I'm fucking doing it. Hell, if Diamond still says no maybe he could call this Tomi guy and get me on the roster.

The music stops and Speck motions me forward again, stalking over to where Diamond is waiting at a table with a couple of the patrons, all of them laughing and drinking. There's a private door to get on and off the stage so I'm not sure why exactly we're out here on the floor with all of the guys watching me walk around but there's a whole lot of interest in my tits and ass as I do walk. Speck sees it all too, walking a little slower so I'm closer to his body and I wish the music were a little quieter so I could thank him.

I've known him for less than an hour and he's already shown me more respect than any other man has since my dad died.

"Well, well. I guess you have the right sort of body for this but I don't see how the hell a dance is going to change my mind," Diamond says as she looks me over, her eyes a little shuttered even in the dark.

She really doesn't like me.

I shrug. "I'm a woman of action so I'll get up there and show you exactly how I'm going to earn the cash."

A couple of guys around us start chuckling and murmuring to each other, and the eagerness is clear in their tones.

Speck takes a seat with Diamond and I walk over to the stairs by myself. The guys at the table are all wearing patches as well, but I can see the difference in them now. They're all members and not prospective like Speck. They have more of a vote here than he does.

I need to impress them all.

The Nasty Song by Lil Ru starts playing as I walk over to the pole, jeering and whistling starting up as the crowd sees fresh meat up here. I take a breath, forget what the hell I'm wearing, and then I let the song take me over.

It's like riding a damn bike.

Muscle memory takes over and my body moves with the music, the heels are nothing to me after near-on fifteen years of dance classes and daily training. I did ballet, jazz, tap, and aerial. The pole is a little different to what I'm used to but the hour class I took last week in preparation was all I really needed to get the technique down and when I move from a simple swing into a Jade Split the whistling stops.

I'm pretty sure the breathing in the room stops too.

There isn't a man alive who doesn't appreciate a woman who can bend, my dance instructor once told me that and I was so fucking confused at the time but I'm old enough to get it now. Every man out there in the crowd is thinking all about the positions they could bend me into, all of the ways they could force their cocks into me, and although it fucking terrifies me for once I'm fucking glad for it.

The money starts to rain down onto the stage.

As I move into a new position I see guys walking away from other stages, all of them drawn to me like a fucking magnet, and I know I'm in.

I have to be.

When the song finally stops I walk out the private door and wait there for a minute until Speck turns the corner.

"Fuck. I don't think I've ever been so fucking pissed off to not be someone's type."

I startle. "I'm sorry, what?"

He grins and shrugs. "You don't want any of what I'm selling and after that dance, I'm fucking heartbroken about it. A girl who can do that shit with her legs? Fuck me. Seriously. You get an itch you need scratched, you call me."

I force a smile and shrug. "I'll keep it in mind."

Diamond walks around the corner, stacks of bills in her hands, and she plucks a single crisp hundred dollar bill out to hand over to me. "We'll see you tomorrow. Wear something white, it's dirty angel night. Guess you'll fit right in."

Chapter Two

Tomi

Rotting corpses.

Is there any smell on the fucking planet worse? Probably not and even with the mask over my nose and mouth I feel like that stink is coating my damn throat.

"We left this shit too long. Shoulda been out here last week to move 'em," Vic says, the shovel in his hands already coated in rotting flesh and bone shards.

"No shit, asshole. Maybe if you could keep your fucking temper we wouldn't be moving bodies in the stinking hot Missi-fucking-ssippi nights," Rue snarls, already over the entire fucking thing.

I get it.

I am too. I'm over dealing with hot-headed assholes who joined the Unseen to act rough and tough when really they're pathetic fucking cry-babies over their egos.

All of it is bullshit.

"Fucking Serpents come around here and we kill them. Simple as that, if they roll into Coldstone they're asking for bullets," Vic snaps again, and Rue drops the shovel in his hand.

Great.

Here we fucking go.

I take a step towards him and Vic looks relieved for about a half second, right before he realizes I ain't stopping the fight.

I'm joining it.

Cole and Axe both ignore us all, heads down and shovels moving like there isn't about to be a beat down, but I don't expect anything less from them. They know the score.

Rue and I are Callaghans.

The Unseen is ours for the taking, only a matter of time before the mantle is passed on to us and we rule it. Rue's already shown his hand, ruthless and cutthroat. He's never been one to fuck around and if there's a body to be buried he's showing up to get it done.

I'm the wild card.

No one expected a Callaghan to go off to college and get a computer science degree. They expected my homecoming even less. I was behind my cousin in patching in but only because I knew our club needed some fucking tech support and I was the only one with the brain for it.

I didn't join this club, I was born into it. I've always thought about the club first, myself second and that's why assholes like Vic piss me off.

Thinks with his dick and his ego.

It's gonna get him killed and I'll be god-fucking-damned if I let him take the club down with him. Shit like this starts wars.

Wars get good men cold and six feet under.

Rue dives at Vic the second his eyes move over to me, the split second of distraction enough to get the man on the ground. Cole swears under his breath but doesn't stop his work, digging and scooping up parts of dead Serpent to slop into the barrel we're filling up. I keep my hand by my gun, ready to draw it if Vic does something stupid.

He always fucking does.

Rue beats the fuck outta him.

He's a scrappy sort of fighter, dirty and fucking brutal, like he'll do whatever the fuck it takes to win. I fight the same way because who the fuck cares about fair? This is a man's world, ain't nothing fair about it.

The crunching of boots has Rue pausing, his fist in the air and Vic choking on blood underneath him as we wait for who the fuck is out here to disturb us while we're getting shit done.

King and Hellion stalk into the clearing.

I let out a breath but the thunderous look on my uncles' faces don't exactly spell out good fucking news for us. Rue punches Vic one last time and then stands up, shoving the asshole onto the ground again when he tries to stand up as well.

Hellion shakes his head at me with a warning look but I shrug back at him. Nothing about what's happening here is a regret for me. Not a damn thing.

"What exactly is happening here?"

Rue is panting too much to speak and it's probably best if he keeps his mouth shut so I answer for him. "We're cleaning up after Vic."

King stares at us all like we're unruly children and I can feel Rue's hackles rising. I don't even have to look at him, I can feel that shit in my bones.

"Why exactly is he bleeding, Rue?"

Fuck.

Rue stares down at him and there's nothing really human left in his eyes. "Because he ran his mouth. Needs to learn a fucking lesson about who the fuck he's talking to."

King stares at his son for a second and I can see the disaster starting there before he even speaks. "Vic's been a member for longer than you've been alive, Rue. Simple as that, it's a pecking order thing."

Oh bad move.

Bad, bad move.

King has been gone for too long. Doesn't know what shit went down while he was in prison, doesn't know all of the ways his son has thrown down for the club. Doesn't know what rules have slipped and let the brothers become too fucking relaxed about shit.

Vic is one of the worst.

"He fucked a Serpent's old lady. That's what happened here. He fucked a married fucking woman who was looking to piss her old man off in the worst way and when that Serpent of hers came looking Vic gutted him without a fucking thought of what that shit could do to this club. He thought with his dick and not his head and put every brother in the line of fire for it. So instead of spending the night at the bar for your homecoming or working on my hog or, fuck, finding my own piece of ass for the night, I'm out here cleaning up his fucking mess. Don't talk to me about the pecking order and do not fucking talk to me about where the hell Vic sits on it. I've been cleaning up his messes for too long."

Vic finally lurches to his feet and stumbles a little before getting his feet right under him. Cole and Axe both stop what they're doing and give their full attention to their Prez, here in the flesh for the first time in over a decade. He's fucking huge too, like being locked up for all that time means he spent it all working out.

He's easily double the size of Hellion.

"That true, Vic? You fucking around on the club like that, risking us all?"

Vic spits blood on the ground, covering Rue's boots and I watch the tick start up on Rue's cheek as he grinds his teeth. He doesn't hold his temper all that well. Doesn't lie about shit either, if he hates you it's right there on his fucking face.

He fucking loathes Vic.

"So I fucked some bitch, who the fuck cares? I took care of shit when it came calling so what does it matter?"

I scoff at him. "You buried his body on our fucking land, asshole. Cadaver dogs ever get brought out here and we're fucked. Now we gotta dig him up and move the body and any fucking sand that mighta touched him too, pray we get it all just in-fucking-case. You didn't take care of shit, you just made the problem ten times fucking bigger."

King watches between the two of us and then motions Vic over to him like they're old friends. I guess his homecoming means he wants things to be a little more fucking peaceful and he's going to talk his old friend's way outta this shit.

I turn away because I don't need to see them both yakking it up, to see the fucking brotherhood on the two of them while we're out here busting our asses to keep shit in line, and as I bend down to grab a shovel I hear the quiet pop sounds of a bullet through a silencer.

I straighten up to find Vic's sightless eye staring up at me, the other one missing along with half his fucking skull.

King slips his gun into his waistband and stalks over to grab a shovel. "Good call, boys. Let's get this shit cleaned up before Keely comes after us for missing my own party. I'll get Hawk out here tomorrow to get the smell taken care of."

Rue stands there like a fucking statue for a second before finally turning and helping move the last of the rotting flesh.

Between the six of us it's still another hour before both bodies are sealed in the barrels, no signs of what's being stored inside and the ground is torn up to hell but there's nothing there to suggest the carnage we've just dug up.

Cole and Axe start moving one while Rue and I snap the shovels and get them jammed into the second barrel with Vic. Thank fuck we thought ahead and got two, originally to get just the shovels disposed of but with some effort we make it work. Hellion stalks off after the other two, quietly directing them on where to go while King watches the two of us work together.

Once it's done Rue seals the barrel up and huffs out a breath.

"Shouldn't there be a vote? If you're killing a brother, a patched member of your own club, shouldn't there be a vote?"

If that isn't my cousin, I don't know what is. Questioning fucking everything, even if he wanted Vic gone, just to make sure that it's what's best for the club.

He's going to make the best Prez someday.

"We're on the edge of war with the Demons right now, and even with other Unseen charters. There's rats in our club left, right, and fucking center. We've got women and children to protect. Speck isn't fully patched in yet and Lawson and Lyndon are still a year away from prospecting. We can't afford to have sloppy bullshit and he's been given chances. Too many of 'em because I was doing time. That's over with now. Everyone toes the line, everyone pulls their weight, everyone lives and bleeds for this club. Vic was only the first to go... there's going to be a helluva lot more deaths before this is over."

The chill down my spine tells me there isn't a word of a lie coming out of him.

I just didn't really see it coming.

The clubhouse is fucking writhing with bodies.

I knew from the parking lot it was going to be bad but I have to force my way through the crowd just to get out to the hallway and into my room. I have a private bathroom, thank fuck, and I take my time to wash the dirt and gore off of my skin. It's fucking everywhere, even with me wearing gloves I can still see flecks of black under my fingernails which is a sure sign I'll be smelling corpse stank until I've scrubbed myself raw.

There are some downsides to the one percent-er life.

I'm scrubbing my hair down for the third time when my phone starts buzzing like crazy on the countertop. It's never a good sign when it blows up and I open the shower door to grab it.

Have you seen the new girl?

It's from Law and I curse him through my fucking teeth.

You're seventeen. Get your ass outta my fucking strip club before someone sees you and we get raided.

I drop it back on the countertop and finish washing up. It takes him a minute but he does eventually reply.

I'm leaving now, King sent me for more booze and the club is the only place that never runs out. But man, you gotta see this girl.

I don't have time for a stripper right now, no matter how badly I wanna bend one over and fuck her into tomorrow. It's been about a week since I last shot my load down a woman's throat and that is at least six days too long. Fucking Vic and his bullshit has taken up too much of my time.

That and Rue going off the fucking rails over King coming home.

I mean, he's only been waiting for this night every second of the day since he was twelve and his pops got pinned for shit he didn't do. Problem was he wasn't expecting the man King has become, the one who has just lost twelve years of his life and now he's got a club riddled with rats who are trying to take our fucking business out from underneath us. To take away everything we've fought and killed and fucking died for.

The club my grandfather started, the brotherhood he built and bled for, these rats want to fucking spit on.

Over my dead fucking body.

Whatever it takes, I'll burn them all out like a shot of penicillin straight into the bloodstream. Whatever it fucking takes.

Send me a photo of her.

I get dry and dressed, checking one last time that there isn't any evidence of my night's work as I pull my shit on. I slip my phone into my pocket and then forget all about this new girl as I get my head together before heading out.

My mom and my sister are going to be out there. My mom doesn't need to be fretting about a goddamn thing and if Trink knew about shit going on… I don't need that sort of fucking headache.

When I slip out of my room Rue's getting out of his too, a frown still on his face but he's clean and freshly shaved, the shadows on his face cleared up just a little.

"What's the face for?"

He grunts. "Diego came in for the party with Luis and Poe just got back from her summer fucking holiday so she's here with Trink. It's a fucking mess waiting to happen."

I cuss the whole world out and rub a palm over my face. "Are you sure you can't get Thorn to budge and just give her your fucking patch already? Mom was pregnant with me at seventeen, it's not that fucking bad."

He glares at me and I shrug. "I'm not saying knock her up, I'm saying protect her from that asshole and all the other ones coming out of the fucking woodwork now she's grown tits."

I walk away before that comment gets me knocked the fuck out because there's no doubt in my mind he's about to start swinging.

He catches up to me before I make it out of the hallway and says, "It's not that fucking easy. There's too much happening in the club right now to just say fuck it, and have her. What if a fucking war breaks out? That's where we're heading with the Demons."

I can't help but say it. "If a war breaks out and she's not yours, that means she's fair game. If you think for a second Grimm might come knocking to call his kid home then you need to fucking patch her."

He doesn't have the chance to argue as we get to the bar, the crowd already fucking rowdy as hell, and there's too many ears around to keep this going. I head to the bar and get us both drinks, walking over to where Keely is fussing over Poe like she's a fucking toddler.

"You're so tiny, did they not feed you while you were gone?"

She laughs and shrugs. "I did some self-defense classes with my sister, learned eight ways to kill a man with my bare hands so I don't think I've worked out so hard in my damn life."

Rue's eyebrows get all low and pissy so I cut the fuck in before he starts his shit. "So now you're a badass and don't need us watching out for you? Good to know, we'll stop hanging around."

She laughs, all sunshine and fucking rainbows, and nudges Trink. "No need for that, just letting you boys know I could kill you all in your sleep."

Rue huffs out a breath and drains his glass. "Duly noted. You two stay outta trouble. The Shreveport charter are here and I don't need to be starting a fucking war tonight."

Keely frowns a little, casts me a look and I give her the slightest shake of my head. Nothing has happened just yet but Diego would do fucking anything to piss Rue off.

Unfortunately, he's figured out Poe is exactly that something.

"Ugh, he's looking over here. I need a drink to get me through this. Is my ban over or do I need to go sweet talk Speck?" Poe says with a cheeky grin and a flirty look at Rue.

I would rather fucking clean corpses up than stand around listening to this shit.

"Trink, don't be an asshole. Just for tonight, sit your ass down and do nothing," I say and walk away from them all, stopping long enough to kiss Keely's cheek.

I don't hang around to hear Trink's reply because I know for sure she's going to do whatever she can to fuck with me and the rest of the club tonight.

Growing up the only girl has made her intent on stirring up shit.

King and Hawk are already setting up for the night in their booth at the back of the bar, a sight I haven't seen for so fucking long but it just feels goddamn right. Hellion is busy joking and talking shit with the Shreveport guys, the alliance he built with them the only thing stopping the war at the moment.

Luis has been trying to reach an agreement with Grimm for fucking years. Their borders run up against each other and there's a helluva lot of overlap in how the heat treats them.

He's spent some time in lock up with Demons and that just makes him suspect to me.

Axe tips his head at me when I get up to the bar, calling an order out to Speck for us both on his account. I take a seat with him, ready to get fucking wasted and forget all about Vic and his fucking bullshit.

Don't get me wrong, I'm glad the asshole is dead.

But this opens up a whole new era of the Unseen Originals, one that means everyone needs to prove their fucking loyalty. I for one think we'll be lucky to keep half the members.

Axe gets a look at me and nods. "Yup. This ain't gonna be a good time so we better fucking drink while we can."

I slap him on the back and take the whiskey from Speck, rolling my eyes at his dumbass story about his week at The Boulevard.

"Ain't no fucking way the new girl made five grand with one dance, stop your bullshitting," I say, cutting his fucking bravado off.

Looks like he's fallen for some new side piece, so a regular fucking Thursday for him.

"I swear on my patch, she did. Diamond about shit herself, she did not want her on the books but the fucking way she moved… fuck, I'd pay good green myself for a private dance."

Axe chuckles and shrugs. "You waste all your fucking money down there 'cause you don't know how to get pussy without paying. Maybe you need to spend a little more time at a real bar and not just the titty one."

Monroe walks through with Diesel in tow and half the fucking room groans inaudibly. I know it for sure because we're all turning away, hoping they're not gonna park their asses with us.

Of course she picks me.

"What's the sour fucking face for, Tomi? Finally caught the clap from those whores you've been fucking?"

Speck curses under his breath and walks away, just turns on his heel and stalks over to serve drinks further down the bar. I set my glass down and face the little cunt.

Dave's kid and born into the club, she's been a fucking nightmare from day one. A different sort to Trink because she's somehow managed to rope Diesel into handing over his patch to her and yet she spends her days desperately following me and my cousins around.

Difference between Trink and Monroe is that my sister just wants to live her own life. Monroe wants to fucking destroy whoever she touches and fuck is she desperate to touch me.

"Only whore I see around here is you. How about you go on back into Diesel's room and leave us all to have a good night?"

Diesel gives me a hard look and I grin back at him because I'm itching for a fight now. He stands up from his seat and snarls, "Shut your fucking mouth."

Axe curses under his breath and starts looking around for backup.

"I'm not saying anything that isn't true so how about you fucking make me. Unless your little whore of an old lady has your balls about that too."

He dives at me but I'm in the mood to fucking beat the shit outta him and serve a reminder of a lifetime to him and all of the other men here.

Callaghans own this place.

Everyone else can fall the fuck into line.

Chapter Three

Angel

I make almost eight thousand dollars in my first shift at The Boulevard.

After I convinced Diamond to hire me with my first dance she gave me an ID pass and information about working here. The tour was short thanks to my unwillingness to do any of the extra jobs and the only other things I needed to know were about the themed nights the club holds. I'm a little nervous about how much I'm going to have to spend on underwear and shoes but the stacks of bills that were in Diamond's hands from my audition keep popping into my mind.

I can do this.

The bouncer lets me in before the club opens and I walk straight to the locker room without really looking around the room that the staff are setting up for the night.

The locker room is full of girls, most of them either naked or wearing the teeny tiny outfits that the bar staff here wear. I find the locker I was assigned and unlock it, shoving my bag inside and grabbing out the supplies I need to take a quick shower to get ready. None of the girls try to speak to me but they all sure do enjoy watching my every move.

I already feel like an outsider.

I try to tell myself it'll get better, I just need to prove myself. If I keep my head down and dance my ass off hopefully they'll come around. I don't need friends but fuck, it wouldn't be so bad to have them.

I only have two slots for dances but my crowd is bigger than any other girl in the room, half the guys there are familiar or wearing patches. Word has clearly gotten out about the new girl.

I change outfits for the second dance, something a little less white and little more sexual with the diamonds and feathers. I'm stashing the other, sweaty outfit into my bag when the door opens and Diamond walks in, a sour look on her face as she stops next to my locker. I keep my eyes on what I'm doing and she huffs out an annoyed breath at me.

"If it were up to me, I wouldn't have hired you. Girls who think they're too good to do extra don't last here and I don't really want to have to deal with the drama but you caught Speck's eye. I'm sure once he's done with you he'll be happy to see you on your way."

My hands are rock steady while I apply the lipstick, a soft peachy color that I know makes my lips look even poutier than normal, perfect to make men think about ramming their cocks between them. I've had enough practice before competitions to learn how to keep my nerves in line and there's already four thousand dollars locked away in my bag. That will always help me to deal with some bitchy attitudes.

"I'm just here to dance and make good money. That's it. I'm not starting drama, I'm not being pulled into it, I'm just here to dance. If it really is a problem, I can move on and work somewhere else."

She looks down her nose at me. "Well now you've caught Speck's eye I can't exactly tell you to leave, can I? You should though. You'll regret it if you don't."

That sounds threatening.

Jesus.

I lock up my shit, checking for sure it's secure, and then I make my way out onto the stage again. The crowd is even bigger than the last time, rowdier and yelling out to me the entire time dancing. The money rains down onto the stage even though I've been out once already and I try not to listen to any of the words coming out of any of their mouths, just focussing on the dance itself and staying steady on the stripper heels. They're new and even higher than the last pair.

When the song finally ends and I collect all of the cash, forcing a flirty grin on my face as I scoop it up even though I'd rather fucking choke than have any of these men touch me.

Speck is waiting for me in the locker rooms when I get out there.

I'm starting to get worried he's into me, something I can't freaking give him, no matter how nice or cute he is. He grins and motions at the green in my arms. "I've never seen a girl make that kinda money in a single night, let alone one fucking song."

I grin at him and shrug, remembering at the last second I'm in a fucking thong and pasties. I fight a blush or, you know, dying of mortification.

I get my locker open and shove the money in my bag before I pull it out and head towards the showers. Speck chuckles at me and calls out, "I'd throw my life savings at that ass too, Angel-baby."

Christ on a fucking cracker, I need to figure out how to let him down. Firm but gentle, enough that he doesn't chase me but not so much that it gets me fucking fired.

"Selling him your ass already? Guess you aren't Miss Prim and Proper after all," Diamond sneers as I walk past her to get into the showers.

I ignore her but she was loud enough for Speck to overhear and he snarks back at her, "You should be grateful. Half your private dances came straight from Angel's stage, she filled your fucking pockets tonight."

Of course. That's why she'll be freaking pissed at me, I'm taking work from her and the other girls. I tell myself I don't care but honestly, knowing they all hate me here doesn't matter either way.

I need the fucking money.

I'll happily be hated around here if it means my stage is the one getting all of the big tips. I'm not here to make friends, I'm here to set my life up and get out from the freaking hellscape I'm stuck in.

I take my time in the shower, scrubbing the gel out of my hair and washing away the glitter and crystals. The water is piping hot and I have to drag my ass out of there.

Speck is gone when I walk out but all of the other girls are in the locker room, dressed and ready to leave. I duck my head, ready to just tear out of there without another word, but one of the girls steps into my path to stop me.

"Hey! We're having drinks tonight, wanna come with? I know being new is really hard here so I thought I'd invite you!" Melody says, twisting a strand of her bleach blonde hair around her finger like she's flirting with me.

I wish I could. I think that would be the quickest way to get them all to stop hating on me but I can't risk sleeping in the underground parking lot I've found while even a little tipsy. Too easy to be attacked and not be able to run or fight back and I haven't been here for long enough to know the risks yet.

"I can't tonight, sorry! Maybe some other time?"

The smile falters a little on her face, like she wasn't expecting me to say no. "Why? You got some boyfriend waiting or something? You could bring him."

I look over her shoulder and find the other girls watching us, whispering amongst themselves. I shift on my feet awkwardly. "It's not that, tonight just isn't good for me. I'd love to next time though."

Diamond smirks and calls out, "I told you, Miss Untouchable thinks she's too good for us. C'mon, Mel, we have shots waiting for us. Leave the frosty little bitch to her night."

My stomach drops as they all giggle and leave me behind. It's not a big deal, I don't need to be friends with any of them. I don't need friends.

I walk out of the club and set my bag into the back of my car, sliding into the front seat and turning it on to let the engine run to warm up a little. I wriggle my feet out of the heels I've been stuck in for hours and sigh at the relief. God, it feels amazing to finally let them breathe.

I drive over to the gas station and grab something greasy for dinner, ignoring the looks from the guy behind the counter. I don't know if I'm being paranoid or if he really has been down at the club and seen me on stage but fuck, I try to get in and out as quickly as possible.

The parking lot is quiet, no one else here tonight, thank God. There's usually not many people here, and they always stay away from me. I'm glad to be able to sleep in the car, only cracking the window the tiniest bit to let in some air and then putting my seat back and throwing a blanket over myself. It's not ideal but it's also safer than I was back home by a long shot

so I don't fucking care.
I sleep like the dead.

Now that my job is secure, I hope, I figure out where the hell I'm going to transfer my college credits to. The simple answer is Southern Miss but Coldstone is too small to actually have a campus and I don't have a phone with internet access to look that shit up.

So I sit outside a takeout place with free wifi and sip an icy cold coke while I search. The freaking heavens must be looking down on me because there's a college campus in the next town over for me to transfer into. I still want to take online classes, to save fuel and because college isn't exactly my scene, but to transfer I still have to show up and sign paperwork.

Oh, and hand over a sizable chunk of my tips. Can't forget that heart-wrenching part.

It's easy enough to get an appointment right away and my shift at The Boulevard doesn't start until nine tonight so I seize the freaking day and just get it over with. There's no point surviving here if I don't have an exit strategy and there's no way I wanna be shaking my tits on stage forever.

The drive isn't that long but with the air conditioner broken in my car and the hot summer sun blasting down I kinda want to die a little. I'm thankful for my tiny shorts and the little cami I'm wearing because my skin is on fire.

When I finally park and get out of the car I catch my reflection in the car window and, lord help me, I look like a hot mess. I run my fingers through my hair as I tie it up, trying to get it off of my neck and out of the way. There's no rescuing the rest of my look. I make peace with that because, hell, who exactly am I trying to impress here?

I'd rather repulse people and keep them the hell away from me, especially here. The office building is older and needs an update but it's clean and welcoming enough. A couple of guys hold a door open for me and make flirty eyes at me but I duck my head as I thank them and scurry through like my ass is on fire.

I just want to get this over with. In and out.

I stand awkwardly over by the door even though there's no

line or anything stopping me from just enrolling.

"Can I help you?" the lady at the desk calls out and I startle into action, stepping forward with my files.

"Uh yeah, I called earlier? About, uhm—"

"About transferring credits? Do you have all of your paperwork here with you?"

I nod and hand it all over to her. She sifts through it all and types into her computer. I rub at my arms a little, the cami I've got on not doing much against the cold in the office. God, from one extreme to another.

Finally, after like a half hour of typing and frowning at what I've given her, she looks up at me and says, "Okay, I think that's everything. Let me call you an advisor. I've assigned you to Finley, he's good at the more… challenging cases."

I swallow and try to smile back at her.

How exactly am I a challenging case?

I don't get the chance to question her before she gets on the phone, her tone cheery and a little flirty as she speaks to this Finley guy. She motions for me to wait, like there's anywhere else I could go right now, and I take a seat. It's times like this I wish I had a phone to mess around on or a book in my bag to bury my nose in but instead I'm forced to stare around the office at the inspirational posters and event fliers.

I wish I were normal enough to enjoy something like a freshman mixer or to join a sorority. It would be nice to have friends.

A man steps into my eye line, a big grin of his tanned face. "Hello there! Welcome to Southern Miss. I'm Finley, you must be Angel."

I smile and tuck a stray strand of my hair behind my ear, nervous as hell about this entire process. "Uh, thanks! I'm not going to be on campus, just here for like… exams or whatever."

He grins at me and motions for me to follow him down the hallway. He's dressed casually but it's all nice clothes. Designer without being flashy. He obviously comes from money because he carries himself with that lightness that comes from not ever having a single thing to worry about or prove.

I'm jealous as hell.

"Are you sure online classes are for you? The workload can be hard to juggle, there's still room in the dorms here. Not a lot but there's some options I could sneak you into," he says as he opens the door to his office, throwing me a wink as he opens the door for me.

My skin crawls.

It always does around this sort of attention. I hate men taking notice of me in any way, let alone this friendly sort of banter, the type where I'm not sure if he's flirting or just always like this.

I'd rather be on stage dancing in panties and pasties than be in this small room with this guy. The stage is safe and quiet and like an island out to sea in comparison to the intimacy of this space.

The chairs are next to each other on one side of the desk.

"I'm not really into the formal stuff. I'm pretty hands-on with my students' schedules and we need to be on top of your course load so this setup and my laptop works best. Do you have yours with you?"

I left it in my car, hidden under my pillow in the trunk. "No, sorry. I didn't realize I'd be talking to someone today. The last time I transferred I didn't have to."

He takes a seat and grins at me when I get myself settled. He's pointedly not looking at my bare arms and legs but that only makes it worse because it's clear he wants to. Hell, I should have worn more clothes but the temperature here is like nothing else. I'm not used to the air feeling like hot soup to walk through.

It's gross.

"You've transferred once already? Not enjoying the classes or other interruptions?"

I rub my palms down my thighs. "I've moved a couple of times. I'm… I'm staying with family now. I'm here for good."

It feels like I should say something to reassure him that I'm not going to flunk out or run away from this. I don't want to look unreliable or like the gutter rat I really am.

My dad used to call kids on the streets that, but he said it with that sorrow in his voice like he wanted so badly to change it for them. I think if the law were on his side a little more he'd have adopted a hundred kids.

Everyone else who uses the term isn't being so kind.

"Having support is really important while you're in college. I think you'd have a lot more if you were staying on campus but family is good too. Are they happy with your decision to move here and attend Southern Miss?"

I force a smile. "Oh, they're thrilled to have me home. Life is great here and I'll have so much support while I study."

He nods as though he's really thinking about what I'm saying and grabs one of the notebooks from his desk. "Look, I think it would be best if we scheduled in some time each semester to keep in touch and make sure you're keeping up with your classes."

That sounds like a pile of steaming shit waiting to happen. "Sure! Sounds great, let's schedule the first one now so I can keep the day clear on my calendar."

He grins that easy grin at me again and fills out a card, handing it over and making sure his fingers brush mine. It's a dick move and one I was expecting so I manage to keep the shudder to myself.

"Call me if you need anything. My office line is on the front but I've popped my personal cell phone number on the back in case you need anything out of office hours."

Sleaze-bag. "That's so thoughtful, thanks."

He doesn't notice my dry tone at all, just leans back in his chair and stares at me expectantly, like he's waiting for me to flirt with him or hand him my number.

Fuck, I might change mine after this meeting.

"Look I've got work and family waiting on me. Thank you for all of your… specialized attention, I'll be in touch."

I see the challenge light up in his eyes and my stomach drops.

Fuck.

I don't wanna be on anyone's radar.

I just want to disappear.

Chapter Four

Tomi

The party for King's return lasts a full week.

It's stupid and it's reckless but the club also needs something to distract the brothers. Something to make them all forget about the rats, the pigs, and the Demons breathing down our fucking necks.

I don't forget it though.

Neither does my family, no matter how fucking wasted we all get, there's no forgetting the betrayal that's going down in my fucking house. The rats that have been sleeping under our roof, the traitors who eat at our table, no matter how hard I party I won't ever forget about that.

I'm a Callaghan through and through, so when I wake up after the party finally ends I've never been so fucking hungover in my life. Well, that's a lie.

I once had to drink Rue under the table to stop him from ruining his own fucking life. That was a hangover I never want to repeat.

Nothing worse than feeling like death warmed up so I drag my sorry ass to take a shower to try to clean myself the hell up. We have church this morning with the Shreveport charter before they head back home and there's more than enough business to cover with them that'll require a sharp brain.

I stand under the cold water for ten minutes before I switch it to hot and scrub up, rinsing the whiskey and beer outta my skin where the shit is leaking outta my fucking pores. I shave the scuff off of my face and throw on the last of my clean clothes. I should probably let one of the biker bitches clean up around here but the last time I let one of them into my room I'd come back to my desk being fucked around with and with the rat situation I can't afford to have people messing around with my shit.

If any of them knows a thing about security cameras and surveillance equipment we'll be in trouble, I need them to stay unaware of just how much of this shit I'm leaving around everywhere.

When I get out into the clubhouse, I find Rue looking like shit warmed up at the bar and when I park my ass on the barstool next to his he grunts at me.

"Church in ten. King wants us to go over some shit before we meet with Luis and his crew. They're leaving today, thank fuck."

I smirk at him and grab the bottle of beer he's nursing, finishing it in one go. "If you're feeling that fucking wrung out you should probably quit drinking, old man."

He scoffs back. "You're older than me, asshole, and you were a fucking pussy. Pacing yourself like a good little bitch."

I shake my head at him, jerking my head at Monroe so she'll bring us more beer. "I'm not trying to forget how fucking pussy whipped I am so I don't need to drink as much as your sorry ass. Maybe you should take up yoga or something. Find your zen."

The glare he sends me as he tips the fresh beer back would strip paint. "Fucking yoga. College ruined you, asshole, are you sure you wanna slum it here with us dirty bikers?"

I chuckle as I shake my head at his grumbling and clap him on the back as King walks out of the chapel and catches our attention, jerking his head at us to follow him.

Just us.

So not regular church then, fuck.

I leave the beer behind because if this is a family meeting and not a Coldstone one then shit has gone south again and I'll need a clear head for it. Rue sighs and sets his down as well and I'm sure his head is fucking pounding without the hair of the dog.

"Shut the door behind you," King says from the head of the table and Hawk is already sitting beside him with a cigar hanging out of his frowning mouth. Hellion is perched on his chair like he's uneasy sitting there, papers spread out around him that he's poring over like they hold all the secrets of the underworld.

Fuck.

"What happened?"

Hawk huffs and scratches at his beard. "Shipment is gone. Third one from the last set that we sent out the day King got home. There's a pattern going on."

Fuck.

Rue steps up to park his ass next to Hellion and starts scouring over the pages with him, cursing over what's there. I sit next to Hawk and keep my eyes on King.

I want to know what he's thinking about this shit more than I need to know the details right now. I need to know what sort of a Prez we're serving under so I can plan out my own recon accordingly.

Vic's death has told me a little, but not everything.

King's eyes are intense as he slowly takes each of us in. The twitch in Hawk's fingers as he flicks the ash from his cigar, Hellion's piercing scrutiny on each and every document on the table, the frown on Rue's face as he joins the dots together, and me.

The stiffness of my shoulders as I sit there and wait for his instructions. The death already etched into my face and the stillness of my body as I wait. I'm ready to shed blood for my club and to bleed for my family. Whatever the cost, I'll pay it.

Rue starts fucking losing his shit and slides a page over to me, rubbing a hand over his face like he wants to scrub it off. Hellion grunts and leans back in his chair too, looking over at his brother-in-arms and blood as he waits for his decision on this shit too.

King says nothing, waits for me to see the evidence put forward.

I look over the note Rue's passed over, the times and details, and it takes me a half second to see that there's a pattern to where the information is coming from.

Church.

More specifically, the chapel itself because that meeting only had the senior-most members of the council, and the meeting with the route only had my blood which means someone has bugged the fucking place. I don't know how they got that shit past us but it's fucking serious shit.

I meet King's eyes and he nods at me like we've come to an agreement. We have.

I'll fucking find this surveillance.

"We gonna go ahead with the meeting? Even with the chance we're being watched?" Rue says slowly, like he's thinking real fucking hard about his word choices.

I keep my eyes on King and he nods. "We go ahead with the meeting and keep our eyes open. Keep our shit under wraps until we can sort out the shipments. We can reconvene later, make a plan once Tomi's had a chance to go through the place."

Hellion grunts and sweeps the entire chapel with his eyes like he's got laser vision and will see whatever bugs have been planted. "Keep shit on topic with Luis, make sure none of our boys let anything slip. I'll let Luis know too."

I nod at him. We coulda really gone to town on these assholes if the other charter wasn't here. Could've made up some stories to throw them off and catch them out, but we'd have to throw Luis and his boys under the bus for that shit and that just isn't King's style.

Integrity and brute fucking force to the end.

Rue and I have a little more planning and smarts but that's for later, for when we step up and make this shit our own. Not for now. Now we're here to shut our mouths and follow orders, learn everything we can from our fathers, and then rule this place when our time has come.

If we make it, that is.

When church finally lets out I'm ready for a fucking drink before I have to go deal with the bullshit down at the bar. Rue has a mountain of jobs lined up at the garage and looks about as happy as a kick in the balls about it. He'd spent the last week trying to avoid both biker bitches from both charters and Diego, Luis's son and a royal fucking pain in both our asses.

We'd managed to keep Poe the hell away from the clubhouse but now she's fucking pissed as hell and ready for blood.

All I have to say about that shit is thank fuck I don't have a woman because Rue always looks fucking miserable and that's not the life I want.

I want to drink my way through every bar, fuck my way through every stripper I ever meet that catches my eye, and then wake the hell up and do it again tomorrow.

Fuck being 'struck.

I grab a beer at the bar and ignore the bitching Axe and Speck are doing over the hot stripper again.

"You sure she's not just playing hard to get? Fuck, I think I'll go fucking bankrupt if I keep going down there. Never seen a woman do that shit with her legs before."

Speck shakes his head and he looks serious as all get out for once in his life. "She's dead serious and she's making enough green that it's in the club's best interest to let her do her thing."

I park my ass down with Axe and give Speck a look. "Since when do you speak for the club's interests, prospect?"

I shouldn't rag on him like this.

Not when Rue's bitch fit at King is still ringing in my ears, clear as a fucking bell, about what it means to be a Callaghan in the Unseen. But it sounds like he's fucking smitten with this girl and that spells out fucking trouble. Not even patched in yet and already getting into fights over a piece of ass?

Jesus fucking Christ.

The doors to the chapel open again and King walks through with Luis and they both clap each other on the shoulder as they part ways. There's a lot of respect there, even if they're not that close anymore thanks to King's time in lock-up. I finish off my beer but before I can flag Speck down for another Luis meets my eye across the room and motions at me to follow him into the parking lot.

I do it without question.

I've known this man for fucking years, long before he took over the Shreveport charter and began cleaning it the hell up but from the second he took over he's kept me in the loop.

I took a bullet for him a few years back in an arms deal with the cartel gone wrong and that's something his pride can't ever forget. I was twenty-one and a prospect, a prince of my club and un-fucking-touchable, and still, I dove in front of him to get him the hell outta the way of that shot. Barely skimmed me but it woulda been nighty-night for him if it had've hit true.

He takes his phone out of his pocket, stuffs it in his pack on his bike, and starts the engine. I frown at him and do the same with mine, only I balance it on his seat.

Then we walk into the trees, close enough that I can keep an eye on the door and who might come looking for us but far enough away that our voices won't get overheard or recorded.

Unless he's wearing a wire.

Even after years of mutual respect, I don't completely trust anyone but my blood.

"Shit's getting busy around here. More eyes on us all."

I shrug at him. "That's the life. If you thought King's release would make shit better around here you haven't been paying attention."

He huffs out a laugh at me. "You sure you're not gonna push to be Prez someday soon? You're too smart to be a VP to a grease monkey."

Someday there's gonna be a reckoning because they all have Rue wrong, every last one of them has decided I'm the brains of this next generation.

Rue didn't go to college because that woulda meant leaving Poe.

We talked about it. We planned that shit out together and made an agreement on how the hell we'd be moving forward long before either of us ever prospected and patched in. There's never been a question in my mind about Rue's presidency.

If they're second guessing his smarts for this shit then… good. Better to be underestimated, for everyone else to underestimate us. It makes them sloppy and it'll only help weed out the rats.

At my silence, Luis huffs and says, "There's something you should know."

I sigh and nod. "I was guessing this wasn't a fucking circle jerk."

He scoffs as he lights up a cigarette and offers me one. I have enough vices in my life so I wave him off and keep my eyes on the doors.

"The last shipment that came through. I usually don't get a look at 'em, I leave it to the boys and let them earn their cuts but shit went down and I decided to ride along."

That gets my attention.

The shipments go from us to various drop off points around the country. Luis and his boys take care of Louisiana and we move a lotta goods that way. The last shipment had been overseen by Hellion, Rue, Vic, and I. It was stored in the warehouse for two days before we moved it along, everything had gone smoothly.

"What about it? Something missing?"

He takes a long drag and then pegs me with a look. "Nah. Something extra was in the container. Six dead bodies."

I turn to face him completely, forgetting the fucking door. "What the hell do you mean, dead bodies? Demons? Or Unseen? I think I'd have noticed if six of our boys were missing."

He drops the butt of his cigarette and lights up another, keen to just fucking chain-smoke this conversation through to the end. "Neither. They were kids. Six little girls, all dead and huddled together like they were being fucking smuggled."

Jesus fucking Christ.

"Someone is pulling extra cash by smuggling little girls across the borders and we're the ones doing the dirty work. Smells like the fucking rats to me."

I spin away from him ready to stalk my ass up those stairs and start fucking swinging until I find the asshole doing it.

Smuggling fucking kids.

That's never been our style, not something we'd ever get into, and the thought of some fucking gutless turncoat rat making cash off of some guy raping a kid that's been moved by me and my fucking family? Nope. Not today and not on my fucking dime.

"You can't just go in there and start shooting. We need to know who the fuck is doing it. We need to start mixing shit up around here, changing our paths and timetables. Only way to figure this out. You gotta lock it down tight. You think this ain't killing me? I've got kids around the same age as the girls in that fucking box."

Typical fucking dead-beat dad, he has four kids to four different bitches. Diego is the oldest and I'm fucking hoping he's the worst of the lot because he's definitely on the road to being fucking taken out.

He's not exactly a fan of being lower on the food chain than anyone else and even being the future Prez of the Shreveport charter isn't enough because it's not the mother charter. He'll never be an Original because he's not a Callaghan and that's something that eats him up inside.

I blow out a frustrated breath and give him a nod. "Leave it with me, I have eyes on that situation and I'll find the fucking rat."

First, I have a chapel to sweep.

Chapter Five

Angel

The truck is hot overnight. Too fucking hot to handle but short of finding a homeless shelter or spending some of my cash on a motel room I have no other options. I'm not at that extreme point of exhaustion yet so I just don't want to spend the cash on a room yet.

I tell myself I'm only going to do that once a month at most, the rest of the money being spent sparingly on food and new outfits for the themed nights at the Boulevard.

All the remainder is being stuffed into my bag.

I get it, that's a terrible way of keeping my money but I can't open up a bank account in my real name without setting off some alarms and opening a bank account with a fake ID is just… too risky. Too fucking risky for me right now so I keep that shit on me or locked up while I dance.

The more it grows the more terrified I get about having it on hand but it's not so much at the moment that I have to immediately worry about it. I just need to keep an eye out for another solution.

My college classes start up again and I find myself set up at the Coldstone library to work during the day. The lady at the front desk is a nightmare, a total fucking bitch the second she lays her eyes on me, but I grit my teeth and put up with it.

My laptop is old and beat to hell so I price up getting a new one the second I connect to the library's slow-ass wifi.

There's no way I'm parting with that much cash.

No freaking way.

I guess that's the real problem with being a stripper and

knowing exactly what your time is worth, there's no way I'm wasting a whole fucking dance on getting a new MacBook when this one will do for now.

So I set up on one of the desks with my headphones on to watch hours and hours of lectures, taking notes until I think my hands are going to fall off of my arms. The library is quiet enough, even when a small group of little old ladies set up a book club session in the meeting rooms, and I get everything I need done for the week in a single session. There's assignments to start working on and I make a detailed plan to get that shit done tomorrow morning, and by the time I have to leave because it's closing the tightness in my chest eases off a little.

I can do this.

I can work three or four nights a week, study during the day, sleep in my car, cut my food costs so I'm only eating when I feel like I'm going to pass the hell out, and I can pay cash for fucking everything.

A house, college, and a buffer so I never have to rely on anyone ever again. I can fucking do it.

My shift at The Boulevard doesn't start for another four hours so I grab my shit and drive to the next town over to shop for some more outfits. Fuck, it feels wrong to even call them outfits. Thongs and bras and a shit ton of pasties. There's a couple of sex shops with decent options and the girls there are nice enough. They stare at me a little when I go through every rack, the list of themes on my phone as I work through all of the choices until I find enough shit to get me through the next week.

The total is fucking heartbreaking.

I pay for it with my stacks of bills and the girl behind the counter grins at me. "Fuck girl, you must be raking it in! The other girls only buy half what you do."

I blush and shrug. "I like having a big collection, I'm fussy like that."

She grins at me and fills a bag up with the scraps of lace, tucking a sampler perfume in there with it. "Have fun girl! I wish I had the goods to make the same green!"

I duck my head with a grin. Fuck, it's the first time someone has spoken to me about dancing without it being a fucking problem. I get into my car with a smile on my face for the first time in forever.

Maybe it's not so fucking bad.

Three weeks into working at The Boulevard and I hit a wall.

I'm tired.

There's never a time where I'm not exhausted now that I'm working until four in the morning every other day and I have to be out of the carpark by seven. There are places I can park during the day but there's a lot more danger with that and none of those places will be dark like the carpark.

I drink a lot of energy drinks.

They're cheap enough and now that I need to stay skinny I choose a sugar free one and call it breakfast, lunch, and dinner.

I force myself to stay up to date with my college classes because that's my ticket out of this life so even when I feel as though my eyeballs are going to fall out of my head I go to the library.

I'm not expecting my whole goddamn life to change.

But it does.

It's a busy night and by the time I finish my first dance and make it out to the locker room my legs are practically shaking underneath me. I picked a hard routine to start with but one I know the clients here go crazy for and sure enough, there's a whole fucking lot of green in my hands.

I'm stashing it away in my locker when someone grabs my elbow, wrenching me around to face them.

It's a biker, one I recognize from the crowd at my stage but I've never spoken to him before. He's wasted, swaying slightly, but the look on his face is trouble. Big fucking trouble for me.

He reeks of stale beer and cigarettes and I choke back a gag, the stink of it coating the back of my throat like it'll never leave me.

He smirks and reaches out to grab a piece of my hair, wrapping it around his fumbling fingers. "I've had my eye on you, pretty little birdie."

The gag comes back in full force, no choking that shit back. "I don't do extra. Please don't touch me."

He smirks at me and he's like all my fucking nightmares come true with his crooked nose and yellowed teeth. "Club property, bitch. You'll do extra if I want you to."

He moves fast for a man who can barely fucking walk, his hand reaching out to grab my throat.

I hear Speck shout from down the hallway but instinct kicks in and I slam the heel of my palm into the drunk biker's nose, the crunch of it breaking is the most satisfying sound.

He lets me go with a roar, blood pouring out of his face, but he recovers quickly and lurches at me. I stumble back, ready to run the fuck out of this place and never come back, but Speck gets to him before he can lay another finger on me.

He takes him down to the ground, restraining him but he doesn't try to hit him at all.

I'm a little disappointed.

"No fucking touching her, asshole! Fuck, keep your head together before it gets you into the shit."

"She's a fucking stripper! I can have her if I want!"

The biker bucks and tries to throw Speck off but the prospect is too strong for him, easily pinning his arms down and holding him to the ground.

"What you want for your dick isn't going to jeopardize club business. Find another pussy to pump."

The biker snarls, "You don't have a fucking patch, you can't do this shit."

There's footsteps behind me as Diamond and Mel both come running, finally hearing the ruckus these two are making. Diamond immediately gets on the phone, speaking in a purr, "You better come down here, Speck's throwing hands at Mav over the new girl. Shit ain't good."

Mel grabs my hand and lifts it up to the light to look at the blood and swelling already there from my jab at the biker, raising her eyebrows at me. "That'll be Tomi. You're kinda fucked now, Angel, you don't ever attack one of the Unseen."

I didn't though.

I didn't and Speck saw enough of the shit that went down that I should be okay… except he's not patched in so his word probably doesn't hold up to the other guy's.

Diamond snaps her fingers in front of my face to get my attention. "Earth to fucking Angel, get your ass in the office!

The boss is gonna be here to deal with you in a minute and I need to get Mav's drunk ass in there too, fuck's sake! I knew you'd be nothing but fucking trouble. Dancing here like you're too good for extra shit, you fucking deserve whatever you've got coming to you."

Mel at least manages to look a little sorry for me but she doesn't say a word as she moves away to grab her shit and head home. She's never actively tried to hurt me or talk shit but she's also never tried to talk to me again since that first night.

Even amongst strippers I'm a fucking pariah.

I take a seat in the office, nervous and sitting there in my freaking thong. Thank God my last dance was freaking themed and I have a full bra on for a little more coverage. Not a lot, but more than the fucking pasties.

Christ.

Am I going to die tonight?

Worse than that... do I care?

The door swings open again and Mav stumbles through, kicking my chair like a fucking child as he passes before collapsing in one of the extra chairs lining the far wall.

I refuse to lower my gaze, totally a dumb move, but I know I'm not in the wrong. They might kill me for the sake of this guy's pride but... I think I can accept that. He's still bleeding, the blood trickling out of his nose at a steady pace, but he doesn't try to clean himself up or staunch it in any way. It's probably a macho biker thing. Jesus, could I have possibly picked a worse guy to punch?

The door opens and in walks another biker. He's huge, tattooed, a nose ring, and piercing blue eyes. Ridiculously hot, like even my broken self kinda wants to pant after him, but also he's clearly the type of dangerous that lands you in a shallow grave.

Yup, apparently I could've picked a worse guy and here he is, ready to murder me for attacking one of his brothers.

Diamond trots in after him, shaking her ass, and Jesus, where did her clothes go? A minute ago she had a corset and a thong on and now here she is, stark freaking naked. She sits down next to me, leaning towards me and I try to control my flinch away from her.

"You're so fucked," Diamond snickers under her breath at me, batting her lashes at the new guy. "Tomi, I'm so sorry for calling you down here for the new girl. I hope you weren't busy."

The guy, Tomi, smirks at her, all sex and innuendo, and I try not to gag. Anyone who likes Diamond's charms must be a total idiot.

He doesn't look my way at all, just surveys the other guy and takes a seat behind the table, rolling his shoulders out and blowing out a breath. I can see him getting ready to start a whole speech on exactly how fucked I am.

Then he looks up at me and he flinches.

The blood drains out of his face but he doesn't say a word.

Complete freaking silence.

I frown at him, no freaking clue why he's acting like this and Diamond looks just as confused.

"Is there something wrong?"

His eyes flash over to hers. "How long has she been here?"

Diamond shrugs. "A few weeks? I told you I was hiring someone I didn't want to but you sided with Speck, remember?"

Tomi leans back in his chair but he still has the look on his face like he's been stabbed in the gut. I keep my mouth firmly shut.

Mav gets pissed off and starts running his mouth. "Who gives a fuck how long she's been here, she's a fucking deranged cunt! Broke my fucking nose, the dirty little bitch. Should bury her or at the very least kick her ass outta here."

Speck scoffs from the door and Tomi sends him a dark look. "You got something to add to this little story?"

The man I'm starting to think of as a friend steps forward and smirks at Tomi. "As a matter of fact, I do. Mav grabbed Angel by the throat after she told him she wouldn't be servicing his shriveled up shrimp dick. My words, not hers. She was a fucking lady about it. But, the way I see it, the girls here are club property and this asshole was tryna damage the biggest fucking money earner we've got. Self defense isn't a fucking attack and Mav's just being a little fucking bitch."

I swallow hard. I know he's trying to help but I feel like he's just made the entire situation worse.

Mav raises bloodshot eyes and snarls, "You worthless piece of shit, you don't get to tell me what's right for this club! You ain't even in it!"

Tomi stares at me like he wants to set fire to my corpse. I try not to squirm under that dark glare of his but after a beat too long he turns his eyes up to Speck's. Something passes between them, some sort of telepathic conversation, and then Tomi finally speaks.

"Speck isn't patched in but he's still a Callaghan and he was put in charge of watching the girls here. If he says don't touch her, then you don't fucking touch her."

"Siding with your fucking blood, fucking typical egotistical—"

"Finish that fucking sentence, Maverick. Finish it and it'll be the last words you speak because Speck might not have the patch yet but I do and I'll gladly slit your fucking throat for thinking with your dick and not your brain about club shit. The girls here are assets, not fucking toys. Get out and sleep it off, don't fucking come back."

Diamond huffs under her breath but everyone ignores her as Mav walks out. Tomi's eyes swing back over to me and I'm pinned to the fucking chair under that gaze. "Everyone out."

When I shift forward he snaps, "Not you."

Oh God. Oh fucking hell, I'm dead after all.

His lip curls at me and… is that disgust on his face right now? Disgust at a stripper from a man who runs the club and, rumor has it, has fucked every other girl here?

"Do you know how to speak?"

I nod and then say, "I only hit him in self defense. I'll never do that kind of shit again, just so long as no one touches me."

If possible, he looks even fucking angrier. "So you're happy to sell your body but not follow through with those promises?"

I don't get what the hell he means. "I'm here to dance on a stage. I was clear during my interview about what I would and wouldn't do."

He scoffs. "Sure. Let's see if you can keep to that, Angel."

The sarcasm that drips from the words is like acid, burning me right down to my soul. What the hell could I have possibly done to this guy?

I hesitate and he snarls at me, "Get your ass outta my

fucking sight."

That gets me moving, my legs working on autopilot to get me away from his anger. Jesus, what a fucking mess.

My legs are still shaking when I finish up my other dance and when I head out to the locker room again I have to force myself to stay calm. I can't freak out and avoid this place now because I need the showers here.

I take all of my showers at the club.

Diamond hates it, hates that I do it before and after. She's been telling the other girls I'm a germaphobe and that's why I'm doing it. Fuck, I wish that's all it was.

I shave everything while I'm in there each night before I go out, careful not to nick my skin. Bleeding wounds aren't going to make me the big tips.

By the time I finish up, my stomach is killing me. I can't eat until after I'm done for the night because I'm still so nervous every time I get up on the stage that I'll puke if there's anything in my gut. Plus being hungry means my stomach is flat and perfectly toned looking, something I've never worried about before but now, now it's all I can think of. I need my stomach flat and my tits perky, just long enough to get me through until I can afford a house and a little buffer. Just enough that I can afford to live and work somewhere else. Somewhere boring.

A coffee shop or something.

Somewhere where there's no tall, blond, tattooed, and pierced bikers with smoldering blue eyes and a handsome face sneering at the very sight of me.

Fuck.

Why am I thinking about him again already?

Right. I need a boring fucking job where my clothes stay the hell on. Except maybe not, I'd still have to deal with customers there and I'm not sure having clothes on would stop them from trying to touch me.

Why does everyone keep trying to freaking touch me?

Chapter Six

Tomi

When I move to leave The Boulevard I stop by the door and look back over at the stage until Angel comes back out to dance. She's popular, a whole fucking crowd here waiting for her to come out already.

She's unbelievably fucking hot.

Even without being 'struck she'd catch my attention. Long dark hair, big blue eyes, the type of lips a man wants to fuck, ass to get ahold of, and fucking great tits. Fuck.

The swing of her hips is hypnotic as she walks out on the stage.

I feel like she's a fucking witch, casting some enchantment over me to take my soul but I hold my fucking ground and refuse to give an inch.

Her panties stay on and she has little star pasties over her nipples but she might as well be riding a fucking cock onstage, the way the crowd greets her. She takes to the pole like she was made for it, lots of fucking practice there. No way is this her first gig, no way she hasn't gone pro before.

Cuntstruck.

No.

Abso-fucking-lutely not.

There's no fucking way I'm being 'struck and certainly not by some fucking stripper. Nope. Fuck no.

I need some goddamn whiskey, straight and by the fucking gallon. I flag down Speck and he frowns as he walks over to me but there's no way I'm letting her run off without a set of eyes on her until I figure out what the fuck I'm gonna do about this situation.

"Watch her."

He shrugs. "I have been from the second she got here. Has something happened? Someone else tried to touch her again?"

It doesn't matter to me that he's my cousin, my blood and someone I grew up with, the fucking longing in his voice just sucker punches me.

"You touch her, I kill you. Simple as that. Keep your eyes on her and call me the fucking second anything happens. I need a fucking gallon of whiskey to forget this fucking night has even happened."

Speck's eyes turn into saucers. "Are you— holy fucking shit, are you kidding me?! Tell me you're just going for dibs here and you're not 'struck? Fuck Tomi, of fucking course you'd be 'struck on her."

I peg him with a look. "I meant what I fucking said, touch her and you're bleeding the fuck out. I'm out, I have too much shit to do to be standing around here fucking gossiping."

I walk out to the sound of him cussing me the fuck out but really he's only saying the shit swirling in my goddamn head anyway.

The motherfucking Callaghan Curse.

I wasn't built for that bullshit. Rue has the patience of a fucking saint with all of the shit he's been dealing with for Poe but I'm not that man. I'm the type that fucks a new woman every night. The type who keeps his shit on lockdown so I never have to worry about child support or alimony.

I'm not going to get stuck with a fucking stripper and all of the baggage that comes with them. Fuck.

I get on my hog and ride back to the clubhouse, ready to get so fucking drunk I forget about today and find some biker bitch to suck me off, but instead I find a parking lot full of motorbikes and music blaring out of the bar.

Fantastic.

The fucking Bay Charter of the Unseen are here.

Just what I fucking need.

I could go inside and see the lot of them. I could spend a few hours drinking with the Boar and his crew, trying to soak up any little clues and signs about the rat problem. I could do my fucking job, the job I've had a handle on my entire life, but the fucking second my eyes landed on Angel everything fucking changed.

I think about turning my bike around and heading straight back to the fucking Boulevard but instead I perch my ass on my bike and cuss myself and the curse right the fuck out because it's happening already. I'm already feeling that fucking noose around my neck choking the life outta me and it's only been a fucking hour since I laid eyes on her.

How the fuck does Rue live like this?

Instead, I clear my calendar.

I'd been meaning to do a full audit of The Boulevard and finding myself fucking 'struck by a pair of tits with a mean right hook just has me moving that shit forward a couple of weeks.

When I make my way through the clubhouse Farrah waves at me, all coaxing fingers and pouty lips just how I like, but my dick says no fucking thanks.

I'm not fucking happy about it.

"Why don't you wanna come play with me? It's been forever."

Fuck it. I glare at her. "It ain't the time, I've got shit to do. Go find someone else to fuck."

The pout goes from seductive to hurt in a split second. Fucking 'struck, I don't need this kinda shit messing up my life. "Don't look at me like that, I've got a job to do around here that isn't getting on my knees. Find someone who's interested."

She storms off and half the bar starts whooping and jeering at her little old tantrum.

"Since fucking when do you say no to Farrah? Your dick broken or something?" Hawk says with a laugh and I give him a look.

"Good fucking morning to you too. Is Mom around? I need to talk to her about Trink."

That wipes the grin off of his face. "What the hell is she up to now? I'm gonna have to lock her in the fucking house at this rate."

It would be helpful to me if he did. "She's been skipping school again. I'm gonna have Speck start following her around. Law's been doing it but he's got his own classes to get to."

Hawk rolls his shoulders back and grunts at me. "Shouldn't be using club resources for this shit. The girl needs to pull her fucking head in."

I shrug at him and check I've got everything I need. Keys, wallet, guns, a knife strapped to my belt and my phone. Ready as ever for a quiet night out in Coldstone. "She's a Callaghan. What exactly were you expecting? We're lucky she hasn't run off to another club to shake her ass on tables and do lines in the bathroom."

He winces and glances around. "Fuck, don't talk like that. It'll just give her fucking ideas. You were too fucking easy, kid. Makes being her pops that much fucking harder."

I scoff and leave him to his drink, jogging down the steps and over to my hog. It's a thing of fucking beauty, custom built by me and Rue over the last couple of years. He's the grease monkey, never happy unless his hands are covered in oil and there's something in pieces in his garage. I'm the tech guy. Too fucking smart not to go to college but I made for-fucking-sure the club knew where my head was at before I left.

I live and bleed for the Unseen.

I'd die for my brothers.

Going to college meant I could learn how the hell to keep us safer. It means I now know how to build security systems from the ground up. I can rig up fucking anything my club needs and if I can't, I know someone who can for the right price. I might not be able to build a rat finding machine but I can put in enough cameras and mics to catch the fuckers out.

There isn't an inch of the clubhouse or MC property I haven't got ears on.

Makes it easier to find out exactly who Angel Valleti really is because I'm going to learn everything there is to know about the stripper who's 'struck me and then I'll get her the fuck outta Coldstone and my club.

No way I'm losing everything to some piece of ass.

The roar of the engine is loud in the quiet, still air of the night. I pass Alby shutting up his garage as I pull out of the compound, Posey dancing around the old Comet in those tiny jean shorts of hers that I'm sure haunt Rue's dreams.

That shit used to make me laugh... not so much right now.

Speck gives me a look when I arrive at the club, flicking his cigarette to the ground and slouching his way over to me like this whole fucking night is just a normal Tuesday.

"Nothing's happened since you were gone, asshole. No need to ride up in here looking for blood."

I shrug and swing off of the motorbike. "I thought I told you to keep an eye on her?"

He groans and rubs a hand over his face. "I got Mike watching her while I escorted a few dickheads out. Shouldn't you be at the clubhouse with the Bay charter?"

"Change of plans. I have audits to do and I need you to tail Trink for a few days, figure out where the fuck she's been going."

He groans. "Fuck, I think I'd rather stick nails in my eyeballs than follow her ass around. Do I have the club's permission to kill whatever asshole she's sneaking around with?"

I wish. "Just don't fucking lose her. Don't interfere or start a fucking riot, just get me the fucking intel and I'll sort her out."

He nods and rolls his shoulders back. He's the shortest out of the cousins but he's already fucking stacked, too many nights of working out instead of studying for school. He barely graduated, only walked the stage because Mom told him she'd tan his fucking ass if he flunked out.

She's followed through with her threats on us boys enough for him to pull his fucking head in. Trink needs a little more of that shit to get her head back into line but, fuck, I think Mom's attention was just a little too preoccupied by her own antics to remember that her daughter is still a descendant of Rogan Callaghan, the original Unseen MC Prez. The man who built the pipeline and ruled the Dirty South with nothing but a revolver and his old hog.

"I'll let Diamond know I'm out. She likes having me around, Dustin isn't pulling his weight now Maddy had the baby."

Fucking babies. Bitches and babies, a single drop of sweat works its way down my spine.

I have no fucking time for that shit. None. Zero. Another fucking reason this 'struck bullshit needs to disappear. I don't need to be locked down by a woman who comes with some asshole's babies. Strippers always come with baggage and I'd put money on Angel having some asshole ex.

She's too fucking hot not to.

I try to keep my mind on the topic at hand because the tone of his voice has alarm bells ringing in my fucking head. "Diamond likes having you round because she wants a patch. She doesn't give a fuck who she gets that shit from, she just wants to be in the life. Stay the fuck away from her and if you can't help yourself, stick to blowjobs. Just a little advice from your blood."

He grins and shrugs. "Maybe I don't give a fuck about whether or not she's into me. Maybe I just want a warm hole and a great set of tits to blow all over."

I shake my head at the asshole because he's gotta get his head outta his ass over this shit soon. There's this mindless greed that the girls around here have because all of Coldstone know who we are and what we deal in. There isn't a member in the charter that's having money troubles, the average cut for a single weapons run is more than most folk make in a year.

It's why The Boulevard is such a win-win for us. The girls get all of their own tips plus a retainer to stay clean and loyal. The drinks in this place make a tidy profit and the laundering opportunities are endless.

We just need the right fucking accountant to smooth things out a little more, then maybe my headache from this place would ease off.

Mike dips his head at me as we pass and I return the gesture. He's a decent enough sort of guy. Here to feed his kids and pay his ex child support. Hears nothing, sees nothing, ready to bury a body at the drop of a hat.

Perfect employee.

The fact that I have a file full of his criminal activity helps to make sure he stays loyal to the club. I'm not the type of man to leave that shit to chance.

I try to keep my eyes away from the stage but the crowd here is unbelievable. It's a fucking Tuesday and yet there isn't a free seat to be found by the main stage. Diamond looks fucking wrecked, the drinks are flowing and even Mel is serving instead of dancing.

"Busy night! The new girl is fucking popular."

My teeth hurt as I grind them together viciously. "Looks like it. Get your ass on over to Trink."

He gives me a look but doesn't bother questioning me. Wise move, I'm beyond not in the fucking mood.

I wait until I'm at the bar, pouring my second shot of whiskey and ignoring the flirty glances from Diamond herself, and then I look over at the show Angel is giving.

Big mistake.

Huge.

My blood turns to fucking ice at the same time as my belly fills with rage-fueled fire. I take the second shot without looking away from the sinful swing of her hips as she twirls around the pole, her ass completely showing thanks to the thong she's rocking. The matching black bra is still in place but the cash being thrown on the stage in fucking stacks is proof that no one is leaving until her tits come out to play.

When she suddenly tips and flips upside down, her legs splitting open in a full fucking show of flexibility, my cock doesn't just come to the party. Nope, I nearly fucking bust a nut, instantly at the edge of coming at the thought of her splitting those legs for me.

I wonder if her pussy tastes just like the honey scent of her.

I wonder if her pussy feels like the fucking heavenly place it looks on the damn stage. I've never been a jealous man. Never given a fuck about what the girls I've been fucking are doing when I'm not balls deep in them.

I'm about a half-second away from ripping some arms clean off of patrons' bodies, the way they're all calling out to her and trying to reach out to touch her. She's far enough away from them that she's safe but fuck.

I don't want them touching what's mine.

"Call her down once the song ends. Send Mel up there for an hour, I wanna talk to the new girl. Get a feel of her," I say to Diamond the second she saunters back over to me.

She frowns. "She's not the type to fuck the boss, Tomi. Forget about her, I know exactly what you like."

I swipe the bottle and stand up from my barstool. "What I want is you to shut your fucking mouth and do as I say. I didn't ask for your fucking opinion."

The sultry look evaporates and I make my way back out to my office before she can even attempt to reply. Fuck, I'm likely to just snap and fucking fire her but that would just be a fucking headache and a half for me.

Keep your fucking head together, Callaghan.

Forget about the motherfucking curse.

The office is small enough that the second she opens the door I can smell her. She smells the same as last time, the sweet honey that has me fucking hungry for a bite out of her, and it just gets my hackles up even worse than last time.

"Diamond said you wanted to speak to me."

She's hesitant. None of the usual bravado or seduction I'm used to and I sound like a fucking asshole when I jerk my head at the empty chair and snap, "Park your ass. You'll be here a while."

She swallows and sits down, her arms wrapping around her bare waist. Fuck, she's still sitting there in nothing but the bra and tiny thong, streaks of glitter covering her body that definitely isn't hers. Mel uses the shit and it's slowly but surely covering every surface of the place, no matter how thorough the cleaners are.

"Have I... done something wrong?"

I shuffle some pages and then place them in front of her. "I dunno, have you? Diamond said you're a good worker but I like to know this sort of shit for myself. You need to fill this paperwork out, I need some references."

She bites at her lip, the first sign of seduction I've spotted in her, but she takes the pen and starts to fill in the forms. "I don't have references. This is the first... dancing job I've done. If I'm not doing a good job, please tell me so I can... fix whatever it is that I'm doing wrong."

Fucking lying bitch. There's a couple of dozen men out there who will back me up that there's no way this is her first fucking stripping gig.

She works the pole the same way I want her working my dick; slow, dirty, and like a fucking pro.

"Why are you in Coldstone? Or do you travel in?"

She bites that lip again. "I travel in. Look, I'm not here for friends. Is there a like... employment reason you're asking me this?"

I lean back in the chair and drag my eyes over her again, slow enough that she starts fucking squirming. "Does it matter? You work at my club, you answer my fucking questions."

She ducks her head and nods, the pen moving a little faster on the page as she fills everything in and then she hands it over.

I huff out a breath. "You're really not gonna tell me where the fuck you've worked before?"

She chews her lip again, the lipstick of hers fucking bomb-proof because it doesn't smear at all. "I've never danced in a club before. I did competitive dance for ten years and a couple of pole classes. That's it, I swear. If I've done something to jeopardize my job here please let me know."

The tremor in her voice pisses me off. "Get back to work, I have better shit to do than listen to some dumb slut's lies."

Her cheeks are bright red as she stands and walks out, her back straight and her legs steady on those killer heels of hers.

I don't know what I was expecting, not from the girl who doesn't want to be touched, but it wasn't that. I don't have time for a fucking mystery but it looks like I have one anyway.

Fucking perfect.

Three

Chapter Seven

Angel

Tomi becomes a regular face at The Boulevard and everything just gets fucking worse.

He sits in a booth with whiskey and paperwork everywhere but his eyes never stray far from me. The other girls take notice of this pretty damn quick and suddenly they move from a passive dislike to a very active hatred of me.

They start fucking with my shit.

Diamond moves my dances around so I'm never doing the same nights. At first I think it's because she wants to get me off of the busy nights to try and mess with my income but then Speck starts writing my shifts up on the menu board when a couple of the regulars complain.

My shifts are never quiet.

Mike the bouncer starts commenting about all of the extra shifts he's getting and when I wince at him he grins back at me. "Nah, I gotta pay for braces for my twins. It's the best fucking thing to happen for my family, girlie."

I give him a smile in return, he's always nice to me and he's never once tried to touch me. Diamond sees the fucking smile and calls out to Mike from the bar, "She's the worst fucking option if you're stepping out on Kara, Mikey. Might wanna pick one of the girls whose pussy isn't so fucking cold."

I glance around but it's the first night in a while Tomi hasn't beaten me here.

I duck my head and keep walking because I don't wanna get involved with that shit at all. I don't want rumors to start. I've lived through that shit before, I'm never going back to that kind of shit… not if I can help it. So I head out to the back rooms to get ready without telling her to fuck off or to choke, which is exactly what I want to do.

Diamond also picks a new fucking theme for all of the nights I have shifts. They're not good themes either, it's all tacky porno shit that means she can dress up in the cheesiest shit. I put my own spin on everything and, though she bitches about it as loud as she fucking can, none of the guys crowding around my stage have a single complaint.

I'm in the locker room in front of one of the mirrors gluing crystals to my face thanks to one of these stupid themes when Speck ducks his head into the locker room and plasters a grin on his face even though he looks like he's in pain. "You're at college right? Like, that's what you're doing during the day?"

I glue the last crystal to my face, just below my eye and start stashing my makeup back in my bag. "Yeah, why's that?"

He steps into the room and keeps his eyes on my face. I'm the only stripper he doesn't eye off and I don't know what caused the change in him but I'm fucking grateful. I kind of think he wants to be my friend.

"Okay so my kid neighbor is here and she needs help with her homework and I know exactly nothing about geometry. Numbers ain't my fucking thing. Tomi usually helps her but he's gotten caught up with club business and she isn't the type of kid to leave alone for too long, ya know? She'll get into fucking trouble here and then my ass is on the line for letting her into the club."

I turn to face him properly. "What the hell is a child doing in a strip club? You didn't think that one through a little better?"

He scoffs out a laugh and picks up my shirt from where it's hanging on the rail and throws it at me. "She's not a child… I mean, she's almost seventeen so she's definitely not supposed to be here but her tits are about as big as yours so she's not gonna be scarred by seeing what goes on around here. Still, put the shirt on and come help before Rue comes down here and skins us all alive."

Rue.

That's the other biker in charge of this place, the one Diamond wants to bed more than she wants air according to

Mel.

"I'm supposed to be dancing in a half-hour."

He nods and waits for me to pull a long dress back on over my head, something flowy that won't fuck with the body paint I've just spent nearly an hour getting on.

He takes me over to the main office, the bigger room that I'd been in when I'd met Tomi. I feel the first little tremors of nerves building in my stomach but when Speck grins at me I force a smile on my face.

I'll fake this shit until I make it.

Before he opens the door he cringes and turns back to me. "Can you do me a favor, Angel? Don't ever mention me talking about how big her tits are. It's better for everyone if that shit stays between us. It's… it's kind of a life or death thing. Just forget it."

Weird.

Does he have a thing for her?

Ugh, I don't have time to think about his love life beyond not wanting to be a part of it.

I nod and he opens the door, ushering me in before him. There's a flash and I duck at just the right time to miss the calculator being thrown at us both but he doesn't see it coming.

It bounces off of his chest like it's nothing.

"Holy shit, I'm sorry! I was expecting it to be Reece comin' in here being an asshole! Fuck, are you okay?"

I straighten up and on reflex jab Speck in the ribs for laughing so hard at the shriek that just tore out of me. "It's fine! Totally fine, I'm here to help with your homework."

I step into the room and scowl over my shoulder at Speck where he's still freaking cackling. The office is way messier than the last time I saw it, piles and piles of bookwork and invoices littering every surface. The girl is set up on the desk on top of it all, sitting in Tomi's chair with her chin propped up on her fist and scowling.

She's as cute as fuck.

"Angel, meet Posey. Flower child, meet Angel. She's our new girl, the money-maker."

I huff at him and take a seat, the same one I was in when I was last in here, and then I smile at Posey. She gives me a grin and says, "I go by Poe. There's no way a hot piece of ass like you knows something as boring as fucking geometry. No way. I need Tomi's grumpy ass to come teach me."

I snort, slapping a hand over my mouth and glancing behind me like he's got the place bugged and will burst in here. Speck roars with laughter and slouches into the chair by the door.

"Angel goes to college during the day, she's probably smarter than Tomi."

I shrug. "I wouldn't say that. I'm good with numbers though, gimme a look at what's giving you trouble."

She sighs dramatically and pushes a workbook over to me. It's all stuff I can do and even with a quick glance at it I can see she's gotten it all wrong so far. When I tell her that, she throws herself back in the chair dramatically.

"Fuck this! Seriously, why was I cursed with a low fucking IQ. You know my sister is a certified genius, right Speck? Went to the best school in the fucking country on a scholarship, she's a fucking genius and I'm over here in this little podunk town like an inbred fucking hick."

Speck chuckles at her dramatics again, and her eyes narrow at him. "Why the fuck are you laughing? You're not any fucking smarter, you barely fucking graduated."

He shrugs. "I don't need to be a genius, I just gotta win fights." He looks over at me, batting his eyelashes. "I do win them, by the way. I win 'em all thanks to growing up a Callaghan. Rue made sure of that."

I shrug again. "I'm sure you do."

Poe scoffs. "Stop fucking flirting, I don't need to know about whose ass you're chasing."

I cringe and grab a spare piece of paper to start working out equations for her, writing out exactly how I'm doing it so she can refer back to it later, and I try to block them both out.

It hurts me a little to know that they all think I'm climbing into bed with the bikers here. To have them all think about me that way… not that there's anything wrong with that, I guess, it's just not something I want.

Poe seems really sweet.

"Don't talk about Angel like that, Graves. She's not interested in my dumb ass or anyone else so don't treat her like that."

I blush a little at the scorn in Speck's voice. His phone starts ringing and he steps out of the room to answer it.

Poe clears her throat and says, "Sorry if that was rude. I'm just… used to the guys coming here to pick a girl out for the night."

I shrug and check my watch, I still have ten minutes left. "It's fine. I'm just here to do a job. I don't want to start anything with anyone."

I glance up to see Poe chewing on her lip. Speck steps back in with a little frown right as she says, "Most girls are drooling over the likes of Speck so I'm sure he's crying himself to sleep over it."

He flips her off. "Poe's just pissed she's still not old enough to hang out with us when she wants too. She's the baby of the family."

"You are exactly eighteen months older than me, Reece, don't be a fucking asshole or I'm calling Keely and she'll have your ass."

He shrugs and flings himself back on the chair in the corner. "Eighteen months still means I'm free and you're stuck doing fucking geometry."

She throws a pen at him without looking and it still hits him directly between the eyes. "Good arm."

She quirks a grin at me. "Thanks! Growing up with these assholes means I'm pretty fucking good at it."

I huff out a laugh at her and side-eye Speck. "You're only eighteen? Jesus. Mel's old enough to be your mom and she's chasing your ass hard."

He grins back at me. "I do love an older woman. If she asks about me, put in a good word, would ya?"

I roll my eyes at him and try to write a little faster, conscious of how long I have left before I have to get out there.

Poe leans forward in her chair to look at my work. "How long have you been dancing here? No one's told me about you, I'm a little pissed I didn't know you were here."

I shrug. "A few weeks. I... uh, I don't really hang out with the other girls."

She scoffs and sits back in the chair with the first page of notes. "Lemme guess, Diamond hates you and now the other girls are being bitches to you? Diamond is a cunt, for real."

I glance around the room like this is a trap and the stripper herself is about to jump out and fire me. "She's not happy that I only dance. She thinks I'm a frigid bitch… she thinks that I think I'm too good to be friends with them all."

She giggles. "Angel, I've only had to meet you to know that you are too good for them and it's got nothing to do with them being strippers. Fuck, if my ass looked like yours I'd be up there taking dumbass men's money too."

Speck groans and stares up at the ceiling. "Don't even fucking joke like that, it'd end in a bloodbath."

That makes no sense.

Poe huffs and then we both jump at the sound of the door snapping open and bouncing off of the wall. Tomi walks through, pausing when his eyes land on me. The corners of his mouth turn down and my heart stops in my chest.

Poe comes to my rescue. "Where the hell have you been? You promised me you'd help with this bullshit!"

I cringe a little at the way she's talking to him, he's built like a freaking brick shithouse, but he just huffs out a breath at her. "You didn't have to distract the dancers to get back at me. Angel, you're late."

I scramble to my feet and duck my head as I walk past him, cursing under my breath at myself. I enjoyed myself for half a second and it bites me on the ass.

By the time I take the stage Tomi is in his booth, whiskey in his hand and his eyes follow my every move.

Poe is gone before I make it back out.

Chapter Eight

Tomi

I spend way too long hanging around at The Boulevard watching Angel.

I make it clear to the girls that I'm doing an audit of the business, something I do on the regular anyway because it's our biggest legitimate money maker, and then I set up in a booth every night where I can see every fucking twirl and shimmy the girl does on stage.

It's a special type of hell because, fuck, can that girl move.

Diamond gives me all of the books, a bottle of whiskey, and the offer of a blowjob in the back room on the first night I arrive. The shock on her face when I pass on the blowjob isn't just clear to me, the girls all see it and start fucking gossiping but I've never really given a fuck about that bullshit.

By the sixth night in a row like this, I'm sure word has gotten around because I find myself joined by my cousin within the first fucking hour.

"You wanna tell me why you're stalking this place now?" Rue orders a drink from Diamond with a jerk of his head and I pointedly don't look at the new girl.

He notices her anyway. "Fuck. New blood and she's exactly your type. Tryna be the first one in her then?"

I blow out a breath and face the facts. There's no fucking way I'm going to get through this pile of bullshit without having someone on my side. I've watched Rue chase his little flower child around for fucking years and I've dug him out of shit more times than either of us would ever admit to.

I don't even have to tell him. The second I turn to face him he sees it on my face. "Oh fuck no. No. Really? A stripper? That's bad fucking news, man."

I scoff and drain the rest of my glass. "No shit. Looks like you're the only one getting a decent woman assigned by the fucking curse. Congratulations. Who'd a thought it'd be Grimm fucking Graves' kid?"

His eyebrows drop down low and I shrug. "I'm fucking bitter tonight, ignore me. Riddle me this, do you feel like you've been shot in the fucking chest all the damn time? Does the curse make you wanna fucking die or is that just me and my cuntstruck self?"

He gestures at Diamond to leave us the goddamn bottle, wise move, and gets to pouring the shit out. I drink it faster than he can pour, my eyes drifting over to rest on Angel no matter how I try to avoid looking at her.

She's the hottest fucking thing I've ever seen.

"It always feels like that shit. Fuck, Posey disappears for six fucking weeks every year, you don't think that kills me? I don't even know where the hell she goes, let alone who she's with. Thorn tells me fucking nothing."

We're not allowed to ask either.

Part of his agreement with King is that Poe is off-limits. No one touches her, no one asks about her, and we all protect her with our lives.

For the life of me, I don't fucking get why.

A group of new guys arrive and the whole damn lot of them walk over to the main stage where Angel is, even the regulars who have favorite girls. It's pretty fucking clear that the other girls are pissed the hell off about it but the booze is flowing and men are ordering private dances left and right thanks to the tease happening on stage.

She's too fucking flexible, gets a man fucking excited.

"So… gimme her story then. What do you know, how are we getting her the fuck out of this club before she starts a fucking riot? Jesus, Mel is looking at her like she wants to stab her eyes out."

I whip my head around to check her out and, yep, the loathing there is clear.

Hm.

That might work to get her outta here.

"I know nothing. Nothing except she won't do lap dances, won't work on the side like the other girls, and she wants as many shifts as she can get her hands on."

Rue shrugs and fills his glass again. "That's a mark in her favor. At least up there they're only looking. Fuck, is she the one that smacked Maverick out last week?"

My jaw clenches violently. "He tried to touch her. She told him she didn't do that and he didn't fucking listen to her. That's how I met her, I've been too fucking busy with Trink's bullshit to be down here all that much."

Rue grimaces. "Guess you've got Speck watching her now? Fuck, this is a mess. You hear about the shipment?"

We're in public so there's not much more that I can say but, "Yeah. We need pest control right the fuck now."

Rats.

Everywhere. At first we were thinking it was prospects but we stopped taking new members and yet here we are, losing shipments left and fucking right. Absolute fucking bullshit, the only thing we should all be able to trust in is brotherhood and yet we're being betrayed left and fucking right.

"It's getting worse now King's home."

If that isn't a fucking mess as well.

Rue lost his dad to lockup at twelve-years-old, now to have him back at twenty-four as not only his dad but his Prez… lotta shit to deal with there. A fucking lot of shit.

He left behind a boy and came out to a man, one raised by his brother and enough fucking demons running riot in his head that it's going to take a little more than a homecoming to mend what's broken.

I get my eyes away from the girl and back onto my cousin. "It's beyond that. They're just starting up after lying in wait. Gotta keep our eyes open and our ears to the ground."

Rue grunts and takes a sip of his drink, muttering and cursing under his breath as he shifts around to get his phone out of his pocket. "Trink and Poe are going to some dipshit's party tonight. Speck just sent a photo of what they're wearing and you need to tell Trink to quit her shit."

I roll my eyes. "What the hell do you think I've been doing? She's a fucking nightmare, doing whatever the hell she can to piss me and Hawk off. Women are more fucking trouble than they're worth."

As if fucking summoned by my words, Diamond sashays her ass over to the table and brings a new bottle with her.

Rue nods at her and then says, "What's the deal with the new chick?"

She blinks at him.

Yeah, he's not exactly known for chasing tail. He keeps any of that shit as far away from Coldstone as he can fucking manage because nothing on this Earth is going to mess with with his little flower.

"Well I'll be fucking damned. I mean, she's hot but I didn't think she was hot enough to tempt Ruin fucking Callaghan. Those tits of hers magic or something?"

I don't like that.

I might be fucking pissed about being 'struck but it's powerful shit and I'm not fucking happy about her talking about Angel like she's a piece of meat.

Rue doesn't even need to look at me to spot it, he just directs the conversation to something a little less likely to piss me off. "She's getting a lotta interest. It's not good for the club for us to ignore that now is it?"

She huffs a little but I can see the temper tantrum melting away now she knows it's just business. It's pathetic how easy all the strippers get hot and fucking bothered about him.

Ain't a woman in this place that hasn't tried to coax my cousin into bed.

"She's a good worker but not exactly willing to go above and beyond. She's on time, dances like a dream, and keeps her shit in line but there's been a lotta interest in getting private dances from her and she won't budge. A bit jumpy, I think in a few months once everyone is over her pretty face and the money dries up a little she'll sing a different tune. They always do."

Rue nods and jerks his head at the bar. "You've got a line waiting. Off you go."

She huffs and walks away with an extra shake to her ass like that'll tempt him.

It won't.

He leans over to slide my glass at me and encourages me to drink the fuck up. "So you've got until the shine wears off to get her the fuck outta here. You think you can handle that?"

I shake my head. "I've never met a stripper without a problem. She's either got a pimp, a drug addiction, or four hungry kids at home. Not the kinda situation I wanna get myself into. I'm steering clear."

Rue nods at me, his face serious for about a second before the mask slips and he's smirking at me. "Then why the fuck are you still here then, brother? If she doesn't have you wrapped up tight then why are you staring at her ass like you wanna spread her out on the stage and fuck her so good that everyone watching knows who she belongs to?"

Goddammit.

He's not exactly wrong but I fucking hate her for doing this to me. I drain the last of the whiskey in my glass and slide the empty glass away from myself because I can already feel it taking effect... like how badly I want to walk over to the guy trying to talk to Angel right now and break his fucking legs.

"Fuck me, things are about to get interesting around here." Rue laughs and I ignore the fucker.

It's not like I've been cleaning up after him and Poe for years.

I'm a nice enough person not to fucking say it to him though.

My response to being 'struck doesn't get any better as the weeks stretch on.

I put Speck back on watch down at The Boulevard even though he'd be fucking handy for keeping an eye on Trink right now. It's probably a shit move that'll haunt me later but the fucking cuntstruck heart has demands and keeping an eye on Angel becomes my top fucking priority.

Even if I do fucking hate her for breathing.

My solution is to drink a lot. A whole fucking lot.

After another night of auditing books at The Boulevard that just don't quite add up I head back to the clubhouse to lose myself in a fucking large bottle of Jack. It's crowded and rowdy as hell for the night which grates on my fucking nerves.

I slump down at the end of the bar, ignoring everyone so they'll get the fucking picture not to bother speaking to me, and I jerk my head at Monroe behind the bar so she'll come serve me a drink. I fucking hate the bitch but if she's on then there's no way out of talking to her.

"If it isn't the prodigal son. Fucked any good strippers lately? I heard there's a newbie down there that has the boys panting after her."

My teeth start aching from all the grinding I'm doing. "Leave the fucking bottle."

She huffs. "You'll never move outta the clubhouse if you keep wasting your cut from the runs on whiskey and titties."

I drink from the bottle and then look around until I catch Diesel's eye. "If you don't come put a leash on her I'm going to throw her the fuck out. Simple as that."

It kills him to hear me talk like that. Kills him because there's sweet fuck all he could do to stop me. I'm higher up the fucking food chain and it's got nothing to do with my blood.

There isn't a piece of tech used in the club that I haven't ordered, programmed, and set up. D's still fucking pissy that I went off to college and still managed to come home and patch in before him.

I've got a brain and he's nothing but a glorified grease monkey, working in the garage and thinking he's hot shit for the patch on his back.

He's all the shitty things Rue isn't, with his head for money and blood and strategy.

"Monroe, get your nose outta club business. Serve the fucking drinks and move on, that's all you gotta do," he snarls at her, but she shrugs at him like he's fucking nothing to her.

Exactly why I don't need a woman.

They're all bad fucking news.

The door to the bar swings open and in walks Trink looking like a fucking porn star wannabe in shorts so cutoff I can see her fucking underwear.

One of the Bay guys whistles and immediately gets punched in the gut because ain't another biker here who doesn't know who the fuck my baby sister is.

Godammit.

"What the fuck are you looking so sour for? STI check come back with bad news?" she laughs, grabbing my bottle and pouring herself a shot in the glass I've forgotten about.

"What the hell are you doing here? It's a school night, go the fuck to bed."

She laughs again and kicks at me under the table. "We can't all be the genius of the family. I've been over watching Poe rebuild some engine, Thorn just came and bitched Pops out and dragged her home. She has the new Vanth Falling EP though and we got to listen to the whole thing twice through. Fuck knows how the hell she got it, that shit isn't out for another month. It's good shit though, Morrison could fucking get it."

I know what it is and there's no fucking way.

I'm not all fucking holier-than-thou about my little sister's sex life but she's seventeen and makes the fucking worst decisions. She lives by the seat of her pants and enjoys nothing more than pissing me and Hawk the fuck off.

If there's a bad choice to be made, Trink's gonna skip off into the sunset with it like a cheery fucking delight.

For a biker, I'm much more cautious than she is.

She got the full Callaghan bloodlines of reckless, raunchy, and fucking rowdy and I'll be in an early grave because of it. She's my responsibility until she's locked down by some other asshole but I'll be damned if it's not going to be someone I approve of.

She grins at the glare in my eyes and tilts her head at the front door, "Hawk wants to talk to you. He's out there with your Prez."

Fucking brat.

I take the bottle with me because there's no way I'm leaving her with that shit and I head out of the clubhouse, taking the stairs three at a time until I'm standing over in the trees with my blood.

I'm careful to make sure it's not the same trees I stood near with Luis.

Can't be too careful.

Rue kicks at the rocks with his boot, a scowl on his face as he looks out past the trees and over the parking lot to Pops' garage. The lights are still on there but only in the apartment, the old man shut up shop for the night.

"Another shipment is gone."

No way.

There's fucking no way anyone could possibly bug that room.

I swept the whole fucking thing, I have the best tech and I'm fucking thorough. My brothers' lives depend on this shit and I did it all stone cold sober, days before Angel clouded my shit.

King nods at me. "I know. I know it ain't you or your tech, but there's rats higher up in this club then we'd like.

Hawk stubs out his cigarette and says, "We're gonna have to start some new protocols."

Rue groans and rubs a hand over his face. "Right. So how's this gonna fall? It's gotta be locked the fuck down to an inner circle no one knows jack about? Who's in and who's out?"

Hellion lights up a blunt and takes a puff, passing it on to Hawk who smokes that thing like it's the last one on Earth.

"Family only for now. Blood is all we can trust until we've got this shit on lockdown. We'll start up family dinners again." King says and Hawk nods.

"Keely keeps pushing for it anyway, makes it a safe option. Tell the men we're trying to keep shit normal for now. Get the club back to family friendly and all that shit so we're covered. Tomi, you need to rig up the back room. Make sure that shit is locked down tight and we can get a fucking plan in the works. Fucking rats in my club. I'm not having this shit touching my girls."

I nod. No way Mom or Trink are getting fucking hurt by this shit.

I have my own suspicions on who it is but when it comes to brotherhood you gotta step careful. Keep your feet in line and make sure no one gets put out or suspicious until we're ready to strike.

Then we'll burn the whole fucking lot of them out.

Chapter Nine

Angel

The situation with the other girls doesn't get any better as time goes on.

Actually, with the crowds around my stage getting bigger and bigger, their attitudes get bitchier and more freaking obvious. Every shift starts with whispers and giggling, and when I shower at the end they all talk about me in the locker room where I can hear them.

"I heard her old man has a habit. She's in here working to keep him in the gear."

"I heard he's her pimp, not her boyfriend. Guess he wants to be the only one selling her pussy."

"Imagine having some man telling you who to fuck and taking your money? Fucking pathetic."

"I wonder if her pussy is any good? Maybe all these men throwing the cash at her don't even realize she's fucking loose and used up."

It's pathetic to me that they're all out there talking shit about me like that. I know exactly what extras they offer and not once have I shamed any of them on that shit. Not fucking once.

I don't want to sell myself like that because I'm fucking terrified of being touched, not because I have some moral high ground. Fuck, they all call me the frigid bitch… I'm actually the broken bitch, that girl who thinks about touching a man and runs the fuck away.

Well.

Mostly.

There's been two times in the last few weeks of a client trying to climb on stage and grab me. Both of them were fucking wasted and didn't really know what they were doing but that's not at all an excuse.

Both times Speck stopped them.

One he simply grabbed by the scruff of his neck and walked him out of the club, the guy drunk enough to not be any trouble. The other guy fought him, gave him a shiner, and when he finally got rid of him and went out the back to grab ice I finished my dance and then went out to find him.

I gave him a hug.

A quick one and I didn't really love it but I felt like he'd been there for me and even though it's technically his job, I still appreciated him respecting my boundaries.

The grin he gives me isn't at all flirty, like my continued aloof treatment has firmly drilled it into his head that I'm not the girl for him.

Which is good because I'm exhausted from weeks of barely getting any sleep in my truck, not enough food, and studying every second I can, so I just don't have it in me to deal with letting anyone down gently. Fuck, no one has babied me about anything since I lost my dad and I think maybe that has made me hard, unforgiving and just over everyone's bullshit.

The only thing that really starts to get to me is Tomi's presence.

I think I've caught his eye and not in a good way.

Well, neither way is good but I think I've pissed him off in some way. He was rude to me back in the office when I'd punched his brother from grabbing me, dismissive when he caught me in his office helping Poe, but now he's gotten freaking malevolent about my presence. The problem with this is that he's constantly at the club now.

I think he's having issues with the books or something because he has a booth of his own to sit in each night and he slams back the beers and whiskeys as he goes through all of the paperwork. The other girls all try to talk to him but he never really talks back to them and he never takes any of them up on their offers of… stress relief.

They all start glaring at me even more, like it's my fault he's pissed off.

I try to stay out of his way.

I hide in the shower and the locker room, I arrive on time but never early, and the second my showers are done I get the hell outta dodge.

He doesn't try to follow me or speak to me, so I count it as a win. I keep my head down, put everything I can into my dances, and I keep my mouth shut.

It works.

It works so well at keeping me under the radar that I become an easy target without even fucking noticing, my head too fucking caught up in being invisible that I forget that there are other men to have to worry about.

I come out of the back door, fishing around in my bag for my keys, my feet moving on autopilot, and I don't even notice him leaning against my car until he speaks.

"Angel, good to see you."

My stomach drops, and I clutch my bag closer to myself.

It's Finley, my college advisor, leaning against my Chevy with a smug smirk across his lips. I'm positive he can't be here to rob me but, fuck, I have tens of thousands of dollars on me right now. All of my savings are in this goddamn bag.

"Hey… this is unexpected. What are you doing in Coldstone?"

He stands up straight and I step around to sling my bag into the passenger side of my truck. Fuck, I should probably just climb in and slide over before he has the chance to grab me or something.

"One of the other students recognized you from the first distance class, he came to have a chat with me about where you're working."

I look over the tray at him, my keys still clutched in my hand like a lifeline. "I don't see how that's any of his business… or yours."

That smirk of his just gets wider. "I guess it's not but I mean, you wouldn't want me to go in and talk to the bikers in here would you? I looked up your details after I saw you here last week. Lots of shit on your application I'm sure they'd be pissed to know about. We should have dinner. Talk things over."

Jesus.

Fucking.
Christ.
Finley saunters around the car with a smug look on his face while I'm stuck there, struck dumb by his fucking threat. Fear curls in my gut but my legs are rooted to the ground no matter how hard my heart races.
"Look, I don't really date but I can give you my number? I'm tired from a long shift tonight and I'm just going to head on home. I'd love to grab dinner with you later though?"
The smile doesn't falter on his face at all, he just stands there grinning like the damn joker. "You've got this all wrong, I'm not exactly asking. You want me to keep my mouth shut about what's in your file? I want you to come have dinner. It's my shout, what girl would wanna say no to that?"
Any girl with half a goddamn brain. "Sure. Okay, I can grab dinner with you. Where are we heading and I'll meet you over there?"
He reaches out and puts his hand on my arm and I know for fucking sure in that moment that he's a shitty excuse of a man.
He sees me flinch.
He does it anyway.
I've spent a lot of time in the strip club, during my dances and out in the locker rooms. I've sat at the bar, in the office, I've helped clean down the stage because of all of Mel's freaking glitter, and not once has anyone forced their touch on me after seeing my reaction.
Fuck, Diamond loathes me and she still makes sure she doesn't so much as brush against me in the hallways.
Since Mav tried to touch me there hasn't been a single biker that's tried to either. Speck keeps a close watch of who is around me and not once has he attempted to touch me. Fuck, he's always as shocked as hell when I talk to him about something that isn't strictly stripping related.
Finley is a creep.
I don't want to go with him but if someone hasn't come out already then they're not going to save me now. The music is too loud in there for them to hear me if I start screaming and now he's got a firm grip of me. I should've run the second I saw him standing there but I need this freaking job. So my

option is go with Finley or die here now.

Fuck it.

I lock my truck up with my bag safely stashed under my seat and then I go with him.

And I'm not entirely sure that's not the wrong thing to do.

The car ride over is excruciating but Finley doesn't try to touch me again.

It becomes clear that he's not a guy girls usually say no to but… this is clearly also not the first time he's forced himself on a girl. He knows too much, like what to say to control the conversation, how to play everything off like he's swooping in to save me from myself because dinner with him is such a fucking privilege.

I'm not expecting much from the restaurant he takes me to, because why would a guy forcing me on a date take me somewhere decent, and you know what? I'm exactly right in that assumption.

The walls are covered in tacky decorations which in itself isn't that bad but there's a layer of dust on everything and the menus are greasy as hell.

I order the bare minimum. A salad and some water. He looks at me approvingly, like I've done it to impress him with a fucking diet when really I just want to get the fuck out of here and if he's paying, which he has to because my money is back in my truck, I don't want him using an expensive meal as a justification to dragging me somewhere else.

Fuck.

I really should have found another way out of this.

Too late now, he's sitting there smirking at me like this is all going according to his fucking plans. When I catch his eye by accident, he smirks at me and motions at the dusty walls.

"I thought you'd feel at home here, it's always been a staple in Coldstone for the low income houses."

Fuck, I wish he'd get hit by a goddamn bus.

I force a smile onto my face and shrug. "My family is from here but I'm not. Like I told you, it's extended family. Look, I'd appreciate it if you could keep my confidential information to yourself. This has been such a nice surprise and all, but it's not really appropriate."

That fucking smile stays put on his face. "It is confidential but if I see a student in danger, I'm contractually obligated to intervene."

Fuck him.

That doesn't sound right but I can't exactly call him out on it either. My phone is a piece of shit and doesn't connect to the internet at all, I only bought it so that I could take calls from The Boulevard about shifts or calls from Southern Miss about my classes.

"When I heard about you dancing I knew I had to come down here and check it out for myself, make sure you're not in any danger."

The sound of his voice alone sets my teeth on edge.

He's the only danger around here but he thinks he's so fucking slick, sitting there and forcing me to back down like this is some fucking game of dominance. There's no fucking way. I'm not ever going to lie down and submit to some piece of shit man ever again.

Fucking never.

I keep my mouth shut for the rest of dinner, nodding my way through his incessant prattling on about nothing and how important he is. Fuck, just listening to him you'd think he was the dean and he keeps dropping names into the conversation except I know and care about exactly none of them.

He doesn't notice.

When he's finally finished with his steak burger and fries, a large root beer float, and freaking dessert he pays for dinner and doesn't tip the waitress. I want to claw his eyeballs out for that, the girl was great to us the whole time, but instead I try to get out of the diner in front of him to get a head start.

He catches up to me easily, putting a hand on the door to stop me from leaving.

"It's early. You should come back to my place."

It's four in the morning. I shake my head before the words are completely out of his mouth. "I just want to go home and sleep."

The grin on his face just gets wider. "Come on now, Angel. I'm sure you can throw in a freebie. Consider it payment for my silence."

I grit my teeth. "I thought dinner was my payment?"

"Dinner was something nice I was doing for you. Didn't your parents teach you any manners? Do they even know where you are?"

I take a deep breath. Then I take two more. How badly do I need this job? Enough to have sex with this man? Fuck. There's only one thing I'd rather do less than that, and that's to go back to the home I'm running from.

There are other strip clubs.

Now I know what I can make, I'll just head to a bigger city. Might be easier than hiding out in this tiny ass town and finding places to sleep will probably be easier too. Shit. There are other options, just not as comfortable as The Boulevard.

I can make it work.

I just need to figure out how the hell to get away from him now.

I give him a half-smile. I can't even fake anything bigger than that. I'd noticed a gas station on the corner of the block, I'll fucking fake nice and make a run for it down there. I'm in great shape thanks to all of the acrobatics I'm getting in with my dancing so unless he's a regular runner, I should be able to make it.

"Good choice. We could make this a regular thing, I've enjoyed our time together so far."

He steps out of the restaurant ahead of me, his eyes on me the entire time, and I have to control my breathing. He's still too close to me. He could touch me, grab me, drag me by my fucking hair. I have to keep my shit together for a little longer.

Then he stops dead.

I glance up and find Tomi standing next to Finley's car, his face thunderous and fucking pissed. I'm scared for a second, he's not exactly the nicest of the bikers I've been around and the 1% badge is there on his cut like a badge of pride, but then Finley puts his arm around me and my skin begins to crawl.

I'd do anything to get him to stop.

Even throw myself at Tomi and pray he's feeling merciful.

"Hey man, I think you're scaring the girl. Maybe you should back up a bit."

I stay rooted to the spot, my knees locked up with terror at his touch, and Tomi looks me over.

"Angel, get your ass over here now."

The spell is broken just like that.

I take a single step, trying to shrug Finley's arm off, and his hand clamps down on my shoulder. My mind starts to white out with terror, his fingers tightening until I know there'll be bruises, and a weird squeak pops out of me.

Tomi moves fast for such a big guy.

One second I'm standing there freaking shaking and the next I'm stumbling towards the car, Tomi shoving me away from Finley as he smashes his face open with his fist.

I keep walking until I find Tomi's motorcycle, careful not to touch it because I know bikers can be weird about that but I stand there in my yoga pants and old band tee until he's done beating the shit outta the creep.

When he walks back over to me, his knuckles a freaking mess and blood splattered all over his shirt, his face is still fierce. I stare at the blood to try to distract myself from that anger.

I'm not sure what I've done wrong.

For the looks he's giving me, it's bad.

"Was he a John? I thought you'd dress a little better for that shit?"

That gets my attention. My mouth runs before I really think about what I'm saying. "Are you serious right now? Are you fucking kidding me?"

He glares at me, his brows drawing down even more. "I hope he wasn't your boyfriend because he's not gonna be happy when you get your ass home."

I blow out a frustrated breath and hug myself, the heat of the night doing nothing to ease the chill in my blood. "I'm not doing extra. He was an asshole who wouldn't take no for an answer. What was I supposed to do? He was leaning on my car at The Boulevard and I could either say yes or get beaten to death."

He turns to look back at the puddle of blood Finley left behind but he's crawled off somewhere else while we were distracted. "You coulda called."

I shrug. "Diamond would've hung up on me. Hell, I think any of the girls would. I'm not exactly popular."

Tomi stalks past me and climbs onto his bike, grabbing a

helmet out of the pack and holding it out to me. "Get your ass on."

Oh God.

I've never been on a motorcycle before but I don't need experience to know there's no way to stay on it without wrapping myself around him. My nerves are already shot to hell and he's going to know exactly how fucking terrified I am if I do.

"Get on, for fuck's sake, I have work to do that isn't chasing around after dumbass strippers all fucking night."

My feet move at the command in his voice and the self-loathing starts roiling in my gut. I've gotten better at shoving that shit aside to function but there's something about his voice that breaks the tethers.

Can't fucking do anything right.

Always fucking trouble.

Be better for everyone if you were fucking dead, Angel.

Why can't you just fucking disappear?

It's all in my own voice too. It's not like anyone else is saying it to me because even Paul didn't say that shit to me. No, he told me how pretty I was. He told me all about how much of a special girl I really was, all while he was breaking me open and playing around with my insides until I was a fucking shell.

He might have thought I was special, but I know for sure that I'm worthless.

"Jesus fucking Christ, put your foot on mine and swing your leg. Right, hold onto me. No, hold onto me properly. Fuck, you've really never done this before, have you?"

It's like an echo of the shit in my head and maybe that's part of my trauma because that roiling feeling settles down a little. He hates me like I hate me and maybe that's comforting.

I sit there and hold him as tight as he asks me to, my entire body crushed against his. He drives like he wants us both to die, the motorcycle eating up the road like a fucking beast, and I don't have time to think about how freaking scared I am to be this close to him.

I'm too busy flirting with death and trying not to answer its call.

I could let go of him right now and just die.

I could.

Fuck, a heady feeling takes over and… is this what being high feels like? My head goes all loopy and light, like I could fly off into another plane if I could find the tether to cut.

We get back to The Boulevard way too quickly.

I get off of the back of the bike with his help and stumble over to my truck. I fumble for the keys in my pocket and he calls out to me from where he's still straddling his bike, looking dangerous and sinful in the early morning light.

"Listen to me, Angel. You're a dancer here which means until the club chooses otherwise you're our property. If some asshole tries to damage club property, I wanna know about it. That ass of yours makes us a lotta money, no one touches it without answering to the club."

Okay.

There's my trauma again.

I shouldn't want to be club property but, fuck, that's the closest to having someone give a shit about me that I've come since my dad died.

I nod and he waits while I unlock my car and check my bag is still in there. It is and the money is untouched, thank God, and before I can slide in he says, "He comes to this town again and he'll be dead and buried here. Simple as that."

The easy way he talks about death should be scary or exciting or... something. Instead, it just sounds normal. Like, of course he'd kill him for touching club property.

I never want to quit this job for that protection alone.

I watch as he drives away, he turns left and heads out to the suburbs which is kind of weird.

I go right.

I head to the inner city with the big parking lot I can park in and catch about an hour's sleep in. I have classes tomorrow and I have to find somewhere to catch a shower too, thanks to my night of terror sweating. I take a deep breath and decide to grab a hotel in the next town over for the night. Sleep all day, get my brain working again. It's not ideal but it'll have to do.

Chapter Ten

Tomi

I call Rue from the road.

"You busy?"

He huffs down the line at me. "When am I not fucking busy? Diesel was too hungover to do his work today, told King he had family shit going on instead of admitting Monroe has him drinking himself to death, but Dave fucking backed him up when I was fixing to go break down his door. He's a pussy-whipped little bitch who needs to start pulling his fucking weight before I fucking bury him. Where the hell are you, anyway?"

I scoff at him but the sound gets eaten up by the roar of my hog. "I might need a clean up. Stick around until I call you with an all clear."

It's something he's said to me a hundred times by now, every last one of them over some dipshit looking sideways at Poe, but it's the first time I've ever had to call him in like that. To warn him that I'm about to shed blood and he'll need to come help clean it up.

"Fuck me, is she okay? Some asshole touch her again? If it was Mav, he's here at the clubhouse. I'll call his ass down here and get him warmed up for you."

There's a reason I'd take a bullet for him. I know he'd take one for me too, without a fucking question, and if some asshole is touching my woman he's going to help gut the fucker with a goddamn smile on his face.

"It wasn't Mav. Some asshole showed up at The Boulevard and forced her into his car. She didn't call because Diamond is a pissy bitch to her on shift. I'm getting the security footage and then I'm hunting the fucker down."

I don't mention that I'd gotten a call from Speck saying he'd seen her get into the car and I'd lost my fucking mind. I'd gotten on my hog and torn off after them, ready to spill fucking blood. I'm already saying way too much over the phone, Rue could be standing in the garage with fucking anyone around, but I don't care about that shit. Not at all.

I want that guy choking on his own blood.

Fuck, If I hadn't been distracted by Angel's freak out I would've killed him right there, taken his body out to the fucking swamp and left him for Cecee.

Something about seeing the woman who's 'struck you shaking like a fucking leaf messes with your head and your goddamn priorities.

Rue grunts. "Call me, I need to get rid of some of this fucking rage and ain't nothing better than beating the shit outta some asshole tryna touch something that ain't theirs to touch."

I get back to the clubhouse and Diamond's car is in the parking lot.

I don't want to fucking see her but maybe I should fucking tear into her. Tell her the petty fucking jealousies that seem to have come over her don't mean shit to me and my business and I'll fucking gut her if she doesn't stick to her goddamn job.

Fuck.

Maybe I should send Rue in for that conversation because I'm not feeling all that fucking diplomatic. I'm too fucking close to this and I'll end up fucking killing the cunt.

I sit on my hog for a while to calm myself the hell down.

Doesn't work.

The doors open and Speck stumbles down the stairs at me, two bottles of beer in his hands.

"Rue told me to give you these, might cool you down some."

I swing my leg over but lean against the seat still. "It'll take more than this."

Speck nods and blows out a breath. "Yeah… I've got more shit that might send you off the rails too."

Christ.

"Axe has a bachelor's party this weekend at the bar. They've booked out the back room, some old friend of his that goes way back."

I know exactly who he's talking about.

Jameson served in the Middle East with Axe, survived war together, and when they both came home with honors Jameson took over his family business down at the ports while Axe patched in with us.

Jameson is a big help with the guns we import.

Not that Speck would know about it, he's not patched in and very few people actually know about Jameson's involvement. We keep that shit under wraps.

"Why am I gonna care about some bachelor party? I'm happy Jameson is marrying Elizabeth, she's stuck by him through all his PTSD shit. Good woman."

Speck blows out a breath and scratches at the back of his neck. "They want some of the girls to go serve them. They have the back room and Axe wants to surprise him with a show."

Fuck.

Jesus fucking Christ.

"I told him Mel or Farrah would do it but all the guys are fucking obsessed with Angel. Diamond's in there trying to convince Axe that Angel ain't worth the effort."

Maybe I won't kill the bitch.

The jealousy might come in handy this once. I don't fucking need this headache today, not with some asshole out there still bleeding who tried to hurt her. I don't fucking want her, but I don't want her dead either. Not until… I know. Fuck. What am I thinking, I do know! Cuntstruck! She's a fucking stripper.

I grab the second bottle of beer from Speck and take the side entrance, bypassing the bar altogether and getting straight into my room. I get my computer turned on as I walk through to wash the blood that's dried on my hands.

Fuck, I shoulda killed him.

I should have fucking killed him for putting his hands on her. If I ever find out she's seeing someone I'll kill him too. I've never been the jealous type before, I've watched my cousin be fucking consumed by it and never wanted that shit for myself, but the thought of any motherfucker putting his hands on her again… Jesus, I need a fucking whiskey and a brawl to calm my shit down.

I don't get the chance to look up the security footage.

"Church!" King bellows down the hall, and even through my closed door I hear it loud and clear.

I leave my shit behind, stalking straight to the chapel and taking my seat while the others all file in at a slower pace. Hellion joins me first, slinging himself down into his chair with a groan.

"We've got runs to get into," he murmurs, and I shrug. It's about time to get back into the real Unseen business. We've been leaving it to the lower members and other charters for too long thanks to King's homecoming and now we have some leads on the fucking rats.

I glance back to see if Rue's ass has made it in yet. I need him to come hunting with me after this shit.

Hellion sighs at me. "Is your head in this or not?"

I scoff and look up to meet his eyes. He's the only one not laughing and joking around, the caretaker uncle as always. "My head's just fine. I've just got some shit going on."

He shrugs. "I heard about the new stripper you're stalking. 'Struck or just enjoying a challenge?"

I let out a breath. It's the first time someone has noticed. Well, someone who isn't Rue and Speck. Those two don't fucking count, I spend every waking fucking minute with one of them. The joys of growing up in an open house for the lost boys of the Unseen. Between my cousins and the twins there's always someone hanging around. It's always come in handy with keeping an eye on Trink but fuck if it doesn't make my skin crawl a little from all the eyes on me right now.

"It's not something I want talked about a whole lot. I'm not looking to settle down with trouble, no matter how hot the package is." Cole hands me a drink and I shoo him away. This isn't a conversation I want anyone overhearing.

Hell nods and drains his beer. "You need to let that bitch go. The curse is nothing but fucking trouble. Liza and Georgie proved that shit."

Liza would be Rue's mom. An addict and a shitty fucking human, she left when he was six and never once came back for him.

Georgie tried to take Speck with her when she left so I guess that was a half-step up but leaving the Unseen isn't on the table for a Callaghan and when Hell made that clear, she still left her son behind to chase some dream in Cali.

The thought of raising a kid here by myself, having them sleeping in the clubhouse or back at my parents' place when I'm locked up over club shit, it makes things clearer.

I'm not fucking touching her.

I finish off my beer in a single go. "Bitches are good at sucking dick and that's about it. I've got no need for a full-time piece. Fuck it, I don't wanna talk about it anymore. I don't need it getting back to Keely and her getting her hopes up."

Hell chuckles and nods. "Yeah, she'd be after some grandbabies in no time. She always was happiest with a bunch of toddlers running around."

No fucking thank you.

King and Hawk both walk in together and I shut my mouth up tight.

No way I'm letting word get out.

I'm fucked enough as it is.

After the meeting I pass the hell out.

I wait until I've had eight solid hours of sleep before I get back on my computer and find the security footage. The guy has been in The Boulevard before which makes it easy to find and run his ID.

Finley Moody.

Some rich dick, not from Coldstone, and nothing comes up on the ID check. He works for Southern Miss, drives a Range Rover, and belongs to a country club.

What a fucking asshole.

He'll be a dead asshole soon. I send his details to Rue and, after thinking about it for a half-second, I send them to Speck too. I need them both on this. If Speck is keeping an eye on Angel, which he will be until further notice, then he needs to know all about the assholes that might be a fucking problem.

He messages back straight away.

Can't take care of him. Angel's student advisor, too fucking messy. I'll keep an eye out instead.

Student advisor.

She's at college?

What a way to find out that there's so much I don't know about her. Fuck, other than the fact she's hot as hell and can work a pole better than any other girl I've ever seen I know fucking nothing about her really.

I don't like it.

What's she doing at Southern Miss?

I hate asking him but I need to fucking know.

No idea but she's good with numbers. Fucking good, Poe passed a geometry test for the first time thanks to her notes.

I don't have enough time to think that through fully. Jameson's bachelor party is being held at Mugshots, the bar the MC owns, and I said I'd drop by and have a drink with them. I don't know Jameson like Axe does but I've met him plenty of times, most of them involving a helluva lot of whiskey, and I've buried some bodies for him.

Enough that we have a mutual respect for each other.

The motherfucker doesn't miss with a long distance rifle and a scope.

I make it to Mugshots early so I can check it out before the party gets here. I want to get in and out because I'm a dumbass about Angel, even though I'm trying so fucking hard not to be. I want to go get my eyes on her and make sure Moody didn't go after her again last night.

If he knows her from college he might have her fucking address too.

Come to think of it, I need her fucking address.

It's already busy, every table full and the food and drinks are coming out at a decent clip. I grin and work my way through the room, greeting the regulars and the townspeople that I've spent my whole life around. Some people might find that a little claustrophobic but to me it's just the way home is. I know everything and everyone so if someone steps outta line I know exactly how to deal with it.

I take a seat in the Callaghan booth, always reserved for one of us, and one of the waitresses comes to my table straight away.

She grins at me, all batting eyelashes and push up bra. "Hey Tomikas! It's been a minute since you were last here!

Something big going on in your world?"

I don't have it in me to flirt back with her. Fuck, I can't even fake it. "I'm a busy man. I'll have a couple beers and that's it."

She deflates with a pout but doesn't push me. "Coming right up."

She's quick about bringing them to me, and when she turns to leave I spot the last fucking person I want at this bar tonight.

Angel walks in in a pair of jeans and an old, washed out band tee. Her hair is already done and her make up so she's not here for a fucking drink.

I want to break something.

She spots me and startles a little, then she pulls herself up and walks over to me with a straight back and a determined look on her face.

The second she's within earshot I snap, "What the hell are you doing here?"

She clears her throat as she comes to a stop in front of the booth. "Diamond told me I had to work the party here tonight. She said it was do this or find a new job and I like The Boulevard."

Fucking Diamond.

I should've killed the cunt last night, of course she changed her fucking tune. Axe probably fucked her until she caved, I need to go punch the asshole square in the jaw.

Angel twists her shirt in her hands, chews on her lip a little more before clearing her throat. "I just wanted to say thanks… for coming to help me. I know you're just… protecting property or whatever but, yeah, thanks."

Her eyes stay on the ground and my jaw locks up from all of the fucking clenching my teeth are doing. Does she even know what she sounds like right now?

Thanking me for dehumanizing her.

It's the first of many signs to come that something isn't fucking right.

I don't see it that way though. I see it as a girl who's trying to piss me the fuck off, get a rise outta me to chase this patch of mine and fuck if that isn't the biggest fucking kick in the guts.

I want her.

She's playing fucking games.

I'm going to end up losing fucking everything to a girl

who's named Angel, looks like just like one but has the fucking devil inside her.

She moves to turn around right as Jameson and his party arrive.

I lose my goddamn head for a second.

"What are you wearing tonight?"

She turns back to me and swallows. "I brought a few options. Speck… Speck said there's different laws about dancing at this kind of bar so I've got a corset instead. Is that… okay?"

I shrug and stand up. "Show me. I'll take you out back, you can get changed and if it's not right you can put something else on."

She bites her lip and jerks her head into a nod. "Thanks. It's… been weighing on me. I don't want to… risk the club or my job."

Another warning sign.

Why the hell does she need the money this badly?

But that thought doesn't stick in my head like it should. Instead, I walk out to the back rooms and I let her into the staff bathroom. Coulson, the bartender here, sees me and gives me a respectful nod. He's a good man, the type who knows his place, and when Angel shuts herself up to get ready I lean against the wall opposite like some kinda chump he doesn't say a fucking word about it.

"You want a drink, boss?"

Good man. "Whiskey. Just bring the bottle and if Rue gets in let him know I need to see him."

Coulson nods and leaves without a word.

Three minutes later Rue stalks out, the whiskey in his hand, and a pissed look on his face. So a regular Saturday night for him then.

"Is there a reason you're stalking the fucking bathroom, asshole?"

I shrug. "Diamond changed her mind. Sent Angel to dance."

Rue groans and opens the bottle, taking a swig straight before handing it over to me. "And she's in there? Getting ready to dance for all your fucking friends?"

My jaw clenches. "Guess so."

The bathroom door unlocks and Rue curses, his eyes dropping down to the ground like he'd rather gouge them out than look at her. I know it's not because he thinks he'll want her. Nope, he's so far fucking gone on Graves that he barely fucking notices tits on anyone else.

Nah, he's respecting me and my fucking rage at the sight of Angel.

A fucking corset.

I didn't even know what one was but there's no fucking way, no fucking way, any woman of mine is walking out in that. Fuck, it's worse than the pasties. White lace clinging to every fucking inch of her, accentuating her every curve, and I want to kill everyone.

"I just got here from the party and they changed their minds, Angel. You head on back to The Boulevard. I have Mel coming over," Rue says, his eyes still on the ground, digging me out of the fucking murder that's about to happen.

I finally look up to meet Angel's eyes.

Her pupils are blown out, her lips are parted and, fuck me, she's breathing in these little pants that make me wanna push her back into that bathroom and fuck her against the wall.

I step forward and she snaps out of the trance, ducking her head and scurrying backwards.

"No worries, I'll just get dressed again."

She snaps the door shut and I start cursing up a storm.

Rue huffs and pulls out his phone to call Diamond and arrange the swap. "You are fucked, brother. You are fucked."

Three

Chapter Eleven

Angel

After being sent away from the bachelor party, I head over to The Boulevard to cover for Mel's shift. It's a long night of dealing with Diamond being pissed off at me and when it's finally over the last thing I wanna hear is her fucking voice. I'm digging through my locker for my shampoo, ready to scrub myself completely before I head back to my Chevy to pass out, and I damn near hit my head when she speaks to me.

"Tomi wants to see you in the back."

I glance over my shoulder at her but the only thing on her face is a smug grin.

My stomach drops.

I pull a shirt over my head and when I move to grab up some pants she snorts at me. "He's an impatient man, you might wanna hurry your ass up. Besides, going in there fully clothed might just piss him off."

Fuck.

I lock up my shit and then head to the office, my hands shaking a little at whatever it is he could possibly want from me. Fuck, I've been dancing my ass off, coming up with new shit so the crowds stay as big as ever around here, I'm always on time, I never gossip or start shit with the other girls… what could I have possibly done wrong?

I take a deep breath before I knock in an attempt to calm my nerves but nothing prepares me for the low tones of Tomi's voice when he calls out to invite me in.

He doesn't sound pissed off.

My hands shake a little more as I open the door and step

in, finding Tomi behind the desk with a bottle of Jack and two shot glasses.

"Take a seat."

Why the hell do my legs get weak at the command?

I stumble over and collapse into the chair, telling myself I'm just exhausted. I've been working harder than any of the other girls and my muscles are feeling it but I know I'm lying to myself.

Tom is wearing a black shirt under his cut, the sleeves short and tight over his arms. The tattoos flex over his muscles and it's clear there's something about this man that draws me in because… I want him. I fucking want him enough that maybe I could touch him and have him touch me.

He smirks at me, still not saying a thing, and slowly picks up the bottle to pour out the shots.

I find my voice, rough and drenched in heady lust, "I don't drink whiskey."

Tomi shrugs. "Do the shots with me. What's it going to hurt?"

Me.

I've never had hard liquor before and he's too intense for me to try it out for the first time. I mean, he's never tried to touch me, not once, but every time he comes into the club he sits in the corner and watches me all night. I think half the reason the other girls hate me is because he doesn't watch any of them anymore. I try to tell them I don't want his attention, I really don't, but that just makes them even more angry.

Diamond keeps snapping at me, like I'm acting 'too good' for him. Fuck, that couldn't be further from the truth. I'm a runaway gutter rat flashing her tits to old men for money.

I'm the lowest of the low.

My own self-loathing pushes me into taking the shot, wincing when it burns the whole way down. Tomi takes his without so much as a flinch, refilling both glasses and pushing mine back in my direction.

Bad idea be damned, I knock it back and this time it barely touches the sides.

He leans back and looks at me through hooded eyes. "This is your performance evaluation, I just wanna go through a few things with you and whiskey might help us along."

I shrug, the warmth pooling in my belly and spreading down my arms from the whiskey an unsettling sensation. I've only really drunk beer before and it takes a bit before the alcohol really sets in.

This was damn near instant.

"You're very popular."

I shrug. "I take my dancing seriously, no half-assing around here."

He pours another shot and I take it before he even slides in across to me, the smirk on his face getting a little wider. "And yet you'll only work the stage. A lot more tips are made in private dances."

"I don't want to do extra. I've been very clear about that," I say, my words coming out in a croak but his eyes still burn as they trace down my bare legs.

"You just wanna be a dancer, not a pro? Fine by me."

Except then he stands up and walks around the desk until he's leaning back on it, the bulge in his pants telling me this isn't the end of the conversation.

I swallow and he chuckles under his breath. "I'm not offering you money, Angel, but I do want you to suck my dick. You got a boyfriend or something stopping you?"

I shake my head, my eyes still glued to the bulge. Jesus. Has he hypnotized me with it or something? The low and sultry tones of his voice are like a balm over that jittery part of my soul, soothing all of my sharp edges until I'm sitting here staring at his dick like it's fucking breakfast.

What the hell was in the whiskey?

"What are you going to do about it then, Angel? What are you going to do about me standing here, wanting you to suck my dick? Are you gonna be the frigid bitch or show me what that mouth can actually do?"

I shouldn't let him bait me into anything.

I shouldn't.

But for once in my life, I'm not scared of touching someone. I could show him… not that I really know what the hell to do but looking at him is like injecting lust straight into my bloodstream.

I want him.

I don't want to want him, but I do.

I sink to my knees and for a second, I think I see him hesitate. Fuck, if he doesn't want this then why bait me? If he walked away right now… fuck, it wouldn't actually change anything. I'd still be here for work tomorrow, the only thing would be that for once the rumors about me would be true.

I would be the girl ready to get down on her knees for some biker she doesn't really know, in the back of a strip club ready to suck him off.

Maybe I should've done this years ago?

Maybe the way to get past the horrible things that were done to me is to just… own them. Do whatever it is I want to do just so long as I find the right guy to be doing it with?

The only flaw in that plan is that Tomi has been the very first guy to interest me and I'm freaking positive that once he blows his load he'll walk the hell outta here.

I guess that's a good thing.

I can't let anyone close to me right now anyway.

"Fuck you're sexy down there, Angel. Hands behind your back. Open up wide for me, gimme that tongue."

I do what he asks, clasping my hands together and sticking out my tongue. I'm sure I look fucking stupid but he grunts as he unzips his jeans and fists his cock.

It's bigger than I thought a dick could be.

I manage to swallow, even with my mouth open and he grunts at me, squeezing his cock until the tip glistens with his pre-cum. "Fuck, sweetness. You want this? You want me to shove this down that pretty throat of yours so you can swallow me up."

I nod my head just a tiny bit and he growls at me, a low and rough sound that has my thighs clenching together.

I didn't even know my body could react that way.

He touches the tip to my tongue, rubbing the pre-cum there so I can taste him, and his eyes are hot on mine as he watches my every move. Not that I can move, nope, he has me trapped with the intensity of this moment. The salty tang of him isn't exactly unpleasant but it's not something I'm used to tasting.

One of his hands drops into my hair and clenches into a fist, loose enough that I'm not in pain, and then he moves me forward until his cock is in my mouth and down my throat just like he promised me.

I swallow around him until he slides further down, cutting off my air completely and I feel like my throat is bulging with the heaviness of him.

He grunts like he's in pain, then he starts to move his hips.

"Fucking perfect. Taking my cock like a fucking pro, barely fucking gagging. It's enough to tempt a man to really fuck these pouty lips, see if I can make you cry so pretty."

The words are like a sexy drawl, all confidence and arrogance that comes from being a big shot in his world. He's a biker, the son of a long line of outlaws, grown up in the life and a clear path to whatever the hell he wants.

I bet he's never slept in a car before.

I don't cry. Not even when his hips start to really move, the tip of his dick nudging at my freaking voice box, and his hands jerking me further down his length. I don't feel dirty or used because the sounds that come out of him… they're like nothing I've ever heard before.

Doesn't matter that he's fucking my throat, I'm the one sending him over the edge. My mouth is the one sucking and swallowing and working him over even as my hands stay clasped tightly behind my back. I chose to be here on my knees and I've chosen to watch his every move, the hitch of his breath and the grunts he lets out, until I'm sure I'm giving him the blowjob of his life.

He pulls back at the last second and comes all over my face and chest. It misses my eyes but my makeup is ruined and I know I must look like every porn video ever with the fake lashes and red lipstick smeared around my face.

The hand in my hair tightens as he grunts and then he tips my head back to look over where he's left his mark.

"So fucking pretty like that, Angel. Do you enjoy being on your knees for me in a strip club like a good little whore?"

The word whore cuts into me like he's taken a knife to my skin, cutting away the last little threads of power I'd just felt, but I manage to keep it off of my face. I mean, he's right. Here I am on my knees in the back room of some strip club, sucking off my boss, so yeah… I guess whore is the right word.

I want to die.

I want to go back to before I'd taken those shots and say no. Why had I let my guard down for a second? Why does his face feel like the home I never got to have and his arms around me feels like the heaven I'll never get to?

He uses my hair to tug me to my feet, no caring touches or tenderness in him at all. This isn't what I want.

He reaches for my panties and I flinch. A full body flinch away from his touch. I can't. I can't have him touching me, not now. I feel so fucking worthless and the shame from him seeing just how broken I am... fuck, I'm about to lose my shit, right here and now, covered in his cum.

He sees it on my face too.

"Fuck, there's the little frosty bitch. I wondered when you'd remember and snap back to your usual fucking ways. Don't wanna get off, Angel? Fine by me, I'm good," he snaps, and tugs his hand out of my hair, buckling his jeans up and turning to the door without another word.

I stare at the ground and try not to fucking die.

I stay in the office for another few minutes, trying to stop myself from crying. When I'm finally sure I won't burst into tears I get to my feet and poke around until I can find a box of tissues, cleaning up enough of the mess he's made of my face that I think I can make it to the showers without completely shaming myself.

It's too little, too late.

The second I open the door to leave the office I find a group of giggling women, all of them fresh outta the bar and witnesses to Tomi's speedy exit.

"Fuck, girl, I've never seen that man look angry after he's blown a load. You must be really fucking shit at sucking dick!" Diamond laughs and it nearly fucking kills me not to cry.

If I can escape my stepfather's house, I can get through tonight without crying or making a scene. I have a plan and I'm going to fucking make it through this. I'll be back here dancing tomorrow night and it'll be the best fucking dance any man has ever seen.

It has to be.

The other girls do everything they can to make me feel like shit.

It's so fucking stupid, I mean I'd bet every last one one of them has fucked Tomi or one of the other bikers for pay or for free, but with all the shit in my head it chips away at me pretty damn quick.

I just wanna fucking leave this place forever but there's nowhere else I can make this type of money safely. Tomi didn't force me to do a goddamn thing, I chose it and when I flinched away he left. He spat fucking fire at me first, but he left.

So I've just got to suck it up and take whatever these women throw at me.

I leave the stage after my last dance for the week exhausted and just plain wrung out. I'm due for a night at a hotel and, fuck it, I might even make it two just to fully recharge even if it does make me wanna cry over the costs. I have three days off from work and I can email all of my lecturers to get out of classes for the same amount of time so I can just… sleep. Sleep and lie around thinking about what I'm going to do the second my cash fund hits my goal. Fuck, that's the headiest feeling in the world. Hitting that number and having a roof over my head, college paid for, never having to dance again… fuck, I just have to keep my head on straight and ignore the bullshit.

When I make it out to the locker room I find Posey leaning on my locker with her phone out, giggling as she texts someone. Her eyes snap up to mine and the grin on her face gets even bigger.

"There you are! I've been looking for you!"

I raise an eyebrow at her but it's impossible to keep the smile off of my own face. "It's a strip club and I'm a dancer, it's not that hard to find me."

She laughs and moves for me as I grab my stuff out. When I head over to the showers she follows me and sits on the bench outside my stall. "If I had've gone looking Rue woulda skinned me alive. He's already pissed we're here but I don't mind it. Means I get to hang out with you."

I'm glad she can't see the stupid smile on my face. Fuck, being friends with her is a weird but lifesaving thing. "What are you doing here with him anyway? Finally convinced him to date you?"

She huffs at me. "Not fucking likely. Nah, there's obviously shit going on in the club because he's keeping tabs on me again. He picked me up from Pops' and is taking me back to

Trink's place but he had to sort something out here first."

Hm. That makes sense. Tomi's been here all the time and I know for a fact that this place is one of the club's best earners. Probably a whole lot of dirty cash being cleaned here too.

I finish up my shower and I throw on my yoga pants and an old band tee. When I make it out of the stall Poe grins at it and says, "The lead singer is the best kind of asshole."

I know exactly what she means by that.

Because doesn't that exactly describe Tomi? The best type of asshole who I wish cared just a little bit more for me. Or maybe less? He cares enough about what I do for this business that he's nosey but there's that secret part of me that wished he cared enough to… want me for more than just my body.

Why the hell am I thinking like this?

I drop my bag down onto the bench next to Poe and grab out my makeup wipes to get rid of the dark circles that didn't quite disappear fully in the shower. She looks at the lace that's overflowing from the open zipper and sighs hard.

"Fuck I wish I could pull that shit off. Maybe if I was a little less tomboy and a little more stripper-chic Rue would notice me. Fuck I hate guys! I hate feeling like this. Ugh."

I glance down at her. "You could wear that stuff. You're eighteen soon right? You could come to the sex shop with me and buy a whole closet full of this type of thing."

She huffs out a breath and her cheeks turn pink. "I'd just look fucking dumb. Plus if word got back to Rue and Tomi? A fucking bloodbath."

Her words are exactly the distraction I need from all of the bullshit I've been dealing with. "Why would it end up in a bloodbath? They're only lingerie."

She huffs out a laugh and stands up, kicking at nothing on the tiled floor. "Thorn got custody of me when I was six. Tomi was fourteen and Rue was twelve, they both got put on Posey watch. Like, kept an eye on me around town and kept me safe. I think Rue's always gonna see me as that fucking dumbass six year old with a shitty haircut, so there's not going to be any sexy lingerie in my future. There's only gonna be rebuilding engines and the fucking friend zone."

I snort at her and a plan pops into my head. A dumb one but I've had a really fucking hard week and I need something… normal. Stupid and fun and something a girl my age would really do.

"Lemme do your makeup. You're going to hang out with Trink tonight, right? Lemme fix you up for the night, might help keep that smile on your face."

She grins at me and it's like looking into the sun, bright and warming enough to sort through my skin and into my bones. Ten minutes later and it's all done, I'm a freaking expert at doing the perfect face in zero time now and when I take a step back to look at my work it hits me in the gut.

She's fucking stunning.

The makeup only enhances all of the beauty she already has but with it on there's no mistaking the fucking beauty in her. The sweet soul and fierce loyalty, she's going to break hearts no matter where she goes, even if Rue doesn't want her.

I give her a pair of my shorts and a cami, the only clean one I've got but, hell, I think I'd hand this kid just about anything she asked for. She's too fucking pure, too kind, too fucking smart for this dirty locker room.

She giggles as she shimmies out of her jeans and bends over to hook the shorts onto her legs, the cheeks of her ass on show thanks to the thong she's wearing.

Speck's eyebrows hit his hairline when he walks into the locker room, turning on his heel and yelling, "Fucking hell Poe, you tryna get me fucking killed or something?"

She snorts at him. "You practically fucking live here, like my ass is going to even fucking hit your radar."

I hide a smile when he mumbles, "That ain't the fucking danger."

Ahh.

So Rue maybe notices her a little more than she thinks, that would explain Diamond's hatred of her.

Sure enough, the moment she gets her ratty band tee over her head Rue stalks in and the look on his face tells me everything I need to know.

Everything.

"What the hell do you think you're doing, flower? Get your ass back in the office, you're not supposed to be out here and you for-fucking-sure aren't supposed to be getting your tits out."

She huffs and shoves the cami over her head, straightening it before she turns around to face him. He rocks on his heels like he's been shot.

Oh yeah.

He's fucking smitten.

"Is it safe to look or are my balls still in danger of being ripped from my body?" Speck says as he turns around and Poe scowls at him.

"Why the hell are you teasing me? Am I not allowed to go out with my fucking friend and look like a fucking girl?"

The two of them keep their mouths shut so I fumble to fill the silence. I don't know why he won't tell her but I guess the very secret, very selective romantic in me wants to salvage this situation. "I've seen how fierce you are, Graves, no doubt you have them all worried about your claws. You look great, I'll grab the clothes back next time you're here."

Her eyes narrow a little more at Speck before she turns to me with a grin. "Thanks! You could come over and pick them up if you wanted? Or I could come drop them off to you if you want? I don't have a fucking beauty like the Chevy but I could bribe Reece to bring me over."

Tomi walks in and it's like all of the air gets sucked out of the room, one minute I'm laughing and joking with my friend and then next I can't fucking breathe.

"It's fine, I don't need them anytime soon. Just have a good night," I choke out, forcing the smile back on my face but Poe's eyes flick between Tomi and I until a frown takes over her features.

"You should come out with us tonight! It's just a dumb club thing but Trink and I are going out after. It would be fucking awesome with you there."

I swallow and refuse to glance at the dark cloud in the room. "I'm beat. I'm getting bad gas station tacos and passing the fuck out, but I hope you have a great time."

Her glare settles on Tomi. "Why are you being an asshole to her? I just wanna hang out with my fucking friends and you're walking around being a fucking killjoy."

I don't want to hear a word out of his mouth, none of the vitriol he'll spit at me, mostly because I think it'll hurt so much worse coming from him. I think all of that shit about myself anyway but he's just… fuck, he just knows how to pour acid into these open wounds of mine.

I shove the last of my shit into my bag and I don't even think about it, I just push forward until I've got Poe in a quick hug. She grips me back hard, even in her shock she's down for the affection, and then I stalk out of the room before I can get my ass torn open by the utter hatred.

I've never hated myself more than right now, than this moment of having something I didn't even know I wanted ripped away from me.

Another short night of broken sleep ahead of me, I start the old Chevy and let the engine turn over for a second before I pull away.

I see the motorcycles go past as I wait to turn onto the highway, Posey secure and safe behind Rue on his hog.

Speck raises a hand to wave and I lift one back at him.

Tomi pretends I don't exist.

I fucking wish it were true.

Chapter Twelve

Tomi

I give up chasing after some fucking bitch who 'struck me but doesn't want me and I get my head back into what I'm supposed to be doing.

Sniffing out a fucking rat.

I'm not fucking around anymore. There's not a single fucking thing I can do to fix my cuntstruck self but there's options for finding the rats. I leave The Boulevard after the best motherfucking blowjob of my life, I swear to God she sucked my soul straight outta my body and swallowed it down that pretty little throat of hers, and I go back to my parents' place for the night.

The shit I need to do isn't the type of thing I want to get disturbed while I'm doing. Keely will be fucking thrilled to have me around anyway.

So I get home, drink a couple of beers with Hawk, and then I pass the fuck out. I wake to the smell of bacon wafting through my bedroom door because my mom is a fucking saint.

I shower before I head down, no need for her to catch me smelling like a fucking bar, and when I eventually make it to the kitchen she's setting my plate down on the kitchen table.

Just one because I'm the only one getting up this late in the afternoon.

"Big night? You've been working too much. I have half a mind to call King and tell him I want my son back."

I kiss her cheek before I sit down, she has every last one of us trained for this shit. "I'm keeping myself busy. You know I hate sitting around with my thumb up my ass when there's shit to be done."

She hums under her breath, checking her watch. "You take after me. Hawk always did prefer the quiet times, enjoying the fruits of all his hard work."

I scoff at her. "I doubt it. Callaghans are made of chaos and ruin, not sitting around with a fucking beer."

She laughs at me as she scrubs the pots and pans. She's already dressed in her scrubs, ready to head into the afternoon shift at the hospital. She works too goddamn much, they don't need the fucking money, but she's always been too wrapped up in her own busy schedule to worry about something as stupid as money.

She always did say, Hawk keeps the lights on and food on the table.

She keeps sharp and ready to stitch him and the boys up just the second they need it.

And that's how their marriage works.

"What are you doing today? As much as I'm sure you missed me cooking for you, you always come home with a plan."

I shrug. "I'm heading on a drive to grab some tech shit. I'm upgrading everyone's shit in batches and it'll take me a fucking week just to get half the guys online."

Keely laughs and wipes her hands, grabbing her purse and leaning down to kiss my cheek before she leaves. "Those old bikers won't ever figure out an iPhone, Thomas. Stick to simple."

I wave her off and listen to the familiar sounds of her getting into her car, the engine starting and then backing out. Something I've heard so many times in my childhood that it'll never leave me, no matter how long I've been crashing at the clubhouse.

I don't care whether or not the Unseen want new tech.

I care about what that tech is going to report back to me.

I clean up my plate because Keely Callaghan didn't raise a disrespectful shit, just an outlaw with no time for the law. Then I get on the road.

The plan is simple.

I get new smart phones for as many of the guys as I can. I tell them all that I'm doing it to bring the club into the present, drag their old fucking outlaw asses outta the Wild West and into the real world, and I make a lotta fucking jokes about it.

Enough jokes that the assholes all just take what they're given without question.

There's plenty of shit that upgrading their phones will tell me. GPS trackers on them all is child's play. I want their fucking keystrokes. I want who they're calling, what they're looking up, the photos they're taking, the texts they're sending. I want every fucking second of their lives for me to sift through until I'm fucking sure that they're not the fucking rats.

I haven't run this shit past King… not really, but I have plans to bring it up with him the second I can get him alone for sure. There's no point in waiting around, this shit takes time and he's not going to say no.

I'm in charge of tech and security for a reason.

When I get to New Orleans, I stick out like a sore thumb.

Doesn't fucking matter. I get in and out of the store and walk out with thirty-five smartphones, paid in cash, and there's one for every member plus Speck and… the twins, Lyndon and Lawson.

I feel like a piece of shit even questioning them but, fuck, if anyone is going to have beef about our club you'd think it'd be Harbin's twin boys.

Their mother is a junkie living on the streets of Mounts Bay, she chose a high over feeding them back when they were kids. Harbin is a decent enough kinda guy but he's never had time to raise them so instead he dropped them off with Keely and Hawk.

Keely never asked questions, just told Hawk he needed to build that extension fucking pronto.

I'd already moved out to college when they showed up but my mom has always kept all of our rooms like fucking shrines in case we wanna come home. It's fucking handy for Rue.

His bedroom window faces Poe's.

Yep, he's been sleeping next door to his little flower from the second she rolled into town at six years old. Fuck, I remember it perfectly. Thorn just up and disappeared for three weeks. It was the same time King was being sent to prison for shit he didn't fucking do and our entire club was in fucking chaos.

Pops moved out the same day they came home and Poe was this little thing, gangly arms and eyes too fucking big for her face.

Rue's obsession started from the very first day.

Motherfucking cursed, at least he knows for sure that he's lovestruck. Poe's been fucking obsessed with him just as much as he's fucking gaga over her.

I bet Poe would never flinch away.

Fuck, Angel has turned me into some whiny bitch. I need to man the fuck up and take care of club business. Then maybe I'll go find some biker bitch to fuck the memory of Angel's mouth away.

Great plan.

Except that the fucking thought of someone else doesn't interest my dick at all. Fuck, I need to go ask Hellion how long it took him to fuck Georgie outta his system because there's no fucking way I'm taking up celibacy.

I get the new phones back home and stash them away in the gun safe in my room.

Trink is home and listening to shitty rock music in her room, if she sees the phones there's no way she'll leave them alone. She's been such a bitch lately I have no doubt she'll be in here snooping around the second I leave.

I bang on her door on the way out. "Are you coming to the clubhouse tonight or what?"

The music cuts off and she flings open the door. She looks like hell, makeup running down her face and her nose is all puffy.

"What the fuck happened to you?"

Her eyes narrow at me. "What the fuck do you think? I'm fucking cursed!"

Jesus Christ. "Girls don't get fucking 'struck, what's happened?"

She rolls her eyes at me and collapses back on her bed. There's shit everywhere, cups and plates on every surface and dirty clothes all over the floor.

Keely would have a fucking heart attack at the sight of it.

"I'm not talking about the stupid fucking curse! Not everything is about you Callaghan men, for fuck's sake! I'm so sick of this stupid family."

I tip my head back and pray for the patience to get through this without snapping at her childish ass. "Why are you cursed then, Trink? Tell me."

She sniffs from the bed. Shit must be bad if she's crying, she's not exactly the type to let her brother see her crying.

Probably because the first boy to break her heart is still breathing through a fucking tube.

Zero regrets about that.

Fucking nothing.

"I can't tell you. Let's just say my last name is ruining everything. Fucking everything! It's not fucking fair that being a Callaghan has set you up for life and I'm being cut off at the fucking knees by it. It's bullshit. I should just give up and find some guy to knock me up. That worked out for Mom."

Deep breaths.

Deep, deep motherfucking breaths.

"Trink, tell me what the fuck is wrong and I'll fix it. Simple as that, when have I ever let you down?"

She scoffs at me. "Fix it? What, by sending Speck after me to spy on what I'm doing? Making Law and Lyn fucking stalk me at school? Fuck, even Poe tells you what I'm fucking doing. When do I get to own my own life, Tomi? When do I get to make my own decisions?"

I have to take a few more big breaths to remind myself that she's a fucking kid. Seventeen years old and never had to face real consequences before, I've made real fucking sure of that. Fuck, Hawk has done everything in his power to make this house a safe place for all of us kids. He and Keely sheltered us all from all of the bad and dirty and bloody parts of the MC.

She doesn't really know what we've done for her.

She sees me as nothing but her big brother, the one who drinks too much and fucks strippers, so of course it sounds like I have an easy life.

She doesn't see all of the death, the mind games, the years of trying to get King the fuck outta prison without getting our clubhouse and businesses raided. I've been shot, stabbed, beaten, and damn near fucking killed for this club and each time I keep my ass the hell away from her and Keely so they don't see that shit.

Maybe I shoulda let her see a bit more of it.

"I'm not going to apologize for taking care of my baby sister, Trink. That's my fucking job. If you need help with something, tell me. I don't want you miserable but I'm also not gonna let you go out there half fucking cocked and get yourself into trouble. It's as simple as that."

She rolls over on her bed until her back is facing me and I close the door behind me. I pass Lawson on the stairs and he gives me one of his trademark grins.

It's easy to tell the twins apart.

Lyndon doesn't know the fucking meaning of a smile.

Law never stops.

"D'you know what happened with Trink? Who do I need to kill?"

The smile slides right off of his face. "Shit. Is she still pissed off? I dunno what happened, only that she called me to come get her from the diner and she was ready to carve some fucker up. You might wanna ask Poe what's going on because she told me I was about as trustworthy as a fucking Demon which, I can tell you, cuts a man deep."

Dammit.

I give him a nod and slap his back as I get past him.

I find Speck waiting for me at the kitchen table, his boots still on and a beer in his hands. "You ready for the party? Where the hell have you been?"

I shrug and grab my keys from the kitchen counter. "I'm a busy man. What are you doing here? You're supposed to be watching Angel."

He grins. "It's her night off. Diamond is being a bitch about her hours still. I'm just grabbing beers from the bar to take to the clubhouse for the party tonight… thought I'd check in with you. In case you've fucking killed yourself over your little backroom fuck last night. Biting that forbidden fruit and all that shit."

I think about smashing my fist into his fucking jaw and I'm sure he sees that on my face. "I'm just saying, for a man who was spouting shit about staying away from her, you're doing a shit job of it."

I try to unclench my fists. I need to get the fuck away from her, I need to get her the fuck outta my head and my town before I fucking lose it. "Call Diamond. Tell her the girls all need to come to the party tonight. No excuses."

Speck stares blankly at me for a second and then groans, shaking his head. "That's a fucking terrible idea."

I pin him to the fucking floor with a single look. "And why's that, asshole? Are you already fucking infatuated by her or something?"

He heaves out a sigh. "No, but she doesn't like crowds. This'll only drive her away."

Good.

I hate this fucking feeling, this tightness in my chest and the energy in my legs like I need to run far away from this fucking situation. It's probably that feeling that pisses me off the most. I'm a fucking Callaghan. I don't run, not from fucking anything, and certainly not a stripper.

She fucking flinched.

"All of them have to be here. If she doesn't show up then she doesn't have any more shifts."

The back door slides open and Rue steps in, grease covering his shirt and hands from whatever he's been working on in the garage. He stops at the sounds of us arguing.

Speck huffs out a laugh. "She's doubled the alcohol sales in a single week, did you know that? Guys are coming and drinking for longer now she's on the stage. Diamond is convinced that they'll quit coming if she doesn't do extra but if anything it's just getting busier."

I clench my jaw and fight the urge to punch him in the face for even talking about her. "Like I give a fuck about what our laundering strip club makes in legitimate income. I want her the fuck outta there."

I don't even care that I'm lying, I'm just in a shitty fucking mood. Trink crying has just made it fucking worse.

He squares up and puts himself all the way into my path. "Fine. Fire her then. Boot her ass out and we'll never see her again, easy solution."

Rue curses and steps up closer to us both. Fuck knows whose side he's on, the three of us are as close as brothers, but I guess we'll be needing a referee soon anyway.

When I don't say a word he knows he's got me, the fucking asshole. "You don't want to risk her leaving. You want to force her into coming into your turf and finding out her fucking story. How about you stop being an asshole and just ask her?"

Rue scoffs. "Because she's a fucking stripper who's 'struck him. You don't think that shit is risky? Just fucking wait. Just wait until your ass gets 'struck and then see how you handle it."

He shrugs. "I'll be a fucking pro by then, after all the shit I've done for the two of you. A conversation isn't that fucking hard, anyway, Tomi. Don't be a fucking dipshit."

Rue pointedly doesn't look at me because he gets it. He gets what it feels like to know your fucking life doesn't belong to you anymore. Hell, he's been chasing Poe around for more than half his fucking life now, never once telling her about the curse choosing her for him and what's going on. He's convinced it'll fuck her childhood up knowing, so instead he just spends all his time beating the life right outta anyone who goes near her and tries to stay the hell away himself.

It was easier for him back when she still looked like a kid. He just treated her the same way he did Trink and was done with it. Then a few years back we get a call to bring her out to the Bay, her school year cut short at the discovery of this sister of hers and she walks out with a guy draped all over her.

He was way too fucking interested and she was smiling at him like he hung the fucking moon for her.

She has Rue's full fucking attention now.

The whole lot of it, every grumpy minute.

I decide I'm done with this conversation and head back into the clubhouse, ready to drink enough to forget all about this fucking night and the fact that Angel exists. Fuck, she probably had gone back home to fuck her boyfriend.

I'm still not convinced she doesn't have one.

I'm really not sure that I won't kill the fucker if I find him.

Chapter Thirteen

Angel

Poe invites me over to her house to help her out with her homework while Tomi is out on club business and can't help her.

She gets the message to me through Speck and he passes on her address, telling me to head there after my early finish that week.

I arrive just after midnight to find two guys sitting on her couch, sharing pizzas and talking a whole lot of shit with each other. They're very obviously twins, identical but not. One of them is laughing and joking, the picture of playful shit-talking, and the other is messing around but quieter, more reserved. When I walk in the quiet one shoves his brother and scowls at me.

I pause in the doorway and Poe ducks around me. "That's Lawson and the scowling dick is Lyndon. Ignore Lyn, he's weird about new people. Trust issues or some shit."

He glares at her and she shrugs. "Tell me I'm wrong, asshole. Angel is here to help us so stop glaring. I'll kick you the hell out too."

She realizes what she's said and bites her lip, glancing over her shoulder at me. "Trink was going to study with us but... she's weird about strippers. It's not you, I swear."

I shrug and try not to be so freaking awkward as I step into the room. "It's fine. I mean, I'm sorry you had to kick her out or whatever, but I don't blame her. What do you guys have?"

Poe hands over a whole pile of worksheets and a textbook. And then heads into the kitchen to grab us all drinks and snacks. When I look the pages over it's all shit I'm good at, thank God, and I get them set up and working in no time. Lawson keeps his eyes on Poe and what she's doing but it feels pretty... familial. They must all be related or something, because he jokes around with her like she's his little sister or something.

Lyndon just keeps staring at me like I killed his goddamn puppy.

After an hour of it I decide I can't take another second of it. "Look, there's only half a page left. I'll get going."

Lawson punches his brother in the arm. "Stop being a fucking asshole."

Lyndon shrugs. "I don't trust strippers. The fact that you can do math like this makes me trust you even less. You're either a spy for the Demons or an undercover cop."

I choke on my coke.

"You think I'm a cop? Are you for fucking real right now? Jesus." My skin is crawling.

Poe watches me closely and shrugs. "Thorn's a cop and he's not so bad."

Lyn glares at her. "That's different. He's family."

I lean back in my chair and try not to shake like a fucking leaf. Lawson rubs at his temple as he works through the equations but Poe and Lyn settle into a full blown out-n-out fight.

"The club don't think he is. Fuck Diesel wants to rip his goddamn throat out, so your argument is a pile of shit."

"Poe, my argument isn't about your brother. It's about whether there's a stripper at The Boulevard that's there to spy on the club and send another brother away for hard time. You want Tomi in lockup? Hell, if it were Rue chasing her you'd care a helluva lot more."

I grab my bag, ready to leave and Poe finally snaps, "Leave Lyn. I'm hanging out with my friend, whether you like her or not, that's what is happening here."

He storms out, leaving his own homework behind like it means nothing to him. Law grimaces and glances up at me. "He's just pissed off, it ain't you."

I shrug because it's none of my business really and I chew my lip as I sift through the last few pages of work. "So uh—

what's a Demon?"

Law chokes out a laugh and Poe buries her face in her hands, her answer muffled behind them, "They're the fucking worst MC that's ever existed. Also for like… reference or whatever… technically my sperm donor is the president of the entire MC. He's literally the worst human on Earth so if you see anyone in a Demon cut, run. Run and call Tomi the second you can."

I nod because, I mean, what else can I do? And we get back to work on the homework. Law is nice enough to me, doesn't start shit or look at me like he's judging me, but I'm still glad to head on home.

Poe grins when I give her a quick hug, thanking me with that big grin of hers plastered on her face.

I stop in at the tiny grocery store at the edge of town on my way back through. It's not exactly a good area but it's open even this late at night and I need some energy drinks to get me through tomorrow morning's lectures.

The guy behind the counter leers at me when I walk in but I ignore him, stalking straight through to the drink fridges. I grab some candy bars too, I'm due for my period and I'm craving the sugar. I know I'll regret it when I bloat but, fuck, Diamond has only given me two shifts next week anyway.

What does it matter if I'm a bit bloated for my online classes?

I turn around with my arms full of crap to find Tomi in the fucking grocery store with me, glaring at me like I'm his biggest fucking problem.

Oh God.

"What the fuck are you doing in here? It's nearly fucking midnight and there's a stabbing every fucking minute in this place."

I clear my throat to try to find my voice. "I was… helping Poe out. Just driving through, I needed shit for class tomorrow. Is there… something wrong?"

He huffs at me and stalks towards me. "Something wrong? Yeah, I'm too fucking busy to be chasing pieces of ass around who can't take care of their own shit."

I frown at him glancing around but there's no one in here but me. "I'm just buying snacks, what's the problem? Is this like a turf thing or—"

He curses viciously under his breath at me. "Coldstone belongs to the Unseen, this isn't a fucking turf thing. This is about me getting home and finding your car parked outside of the shittiest fucking store in the whole town dressed like you're for sale. Pay for your shit and get out of here. Stop making fucking trouble for me."

I nod and walk past him, still confused over what his problem is. I didn't ask for him to come looking and I'm in jeans and a hoodie, even though it's hot as fuck out.

The guy behind the counter rings up all of my shit, smirking at me the whole time but I ignore it, handing my cash over and taking my change.

I'm silently begging him not to say something that'll prove Tomi right.

Of fucking course he does.

"Hey, don't you work out at the strip joint? Yeah, you do! You're the hottest one there! Fuck, you must have some sexy fucking titties under that ugly sweatshirt-"

He's interrupted by Tomi's fist breaking the glass on one of the displays. I jump a mile into the air and the guy shits himself, jumping back away from me like his ass is on fire.

"You ever speak to her like that again and I'll cut your tongue outta your head and feed it to you, you hear me?"

The guy nods and clutches at his chest like he's having a heart attack, all fucking terrified now he's faced with the giant, tattooed biker. I don't see him as the scary guy I once faced but this guy sure does.

He was just speaking to me like that so it makes no sense that he'd be defending my fucking honor. I mean… I am just a stripper. I'm a woman who sells her naked body on stage for tips.

Tomi had just said it to me himself.

Piece of ass.

I blink at them both until Tomi barks at me, "Ass outside, Angel. Get in your fucking truck."

I do exactly what he says, leaving without checking to see if he's following me, but when I start the Chevy and wait a minute for the engine to warm up, he stalks out and charges right up to my window.

I wince but I roll it down.

"Make sure you're at the club party. Everyone goes and if your ass isn't there I'm coming to find you."

What the hell does that even mean?

I don't get the chance to ask, he just turns on his heel and stalks over to his motorcycle, swinging onto it and letting the engine roar to life under him. When I just sit there staring at him, he waves his arm at me to go ahead, waiting until I'm on the road before he leaves himself.

Diamond calls me to tell me about the party.

There's no fucking way I want to go but Tomi's words are still ringing in my head so I know I have no choice.

I spend the day before at the library doing my classwork and I have a headache by the time I have to leave and head over there. I stay in my car for a good five minutes convincing myself I'll get the hell through this. If Poe isn't here I'll just find Speck. Hell, if he's bartending like he's told me he usually has to, I'll offer to help him just to get a slab of wood between me and the drunken bikers.

There's a lot of them.

Every last one of them is loud and drunk and fucking huge. If any of them try to touch me there's no way I can stop them. I wouldn't stand a fucking chance.

I finally get out when Mel parks up next to me, Lana and Farrah piling out with her as they all giggle and laugh together.

I'm almost jealous.

The bonfire is bright and the other girls disappear into the crowd the second they get there, mingling with the crowd of bikers as easy as breathing.

I wonder how long I have to be here for?

I'm hesitant as I tiptoe through the crowds, trying to be small and inconspicuous.

"Angel! Hey! Get your ass over here," Poe calls out.

Thank God.

I dart over to where she's standing in the parking lot by the bonfire, a beer in her hand and a friend standing there with her. She leans down to snag a beer for me from the barrel. I try to ignore the looks her friend is giving me, the loathing not even a little subtle.

I'm guessing this is Trink.

"Can you quit it? We're trying to have a good night," Poe snarks at her and then turns to me with a grin.

"I wasn't expecting you to come! You haven't been to any of the other parties… they're kind of boring, except for the free beer."

I shrug and force a smile on my face. "I was, uh, invited… I guess. I didn't even know these parties were happening."

I down the entire beer in two gulps. I need the courage and something to lessen the nerves a little. Poe giggles and hands me another.

"Is there a guy you're sweet on or something? Reece seems pretty freaking interested. I've never seen him tail a girl like he does with you."

Trink scoffs. "He tails you like that too, Posey, you just never notice him."

I shift on my feet, too uncomfortable with this conversation. The only man to ever catch my eye is standing on the other side of the parking lot, glaring over at us like he wants to murder me for daring to speak to his sister.

If he enjoys fucking strippers so much then why does he loathe me so fiercely?

It's not a question I want to linger on.

Fuck, I know exactly how easy it is to hate me.

"Uh, no. No boyfriend. I'm not really interested in getting caught up into anything at the moment. I just... I want to finish up my college classes."

Trink's eyebrows raise. "You're going to college? How do you find time for that? I thought the pole work was full time."

Poe elbows her hard. "Can you quit it? Angel is my friend, stop acting like an asshole."

I raise the beer back to my lips, pausing before I take a sip to say, "It's fine, Poe. This is Trink's home. If I'm not welcome I'll head out."

Then I finish the bottle and drop it into the trash can, giving her a quick hug and walking off to find Speck. Poe and Trink start arguing the second I walk away and I cringe. I really don't want to be here, I don't want to start shit, I just want to go pass out for the night.

Hell, I was planning on getting a hotel room for the night and getting a good night's sleep in for the first time in weeks and instead I'm wasting my time here, drinking terrible beer and trying to avoid stray hands.

I find Speck talking to Rue over by the door to the clubhouse, another biker I don't recognize standing there with them. I don't want to interrupt them but they all fall silent the second I walk over.

I feel like a fucking pariah.

"Is there an amount of time I need to be here for? I'm pretty tired, I want to head out," I mumble and Speck pushes off of the wall towards me.

"Come with me, I'll get you something to eat first."

There's a laugh and joking around me, some guy talking about exactly what it is I'll be eating, but I nod and follow him into the clubhouse. I don't know why, but I do trust him. I trust him enough to follow him into the country's most notorious MC clubhouse to find food.

"You've had too much to drive home without eating first," Speck mumbles and I smile.

"I've had two beers, settle down. I'm just... not one for parties."

He nods and starts piling up a burger. "Are you one of those fucking weird chicks who don't eat anything but lettuce?"

I'll eat fucking anything. Right here and now for free, I'd eat anchovies on pizza if that's what is on offer. "Gimme the lot. I like my burgers stacked."

He throws his head back with a laugh and opens up the fridge. "Well, let's fucking find the lot then. I like a woman with an appetite."

I laugh at him when he wiggles his eyebrows at me because it's clear he's not actually flirting, he just wants me laughing and enjoying this shit-show a little more.

I perch on the countertop and talk shit with him, just random bits of information that mean nothing but also are the foundations of a friendship. He hates tomatoes. Enough that when I ask for extra he pretends to gag which only makes me laugh harder. I tell him I hate beer that much too and he refuses to believe me.

"You drink it too smooth to hate it."

I scoff. "It's free alcohol, you learn to just swallow."

He cracks up and flips the hamburger patty onto the pile of salad and bread he's constructed, smothering the whole thing with sauce and then slides the plate over to me.

"Aw man, the dirty shit I could say to that… you're lucky you're off limits, Angel. You can sleep here if you want, you know. There's plenty of beds here and I'm the only one in the bunk room. You could even have the top bunk, I'll go to the bottom."

It doesn't sound like an invitation to fuck him but I can't risk sleeping on a bed around him anyway. My demons might come out to play and then he'll find out just how fucked up I really am. "It's fine, I didn't exactly pack spare clothes. Besides, aren't you trying to fuck Mel? Can't do that if I'm around cramping your style."

He smirks at me as I take a bite."I'll just fuck her behind the bar, you wouldn't even know it was going down."

I pull a face and chew, swallowing before saying, "Remind me not to drink here again. I do not want your fucking sweaty-balls-beer."

He roars with laughter again, his head thrown back as he chews on his own burger. The crash of the kitchen door slamming on the wall scares the ever-loving shit out of me.

Tomi looks fucking enraged in the doorway, huffing and fucking puffing like he just ran here or something and Speck's face isn't great.

"What the fuck are the two of you doing in here?" he snarls, and I shrink back onto the kitchen counter like I can scoot away from his anger, far enough that he can't reach me.

He glances over to me and then down at the burger. I push it away from myself, like I've been caught stealing it or whatever. "I'll leave. I should go now anyway."

I move to jump down but he steps towards me as if to stop me and I shrink back again.

"Speck, get the fuck out," he says, his voice low and dangerous.

I glance over at Speck and try not to fucking whimper when he blows out a breath and walks out without a word.

Okay.

So he's definitely not my friend. Friends don't abandon each other like this, they don't leave you to fend for yourself against an enraged and bloodthirsty biker who looks about ready to rip my fucking head off about eating a damn burger.

"What the hell do you think you're doing here?"

I rub my palms down my legs. "At the party? You told me I had to be here. Or do you mean the kitchen? I was going to leave but Speck said I had to eat something before I drove. He made me a burger and we were just eating together. That's it. That's the whole story."

He stalks forward and I force myself to stay still, no matter how badly I want to jump down and run the hell away from him. His nose ring catches in the light as his nostrils flare at me. I'm so freaking scared that he's about to murder me that it shocks me when he finally relaxes.

"Didn't find the right guy to work for tonight?"

I frown at him. "Why do I have to keep telling you I don't do extra? I've said that from the word go, I don't take on any other work."

He steps forward and rolls his shoulders back. The slow and easy smirk that stretches across his lips is seductive and my poor fucking heart can't take it. I've gone from terrified to aroused in under a minute and my rib cage is hurting from the pounding in my chest.

"You did though, didn't you? You gave me something extra. Difference is you did it for free."

I swallow hard against the bile creeping up the back of my throat. "I don't care what other women choose to do with their bodies, that's their decision. I'm not for sale. If you want me to dance then I will, but that's it. What happened in your office, that was… a mistake. I made a mistake."

He steps forward again until his body is snug between my legs, his hips touching my thighs and his hands planted down on either side of me. His face turns up towards mine and his lips get close to brushing my own.

The panic is there but this time it's different.

I'm not scared of his touch, not how I usually am, but I am terrified of what this moment means. Why is he so fixated on me now when he's always hated so much as the sight of me?

"Name the price I have to pay to fuck you right here. I want to push you back and fuck you on the countertop. What'll it cost me?"

Jesus, Lord have mercy. My pussy wakes the fuck up at that. I didn't even think I could get wet and now I'm fucking dripping for him. Except—

"I'm not for sale. Can you... can you move please? I'd like to go home."

His jaw clenches and he grabs my face, moving me until I'm staring up into those stormy blue eyes of his and panting. "Is there a boyfriend waiting up for you? Is that why you're pretending you don't fucking want me?"

"Pretty sure I said I'm not for sale. Get your hands off of me," I say, breathy and I swear my nipples try to cut through my shirt to get his attention.

"Your pupils are blown all the way out, Angel, but I'll keep it between us. Wouldn't want all of my brothers knowing how easy it is to get you to change your mind."

I don't care what my pupils are doing, I just want to get out of here in one piece. "I'm going to leave. Let me know if that means I've lost my job and I'll go someplace else."

I have no choice but to slide down his body to get off of the counter and, my God, the feel of his rock hard body against my own is like a special form of torture. I wasn't expecting to find a biker who looks like a fucking cover model, the dirty blonde hair and the nose ring, fuck. Without the tattoos he'd look like a fucking surfer.

He licks his lips and stares down at me and then it's like the alcohol clears and he remembers who the hell he is and what exactly I am.

"Fuck. Get the hell out of here and try not to bend over for my cousin's cock on your way out. You're practically begging for him to fuck you in my goddamn kitchen."

His kitchen? I'm fairly certain this is the MC's kitchen but I keep that little tidbit to myself as I flee.

Poe grabs my arm on the way out and her eyes are all sorts of worried. "Angel, what the hell happened to you? Did someone hurt you? Jesus, Trink go get Tomi."

Oh fuck. "I'm fine. Honestly, I just don't feel well and I wanna go home."

The doors behind me open again and Tomi comes stalking out. I rip my arm out of Poe's grip and take off for my truck before anyone can stop me again. Speck calls out to me but Tomi's words ring in my ears and I hightail it out of there, not stopping until I'm locked in my car, the engine running and my breath heaving out of my chest.

Holy shit.

Am I crying right now?

Where the hell have these tears come from? I have no clue but they're streaming down my face, like a freaking stream just overtaking me completely.

Maybe Coldstone isn't for me.

Chapter Fourteen

Tomi

I get all of the phones ready to be given out.

I cover every fucking base I can think of. Tracking their GPS, their keystrokes, alerts if they're changing SIM cards, logging every password they might put into a website or an app, and I make the camera and mic remote accessible so if they go somewhere they shouldn't be I can figure out what the fuck they're doing. I'm not sure what will be the most useful because half the guys barely know how to text, but I want to be sure I've thought of everything.

It's a good distraction from all of the bullshit going on in my head because I'm a fucking mess. I don't know how the hell Rue survives this, how he deals with feeling so fucking angry and out of control all the damn time.

No wonder he's so fucking grumpy.

I do the entire lot of the work in my childhood bedroom where I'm absolutely positive there's not any fucking bugs. I've swept the place enough times to be sure, I've torn the whole fucking house apart twice in the last week.

Keely is good about it, no doubt Hawk has told her about our plans, but I just can't shake the fact that maybe someone is in this fucking house and planting bugs.

I'm fucking paranoid.

Sunday night finally rolls around and Keely makes us all dinner and before taking Trink down to the den to eat quietly together. Trink is obviously still a little afraid of King because she doesn't argue once, just grabs her plate and follows Keely out.

Law and Lyn are both out running errands for Keely so around the table it's only the Callaghan men, only the blood we can trust.

Speck still looks a little shocked to be at the table.

I flick the switch on the jammer I made myself, just in case, and give King a nod. If I missed a bug, this will stop that shit from working.

There's silence for a moment, only the scraping of forks on plates to be heard.

Finally, Hawk huffs and starts shoveling food into his mouth, "Let's get this shit over with sooner rather than later. Anyone have any fucking leads?"

Speck looks around at everyone like a fucking idiot and Hellion death glares him into silence. Fuck being the youngest, unpatched project of the family. I'd be fucking swinging.

Rue takes a swig of his beer and says, "I've got a few. Nothing concrete but I'm working on it."

I know all about his hunches and I think he's fucking right in them but that's for him to chase.

I've got my own shit to handle. "I have a plan. I'm bugging everyone's phones, I'm bugging the entire clubhouse, and everything that is club owned."

King and Hawk both nod without a word, all the go ahead I need and Hellion scoffs. "You and your fucking computer shit, you're not going to catch fucking Dave doing anything on his phone."

I shrug. I don't need them to understand what I'm doing.

I just need them to fucking shut up and do something when I catch the assholes in action. Rue shoots me a look from across the room, the warning in his eyes clear as a fucking bell. I need to tone my shit down but, fuck if that isn't impossible.

I know my shit.

Hawk sets his beer down on the table and blows out a breath. "Is there anything you can do about the Boar's phone? Tracking that would be the fucking game changer."

King blows out a breath and tips his head back so he's staring at the ceiling, his lips moving like he's silently praying or some shit. Clearly this isn't the first time he's hearing about Hawk's suspicions of the president of the Mounts Bay charter of the Unseen.

Rue looks between the two of them and says, "Is this a rat thing or just a general keeping an eye on the asshole?"

Hellion gets up for another beer, offering one to Hawk who takes it with a grunt.

King finally turns his gaze back to his son and cocks his head a little. "That man has walked the line one too many times to have our trust. He might not have betrayed the patch but fuck has he come close. We'd be stupid not to keep an eye on him… especially if Tomi can get it done without having to leave the state or trusting anyone in the Bay's charter."

I nod. "Easy done."

Rue blows out a breath. "You really think he's dirty? Fuck, even if we find something it's not as simple as taking out a fucking rat. If we kill him we'd have to face the Twelve. That ain't shit to take lightly."

Hellion snorts. "At least it's not the fucking Family."

Jesus Christ.

Like we need the added headache of Mounts Bay's twisted fucking politics. Rats in our club and the Demons fucking stalking us is bad enough, we all heard about what goes down in the Bay and Coldstone isn't equipped for that kind of warfare.

Rumor has it, the Jackal stepped out on the Twelve and got his fucking head cut off.

He ran the biggest fucking drug empire in the country and even he couldn't face the rest of the fucking Twelve and come out alive. The Lynx too, she tried to betray the Wolf and got taken out like she was fucking nothing.

After that the Family formed and I'll be fucked if our club goes against them, if the Boar needs to die we'll have to approach them for a fucking parlay. Jesus Christ, this is turning into a fucking mess.

Rue slides a beer across the table at me. "One step at a time, brother. First we find the rats, then we burn them out. Whatever it takes."

I start getting the phones distributed through the club easy enough. King tells the men we're upgrading everything because of the bump in income over a big arms deal he's done.

A lotta questions about the deal which stops people giving a shit about the new tech.

I keep my head down and my eyes on my fucking computer until something flags. I'm impatient for it but the week goes by with nothing until Friday.

Jameson calls me at midnight.

"I've found some good fishing holes down this way, you should book a trip."

I hold my cursing in.

It's all a code, something we came up with way back when he took over his family business and started working with us.

Something is up with our shipment.

"Sounds like a plan, man. I've been meaning to head out fishing. I'll pack my shit and head down."

He lets out a breath and murmurs, "Bring a couple of your friends, make a day of it. You know we'd love to have y'all stay for dinner."

Fuck me.

A big find then.

I talk bullshit with him for another minute or two to calm his nerves and then hang up, flicking a text to Rue to get his ass moving. There's no one else I trust like him to back me up and if we're heading down to Biloxi then I need someone sharp.

I text Speck, too.

Now that King's decided to have him in the fucking loop about the rat shit a little more I can start giving him bigger shit to do. I don't really want him off of Angel duty, I need a set of eyes on her, but there's something still fucking needling me about the two of them laughing and eating together the other night.

I'd never heard her laugh before.

Fuck, I've barely seen her smile.

I meet them both in the parking lot, armed to the teeth and ready to spill blood for our club, the joking asshole persona of Speck's has simmered right down.

It's been a while since I saw the real Callaghan in him.

It's clear as hell now.

The drive down to Biloxi is a long one but my hog eats up the road like it's fucking nothing. I take the lead and make

Speck take the rear, Rue in the middle like he someday will be when he steps up as the Prez. He hates that shit, never wants to be protected, but he knows better than to argue with me about it.

It's protocol for a reason and there's been a target on his back from the second he took his first breath, it'll be there until his last.

We get to his place and park up behind his place where the hogs aren't visible from the road. We all strip out of our cuts and pack them away in the saddlebags on our motorcycles. We're extra fucking careful about this place. There's a reason we don't go down for the real shit we do.

Jameson meets us out in the front of his house, carrying beers with a grin on his face. "How was the ride?"

Speck grins and shoots shit with him for a minute while Rue discretely looks around. Nothing's changed around here except the house has been repainted, and there's actual fucking flowers in the garden.

A woman's touch.

"Come in! Elizabeth is out visiting with her parents before the wedding. Her granddaddy is too old to travel."

I nod and stalk into the house, kicking the dirt off of my boots before I walk in because Keely raised me right.

Outlaw, sure, but I still have fucking manners.

We walk into the kitchen area and he takes a seat.

We have no reason to believe this place is bugged but Jameson saw enough shit serving overseas to be extra fucking careful about shit. A little paranoid some would say but with everything going on in the MC that shit is smart.

"These are the photos I was telling you about. The ones from the fishing trip. A lotta big fish out there."

I take what he's handing over and try not to lose my fucking cool.

More kids.

More fucking kids in the shipping containers, only this time they're alive and sitting on white sacks.

I sift through more of the photos and yep, the sacks are drugs. Someone is using the fucking pipeline and our club to run fucking children and drugs across the country.

"It's a catch and release thing, I don't usually have any

need for them so I let them go. The freezer here is full enough."

Right.

He let the kids go. I don't ask questions about it because I can't without risking us all if the place really is bugged but I know Jameson and I know he has contacts he can use to get them home safe.

I don't want to think about the girls that don't have homes to go to.

Hopefully they're not selling themselves on the fucking streets.

Rue just barely contains himself. I get it, hearing this shit from Luis was bad enough but to fucking see the evidence? Fuck these rats. Fuck them for using our shit for their own fucking profit instead of starting something for themselves.

And to see kids is fucking disgusting.

Again, I'm an outlaw not a piece of shit.

We stay there long enough for it to look as though we've spent the night drinking together, eating a late dinner, and shooting shit. There's more than enough we can talk about with him that doesn't put any of us at risk. Speck asks way too many questions about guns and Jameson is good about it.

Rue is quiet.

I get it. This shit is hard knowing that it's probably Grimm having a hand in trafficking the kids, everything coming back down to Poe's fucking bloodline. She's a good kid though. She's been raised right and protected from his shit.

Rue needs to worry a little less about her last name.

He'll change it the second he can anyway.

The ride home is twice as long as the ride down there, all of our heads full of shit we wish we didn't have to think about. I try to figure out what the fuck else I can do to lure these motherfuckers into showing themselves but there's limits to what I can do.

I have to wait.

Watch and fucking wait.

I get home, frustrated and full of rage I can't do shit about, only to find Angel wet and pretty much naked in my backyard.

What.

The.

Fuck?!

Worse than that, there's a whole pile of other people out there, half of them from Trink's school and a lot of them are guys.

All of them are getting an eyeful of her.

Not fucking happening.

I hear Rue start muttering behind me and Speck starts cursing up a storm but I ignore them both to storm out into the backyard like my ass is on fire.

The guy talking to Angel, leaning in and leering at her tits, sees me charging towards them both and shits his pants. Just fucking loses his manhood and melts into the crowd like a pathetic worm.

Angel frowns and swings around to see me, her hand clutching at her beer a little tighter. "Oh. I didn't think you were going to be here. I can leave."

Her whispers are low enough that I might be the only one hearing them, especially since everyone is taking big steps away from us both. "You need to get a fucking towel and march your ass upstairs to put some fucking clothes on. Now."

I turn around and yell, "Trink, who the fuck are all these assholes? Send them the fuck home now before I start swinging!"

That clears the pool area pretty fucking fast. I keep myself within arm's reach of Angel at all times, using my body as a shield as she bends down to grab her towel. Fuck me, her ass is hardly covered by those bikini bottoms.

"Why the fuck are you being such an asshole? She's not fucking hurting anyone being here for my fucking birthday! God, you are such a fucking asshole, Tomi! Angel is my fucking friend, she can come here if she wants to!"

I ignore Poe's whining and the second Angel has the towel around herself I get a hand hooked into her elbow and start pulling her back into the house. She tries to get to the door but I tug her until she follows me up the stairs.

Chapter Fifteen

Angel

I'm still busy trying to survive being homeless and working all night during my midterm exams when Poe messages me about her birthday.

I didn't give her my number so I'm guessing Speck handed it over to her but having to think about a party when I'm overloaded with my workload is just too much for me.

She moves the date for me.

I kind of want to cry over how much she wants to be my friend, how much she's willing to do to be my friend, and so even though I really don't want to be around her friends I say yes.

Poe promises me three times that Tomi won't be there. I think she's scared he's hurt me or something when really it's just that I'm broken and he might be an asshole but he's also way too fucking good for me.

She messages me to meet her over at her place and I suck it the fuck up and text her back to say I'll be there.

If I'm going to stay in this goddamn town, which I'm planning to, I need some friends and she's been the best option so far.

I throw on a swimsuit and then a dress over that, slipping flat shoes on because anything with a heel has been ruined for me now. The second I hit my goal and quit dancing at The Boulevard I'm throwing all of the heels out.

Poe lives out in the suburbs, a few streets over from the Unseen clubhouse, and the two-story townhouse is really nice. I didn't really get a good look at it the last time I was here.

It's older, the paint peeling a little and a little overgrown, but it's clean and the street looks safe. I'd kill to live here, to have grown up in a place like this.

There's cars everywhere already.

I park up my Chevy and take a deep breath before I get out, taking my bag in with me. I'm dancing tonight so I'll use that as an excuse for why I'm carrying it around.

I feel stupid knocking on the door, especially if there's already people around everywhere but Poe is the one to open it up. She's already standing there in a tiny bikini, a bottle of beer in one hand and a grin across her face.

She looks adorable.

"Now what the hell is a sexy piece of ass like you doing wearing that dress? I can barely see you've got tits under it."

I scoff at her and steel myself for the hug I know she's going to give me. She doesn't. She just takes a step forward and shuts the door behind her.

"Are we not going in? Is the party being held on your porch or something?"

She scoffs and gestures to the house next door. "Trink has a pool, the party is over there. I decided to be fashionably late because I'm a classy bitch."

Oh.

Shit.

I chew my lip a little. "Are you sure Trink is going to be okay with me being at her place?"

Poe shrugs with a smile. "I really just couldn't fucking care less. Trink's just… going through some shit at the moment. It's made her a little bit of a bitch. Don't get me wrong, she's my bitch, but she's also wrong about you. Let's head over before you change your mind."

I sigh and lift my bag a little. "I don't wanna take this over there or leave it in my car. Is there somewhere safe you can leave it locked up here?"

Poe frowns a little but shrugs. "Sure. Lemme put it up in my room."

I wait on the porch for her and then we walk next door to Trink's place. I'm a complete dumbass though because I fail to remember that Trink is both seventeen and Tomi's little sister.

It's only when the door opens that I realize I'll be meeting their parents. Tomi's freaking parents.

Oh god.

The woman standing there looks a lot like her children but her eyes are softer and more kind. "Well hello! Your face isn't one I've seen before."

I sputter out, "Uh, I'm Angel. Poe's friend."

"Keely isn't going to slam the door in your face, Angel, if she doesn't like you she'll be a lady about it."

I blush as Keely chuckles under her breath. "And hello to you too, birthday girl! Sweet seventeen and never been kissed, I'm sure."

Poe darts forward and gives her a hug, cackling like a crazy person. "Absolutely. Virgin fucking Mary thanks to your dumbass boys."

Keely chuckles at her as she hugs her back, all warmth and familial love.

"Thank you for having me over, I appreciate it." I fumble with words, too awkward and unprepared.

Keely smiles. "You're always welcome. This house is always open to all of Trink and Poe's friends. All of the 'dumbass boys' friends too."

Oh God.

What are the chances Tomi told his mom about me? He wouldn't have. I mean, he wouldn't be going around and telling his goddamn mother about his conquests, right? That would be weird.

While I'm busy freaking the fuck out, Poe grabs my elbow gently and starts walking me through the house and out the back.

She snorts at me when I don't say a freaking word about it. "Stop freaking out, Keely is great. C'mon, I'll take you out back to the pool. Best freaking pool in all of Coldstone, there's a slide on it which Trink pretends she's too cool for but a pool slide is always fucking cool."

I don't get to see much of the house except that there's family photos everywhere. Dozens and dozens of them on every surface and when we walk outside there's a huge Unseen emblem painted on the bricks.

It's really nice out here.

The pool is huge, there's a table full of food, and barrels of ice and beer everywhere. There's too many people here for me to be comfortable, and when Trink sees us walk in together she rolls her eyes at Poe.

Right.

I'll steer clear of her.

"Let's go for a swim, that'll settle your nerves. Then we can grab food and I'll introduce you to some of my friends."

She sounds so goddamn hopeful that I have to take a second to get the hell over myself. She's my friend. She's trying to include me in shit.

No one here gives a fuck about me and my job.

So I strip out of my dress and jump into the pool with my friend. We act like idiots, splashing and swimming and just having fucking fun. Poe swims to the edge to grab us beers and we sit on the edge with them and talk about random bullshit. I tell her about the noise my car is making and she tells me about the car she's rebuilding with her sister's boyfriend.

Once the sun has gone down and all of the outdoor lights are glowing some of the guys from Poe's school start trying to talk to us both. I don't really want to talk to them but Poe does a great job of keeping them at bay, insulting them all and reminding them that this house is owned by the VP of the Unseen.

Not a smart idea to fuck with the girls here.

When she ducks off to the toilet, one of the guys decides to try his luck with me.

Right as Tomi, Rue, and Speck arrive.

All hell breaks loose in the blink of an eye, and I'm marched up the stairs by a fucking enraged Tomi.

Tomi walks me through a bedroom and into a small private bathroom. I don't get the chance to see anything really, just the tight lines of his jaw as he clenches it at me.

I don't know why he's so fucking pissed at me. "I'm sorry I came here. I should've just-"

"Shut the fuck up, Angel. Just shut up. Get your ass into the shower and rinse the fuck off."

I frown at him but he doesn't move, just stands there in the doorframe with his arms crossed over his chest until I give in and strip down. He's seen me naked… almost, but I still blush over it. I duck my head under the spray of water and rinse off quickly, hesitating over whether or not I should use his soap.

"Hurry up and get clean. We need to talk."

Great.

He's got that whole caveman thing going on again. I didn't even do anything wrong!

I scrub down, trying not to breathe in the scent of his soap, vowing to myself that I'll take another shower the second I get the chance. The smell of him makes my chest ache in the worst way. I don't know when or why he's gotten his claws into my soul but he's in there so deep I can't dig him out, no matter how hard I try.

I rush through the rest of the shower, worried about what the fuck he's going to do once I'm clean. Throw me out in the street naked, probably. That would be fucking shameful but at least I could make it over to Poe's house and beg her for something.

She'd also probably come over here and stab Tomi for me.

That makes me feel a little better.

I shut the water off and pull the curtain back, holding it over my body. "Can you pass me the towel, please?"

He just stares me down like he's playing with me, baiting me into breaking the fuck down.

Fine.

Like I care that he's going to get a look at my tits and the brand spanking new wax job I did last night. It's not like he hasn't seen it all before.

I step out and reach for the towel, my skin burning where his eyes drag over every inch of me. I hear him curse under his breath but I don't give him any more of my attention. I'm not playing into his games… well, not any more than he's forcing me right now.

His breathing is still fucked up, his chest heaving as he takes in every inch of my skin that's on show. I don't… hate the feeling. I'm not trying to get away from his touch so I guess that's a win.

"Drop the towel."

I swallow but my hands move at his command. My body

is still wet, the droplets covering every inch of me making my skin prickle with cold.

"Get on your knees."

Oh God, I can't live this down again. I can't suck him off again and go through the aftermath.

"Do it right and I'll eat your pussy so good you'll come harder than you ever have before."

I swallow.

I've never come, not once in my life.

I can't stand touching myself, not even now that he's been having this effect on my body. But… fuck, I'm already here. I'm already naked in his bathroom with the whole party out there being disbanded thanks to his temper over me being here.

The damage is already done.

I sink down to my knees on the bath mat, my hands already moving behind my back.

"No, you do it. Unzip my jeans, remind me of what that mouth of yours can do."

I stare up at him but he isn't smirking or showing any emotions at all. He just stares down at me through his hooded gaze until I reach forward and do as he says. His cock is already straining behind the zipper, as hard as stone and leaking a little when I finally get my palm wrapped around the girth.

It feels even bigger in my hand, the blood red color of my nails stark against the soft skin and veins. I lick my lips before I suck him down, and he takes a fistful of my hair, shoving his hips forward to slam his cock all the way down until I'm forcing my gag reflex down and swallowing to take him further into my throat.

"This fucking mouth. I could fuck it all goddamn day, fill your belly with my cum and just keep going until you're fucking stained with me. Fucking ruined."

I start to suck him with everything I've got, angry and ready to make him come just to get a little power back. He talks about me like I'm something dirty and to be used.

Maybe I want to use him a bit too.

He grunts and tightens the fist in my hair, tugging and pulling me over and over again as he rocks his hips and pumps into my mouth with all that he's got. I can't help but look up at him, to watch him lose himself in the wet heat of my mouth.

I choke a little when he shoots down my throat, the taste not something I'm used to, and this time when he drags me to my feet he doesn't give me the chance to flinch away.

He kisses me.

He hauls my naked body up against his and takes over my mouth, biting my bottom lip and tugging it with his own until I open my mouth to his and he can taste himself on my tongue.

I can count on one hand the amount of times I've been kissed.

It was never like this.

His hands run down my sides until they reach my ass, cupping it to haul me up and into his arms, my legs curling around him on instinct. My bare pussy rubs against his shirt and I can smell my own arousal, clean and sweet, between our bodies.

"Did you flirt with any of those boys out there?" he growls against my lips and I answer without thinking.

"No, I'm not interested in anyone."

His eyes narrow and his palm cracks down on my ass, the sting of it jolting me and forcing me to rub against his chest. "You wanna rethink that? You're dripping down my shirt, I'd say you're more than fucking interested."

I'm too far gone to blush or get embarrassed, I just nod my head and when he crushes his lips to mine again I kiss him right back.

He walks us both out and into the bedroom again, laying me out on the bed and yanking my legs up, spreading my pussy open as he stares at it like he wants to tear into me.

The first trickles of fear start up in my gut and I have to say something. "What are you going to do?"

He glances up at me, his eyes glazed and his tongue darting out to swipe over his bottom lip. "I'm going to eat this pussy until I've had my fill. I'm going to make you come, over and over again, until you forget about those fucking assholes that were trying to get inside you."

My legs start to shake a little and I collapse back onto the pillow, throwing an arm over my eyes and taking a deep breath. If I hate it I can just... leave. I can walk over to Poe's house and I can leave.

He doesn't attempt to ease me into it. He attacks my pussy the same way he's always treated me, a firm and rough demand, but the feel of his tongue parting my lips and dipping inside is like nothing I've ever felt before.

He licks and sucks at every part of my pussy, his arms curling around my hips and holding me still once my shaking legs turn into a full body tremble. When his tongue circles my clit a gasp rips through me and I really start to squirm.

When my very first orgasm finally takes over me, I'm practically sobbing. My entire body is overwhelmed with sensation and overstimulation, and I think I'm going to embarrass myself when he finally looks up at me.

Except he doesn't.

No, he keeps going. He lays there on his childhood bed and pushes me over the edge three, four, five times until I'm gushing all over the sheets and his face is dripping with my arousal.

My brain is broken.

He sits up and I'm expecting him to get up and leave, or tell me something fucking awful about myself that'll ruin this whole thing, but he doesn't.

He sticks his fingers inside me.

The last ripples of pleasure evaporate and panic drenches my entire body, the sweat turning cold and my body clenches up for an entirely different reason.

His eyes are hot on mine as he freezes, his fingers slowly slipping out of me but the damage is done. My heart is beating so hard it feels like it's trying to pound right out of my chest.

"I can't," I croak, and his brows draw down low.

"Why?"

I don't have an answer for that. Not without breaking open my ribcage and exposing all of the damage that's been done to my soul. He's gorgeous and he's strong and he's loyal to his family.

And I'm a piece of trash, gutter-rat stripper with trauma by the bucket load.

"Could… could I have a shirt? Just to get down to my car?" I whisper, and the frown on his face gets darker, more malevolent. Tears fill my eyes but I blink them away.

He pushes up off of the bed and strips off his own shirt, throwing it at me. "Get the fuck out. Just get out and quit wasting my fucking time, Angel."

Chapter Sixteen

Tomi

I swear I can taste the sweet honey of Angel's cum in the back of my tongue for days after I ate her out on my childhood bed.

Every morning I wake up, hard as stone and leaking on my sheets. The image of Angel's lips wrapped around my cock as I fuck her mouth is the only thing I see when I shut my eyes. Fuck, this 'struck shit is hardcore. I can't stop thinking about her and I just get angrier and angrier the more I think about it.

She's a fucking stripper.

She flinched away from me, but only after she'd given me the blowjob of my life. No way the girl hasn't gone pro before, that was too skilled to be an amateur.

Twice she's fucking flinched.

It doesn't matter how hard I try to cut the fucking ties, I still find myself pulled back to The Boulevard. With Speck busy dealing with rat business I lose my set of eyes on Angel and I'll be fucked if I'm leaving her without someone tailing her.

My time there is justified because the books are a fucking mess.

No matter how much I try to clean them up, nothing ever adds up and I fucking curse myself out for letting people who barely know how to count touch them.

So no matter how much I want to sit out in my booth and stab any fucker that looks at Angel, I stick to the office and sift through the accounts and the piles of invoices with only a bottle of whiskey and a bad mood to keep me company.

It's a little after two when there's a quiet knock at the door and a pause.

No one knocks like that around here.

I call out and when the door opens Angel scurries inside, stripper heels and nothing much else on.

She doesn't walk around here in her getups. Not ever, she always puts clothes on between dances. The other girls give her shit for it but she always does it. We also haven't spoken since the pool incident, she hasn't once so much as tried to look at me and now she's scrambling into my office like the hounds of hell are on her ass?

Alarms bells start sounding.

"What's happened?"

She walks right over to me behind the desk, bypassing the chair entirely, and if she wasn't shaking so hard her teeth are chattering I'd think she was coming here to ride my dick.

"Angel, what the fuck happened?"

A weird noise starts up outta her throat, like a high-pitch keening, and my patience snaps. I stand and tug her into my arms, getting my shit covered in Mel's goddamn glitter, and I push her into my chest, banding my arms around her and squeeze a little.

The keening stops but her words come out in a series of little gasps. "Are— I mean, do those other bikers belong to the Unseen? I haven't... seen them here before."

Fuck's sake.

The Shreveport charter are in town and I know who the hell she's talking about without another word which is good because she's being so damn hesitant. "What did he do? Angel, what the fuck did he do?"

She looks up at me, her eyes all electrified with terror, and fury sweeps over me.

I don't fucking care if I'm cuntstruck, no fucking way am I letting someone scare her like this. She's mine. Whether that's the biggest fucking tragedy of my life, that changes nothing. She's mine and no asshole is going to fucking touch what's mine.

"It was the big one, I don't know what his name is, he came up to me when I was trying to leave the stage. Told me he'd see me back at the clubhouse tonight. I told him I don't do extra and he said I belong to the club so he'd fuck me if he wanted to. Tomi, I'm not—"

"No, you're fucking not. Go get your clothes on, take a shower, whatever you do between sets. I'll sort this out, don't even think about it anymore. Stop fucking shaking, Angel, I'll take care of him."

She takes this deep gulping breath that damn near takes my knees out but after another one she pulls away from me, her hands on my chest as she pulls away. They linger there like she doesn't want to let go of me.

Two things set like stone in my head.

I'm fucked over this girl.

And Diego is fucking dead for scaring her like this.

I walk her out of my office, all the way over to the locker room and I wait until she's locked in the bathroom there before I stalk back out to the bar.

I will kill that cunt.

I take a seat at the bar where I can watch Diego and what he's doing at the front of the stage. There's enough of the Shreveport charter here that I need to cool my fucking jets. I'm a good fighter but probably not good enough to take on sixteen men in public.

I need to call Rue down here now.

Two against sixteen is doable.

The minute she gets an eyeful of me Diamond huffs and shakes her head. "I told you having her here is a problem. You should tell your cousin to stop thinking with his dick and inviting trouble in all our lives."

I give the jealous bitch a look and I watch as she gulps and scurries away. Just because I'm the friendlier Callaghan doesn't mean she can tell me what the fuck to do and from the moment Angel 'struck me I've been on edge.

Diego is laughing and doing shots with a couple of the other Shreveport brothers. Luis is too busy talking business with Hell to give a shit about the girls or what his asshole son is getting up to.

Too bad.

Mighta saved Diego from getting his asshole torn open because I'm about to fucking ream him. If my threats aren't enough I'll actually gut him. I'm not in the mood for his bullshit and the only thing stopping me from walking over there and slamming his face onto the table until his nose shatters is knowing just how fucking persistant the cunt can be.

His obsession with Poe has everything to do with Rue and nothing to do with the kid herself.

So I can't show my hand here or I'll be dealing with a bigger problem. Fuck, his constant stalking of Posey when he's in town is beyond annoying, it's enough to know that someday I'll be helping Rue bury his body somewhere because Diego can't help himself. One day he'll strike and on that day, he'll be fucking dead.

The curse is a fucking powerful thing.

And my lovestruck cousin isn't going to fucking stop until Poe is safe, happy, and his. The kid just has to grow the fuck up first.

"Jesus. She came to you?" Speck says as he slides onto the barstool next to mine.

I nod and he grunts at me, "You might actually be winning her over."

I side-eye him as I take a sip. "Why would you think that?"

"Well, she came to you and not me. That's a first. She also didn't run screaming outta here and after what he said, that's what I thought would happen."

I set the glass down. "He touch her? Did he do anything except talk to her?"

He shakes his head. "One of the guys stopped him from following her onto the stage. Shoulda fucking known he'd be obsessed with her, it's like he knows when a woman belongs to a Callaghan."

It's the first time he's said that and my hackles haven't gone up.

She does belong to me. One way or another.

"I want to see what he does when she comes back out. I'll talk to him once I see it with my own two eyes."

Speck groans. "Should I call Rue and let him know we're starting a war here tonight? Just to warn him? Because you'll kill him. Fuck, I nearly killed him and she ain't even mine."

The rage in my system starts pumping until I'm sure it's replaced all of the blood in my system and now I'm fucking itching to beat the life outta that piece of trash. Nothing but a fucking clown, talks himself up but doesn't actually pull his fucking weight. He knows he's on the path for being president when Luis steps down but only because of his blood.

Fuck, I'm going to be on the Council someday because of my blood but I have done everything for my club. I went to fucking college and dealt with dumbass frat boys and bimbo sorority girls who wanted a taste of the dirty biker life before they married some fucking suit. I've always thought long-term and not about how shit makes me look. I couldn't give a fuck about looking like some dangerous biker... I'm too busy being one.

The song changes and my attention shifts back to the stage as Angel walks out and the nerves are right there in every fucking line of that body of hers. She's practically vibrating with it and there goes my fucking control.

I stalk forward ready to reach down Diego's fucking throat and yank his spine out, but when Angel sees me coming something calms in her and the shaking stops.

Fuck if that doesn't change something.

Hell, she might have flinched at me twice now but she's still coming back for more. That has to count for something.

I decide right then and there that I want it to count for something.

Diego starts calling out at her and I wave Speck off when he starts cussing him out under his breath. I'm calm now, I'm thinking clearly and I know what I need to do.

"Don't call him. I've got this under control."

I motion at Mike to get him to bring Diego over to me. I'm not walking over to the cunt, he's in my fucking bar.

Diego frowns and tries to snarl at Mike, only stopping himself from taking a swing at the bouncer when he looks up and sees me. He stalks over to me with a snarl on his ugly fucking mug.

"The fuck do you want, Callaghan? I'm trying to enjoy the show."

I take a sip of my drink, all fucking casual, and say, "You're welcome to enjoy the show but if you try to put your hands on one of my girls again you'll be answering to me. You're not going to enjoy that shit either."

His lip curls up even more at me. "Who the fuck do you

think you are, telling me what to do? She's club property. I'll fuck her if I want to."

Over my dead body will this cunt touch her. "This is your last warning about my girls. That one dancing up there, you hurt her or scare her off? That's the income of this place cut in half. Means the extra cash we put through starts looking suspicious and it affects the club. You stay the fuck away from her or I'll be fucking dealing with you."

His face shifts, the disdain for me and my club clear, because he doesn't fucking deal with being told no. Not ever, he throws the spoiled fucking biker version of a tantrum.

Shedding blood and fucking with business.

"If she's dancing here she belongs to the club."

My jaw tightens and I take a step in towards him, ready to just fucking kill him and be done with it. Fuck, Luis would never forgive the club and it'd be war but fuck would it be worth it. Speak of the devil, he's heading towards us with a frown at the murder on my face.

"She belongs to the Coldstone charter. You touch her and you answer to us. Nothing your daddy can do to save you."

Luis stops at Diego's side and tips his head to me. "He'll leave her alone. Plenty of pussy for him to chase that isn't your money maker."

I nod at him and jerk my head towards Diamond at the bar. "All the other girls do extra, for fee or free, for the club. I'm not forcing our money maker and fucking with my business."

Reiterating to cover my ass because Diego is still eyeballing Angel and I'm going to rip his throat out with my bare fucking teeth like a savage if he doesn't quit it.

Luis nods and claps Diego on the back, "Plenty of hot pussy around for you to have, son. If she ain't playing then leave her be."

Diego's lip curls at me but I walk away from them both and find a seat in the front fucking row to watch the rest of Angel's dance.

Her eyes meet mine and her body goes from that smooth and fluid way she dances to languid and liquid, like molten fire trapped in the most fucking sexy body that's ever existed.

The men around us quieten down a little and I know if I break her eye contact I'll see them all taking notice of the change in her from hot piece of ass to a fucking siren, a fucking nymph out here trying to put every man in here under her spell.

It's working too.

A slow blush starts on her cheeks as her hips ride that fucking pole, the bump and grind of it has my cock leaking in my jeans.

I've sold my soul to a stripper.

I'm not even angry about it anymore.

Chapter Seventeen

Angel

My college classes really start kicking my ass.

It's a hard pill to swallow because I've always been so damn good with my classes, I got my GED at sixteen and never found this stuff hard, but I guess with the small amount of sleep I keep finding myself existing on my brain just doesn't have enough time to recover and function properly.

If that isn't bad enough the noise the Chevy keeps making just gets worse and worse until I have to face the facts. If I don't get it looked at soon the damage might end up irreparable. It's an old classic but, more than that, it's a piece of my dad and not something I could ever bear to lose.

I count some money out from the stash in my bag. I haven't counted it in so long that it's kind of a shock to see how much is really sitting in there, I really should get around to counting it and making a plan on how the fuck I can deposit it into a bank.

I need to do that to be able to buy a house.

I pull one of my dad's old sweaters on to cover up a little before I drive over to the garage in town. There's technically two, but the other one is across the street from the clubhouse and I don't want to get in Tomi's way by being on that side of town. He told me to stop wasting his time so… I guess that's what I'm trying to do.

Half an hour later and I know I'm kind of screwed.

The guys there had been so freaking rude to me. They've all obviously seen me dance at The Boulevard and when I stumble over my words, explaining a sound to guys in an closed space when you're touch-phobic and generally cautious around men is fucking hard. They all crack jokes about my ass and tits, and how my boyfriend should be able to fix this shit for me.

I nod along like their words don't piss me off because there's nothing I can do about it.

Except that when they give me a price it's a week's worth of tips for me. My eyebrows shoot to my hairline but the guy just shrugs at me.

"We both know you can afford it. Don't walk in here being a cheap little hussy."

My stomach drops and I walk out to the sound of them all laughing. It's not like I can't afford it but… fuck, I don't want to be put a week behind in my plans. I already feel like the walls are closing in on me, every other day I'm getting catcalled leaving the club or having some guy trying to climb on stage after me.

I need to get out of there.

I arrive to work with my head in the fucking clouds, freaking the hell out about what I'm gonna do about my car, and I make it through my first dance in a fucking daze.

There's a two-hour break between my sets so I throw clothes back on and sit in the locker room, chewing my lip and staring off into space while I try to figure out if I can make it work.

If I don't get my truck fixed now and it blows up, I'm fucked.

I could buy a new car to get me through… but where would I leave the old Chevy until I got my house? Are there any costs I could cut to cover the mechanic bill without losing a week's tips?

I want to throw up by the time Poe and Law find me sitting there.

"Oh shit, did someone try to touch you again? You'd think the dumbasses would learn."

I glance up and smile at her, quirking an eyebrow at them both. "What are you two doing wandering around here? Rue'll be pissed if he finds you out here, Poe."

She shrugs and slings herself down on the bench next to me. Law sits down on the other side of her, huffing a little.

"Law's on babysitting duty tonight. I tried to go out to a movie with a guy from school, didn't end well."

I glance over at her. "Really? What happened?"

Law scoffs at her and makes an oof noise when she elbows him in the gut. "He stood me up. I think I'm turning into a fucking leper. No one wants to be within a fucking mile of me and it's making me fucking cranky. Maybe I'll move to the Bay with my sister. She has better luck with guys over there."

Law winces and I give him a look. So he's in on this little secret of Rue's. I wonder if the biker is the real reason guys give Poe a wide berth. I don't blame them, he's kind of... terrifying.

That shit runs in the family.

"Anyway, I called Law to come get me because Rue yelled at me for going in the first place and Trink is still... pissed off or whatever. Then I sweet talked him into bringing me here to see you! I feel like you're a fucking ghost half the time. Impossible to fucking find unless you're working."

I shrug. "Sorry, I've been busy. My car's still fucking up so I took it to the garage in town and now I'm freaking the hell out about paying for the fucking thing."

Poe frowns at me like she's wounded. "How much did he quote you?"

After checking my watch, I sigh and bend down to do up the straps on my heels. I've gotta get back out there soon. "Nine grand. I can pay it but taking that money out of my savings is going to hurt."

She scoffs and holds out her hand. "Gimme your keys. I've never met a car I can't fix and I'll only charge you for parts."

I straighten up, chewing on my lip a little as I figure out what the hell to say to her. She takes my indecision the wrong way.

"What, you think because I'm a girl I can't do it? I've grown up in a garage, I could fix the Chevy in my fucking sleep. Law, tell her I can fucking do it."

"Posey Graves has never met a car she couldn't fix, and that's a fact. She's fixing shit that no man could, I'm telling you," Law says, his eyes firmly on the ground now I'm up and getting dressed. It's very nice and respectful, not what I'm expecting out of a seventeen-year-old guy.

"I'm not doubting you at all, Poe, it's just… I feel bad for not paying you for your time! Well, that and the fact that my car is all I've got left from my dad so it's kinda like my security blanket. I can't stand the thought of not having it."

The fierce look on her face eases off. "Yeah, it's a beauty. Honestly, I'm excited about getting under the hood. I haven't seen a '69 in such good condition before. Besides, you're my friend. You don't have to hang out with me and yet here you are, talking to me while the other girls are hating on me."

I huff out a laugh as I strip my shirt off, shoving it into my bag and grabbing her my keys. "They hate me too. Guess they don't like girls who are on the Unseen's radar, good or bad."

Law gets up and walks away, muttering under his breath about how much he enjoys breathing, which doesn't make sense.

Poe ignores him as she giggles at me, all sunshine and joy, and my heart clenches at the sight of it. She's a stunning girl, one that must get a whole lot of attention, but it's her attitude that knocks the breath right out of you. Standing here in the tiny dark back room of a strip club with a half-naked woman, she looks like she's totally at peace with her life.

I'm only writhing with jealousy on the inside.

I start fixing up my makeup, fussing just to make sure it's perfect.

"Thanks. I really appreciate you taking a look, let me know if there's anything I can do for you in return."

Poe shrugs and turns as if she's going to leave but she only makes it a half step before she turns back. "Are any of the girls here sleeping with Rue? You see him here often?"

Oh God.

"Tonight's the first night in a long time. I know Mel is obsessed with him but I've never seen or heard anything. Are you dating him?"

She grins at me and twirls the keys. "I'm seventeen and this fucking close to being allowed to date. This close. Thanks, Angel."

I smile and get back to my makeup, rushing a little now I'm going to be late.

Poe makes the arrangements for my car and messages me to tell me she'll have it picked up from The Boulevard after my next shift.

It kills me but I book a hotel in the next town over for the week so I'll have somewhere to sleep. I reason with myself that it's worth it to keep the Chevy and with a week of decent sleep I'll be able to get a heap more of my classwork done so it's definitely worth it.

Poe's parts estimate comes in at just under two thousand dollars so I'm still way ahead of the original quote.

I spend the day checking into the hotel and unpacking my shit into the tiny room. There's no safe, the room is too cheap for that shit, so I have to keep my cash on me still.

I don't think I could actually bear to not have it on me, the more that pile grows the scarier it is to think about losing it.

I bite the bullet and finally pour the entire lot of it out on the bed.

I count the giant stacks of cash and, holy shit, I'm only like twenty grand away from my goal amount. I've already paid for the hotel for the week so if I can keep the rest of my expenses down that's only like two more weeks left of dancing. Fuck, if I choose to do three more I can have a nice little extra buffer and then I'm out.

I'll be free to buy a house, finish college, find some swanky accounting firm to hire me, and then live a normal fucking life.

A life that belongs to me and no one else.

My hands start to shake. I rub them together and take some deep breaths but I can't keep the tremble out of them, no matter how hard I try.

I'm so fucking close to being done with this shit.

I need to figure out how the fuck to deposit this shit into a bank as soon as I possibly can. I need to start looking at houses and find somewhere right the hell now.

I take a shower at the hotel and get ready for the night there, happy to be somewhere private and without the bullshit the other girls put me through. They haven't been so bad lately, just vocal enough that I know they all hate me but nothing that really makes me take notice of them.

When I'm finally dressed to the nines, my hair is perfect and my cosmetics make me look like a naughty school girl. My hair is in pigtails and I'm wearing a tiny skirt that just barely covers my ass, I'm sure this'll get me a shit-ton of tips tonight.

I'd rolled my eyes when I saw the posting Diamond had put up with the theme but the more I look at myself in the mirror, the more I'm convinced this is going to be a big night.

I throw a long coat over the whole look, double check my money is secure in my bag, and then I lock up the hotel room, walking quickly to my car. I feel a little fucking teary over the thought of giving her up tonight but it's for the best.

I get halfway to The Boulevard when I have to pull over to answer my phone. I find a parking lot and cut the engine, cursing under my breath about the damn thing ringing. It's around the time Diamond calls when they need me to come in early for an extra time slot on the main stage but I'm too far out of Coldstone still to be able to make it in on time.

"Hello?"

It's definitely not Diamond.

"Is that Miss Vaughn? It's Officer Daniels at Maryland—"

I hang up.

I hang the phone the hell up and then I immediately pull out the battery, grab the sim card and fling my car door open to smash the thing under my heel. I throw it into the trash can next to my car. I take the sim card and drop it in my half drunk can of energy drink and then I throw that into the trash as well.

Then I start my car and drive the hell away, my heart fucking racing in my chest.

Did they track me?

Fuck.

Have they been tracking me for a while? If they know about The Boulevard I'm fucked, like truly just beyond fucked.

The shaking gets worse.

By the time I wobble up the steps at The Boulevard to start my shift I'm fucking rattling around like a crackhead.

Diamond notices when she walks into the locker room as I lock my bag up and says to me with a smirk, "If you're tweaking you need to stay the fuck outta my club."

Her club, fuck, Tomi would kill her if he heard her saying that shit. "I'm not. I got some news this morning and it's nerves."

She scoffs. "Sure thing, Angel. Keep your tweaking ass in line."

I do.

I'm a fucking professional at faking shit until I make it, fuck that about sums up my entire time here at the strip club.

So I dance my ass off, the outfit just as popular as I thought it would be and the green raining down onto my stage faster than it ever has before. I wait until I'm done for the night before I start thinking about what the fuck I'm going to do if they've really found me. Fuck.

I'm fucked.

Tomi stalks into the locker room as I'm coming out of the shower, my hair still dripping wet. His eyes drag over my bare arms before he snarls, "What the fuck are you on?"

I sigh. "Nothing. I just… Jesus, I just got some news this morning. It's not a big deal. Test me if you want."

He stares into my eyes like he's looking for the lie. I stare back at him, unwavering and honest because I have nothing to hide.

I'm just freaked the fuck out.

"There's a lot of shit that ain't adding up about you, Angel. You wanna start being fucking honest about it?"

Chapter Eighteen

Tomi

"Hey Tomi! Diamond is busy behind the bar but she wanted me to tell you that Angel is strung out tonight. She's been shaking like she's coming down from a bad high." Mel actually manages to look like she gives a fuck when she says it too, if I gave a shit about the girl I'd be impressed.

Instead, I'm fucking livid.

There's no way it's true, Angel hasn't fucking once looked like she's tweaking and Diamond is a fucking cunt about her at the best of times. I'm sure this is just her next move to fuck with my girl.

Fuck.

Not my girl.

She mighta 'struck me but she definitely doesn't have me… yet. Fuck, I don't want to think about how fucking obsessed with her I already am.

I get into the locker room as Angel is coming out of the shower, all pink and clean, the smell of honey wafting out after her.

Her hands are shaking so bad the makeup bag in her hand is rattling.

I lose my fucking cool and snap, "What the fuck are you on?"

She sighs and she looks tired. "Nothing. I just… Jesus, I just got some news this morning. It's not a big deal. Test me if you want."

She stares at me, unflinching, and here in the shitty lighting of the communal bathroom she just looks… young. Really fucking young and scared, as if the shaking has everything to do with some danger she's facing and nothing to do with a high.

My patience with this whole fucking thing is wearing thin.

"There's a lot of shit that ain't adding up about you, Angel. You wanna start being fucking honest about it?"

The tremors get worse.

She's standing there staring right through my eyes and into my soul, and shaking like a fucking leaf.

Someone is fucking with this girl and when I find out who the fuck it is I'll be slitting their fucking throats.

She hesitates and then brushes past me to get to her locker, hunching over the combination a little before she opens it up and pulls out her bag.

Finally the warning bells start to get my fucking attention.

"Is there an asshole boyfriend taking your money? Knocking you around some?"

Angel startles at the sound of my voice like a damn rabbit. My teeth clench at the sight but I try to look a little less fucking pissed. She barely ever talks about herself and never talks about what happens to her when she leaves here so I need her to fucking trust me right now.

The shaking is fucking killing me.

"What? Why?"

Deep breath. "You make double what any other girl here does. All the other girls are pissed over how popular you are so I've started keeping tally. You're on almost ten g's a week, how the fuck are you still walking around here with a flip phone and a busted ass bag?"

Her eyes drop down to her bag and she curves around it a little more like she can hide its ratty appearance from me now that I've started taking notice.

"I don't have a boyfriend. No one is taking my money from me… except my truck, which needs some work."

Mel tries to walk in but I stop her with a look, waving her the fuck out. Rue and Speck walk out of the office behind her but when they get an eyeful of me they shut the door, wanting nothing to do with whatever is eating my ass.

Smart.

"Do you owe someone? You got family in the hospital or

something? You're not on drugs, I know a tweaker when I see one."

She pulls a sweatshirt on over the thin cami she had on, wincing and rubbing at her shoulder a little. She's worked every other night this week thanks to Farrah's time off, she's danced her ass off without a fucking word of complaint over the long hours, and there's no doubt she's a little fucking sore. Diamond put her on all of next week too.

I hate her dancing here but it sure does make it easier to keep an eye on her.

"Nope. I'm single, sober, and just trying to survive here, Tomi. Is there anything else you need? I'm really just fucking… beat. I have classes early tomorrow and I'll be dancing tomorrow to cover Farrah. Please just— please let me go home."

She slings that shitty bag over her shoulder and pushes the wet tendrils of her hair away from her face. Fuck, what is with this fucking lighting making her look so fucking fragile?

I step aside and let her pass, my mind already planning out exactly how I'm going to tail her carefully the whole fucking way back to her place. I'll run the address and find out who she lives with, where she grew up, fucking every little piece of her life until she's not such a mystery to me anymore.

I watch the security cameras until I've seen her get into a cab and then I dig my keys outta my pocket, ready to get out and follow her home.

My phone ringing in my pocket stops me.

I think about ignoring it, just fucking forgetting all about my responsibilities at the club but the patch weighs heavy over my shoulders and I answer it, cursing under my breath.

"Get your ass to Mugshots. Grab Rue and Speck, be discreet about it."

King's voice is rough but the tenseness of his is radiating down the line. "What the fuck has happened now?"

He grunts down the line. "The whole place was just shot up. Glass and bullets fucking everywhere."

When we walk into Mugshots it really is fucking torn the hell up.

Rue explodes the second he sees the damage. "Fuck. Fuck! Was anyone hurt?"

King stalks over to us from where he was looking over the bullet casings with Hawk, the crunch of glass loud under his boots.

"Coulson was here but he was out the back, managed to get down the back alley and call me without them fucking seeing him. He's rattled as hell though, I got Hellion to take him back to the clubhouse for some whiskey."

Jesus.

"Have the cops been here yet? Any witnesses?" I say, staring at the tens of thousands of dollars worth of damage. The club can afford to cover the costs without even feeling the hit but some asshole is costing us green.

King shakes his head. "We're keeping the cops outta this. The less eyes on us all the better."

Rue nods at him and leans down to pick up a shell. "They walked in here and shot the place up. They had to have an in… or this is one helluva coincidence and Coulson has a hit out on him we didn't know about."

King shakes his head again, his face fucking sour. "Can't have been a hit. Everyone knows the bar's empty by three, it was a fucking fluke that Coulson was even here. He was trying to figure out where the missing money has been going."

More missing fucking money.

What a mess.

Hawk stalks back over to us. "Tomi, get your ass back to the clubhouse and keep watch on your computer shit for what's going on here. Someone has gotta say or do something after this. Rue, Speck, grab a broom. We need to get this shit cleaned up before anyone notices the fucking bullet holes."

I give him a jerk of my head and turn on my heel to get my ass outta there, ready to check fucking everything for a clue over who the hell is responsible for this shit.

The clubhouse is fucking quiet when I get back there, the air heavy with the unknown threat of stray motherfucking bullets. I clap Coulson on the shoulder as I pass by him but he's already too fucking wasted to notice much that's going on around him.

I jerk my head at Hellion until he follows me into the

hallway. "Did he say much?"

He looks around, his words chosen carefully. "They took down the front door and they didn't say anything specific. Any leads down there?"

I shrug. "Not really. Just a whole lotta casings."

He nods and stalks back over to our bartender who's swaying on his barstool, the whiskey in his hand spilling everywhere as he tries to get the shit down his throat.

I spend the rest of the night going through the security footage… nothing.

I mean, sure, I can see the guys. They're standing there in our bar wearing black and balaclavas, not a single patch or recognizable feature between the three of them.

I check all of the phones and there's been phone calls a-fucking-plenty, enough to keep me busy for a few nights going through. I pass out for five hours just to reset and then I head back to The Boulevard with my laptop.

If some asshole is shooting up buildings owned by the MC then there's no fucking way I'm leaving Angel exposed like that. No fucking way.

Speck meets me there, his face just as tired and fucking grumpy as mine. "Cocksucking fucking Demons… I'm over this shit."

I scoff at him and get my shit set down in my office. I switch the security monitor in there on so I can keep an eye on shit while I work, mainly when Angel gets here and where she's waiting around between dances.

"This shit is a part of being Unseen, if you can't handle it you better hope some college is dumb enough to let you in because Keely will skin you alive if you try to move home with fucking nothing."

He scoffs at me as he flips me off, walking out and getting to work watching the bar. No matter how much shit I give him, he's a fucking good kid. He's going to be a fucking great brother, never flinches before the hard shit or shies away from an order.

An hour after the club opens the cab holding Angel arrives, pulling my attention away from the keystrokes reports. She barely pays attention to what's happening around her but that's not what catches my eye. Nope, the warning bells are fucking screaming in my head now.

Rat be fucking damned, she has my full fucking attention.

I stop her in the hallway and jerk my head at her so she follows me into my office, shutting the door behind her.

I don't have it in me to be subtle or gentle with her. "Where the hell is your phone? That one is even fucking worse than the last."

She looks down at the busted ass burner clutched in her hands, the blood red of her nails starkly luxurious against its shitty cover. Her hands still have that fucking tremble, only now her lip has this little fucking quiver that I don't wanna ever see outside of the goddamn bedroom. "I broke the old one. No big deal."

I feel like anytime the words no big deal come outta her mouth it's a giant fucking warning sign and it's a big fucking deal.

"Did you break the old one or did someone break it for you? Stop fucking lying to me, Angel."

She blinks up at me like this is all out of left field. "I broke it. What the hell has happened? Why do you suddenly care about my shit? I do my job well and I'm no trouble to you, why am I the only girl here you question like this?"

She's still standing there by the door with her trembling fucking lip and I lose my goddamn mind. "Why? Why do I care? Because you showed up here and messed with my goddamn stripclub. You're nothing but fucking trouble! Tell me what the fuck is going on with you so I can get you the fuck outta my head. I'm sick of wanting some stripper who blows hot and fucking cold all the damn time!"

Her face crumples for a split second, just long enough for me to swear I'd seen it but it's replaced with something I've never seen on her before.

Rage.

"I didn't ask for you to want me! Hell, I'd rather you didn't! I am nothing but trouble and that shit isn't going to stop any time soon! There's hundreds of girls in this town that want you and aren't dirty strippers. Bring one of them back here to drop down to their knees for you."

My jaw clenches as rage fills my fucking veins. It's as if her words are a knife in the fucking gut. "Shut your fucking mouth. You're mine, end of fucking story and you're gonna stop fucking dancing."

I don't know where those words came from but the second they leave my lips I know it's all I want. I fucking want her and I want her out of this place. I want her in my goddamn bed and impaled by my cock three times a fucking day for the rest of our lives.

Fucking cuntstruck.

"You're firing me? It's the last you'll see of me then. I need the money."

This fucking girl. This fucking stripper. "Why? You tell me why the fuck you need that kinda money and I'll fix the fucking problem."

She throws her hands in the air. "Are you God or something? I don't see how you can fix my shit."

"If I take on your problem, my brothers do too. You got something that needs to be taken care of and it's fucking done. No one takes on the Unseen. Who the fuck is taking your money?"

Her eyes squeeze shut. "I don't want trouble."

I want to throw her over my fucking shoulder and carry her home. If she wasn't so fucking touch-phobic I would. "I'll sort them out, just fucking tell me."

There's a knock at the door and then Speck's voice carries through the solid wood. "Is Angel in there? She's due on stage."

Her eyes open and she whispers, "I can't."

Chapter Nineteen

Angel

My stomach is in knots after my showdown with Tomi.

I get through my dances, I've danced under worse pressure to perform than this, but I still just feel as though I'm losing my fucking mind.

He said he wants me.

He said I belonged to him.

Hell, I've heard those words a hundred times before and it was always fucking terrifying to me. Terrifying. What is it about him that makes me want to push through the fear and the panic to… let him own me. I think maybe I want to own him too.

As soon as I think that I want to vomit.

He's a biker and a fucking hot one at that. He has a family and a job and a whole-ass fucking life that has exactly nothing to do with me.

I have nothing to offer him.

When I get off from my last dance Law meets me at the back of the stage, his eyes on the ground and very far away from me.

"Tomi and Speck got called out. Rue sent me down here to keep an eye on you until Tomi can get back here for you."

I clear my throat but my voice still comes out all thready. "Uh, thanks. I'll just— uh, grab some clothes."

He walks with me to the locker room, still not looking at me, which I kind of find sweet. It's a little like Speck, that respect they all have around me.

For bikers, they're very considerate.

I get a bra on and a pair of shorts while Law stands with his back to me, watching the door and running his mouth at a mile a minute.

"They got called into the clubhouse. Nothing to worry about, he'll be back soon."

I don't get why he's acting like I'm waiting around here for Tomi. After our little chat in the office I was planning on grabbing my shit and running out of here the second I was done for the night.

I shrug at him even though he can't see me do it. "Honestly, I'm good. I'm going to call a cab and head home. No big deal."

Law blows out a breath and scrubs a hand through his hair, glancing over his shoulder at me and then turning once he realizes I'm mostly covered. "Tomi was very clear about keeping you here until he gets back. I volunteered, it's no problem at all."

I chew my lip a little, trying to figure out how to get him to let me go but he misreads me and just tries to reassure me instead.

"My dad is back in Coldstone to see me and Lyn. Makes shit a little… uncomfortable around the clubhouse. He's from another charter and there's always tension with the crew over in Mounts Bay. Anyway, I'm happy to hang here and keep an eye on you."

I nod and pull a shirt over my head. I don't realize until the last second that it's one of Tomi's, the one he threw at me after Poe's birthday and has the Unseen patch on the back, until it's on and Diamond is scowling at me.

"He give that to you? If you took it from him you're gonna get yourself killed."

I falter but Law's lip curls at her and says, "You really can't see a fucking thing that's in front of you, can you? Tomi will do more than fire you if you keep it up, Diamond."

She huffs and walks off. I let out a breath and sit next to him, careful to leave enough space between us that we won't touch and he grins at me. "Ignore it. They're all just writhing with jealousy over you and him."

I shrug. "Is there really a me and him? I'm not sure what he's trying to do but I'm just trying to survive."

He grins and gets out his phone, tapping away at the screen

and then flipping it over to show me a text from Tomi.

A bullet between the motherfucking eyes. You touch her and that's what you get.

I blink at it.

He chuckles and tucks the phone away. "I was raised in Keely and Hawk's place. They all call me and Lyn 'the extras'. The extra kids they took on to keep us safe and, fuck it, loved. Tomi's been the closest thing to a big brother we've ever had and, I promise you, he's dead fucking serious about killing me if I touch you. I'd say what he's trying to do is keep you for himself."

Oh hell.

Oh hell in a handbasket, this isn't fucking good.

There's a whole lot of shit Tomi is going to lose his mind over when he finds out I've been lying to him and the club. If he really does… want to keep me, I'm fucked.

Royally, totally, completely fucked.

Good thing I'm great at thinking on my feet, something you learn as a gutter rat pretty quick on the streets.

I clear my throat. "I'm actually really tired. Is there any way you could drop me off home? I can talk to Tomi tomorrow or whenever he's not busy with the club stuff."

Law frowns a little and grabs out his phone, tapping away with a little frown that looks so out of place on his face. "Okay, yeah, Tomi said I can drive you home."

There's a nice block of apartments a few streets over from the hotel I've booked for the week. As long as I can convince him not to walk me to the door then I'll be okay.

I smile and grab the rest of my shit together. Once I'm ready I nod at Law and he starts running his mouth again, lots of shit that just doesn't make sense to me but I smile and nod along anyway.

He gets three steps out the back door before he abruptly stops, cursing viciously under his breath. "Get back inside, Angel."

I turn around but the door has auto-locked behind us.

"There's that sweet ass. Get lost, kid. We've been waiting too fucking long to get a piece of that bitch."

Law's shoulders are pulled in tight but he doesn't react in any other way. I glance around him and see three guys, all of them older and bigger than him. They're all regulars, never been the type to try anything but I guess they've wanted to.

"Stay behind me and get Tomi on the line. Or Rue, you got his number?"

I don't, I don't even have a working phone but Law just throws me his own phone.

I dial with shaking fingers, thankful I can remember the number and the dial tone is loud in my ear as Law presses me back into the door with his body. Even knowing the gesture is protective, my heart starts to thump in panic and I want to puke.

"You got her home safe or not, dipshit?"

"It's me. We need help."

He curses down the line right as Law lurches away from me and throws himself at the guys. He knocks one over and punches another in the face with a sharp right hook. He's stronger than them, faster, and better trained, and I watch on as he effectively and freaking brutally takes the three of them on and wins.

I've definitely been underestimating the smiling, happy twin.

By the time the roar of the motorbikes hits our ears Law has one of the guys out cold, another groaning and choking on his own blood next to him, while he straddles the last guy and beats on him.

My legs hold me up until the motorcycles park and Tomi comes stalking over, then I slide down the door until I'm parked on my ass on the gravel.

"The fuck happened, Law? Where the fuck was Mike?"

Law smashes his fist one last time and then stands, his chest heaving but other than a ripped shirt and bleeding knuckles he looks just fine. "He's inside watching the floor. There's been a big crowd tonight, no way I could grab him without risking the other girls."

Rue curses and stalks inside The Boulevard without another word.

Speck spits on one of the guys as he passes. "Lemme guess. They wanted something that wasn't for sale? I know Brandon, he's a fucking piece of shit."

Their words are all sort of… wrong as they make it to

my ears. Disjointed, like they're making their way through a tunnel to get to me.

Oh.

I'm in shock.

"Angel. Can you get up or do you need some help?"

I startle and flinch back at Speck's voice but he doesn't attempt to touch me or get too close. Just stands there and waits for my answer.

Law and Hellion start scraping the guys up while Tomi gets on the phone. "Yeah, we need a clean up. Three guys attacked one of our girls. Law walked in on it, dealt with it. Yeah… yeah, we'll get her home safe. She's not interested in your kinda help."

That's not exactly what had happened but I'm sure he has his reasoning for… tweaking the truth.

"I'm… I'm okay. I just need a minute." My voice sounds hollow and kind of wrong in my own ears but Speck doesn't comment, just nods and leans against the wall next to me.

"I'll take you back to the clubhouse when you're ready. It'll be best to keep you close for the night, just in case. There's a bunk room that you can crash in… or Tomi's room, whichever you want, Angel."

I nod and scrub my hands over my arms. I don't want to be lost in my own head after this but, hell, the clubhouse is still freaking terrifying to me. I'd take a night with the cattiness of the strippers over the looks from the bikers there.

Tomi stalks over and pulls me to my feet, his eyes fucking furious as he takes me in.

"Help the others, Speck, I'm taking her home."

The club is pulsing with music and laughter and life.

I'm instantly uncomfortable. The last time I was here I barely saw anything thanks to the warm beer and the crowd, but the entire bar area is freaking overflowing with bikers and women now.

There's hands everywhere and as I walk through behind Tomi there's more than one set of hands grabbing at my ass. I plaster myself to his back, trying desperately to keep away from the men, and when we finally make it to the hallway he glances down at me and snaps, "Why are you still fucking shaking?"

I roll my eyes. "Did you not just see the amount my ass got groped? Fuck, if I didn't have shorts on I probably would have had fingers inside me thanks to your fucking brothers."

His eyebrows draw down low. "Get your ass in there."

Great.

He's just been reminded that I'm a woman who sells her body on a fucking stage and now he's pissed about wanting me again.

What the hell is wrong with me? Why can't I ever keep my shit to myself? "Look, maybe I should just—"

"Angel. Get your fucking ass in my room before I throw you in there myself."

It's terrible and probably a sign of Stockholm Syndrome but that just sends a shiver down my spine, the deep growl just taking over my body until my nipples are peeking through my shirt and my thighs are clenching together.

Why does he just keep getting that response out of me?

Maybe it's just my natural response to always being in danger around him, maybe my instincts have gotten all messed up and now all I know how to do is fuck or flight.

I've been choosing the second option for so long, the first one never really something I craved, so now I've found the man that has changed the response I'm kind of… scared. Scared about how much I think I want with him.

I don't deserve a second of his time.

Gutter rat.

His eyes drop down to my tits and even in the shitty lighting of the hallway I can see his pupils dilate. "If you want me to throw you around, Angel, you only have to ask."

I take another step backwards, farther into his room, and even though I'm still fucking scared, he's already proved to me that he'll stop if I want him to.

Maybe this time I won't want him to.

He watches me, his eyelids dropping down low and his eyes smoldering. I don't know how to tell him that I want him but, I mean, I'm a stripper right?

I drop my bag to the ground and pull his shirt over my head, dropping it and watching his eyes flare wide.

He's seen it all before, they all have, but he stares at me like this is uncharted territory he's fucking dying to explore. I get my denim shorts down my legs before he moves, stalking into the room and slamming the door shut behind him.

I hope it has an auto-lock or something, because Tomi doesn't stop, he just charges up to me and pulls me into his arms, his hands going straight to my ass, grabbing it so hard I'm definitely going to have bruises.

When he kisses me it feels like a punishment to us both, bruising and hard and all-consuming until I'm fucking shaking with need.

One of his hands slips around my body to dip into my panties, finding my pussy wet and when a stuttering gasp rips out of my throat he breaks away from the kiss.

"No more fucking flinching," he snarls, and I pull his head down so I can kiss him. His lips are like a fucking drug, numbing me out until I'm not just okay with his hands on my skin, I fucking crave it.

Even when he pushes two fingers inside me, I can't think about the fear still creeping into my mind, all I know is the feel of his tongue stroking mine and the hand on my ass kneading my curves like he wants to take a fucking bite out of me.

His fingers work me over, his thumb pressing down on my clit in maddening circles until I'm gasping and clenching around him, my legs like jelly and only my arms around his neck keeping me standing.

He moves his hand away and my pussy clenches at the loss of him. "Get on the bed, I want to taste you."

I turn around in his arms, gasping when he slaps the bare part of my ass peeking out of the thong. His bed is unmade, piles of shit everywhere in the room like he really is some outlaw too fucking cool to clean up after himself.

When I lay back on the black sheets I can smell him there, no perfume thank God. He strips down until he's naked, his cock already hard and straining against his belly. I have to calm my breathing down a little but… I also really want him to fuck my throat.

I never feel more powerful than when he's grunting and pumping his hips as he fucks my face.

I try to sit up but he presses me back down onto the bed

with a palm to my chest as he crawls over me.

I don't understand how that makes my pussy get even wetter but nothing about tonight makes any sense.

"Stay fucking still. When I want you taking care of me, I'll tell you."

I throw an arm over my eyes, just like last time, and wait for him to eat me out. I haven't let myself think about last time, not the parts where it was so fucking good before my trauma ruined it, but now thinking back… Jesus, the man can really use that tongue of his.

"Angel, get your fucking arm away from your face. Eyes on me."

I take a deep breath and meet his eyes, my heart stuttering in my chest.

He doesn't even bother taking my panties off, just moves them to the side and holds my eye contact as he falls onto my pussy, licking and sucking, grabbing my hips to drag me closer and closer to his lips and tongue. It feels a little like worship, like he's been craving the taste of me just as bad as I've wanted his touch.

Why didn't I do this before?

Why did I flinch away from him?

I come twice more before he finally moves away, my pussy so fucking wet that his face is dripping and he climbs back up my body to kiss me and share the taste between us. I groan into the kiss, wrapping my arms around his neck as he grinds his cock into my pussy, making my groans turn into moans, low and throaty.

When he moves away to grab a condom, it finally sinks in that we're going to fuck. Right as I'm about to think about maybe panicking he says, "Hands and knees, Angel. Show me that ass."

Oh.

Right.

My brain switches back off. I hope he's not planning on sticking it in my ass just yet, I feel like I need a whiskey or twelve before then, but again, my body moves at his command.

My arms and legs are trembling by the time he settles onto the bed behind me, sliding a large palm down my spine and then smacking my ass again.

He clearly enjoys the sight of my ass in the thong because he strokes a finger down the seam of my ass, hooking it out of the way and tugging on the lace as he lines his dick up with my pussy.

I feel just a little bit of fear.

Then he's inside me, groaning and slamming his hips into my ass

It just feels… really fucking good. Really fucking good, like he's lighting me up from the inside out and my pussy is clenching around his cock like it never wants to let him go. My arms collapse until my face is buried in his pillows and all I can smell is his scent and all I can feel is the way he's using me, and the sounds of him grunting and cursing and moaning about how tight my pussy is… it kind of feels like heaven.

I come again, gasping and sobbing, and before I come down, he pulls out, flipping me over and sliding back in as he stares right into my eyes, a hand slipping between us to press on my overstimulated clit, grunting and biting at my lips like he wants more, more, fucking everything I have to give him.

I think I fucking squirt, I come so hard.

He roars when he comes too, louder than I've ever heard him and right in my face as his hips just keep pumping into me. My heart is hammering in my chest, whimpers falling from my lips as my body shakes with aftershocks.

There's silence for a second, peaceful and heavy with only the sounds of us both panting to be heard.

"You're fucking mine, Angel."

I should just let it go but the orgasms and intimacy have broken my brain. "I'm not. I'm really not yours."

He rolls away and the way he makes sure none of his body is touching mine is like a bucket of cold water over my head.

I swallow and lay there, praying I'm wrong.

Of course I'm not.

"We're done here. You need to get dressed and get out of my room."

I take a deep breath. There's no point arguing with him, he never backs down and how can I explain to him that I have nowhere to go? I sit up and straighten up, my bra and panties are still on, he didn't even bother to take them off of me.

Moments ago that felt sexy, like he couldn't wait to have me.

Now I know he just wanted to get me out quicker.

"Not going to say a fucking word to me?"

I scoff at him and shove my legs into the denim shorts. God, they're so skimpy. Walking out of this place and having to walk past his biker brothers… every single one of them is going to know.

I'm fucking disgraceful.

"There's nothing to say. We're done here." I'm proud that my voice doesn't break. I refuse to look at him until my eyes clear a little. I pull his shirt back over my head, not wanting to wait around long enough to grab another one out of my bag.

Shit.

Okay, my bag is on the floor. It's fine, zipped up still, nothing has been touched. I grab it and sling it over my shoulder.

He hasn't moved, still splayed out and naked, his skin flushed and sweaty. He looks like a freaking cover model, especially with that smirk across his lips. Of course he's smirking. He's fucked the frigid bitch stripper, the one they've all tried to get, and now he'll have some fucking trophy.

How could I be this freaking stupid?

"Do you need me to call you a cab? I'd drop you home but you're too stuck up to tell me where the fuck you live."

I shake my head. If I can survive Paul, I can survive tonight out on the street without my car. "Don't concern yourself. You might even find time to go out to party and pick up some other girl to blow a load in."

His eyes narrow.

His lip curls.

I walk out and shut the door quietly before he can say anything else. I don't want to hear any of it.

The walk out of the bar is as bad as I thought it would be but there's something about Tomi's shirt on my back that keeps anyone from actually grabbing me. Rue frowns at me from across the room but I duck my head and keep going, the crowd slowing him down enough that I can make it out without having to fucking talk to any of them.

I don't see Speck.

Thank fuck.

There's so many people at the party that the parking lot is packed as well, none of them taking notice of some stripper with tears running down her face. Goddammit, why am I crying again?

I get across the street to the garage there, my Chevy still up on the jack from where Poe's been working on it, and I duck down the side of the building to stay hidden while I try for a cab.

It's too late to get one.

Or too early, I guess.

Fuck.

There's no way I'm walking back into that fucking building, no way I'm going to risk one of those men touching me while I hunt around for Speck. The new phone doesn't have his number in it anymore, or Poe's, and they're the only two people I can think of that would help me.

So I slump down on the front step of the garage, my bag between my legs with the strap wrapped around them too so no one can grab it without waking me and I let my eyes drift shut.

I don't even really notice myself slipping into sleep.

"Are you high?"

I startle and scramble to my feet, one hand clutching at my pepper spray in a panic and the other tightening around my bag like it's a shield.

"Ah, oh God, no. No, I'm not high. I was just… fuck, I was just sleeping. I'm sorry."

He looks at me like I'm highly suspicious, and my mouth just keeps running. "I know Poe and she has my car here. That's why I stopped here. Oh God, I didn't mean anything by it."

He frowns at me, his eyes shifting back up to my car, clearly visible through the dusty window. "I mean, it's a beauty. A good old classic but I'm not sure it's worth guarding overnight. This place is secure enough to keep anyone out and I'm usually a 'shoot first' kind of guy."

Fuck.

I need to think fast. "I got kicked out of my apartment. There's a few days in-between me moving out and being able to move into my new place. I just had a fight with my… well, with a guy and he kicked me out of his place. I was, uhh, I was staying with him for the week."

The frown deepens a little. "Is there no one else you can go to? There's a hotel down the street, you know."

I stayed there once and the bellboy tried to break into my room. Never again. "I didn't want to wake any of my friends up and worry them. It's only one night, I didn't think it would be a big deal to sleep here. I'm so sorry, I should have realized it was trespassing. I'll go."

His arm comes out and I flinch back but he doesn't try to touch me, he's just turning the lights on so he can get a better look at me.

His face hardens at the flinch. "This guy of yours hitting you?"

I shake my head. "Not... not this one. Look, please don't call the police. I swear I didn't try to get in. I just sat on the step and I'll never come here after hours again. I swear it."

He shakes his head. "You look like a child. Posey said she met you out at The Boulevard. Are you old enough to be dancing there?"

My spine snaps straight. "Yes, sir. I am. I'm just... tonight isn't a great night for me."

He nods again slowly and grabs out his phone. My stomach drops and tears fill my eyes again. Dammit, I'll need my fake IDs to stand up against a full police check. Fuck, I should have just walked into town or something.

"Yeah, well, I didn't want to wake you either but I have a little girl here at my garage who needs a bed for the night and a friend. Poe knows her, she's been working on her car... yeah, that would be her. Come pick her up and get her something to eat, she looks exhausted... yeah, sure."

He hangs up and I try to pick my jaw up off of the ground. "That was my grandson, Briar. He and Poe live further out in the suburbs, only a few streets over from here. He's a cop, he's not going to hurt you but my guess is he'll wake Poe and they'll both come to get you."

I blink away the tears. "I really... I can't thank you enough, sir."

He scoffs but it's a gentle sound. "My name is Alby but you can call me Pops. You seem like a good girl. You need to stay away from that guy who kicked you out, no decent man ever does that to a woman."

I nod. "I'm trying to, sir- I mean, uhh, Pops. I just keep making dumb choices."

Chapter Twenty

Tomi

You know what's worse than fucking flinching?

I'm not. I'm really not yours.

Fuck, I was this fucking close to opening the fuck up and telling her about everything. Telling her about the curse, about the way she fucking owns me, the ways that hearing her voice down that phone all thready and terrified had me ready to fucking spill blood in her name for the rest of my goddamned life.

I'm fucked.

And she laid there, panting and sweaty and fucking stunning, and as good as told me she didn't fucking want me beyond a good fuck.

Okay, a fucking great fuck.

The second she leaves, I throw my clothes back on and make it my fucking mission to get blackout drunk. I should have a shower to get the honey-scent of her off of me but, like I said, she's got me fucked in the head so when I wake up in my bed the following afternoon I can still smell her on my skin and my sheets.

I lay there and fucking stew in it.

I hate her.

I want her.

I want to hate her so much more than I do but instead I'm laying here fucking worried about her.

Finally I get my bitch-ass up and take a shower, shave while I try not to look at my bloodshot eyes too much, and get dressed.

When I leave my room, I find King in the chapel with the door wide open. I hesitate for about a half second but the whole fucking deal of being a man is owning your bullshit.

"You got a minute, Prez?"

He glances up at me and nods with a frown. I step into the room but I don't close the door. I'll keep my voice down but I don't want anyone getting suspicious about our conversation.

It's not about the fucking rat.

"It's about the shooting at the bar. I've been thinking about it and I need to triple the security at The Boulevard."

King nods and leans back in his chair. "You think they'll hit there next?"

I shrug and pause for about a half second before I answer him honestly. Owning my fucking bullshit. "I don't wanna talk about it with Keely or Hawk yet but... I was 'struck. Angel is working down there and while there's even a fucking chance that she could get caught up in this... I'd just rather there's extra eyes. It makes sense that if they've hit the bar and the shipments it's only a matter of time before they go after the garage and the titty bar. Rue will keep shit on lockdown at the garage and I'll get over to The Boulevard when I can but right now, I've got to be where the club needs me and that isn't always with her."

He stares at me for a half second and then says, "A stripper? You've been 'struck by a stripper?"

I huff out a breath. "Yup. The curse strikes again, there's no fucking chance of this ending well but I'll be goddamned if I can't stop looking out for her."

King nods and looks out of the door. The bar is quiet, no guys loitering around at the moment. Everyone is on edge and has a job to fucking do. Beer will just have to wait.

"She's the new girl right? That one who broke Mav's nose for trying to touch her? What's her story?"

I do not want to talk about her, especially not with my lost uncle, the one I haven't had all that much to do with thanks to prison but he's also my Prez and if shit is going to go right around here then we need to have some form of a good relationship.

"Yeah. She's a fucking vault. Won't talk to anyone about anything, except maybe Poe. She's twitchy and flighty. Speck thinks she's got an old man somewhere beating on her but nothing we've tried to get her to talk has panned out and we've been too busy with club bullshit to tail her properly."

He nods and leans back in his chair. "Don't write her off. Keely was a good girl but that also made her dangerous for a long time. Your pops spent a lot of time dancing around with her before we knew she was it for him. She coulda easily been too straight for this life but she's fucking perfect. Strippers don't always mean drug addicts and whores."

Something fucking snaps in my head over him calling her a whore, even if he wasn't directly saying it, and he smirks at whatever it is my face is doing. "Yeah, you're fucked. Either way, the curse has you locked the fuck down."

I get up, ready to get back to my work and find these assholes and he calls out to me.

"Tomi, if she is bad news... you'll get over it. I know you're pissed off about it now but Callaghans always move on. I'm better off now than when I was trying to sort shit out with Liza. It's not the fucking end of everything, even if it feels like it."

That's way too much emotion for me but I can't say that to my Prez. I just nod my head and walk my ass outta there, keeping my ass moving until I get to my hog. I need to take the long way to The Boulevard, let the fresh air clear my head until I can deal with Angel without losing my shit.

My face must be fucking terrifying because everyone scatters the second I step into the strip club. It's probably for the best, the ride over barely took the edge off of my mood.

I lock myself into my office and get back onto my laptop, trying to keep my attention on the stats and not the hot piece of ass destroying my life, slowly but surely.

Huh.

Lawson switched out his SIM card.

That's not that big of a deal but he switched it out, called his dad and then switched it back to the club-issued SIM.

What the fuck is he up to?

My attention is so focused on that twenty-eight second phone call between Harbin and Lawson that I almost miss Angel arriving to work.

In a police cruiser.

I squint at the security cam but no matter how I change my gaze it doesn't change the fact that Angel is climbing out of Thorn's patrol car and leaning back into the window to speak to him, a smile on her face.

Is she... is this her version of a walk of shame? Did she fuck me and then run off to his bed? My vision turns blood red.

Not on my fucking watch.

I call him.

"What a coincidence, I'm just dropping one of your girls off."

"I know, I'm watching you right now and you better be real fucking careful on how you answer this next question. Did you fuck Angel last night?"

He groans. "Are you kidding me? Are you really getting all fucking territorial about a piece of club ass?"

The door clicks open and shut, her footfalls easy to distinguish against all of the other noises in the club. I'm primed for her, always listening out for her presence, and isn't that just the fucking worst thing for this cunt down the line.

"Answer the fucking question."

He sighs. "No, I didn't. I would though, if she wanted me, have you seen the ass on her? What am I saying, of course you have. Alby found her asleep on his front doorstep last night. She didn't have anywhere else to go, no car thanks to Poe working on hers, and the cabs don't go out to that side of town after two in the morning. She was fucking terrified and I took her in for the night. She's staying with me until her house is ready next week."

What the actual fuck?!

It's hard, but I manage to unclench my jaw enough to tell him, "Don't fucking bother. I'll sort her out."

Thorn laughs. "It's no fucking problem, she's—"

"She's gonna get you six foot under if your mouth keeps fucking running. I said she's good. Don't come back here unless you're feeling ready to meet your fucking maker, asshole."

I hang up.

Then I throw my phone at the wall so hard the screen shatters.

I can't go out and confront Angel the way I want to.

I want to walk out and throw her over my fucking shoulder, drag her into my office and force her to tell me everything.

Who is taking her money?

Why is she fucking flinching?

Why the hell is sleeping on a fucking doorstep a reasonable option to her?

I'm fucking enraged so I make probably the first good decision when it comes to Angel and I leave her the hell alone for the night while she dances.

At first, I put the warning in my gut down to feeling shitty over Angel's shit but as the night stretches on I know something's up.

The curse is handy like that.

Sure, I'm probably cuntstruck but I also can tell when shit is going down.

I know before my phone starts ringing that something is happening.

Something is very fucking wrong, something in this town is about to go off and fuck knows what the hell it actually is but I feel like I'm going to fucking puke.

The door to my office bursts open and Rue's face is fucked up. "You feel it too, right? I'm not going fucking nuts, am I?"

I mean, we could be wrong. There's so much shit going on in the fucking club at the moment it could be paranoia but the fine tremble in his fingers on the door handle tells me it's not.

Something is happening.

Something fucking bad is happening.

I get the camera feed of Angel dancing on my screen but she's fine, just gotten out on stage and there's security fucking everywhere around her.

She's safe.

"Call Poe. Call Poe and I'll call Keely." I say and he nods, the phone already halfway to his ear.

"What's up?" she answers on the first ring.

"You okay? Where are you?"

She hums under her breath. "I've just gone on my break at

work. Are you okay?"

"Yeah, just stay safe. Something is happening."

She hums again. "The curse singing to you? I'll keep an eye out, baby."

I hang up and immediately call Hawk's number.

Voicemail.

Fuck everything.

I turn to find Rue talking to Poe, mumbling a few threats about keeping her ass at home and I get back to calling down the list.

Trink is in a bitch of a mood but fine.

Speck doesn't pick up.

Hellion doesn't either.

I grab my keys and start out of The Boulevard, yelling over my shoulder at Axe to keep the place locked down. He frowns at me but nods, solid in the orders. I don't want to leave Angel but Axe isn't on my fucking watch list and there's something happening.

I try Hawk again and this time he answers. "Where the hell are you?"

I get my ass on my bike, leaving the helmet tucked in the bag, and jerk my head at Rue. "Something's going on, Speck and Hell aren't picking up. Mom's fine, and Trink and Poe. Have you got eyes on King?"

He grunts, "Yeah, and Lyn but Law was helping Speck with the bar today. He wanted extra green for the hog he's trying to buy. King can feel it too, get your asses over to the bar. We're on our way too."

Jesus fucking Christ. I'm on the road without thought, the motorbike flying underneath me and Rue coming in hot behind me. It's a fifteen minute trip between the clubhouse and the bar, we make it in eight.

"What's the plan here?" Rue says, and I shrug.

"Shoot first, ask questions later."

My phone buzzes in my pocket and I check it as I swing off of the hog.

Angel just got off the stage. I'll keep her in your office until her next dance. I'll keep her safe, brother.

Fuck.

I didn't realize Axe had noticed my fucking obsession but I

guess I'm not as slick as I thought. I have to just fucking pray he isn't one of the rats and I haven't just left her to fucking die.

My heart is fucking screaming in my chest.

I'll need to come to terms with the fact that she was my first fucking thought when the feeling hit my gut, that I only called Keely first because of habit.

I wanted to call Angel.

Fuck.

The bar is closed for the fix up so the parking lot is empty, except for Hell's hog and Speck's old truck. He must have given Law a ride over here.

Something tightens in my chest but I try to talk myself down. They're here. They're probably just busy, there's a lot going on here and if they're cleaning the place out after the shooting then of course they're not going to pick up on the first call.

I glance at Rue but he's still just as fucking worried, shifting straight into the future Prez the club needs. "We go in slow. Just in case. The worst that happens is we're both fucking laughing about this tonight over beers."

True.

I give him a nod and draw my gun.

The club has owned the bar longer than I've been alive, I was a fucking toddler the first time I came here. I know every inch of the entire property, I know which of the wooden floorboards will squeak, I know how to open the back door without a sound.

I go first because it's protocol.

We walk through the back rooms and there's nothing. It's not until I creep around the corner that I thank God for this fucking curse. Whatever it is, however I got it, I'll take the fucking pain of being cuntstruck every day of the damn week because I'm here at exactly the right fucking time.

Speck has a fucking gun to his head.

There's group of fucking Demons standing there laughing as they're about to fucking execute my cousin, kneeling there with Hellion and Law, beat to hell like they've been fucking tortured.

I take the guy holding the gun out with a headshot.

His friend sees us and pulls a gun but Rue gets him first.

Law dives onto the ground as bullets start flying everywhere and then I see him tug Speck down with him. Hell kneels there like he's fucking hoping a bullet takes him and Rue starts cursing the asshole out.

"Get your fucking head outta the way, you dumbass!"

Finally he slumps down onto the ground and grabs a stray gun, killing the one of the guys from where he's ducked behind a turned over table.

I might lose my mind a little but I walk out into the bar as if I'm fucking bulletproof, ignoring Rue's cussing as he follows me out. We're assholes but we'll die together if we have to, just to have each other's backs.

Three more down and Rue takes the last guy down with two shots to the back when he tries to run.

I feel relief for about a half a second.

"Tomi! Tomi, Speck's shot."

My brain just fucking short circuits. Just shuts down but I'm moving on instinct. I've learned a lot from my mom over the years listening to her stories and little things she'll say to me about packing wounds.

When I look at my cousin's chest I'm fairly fucking sure there's no saving him.

I try anyway.

I know Rue will be calling 911 for him and there'll be a helluva lot of paperwork to do about this shootout but I couldn't fucking care less. I'll do time if I have to, I just need Speck to fucking live.

The blood just pours outta him, no matter how hard I pack it, and by the time the EMTs arrive I'm covered in blood. Beyond covered, it's dripping from every inch of my skin and Speck's face is the color of a corpse.

I'm fucking sure he's dead.

I don't even notice my surroundings until they have him loaded up and out of the building, working so goddamn fast but he's dead. There's no fucking way he's coming back from that. No way.

I stand up and find Rue staring at me with blank eyes. The type you get when you see your brother, your blood, bleeding out on the dirty fucking floor of a bar.

Law is shaking like a fucking leaf while he's talking to

Thorn, standing there in full uniform and taking notes. His face is fucking grim, the frown etched so deep into his skin I don't think he'll ever look happy again.

Hell is behind the bar chugging a bottle of whiskey like it has all of the answers, one of the other officers trying to stop him or talk him down but that's not going to work out for him at all.

The Demons are still all lying around wherever they fell and all at once I'm taken over with a calm sort of rage. I'm not ready to ride off into the sunset and find me some Demons to gun down. Nope, I'm feeling a fucking evangelical need to find and destroy whoever helped these fucking rat cunts into my town and my fucking bar to kill my fucking blood.

I turn on my heel to leave and Thorn calls out. "I need your statement. There are men dead here, Tomi, you gotta come in."

I scoff at him. "No, I for fucking sure do not need to come in. I need to go call my mom and tell her Speck's coming in. I need to clean up and head to the hospital myself. I need to go sit and wait to hear if they can save him. That's what I need to fucking do."

Rue slaps me on the back and nods. "I did the shooting. Tomi did all the saving, you can get his statement later."

I meet his eye and he gives me a nod. I'm the one who can find this cunt so he'll man the fuck up and take the fall. That's what this club fucking does, that's what being a brother means.

I leave without another word, riding like a bat outta hell back to the clubhouse and stalking straight into the shower without stopping. King calls out to me but I ignore him, something I would normally get my ass reamed for but today is not that day.

When I'm clean enough to handle the computer I stalk back out in a pair of jeans to find Hawk and King waiting in my room.

"What exactly is the plan here? We can't just ride off to Texas, as much as I fucking want to right now. Tell me where your head is right now, Tomi." King says, his hands on his hips as he takes some deep fucking breaths.

I get it.

I do.

He did hard time for the good of this club and came home to the problem being even fucking worse than when he left. But the thing is, shit has changed around here.

"I'm going to fucking find them. I'm going to find out whoever let those cunts into my fucking town and into that bar because they didn't roll up there without information."

Hawk lights up a cigarette and perches his ass on my bed. "And how exactly are you going to do that? Is that fucking computer of yours a crystal ball?"

He's pissed off, I always know just how irritated he is by how much he rags on me for knowing how to use this shit. It's fine.

"No, it's not but the security cams I've installed fucking everywhere around our properties might just help out with the problem."

King frowns and uses his foot to clear my couch. The entire room looks like a frat house but I don't give a fuck. "What are cameras going to pick up? I mean, we know they got in there because the door was fucking open thanks to the cleaning."

"There's three different leads right now and I'm following all of them until I find out who the fuck did it."

Hawk tips his head back and blows a stream of smoke out at the ceiling. "Who shot up the bar last night, that's a lead. Did they do it trying to hit someone or just trying to fucking get some of us alone."

King nods. "Was it a random choice or did they want Hellion and Speck there?"

I start going through the files. "Or Law. Is this about Coldstone or is it about Mounts Bay and Harbin?"

King scratches his chin. "Third option?"

I don't want to vocalize it, not at all, but I do. "Hell was supposed to be there by himself. Speck and Law went because Law wanted to earn some green."

I don't have to say another word.

Because we're all too busy trying not to think about the fucking worst option.

Is Harbin's son a rat?

Chapter Twenty One

Angel

I wake up to Poe's face about an inch away from mine.

"What in God's name do you think you're doing sleeping on the goddamn street instead of calling me? We're supposed to be friends, Angel. Friends call when they need a fucking couch for the night."

I blink at her but she just hovers over me like I've kicked her goddamn puppy. "I'm sorry. I… I actually couldn't call you. I lost my phone and I haven't exactly memorized your number. Look, I just— I had a bad night."

She frowns a little harder and then sits down on the couch next to my legs so I'm pinned in. "What happened? You went home with Tomi right? What the hell is going on with him?"

I groan and fling an arm over my eyes. I didn't even get the chance for a shower last night when we got back here, Poe just led me upstairs and into her room, throwing a pile of blankets on the couch when I told her I couldn't share the bed with her. She was nice enough not to question me about it.

"Did he… hurt you? It's— I mean, I love that asshole like a brother but if he hurt you I'll castrate him. I know how, my sister taught me. She says all girls should learn how to."

My arm slowly slides away from my face and I give her a look. I'm both shocked and impressed.

I can't imagine this grinning, sunbeam of a girl hurting anyone but… yeah, that's a fucking deadly serious look on her face.

Huh.

So Rue needs to watch out for his dick then.

Noted.

"He didn't hurt me. Not... not like that. I don't talk about this shit, Poe, not with anyone."

She shrugs. "I'm pretty damn good at keeping secrets. I swear, I'm a vault."

She's so damn sincere. I take a deep breath. There's truths I can give her without giving her everything. Maybe just enough that she understands me. "I don't like… touch easy. I don't like the feel of people touching me at all. It takes me a long time to get over that."

She nods. "I noticed. Speck told me not to ever touch you, he knows I'm a hugger."

I give her a wry grin. "Yeah, I noticed. So I've gotten better about it since I moved here. I can hug you sometimes. I've hugged Speck too."

She nods and stands up, stalking over to the window and opening the curtains to peer down at the Callaghan house. It's like she's giving me a little space to get my shit together and I appreciate the hell outta her for doing it.

"I had sex with Tomi last night."

She makes a little squeaking noise which ends in a gag. "Ew! Gross! He's like my brother, that's disgusting. Wait, you let him touch you? Thomas freaking Callaghan, the boy who got so fucking wasted at his sixteenth birthday he puked in the fucking pool… that I was swimming in? That Tomi? Christ, I just fucking can't. I can't. I thought you guys hated each other? I thought he scared you or something?"

Goddamn my freaking body, I blush like an idiot. "Yeah. That one."

She gags again but at least I'm not feeling awkward about it anymore, just embarrassed. "Right. Okay, so you fucked Tomi. Why does that make it a bad night? Oh fuck, please don't describe anything to me!"

I snort at her dramatics and then groan. "It wasn't the sex. It was after that. He kicked me out… said girls aren't allowed to sleep in his bed. There was a party going on and I didn't really want to have to face Speck or Rue during my walk of shame so I just… walked over to the garage. I'm staying at a hotel for a few days while I wait for my house to be ready. I wasn't expecting anyone to be there and then Pops walked out and scared the fucking shit outta me."

Poe's eyes narrow and she sits down on her bed with a huff. Hell, she looks pretty fierce like that, without the big grins and bubbly personality she's fucking… intense.

"I will have Tomi's fucking balls for this. I will cut them the fuck off."

I scoff at her. "Why, because he fucked a stripper? Poe, he's well known for that shit. He didn't force me into anything, I should have known that he was just hoping to get laid. I was the fucking whore that spread her legs for a biker and then cried when he kicked me out. I'm the dumbass!"

She stands up and props her fists on her hips, staring down at me like I'm a disobedient asshole. "If I catch you talking shit about yourself like that again, we're fighting and I'm warning you now, I can kill a man with my bare fucking hands. I'll kick your ass six ways to Sunday."

I groan and sit up. "I'm not trying to sound all fucking sorry for myself but like… what exactly was I expecting? I am a stripper, Poe. That's exactly what I am."

She throws her hands up into the air. "So fucking what? Hell, I'd totally be one if I could! I've seen how much money you make, fuck, I'd suck a dick for that kind of green!"

The door opens and I just about die when Thorn's frowning face pops into the room. "Take that shit back right now Poe before I lock your ass up for the night."

She scoffs and throws herself backwards on the bed. "It'll be the only way I get some damn action in this dumbass town!"

I feel so freaking awkward sitting here with the two of them arguing like this, my skin begins to itch.

I try not to think about him being a cop.

I sit up on the couch and scoot my ass to the edge. "I'll just grab a cab back to the hotel now I can. I'm really sorry again for disturbing your night."

Thorn shrugs and steps into the bedroom properly. Poe glares at him from where she's lying but he ignores her completely. "It was no trouble. I can drive you on my way to my shift this afternoon. Unless you have work? It's no trouble at all."

Poe sits up sharply. "She'll need a lift to The Boulevard

tonight and I'll get Speck to give her a ride back here when she's done. She's crashing on my couch for the rest of the week."

I shoot her a look but she only gives me sass back.

Thorn doesn't even question it, just shrugs and says, "You better be at school every day, Poe. If you start slacking off I'll put you under house arrest."

I open my mouth to argue, I've paid for the hotel already so I don't need to crash anyway, and Thorn shoots me a look. "Girls like you shouldn't be sleeping at a hotel by yourself like that. We can swing by and grab anything you left there before your shift. I'll talk to the reception to get your money back."

I have no choice but to nod. I don't really want to talk to him while he's standing there in uniform.

I can't.

Poe cackles like a freaking witch and dances around as she teases him. "Stop looking at him like you think he's about to fucking arrest you. Thorn's not like a regular cop, he's a cool cop."

He huffs at her and clicks the door shut after himself.

I give her a look but she's too busy being an idiot to take notice of me. "If you wanna get back at Tomi for being a shithead, please don't fuck Thorn. I just— I can't deal with that at all. Nope. Gross."

I collapse back on the couch and pull the blanket back over my head, cussing her out when she only laughs harder at me.

It almost freaking kills me, but I let Thorn drive me to The Boulevard in his police cruiser. My hands shake the whole time but he's nice enough not to comment about it.

When the car stops in the parking lot, he smiles at me and it strikes me how different he looks to Poe. Their coloring is completely different and his smile is nice enough but it's not the same bright one she has.

"I'll grab you around four, is that okay? If not, I'm sure Speck can drop you off."

I nod and get out, clutching my bag to my chest a little. As an afterthought, I remember my goddamn manners and lean down to say, "Thanks again for the ride and for grabbing me last night. I really can't thank you enough."

His phone starts ringing and I get my ass moving, my first dance starts in less than a half hour.

I get let into the back door by a biker, one I don't know, and he checks my ID carefully before he lets me pass.

"What time is your shift?"

I startle, fumbling over my words. "My first dance is at midnight and then I'm on again at two. Is... is everything okay?"

He hands it back and jerks his head at me to pass. "Extra security on from here on out. You're fine, just so long as you're here for your shifts and that's it."

My stomach drops a little. Why would they need extra security? What could possibly have happened? Fuck, is it Tomi?

Why is he the first person I think of? Jesus, him or Speck... even if it were Rue, I'm going to be heartbroken if any of them are hurt.

It would destroy Poe if anything happened to him.

I get through my first dance easy enough but when I walk off stage there's something in the air, all the bikers in the room are on edge and the ones who are working are watching the room like they're expecting a bomb to go off.

Something fucking terrible has happened.

My stomach drops to my knees.

I take two steps towards the locker room when the big guy from the door calls me over to Tomi's office. I feel relief for a split second but when I get over to him and look in, Tomi is nowhere to be seen.

"I need you to wait in here between your sets. I'll be on the door, no one will disturb you."

I chew on my lip a little, my stomach a fucking mess. "Can I grab my bag? I need my phone and to stash my money."

He nods and then walks me over to my locker, never touching me but also never letting me out of his arm's reach.

What the hell is going on?

I don't have Tomi's number, I don't even know what I'd say to him, but I do have Speck's. Poe had given it to me to grab a lift with him tonight if I needed to.

It takes me three tries to put something together but I text him.

Hey, things are really weird here tonight. Can you just text me to say you're okay? And if everyone else is okay?

Nothing.

The entire hour between my sets there's no reply from him. I tell myself it's fine, he's a busy guy and I'm like, just barely his friend.

The biker at the door lets me out of the office for my next dance, giving me two minutes to pee and freshen up before walking me back out to the stage.

Whatever is going on, they all know about it now.

The tenseness is now fucking malevolence in the air, everyone riding their own waves of rage and there's no bikers in the crowd anymore. The only Unseen in the building are the ones who're working. I make a lot of money with this dance, a lot of the guys at the stage are younger and drunk as hell and without the bikers sitting amongst them they're a little louder and rowdier. My knees start to shake just a little and I have to forcibly calm myself down before my song starts.

It's the longest dance of my life.

When I get back out to the locker room with my scowling guard Mel is crying as she gets dressed, deep sobs that shake her entire body.

Diamond stomps over to me and snarls at me, "Tomi is picking you up tonight. You need to go sit in the office and wait there for him, no walking around, no showering, just go there right the hell now. Don't leave or he'll be finding you and dragging you back to the clubhouse by your fucking throat. His words not mine, I hope you run and he guts you."

She walks off and I try not to panic. I mean, I haven't done anything wrong. I haven't betrayed the club or stolen anything... I just come here and dance. That's it.

Why would he be so damn worried about where I am?

I manage to grab my bag before the biker locks me back up into Tomi's office. I pull on a pair of yoga pants and an oversized sweater. I feel like I need the armor, like whatever is going on tonight is going to be so bad I'll need to freaking hide from it.

It's almost seven in the morning before Tomi comes for me.

He looks so fucking bad I want to cry but he doesn't look at me. "Grab your shit."

I stand up, already packed and ready to go but I feel so fucking dirty with the glitter and hairspray still coating me. "Can I grab a shower now you're here? I'm guessing everyone's gone anyway."

"We don't have time for that."

I follow him out of the office and find that no one has gone home yet. Great. Diamond is glaring at me like I killed her fucking puppy and the other girls are all still sobbing.

I don't know what the fuck is going on.

"I can't get on your bike like this."

He doesn't snap at me, he barely reacts, he just strips out of his jacket. Diamond gasps but I ignore her. Fuck, I try to forget she exists.

He holds it out to me and says, "Put it on."

I do and then I follow him out, trying not to piss him off. I kind of get the feeling he's holding his shit together by a thread and I don't want to cop whatever it is he has to say.

Not today.

I check my phone but there's still no reply to my message and bile creeps up the back of my throat. Surely not.

Please, don't let it be that. "Where's Speck?"

He hands me a helmet and says in the same empty voice, "Hospital. He was shot tonight, point blank in the chest."

My stomach drops. "Oh my God. Oh my God, who shot him? Jesus Christ."

He frowns and turns away from me. "Put that on and hurry up."

I fumble a little with the straps but I get it on, climbing onto the motorcycle the same way he'd shown me last time I'd been on it.

The drive over to the hospital is short enough and I do my best to just hold onto him without crushing my body up against his but if my grip loosens even a little bit, he grabs my hands and moves them around himself more so I give up and just hold onto him like he's a freaking life raft.

I'm crying by the time he cuts the engine.

I duck my head so he can't see the tears, and then I follow him into the hospital. The nurses all seem to know him, half of them calling him by his name as he navigates us through the building with ease.

When we stop in the ICU Tomi pauses at the door for a second like he's psyching himself up to walk in there.

I feel like an intruder.

This is a private moment and here I am witnessing it, seeing him during something so traumatic. He must be feeling so fucking bad right now, so exposed, and I'm just tagging along because I need a couch to sleep on.

Fuck.

"Why am I here?" I whisper and Tomi shrugs.

"I need to know where the fuck you are. I need eyes on you all night so I know you aren't targeted next. Rue's heading home in a minute to sleep, you can take the pull-out and I'll sleep in the chair if I need to."

Oh.

Right. I guess if they're going after club assets and I am now making the most cash, makes sense that they'd want to protect me. Jesus, that must be why Diamond is so pissed off, she's out there on her own and I get an armed brother to myself.

He steps into the room and I follow him in on autopilot.

Rue gives me a grimace of a smile as he rolls up out of the chair, his back cracking and shifting as he moves. He's clearly been here for a while, sitting in that chair and just... watching his cousin breathe.

Fuck, he's a mess of tubes and wires, everything beeping and looking vital to his survival, tears start up the second I get a look at him.

"Are you crying right now?" Tomi whispers, and I swallow.

"I can't help it. He's... my friend. Why did this happen?"

Rue claps him on the back and walks out, his phone to his ear as he checks in with King. I subconsciously lean into Tomi, seeking comfort or just to know that he's okay. He doesn't complain, or move away. He just stands there and lets me lean into his back.

He smells like a garage and gunpowder.

"You're shaking," he murmurs and I blow out a breath, trying to calm my nerves.

"This shit scares me. Were you with him when he got shot?"

He steps away from me and over to look at Speck's chart. I glance at it as I pass and I see all of his details. Jesus, he's only eighteen years old and now he has a machine breathing for him and his rib cage is hanging freaking open.

A six-hour operation to save his life and it still might not be enough.

I feel sick.

"I was there. I held my fucking shirt in his chest to try to stop the bleeding. Doesn't matter, that's what this life looks like. You look like you're about to pass the hell out, just lay down on the pull-out bed and get some sleep."

I don't want to make any more trouble for him so I do as he says and, even with the beeping and the door opening every few minutes with nurses and doctors coming by to check Speck's vitals, I still manage to fall into a deep sleep, not waking for hours.

Chapter Twenty Two

Tomi

The day passes too fucking slowly.

Angel sleeps the whole day away which is a good thing, but she twitches and jerks around in the pull-out bed like she's being fucking murdered which, combined with the mess Speck is in, means there's no chance of me sleeping.

Instead, I sit and fucking stew on the rat problem.

I'd managed to get through all of the footage for the bar with nothing. Fucking frustrating, but I'll be back to looking through it once my shift here is over.

The hours crawl by.

Rue steps back in around three in the afternoon, looking like a pile of ass but at least he's clean and, most importantly, he hasn't been locked up for the shooting.

"Any news?"

I shake my head. "Nothing. His vitals only dropped twice so that's a good thing, I guess."

He nods and steps in, his eyes tracing over Speck like there'll be some sign he's going to survive. I know the feeling, that's all I've fucking done all night.

"She looks exhausted." he mumbles and I glance down at Angel. She's mumbled and thrashed around all day like she's been chased around in her dreams and even with the sun streaming through the windows she's still asleep now.

I'm going to figure her the fuck out. Just the second I get the fucker who is responsible for Speck's shooting, I'll fucking gut him first, then I'm finding out every little scrap of information I can about Angel and I'm deciding once and for all if I need to cut her out.

"Take her for food. Grab a shower, spend time with her, whatever. Just go and live for a few hours. I've got him," Rue says, rubbing a hand over his face.

I shouldn't ask him but I do because I have a newfound respect for the curse. "How'd Poe take the news?"

He blows out a breath. "Not… great. Thorn told her she couldn't come here with me today too, so she's extra fucking pissed. He had a lot of questions for me about Angel, too. You should keep that in mind."

I shrug, I don't fucking care what he wants to know, he's not fucking seeing her again. Fuck, I'm going to make sure he doesn't lay eyes on her again until I've figured her the fuck out.

I roll up out of my chair and walk over to gently shake Angel awake because she hasn't stirred at us talking at all.

Her hand shoots up to punch me square in the nose but my reflexes are faster and I manage to dodge it.

"Oh my god, I'm so sorry!" she squeaks and I startle when Rue starts fucking laughing.

Laughing.

The asshole, but he rarely fucking laughs these days and I definitely wasn't expecting it today of all days.

"She's got a great arm on her, can't wait to see the damn bruises you'll be coming home with."

I glare at him over my shoulder but he just smirks at me, shaking his head as he slumps back in the chair I've just spent all day in.

"I'm—Tomi, I'm so sorry—"

I cut her off. "We're leaving. Breakfast and then we're going back to the clubhouse until your shift starts."

She nods and shifts, stretching her arms up and over her head until a small sliver of skin shows above her pants before dropping down to feel for her bag that's stashed under the pull-out bed. Look, I'm not stupid, I know she works as a fucking stripper and I can see close to fucking everything she has on offer any night of the week but that little strip of skin just there?

Nearly brings me to my goddamn knees.

I'm not expecting it and it fucking hits me in the gut,

winding me until I think I'm about to embarrass myself here in front of my asshole cousin.

"Get your ass moving, I'm hungry," I growl and stand back up, trying to stop myself from rearranging myself in my jeans. Rue spots it, even without taking a good look and starts cackling again.

Asshole.

Next time he murders someone for looking sideways at Posey fucking Graves I'll be leaving him with the cleanup. The whole lot, I'll do exactly fucking nothing for him... except maybe scrubbing the security cameras and covering for him with the club.

Asshole.

Angel follows me down to my motorcycle and climbs on without hesitation, a little smoother getting on now she has a little practice.

I stop at the tiny diner on the shitty side of town. It does breakfast all day and no one will expect to see me there so it's a safer place for Angel.

I pay for her food and she blushes when she thanks me, fumbling over her words. Fuck, she must be tired. She's acting more... human today. Less cold, less heartless, and more open than I've ever seen her.

We eat together and I find myself talking to her. Actually talking to her, no snarling or judgment and it's a slippery fucking slope.

"Accounting? Why the hell would you wanna do that?"

She giggles and picks at the bacon with her fingers, the eggs and toast already demolished. "I'm good at numbers. Plus I want to go into taxes. Like, auditing probably because I just find the whole process... like a puzzle. There's always a loophole or a way to do things to save more money and I love that shit. It's weird, I know, but... I just like it."

It's stupid. It's so fucking stupid, I know it before I say it, but my dumbass mouth runs with it anyway. "So, if I gave you the books for the club, you could look over them? See if there's anything we could do to save some green?"

I don't tell her about the missing money.

She swallows and shrugs. "I could. I'm not certified or anything yet, I still have classes left to go but... yeah, I could do it. I could pick up the basics and if the guy you're going to now isn't picking that shit up I can let you know so you can find someone new."

I nod and finish my coffee. I'm dead on my feet but I still have a few hours left before she goes to work and I want to go over the security footage again.

When we leave, she drops a twenty on the table as a tip and smiles at the waitress. She's still careful to make sure no one touches her but when she walks, she tucks herself in a little closer to me as if she's using my body as a shield.

I like it a little too much.

I give her my helmet again and I wait until she's wrapped around me fully before I start my hog. She still smells like honey and sunshine, even after a night of sleeping in the hospital and I want that smell all over my fucking sheets again, just in case it's faded some.

This is starting to get outta hand.

When we get back to the clubhouse it's still like a fucking ghost town. King has every single member out on the streets either looking for intel, guarding our assets, or out of the fucking way because they're on our list of possible rats.

I duck my head into King's office on my way through, Angel looking around at everything like she's fucking terrified.

He barely looks up from his paperwork as I speak."Rue is in with Speck. I'll go back tonight. Any sign of Hell?"

He grunts at me. "He's sleeping his hangover off at Hawk's. Keely's with him to make sure he doesn't choke on his own damn tongue. Did you find Angel?"

Jesus. I nod. "She's going to stay here until she starts her shift tonight."

His eyebrows shoot up and he finally looks up. He can't really see her past me but when she peeks out from behind me he quirks an eyebrow. "Make sure you call Keely. She's fit for a fucking heart attack and Hawk's turned into an asshole about it."

I give him a curt nod and start back down the hall. Angel scurries after me, King's chuckle following us both down. I feel like a fucking teenager, the curse is fucking worse than just the obsessing... you have to deal with smug, asshole family members too.

Utter fucking bullshit.

Angel is uncomfortable as fuck when I unlock my room, kicking the door open and wincing at the state of the place. She doesn't seem to notice the mess though, just stares around at the piles of computer shit and weapons I have littering every damn surface.

I get her all of the financials for the bar and set her up on my bed with my laptop and an energy drink. I grab a shower and pull on clean clothes, ready to fucking pass out but there's no time for that shit. I do make time to text the head biker bitch to get her to come grab some of the dirty laundry that's everywhere.

I never let people into my room so I'm sure there'll be a fight over who gets to come do it. I haven't fucked any of them since I laid eyes on Angel and there's been some talk about it. Fuck, maybe not the best idea to have anyone come in but... well, Angel has made it clear she's not fucking interested in being mine. Maybe I'll fucking test that theory.

I park my own ass at my desk and get back to trawling through the security footage.

Anna walks in wearing a tiny pair of shorts and a halter crop top to grab the piles of dirty clothes on my floor. Angel stiffens but keeps to her work, tapping away quietly.

I keep an eye on Anna and when she opens her mouth to speak to me, I shut that shit down with nothing but a look.

Angel sitting on my bed wouldn't be a deterrent for Anna, she'd probably enjoy the audience.

When she finally leaves, Angel lasts about thirty seconds before snapping, "So do you always have women in here picking up after you?"

I purposefully don't look up from my own work. "Why would you care?"

She sniffs a little, turning her fucking nose up at me. "I don't. I was just going to say they aren't exactly doing a good job."

Frigid fucking bitch.

The warm and open girl who woke up at the hospital is long gone, the same old Angel back in her place. I go back to ignoring her to work on my own shit but now I'm fucking fuming.

We sit in silence for another hour but it's not as comfortable. She's jittery and twitchy, and I'm one step away from snapping at her, pushing her buttons until she drops back down to her knees for me. Fuck, she sucks dick like a pro and that's the type of release I need right now.

Maybe then she'd calm the hell down.

"Tomi?"

Her voice snaps me out of my little daydream, the hesitant tone wrenching me back into the reality of the situation. "What?"

She flinches at the tone and I grind my teeth together at the sight of it. "Angel, tell me."

She swallows twice before she manages to get the words out. "The guy who does your books... do you trust him?"

And in four simple words, she has my full attention. "What have you found?"

She blanches a little and stumbles over her words. "It's—I mean, it could be nothing—"

"Angel, what the fuck have you found?"

She huffs. "If the IRS checked these books tomorrow your club would be fucked. Also, there's money going missing... a lot of money. It's... I mean, it's clear to me and any auditor but I guess to someone who didn't know—"

"How much money is being taken? Explain it to me."

She does.

She walks me through exactly how Maverick is stealing tens of thousands of dollars each month from the club and the sloppy way he's hiding it. And then she walks me through the hack job he's been doing with our taxes and just how royally fucked over we'll be the second an auditor comes knocking.

More than that, she's given me a fucking lead.

I start tracking his movements for the last month. Easy enough to do now I have the security up everywhere and sure e-fucking-nough, there he is.

Three Demons and a wad of fucking cash.

I call King from my computer. "I've got it. I've found the best drop off route."

I stick to the agreed on code, even with the whole club out there looking for clues about the Demons. Just in case, I don't want Maverick making a fucking run for it and having to chase the cunt.

I don't want to leave Speck exposed like that and there's no fucking way I'm leaving Angel.

I've accepted that now.

He grunts down the line and hangs up, two minutes later he comes through the door. Angel startles on the bed but he ignores her. "You sure?"

I nod. "Without a doubt. There's no way anyone could get stopped."

He nods and walks over to look at the screen. I have the still of Mav standing there and King's face turns to fucking stone. "Call Rue and let him know we're going to check it out. Hawk too, but leave Hell to his hangover."

I nod and murmur, "Keely and Trink with Speck?"

He nods. "We have guys coming in from the Bay for backup. I'll station them close by."

I nod and glance at Angel. She's still glaring at the laptop screen. "I'll get Angel to work, Axe is there to keep an eye on things. I'll catch you up on the drive."

He glances at her too and then nods.

Time for Mav to meet the Captain.

Serves the traitorous cunt right.

We get out to the swamp a little after midnight.

Rue and I drive in my truck together, silence in the cab for the whole drive. Sometimes you just have to get your shit together and spill the blood your club needs you to.

I don't have any fucking hesitation in me.

Not a fucking drop.

When we pull up, King is already there waiting. Hawk both arrives a minute or so after us, Mav hogtied in the back of their truck, gagged and fucking livid.

Good.

The cunt deserves worse.

"I've been in this club for twenty fucking years! You think I'm the rat?" he says, struggling against Hawk but there's no budging him. King might have gotten huge in prison but my pops has been a brick wall since birth.

King stops in the bayou, his boots slowly sinking just a

little into the soft swamp dirt, and I keep an eye out on the water, my hand hovering by my gun. "I don't just think you're the rat, Mav. I fucking know it. You thought you were slick, getting away with shit while I was in lockup, getting fucking sloppy."

Mav wrenches his body, trying desperately to get out of Hawk's grip, and Rue finally fucking snaps and steps forward to punch him in the face. One quick blow has blood pouring out of his nose and a string of vicious curses. Good thing we're out in the middle of bumfuck nowhere because he's squealing like a pig.

"King, I've been loyal the entire fucking time you were gone. I haven't fucking leaked a word to any other club, I've been on every run, spilled blood for my brothers, what else could I possibly fucking do?"

King throws the rope over the tree and starts tying it off. Mav watches him work, the sweat on his forehead running down his face and mixing with the blood pouring out of his nose. He looks worried and a little confused, nowhere near the fucking terrified he should be.

It's fine, he'll figure it out once he's up there.

"We had someone go over the books, Mav, you thieving piece of shit. You've been skimming from the fucking top for years and writing it all off. I always did wonder how you kept your hog looking so fucking good with all of the gambling debts," Rue says, lowering the tailgate on the truck and pulling out the buckets, their contents slopping around.

Now Mav is looking a little more worried.

"Skimming from the top gets me excommunicated, not fucking strung up in some swamp. I had debts, I needed some fucking money and I knew there was no way the club would help me out with that. I saw what happened when Vic asked about getting extra."

King takes a step back from the tree to admire his work. It's good, should be strong enough to hold, even with all of the struggling. I smirk at him, waiting for the signal to get moving but the Prez takes one last moment to study his traitorous brother.

"We have the footage of you making a deal with the Demons. You might not have been a rat this whole time, that might have been the very fucking first, but you sold us out. Coulda gotten a lot of men killed. Fuck, you have my prospect in the fucking hospital getting open fucking heart surgery. I'd have put a bullet in your brain for that alone but the fact he's my blood? A Callaghan, set to take over this club someday? You gotta pay the price and it's gotta be the fucking Captain."

Now he's shaking.

Only the Callaghans know about the Captain, know exactly how we torture and kill the worst of our enemies but there's rumors about her aplenty. Everyone knows something evil happens out here in the swamp.

"She's grumpy tonight. I've already given her a snack, just something small to get her excited about the main course."

"King, I didn't—"

"You did. We have it all on camera too. String him up, boys."

I grab one side of him and Rue takes the other from Hawk, walking him over to the tree and holding him in position as King starts to tie him up.

"You'll fucking pay for this. The whole club too. You think the Demons are just fucking around? Grimm Graves is going to fucking destroy everything your daddy built and make it his own personal playground. You think I wanted to hand that information over? He's fucking insane. He's mentally unstable and if you go against him then you'll end up dead too. There is no getting out of this, King. Patch over or die trying to stay Unseen. They're your only options."

King tightens the last rope around Mav's arm and then punches him in the face, the crack of his cheekbone breaking as loud as a gunshot through the warm night air.

"I live Unseen. I'll die Unseen. If that death is handed to me by Grimm Graves himself then I'll have died protecting my family and my club. That's the life I wanna have, the death I'll be happy to have. You get a death out here in the swamp like a fucking coward, your memory nothing but an old story we'll tell our kids about how traitors die. Stinking and screaming."

Rue grabs a bucket and hands it to me, then grabs the second one for himself. The chicken blood and livers fucking stink, King wasn't wrong about that, and when we pour them over Mav's head he starts gagging and hacking up his guts like a fucking pansy.

It takes a matter of seconds for CeCee to come out of the water.

I back up a little, completely aware that I've got some of that stinking mix on my clothes too, and Rue grabs the buckets up to throw them in the truck again.

"You wanna watch it or are you heading back to the club?" Hawk says, a cigarette hanging out of one corner of his mouth.

I shrug and stare as the gator slides on out of the water, her body twice the length of mine and her jaw already snapping at the scent of Mav. I can't think of much worse ways to go.

"I'll stick around with Rue, make sure he's definitely dead and gone. You two go and get cleaned up, head back to the hospital and take over for Hell. We need someone watching Speck at all times. Blood only," King says, and I nod.

We stay long enough to watch the first leg get torn off.

I need that much to get me through another night at Speck's bedside.

Chapter Twenty Three

Angel

My night at The Boulevard is the same as the night before except this time I'm smart enough to take my laptop with me to study while I'm locked in Tomi's office. I've already missed a full day of study thanks to the hospital trip and looking over the club books. I still haven't managed to get through them all but I've made a dent in it.

The Unseen are a very wealthy club.

You'd never really guess it from how rough the guys all are, none of them really scream rich, but the money The Boulevard brings in alone makes my nightly income look like child's play. The garage that Rue runs is known for custom motorcycle jobs and extremely specialized repairs. They handle all of the classics, the shit people shell out a lot of money for, and Rue is definitely a big earner.

Even the Mugshots bar is raking the cash in.

Add onto that the money they're very clearly laundering, they're all fucking loaded.

There's a few ways to sort the laundering issues out and I'd started making notes about them before we ran out of time and the day was up. When I got into The Boulevard I'd finally had time to grab a shower and Tomi had stuck around long enough to see me in and out of it. When I opened the stall to find him glaring at his phone screen I'd tried not to look shocked at him.

Whatever is going on has him really fucking worried.

He disappears right after that to go look at the new route he'd been talking to his club president about planning. I'm smart enough not to ask a single question about it, but he's very clear on what he expects from me.

Stay where Axe can see me at all times.

Tell him the second something happens.

Do not leave The Boulevard with anyone who isn't a Callaghan and sent by him.

The shooting has scared me enough to listen to him and do exactly what he says without question. I mean, Axe is nice enough. He doesn't ever try to touch me or look at me, he only ever speaks to me respectfully.

He seems just a little bit scared of me.

Well, maybe not me exactly but clearly he's been told by Tomi to keep a close eye on me thanks to the asset I've become to the club. I don't really get it but hell, I'll take it.

So I do my first dance and when I get off stage Axe hands me a hoodie, waiting until I have it zipped all the way up before leading me over to Tomi's office.

"You need anything? I can get Diamond to bring you a drink or whatever."

I try to hide my cringe. I would never accept a drink from that woman, it would probably be poisoned. "No thanks. I'm fine. I'm just going to study, I swear I won't be any trouble to you."

He huffs out a laugh. "No trouble. Just yell if you need something, you're gonna be as bored as fuck in there all over again."

I shrug at him. "It's not so bad. I'll get a heap done, Tomi's probably doing my classwork a favor."

I sit in my usual chair, no way I want to sit in his, and even though I know I should be studying I spend the whole time working through the Unseen books. When Axe kicks on the door to grab me for my next dance I startle, no idea that almost two hours have already passed.

I go out and do my thing, the crowd much smaller tonight than it has been in all the months of me working here. I still make a decent amount and when I walk off stage I find Tomi waiting there instead of Axe.

I stumble over my own feet at the sight of him.

He's showered since I last saw him, his hair slicked back and a soft black tee stretching over his wide chest, tight around his tattooed biceps.

He has no right to be so hot.

No right.

He smirks at the dumbass look on my face, handing over the hoodie for me to slide into and it's only when I pull it on that I realize he's switched it out with one of his ones, the Unseen patch clearly visible across the back.

"Diamond wants you to fill in for Farrah again so we're sticking around for another hour."

I nod and then follow him down the hall. I don't know what it is about him but I find myself standing closer to him, tucking my body in behind him and he always shifts until he's covering me like a shield… protecting me even when there isn't any danger in the room.

He lets me into his office when he gets a phone call, standing in the doorway as he talks to his mom about Speck.

I try not to look as though I'm listening in but I'm desperate to know if anything has changed.

"I can do another shift there… Well, is Hawk staying there with you? I don't want you by yourself… okay. Okay, I'll come tomorrow night… is she at Poe's… is Thorn home… I know but it's my job to make sure you're both safe… nah, Rue will go and stay there tonight… okay, I will… call me if anything changes."

Mel and Diamond giggle obnoxiously as they walk past, glaring at me once they know Tomi can't see them. I don't know why the hell they try to hide it from him, it's not like he gives a fuck about me.

Other than adding me to the notches on his bedpost which, again, he's already managed to do.

I roll my eyes at them but Tomi sees that and glances back over his shoulder at them both. I hear their footsteps speed up like they're hotfooting it away from his anger.

I grab my laptop and get it set up again, ready to just work quietly and not get in his way.

He waits until the door is shut before he starts in on me, the accusing tones harsh in his voice again. "You should have told me you didn't have a place to stay."

Typical.

I sigh and keep my eyes on the screen, tapping through the

spreadsheet to make sure my numbers are all correct. It's hard to do with him staring at me like he is.

His eyes are too intense for me.

"It didn't matter then and it doesn't matter now. I'm my own person and I'll sort my own shit out," I say.

"You'd rather sleep on the street than tell me you've been kicked out of your place? Angel, that's just fucking stupid."

I refuse to look at him, to see the loathing and hate that I know he'll have all over his face. "Look, it's not your problem. I don't blame you for showing me the door when… you were done. It's whatever, why are you even bringing it up? You don't owe me anything. I've got a job to do, you've got a business to run."

At the mention of my job his eyebrows draw down a little and I brace myself for whatever he has to say about it.

I will not let him make me feel guilty about my job.

I already hate myself, I don't need the fucking guilt too.

"Angel, my business is keeping you safe."

I swallow and look down at my nails. One of them is chipped from my first dance and my knees are a little sore from it too. There's limits to what a body can do without proper rest, good nutrition, and time away from the pole. I'm quickly discovering that I'm running into the end of the line for what I can do without burning out.

I need to be more aggressive in my saving.

Maybe there's something in the air, or maybe I'm just a glutton for punishment, but I just have to question him.

"Why me, though? Because I'm your biggest asset? You know Diamond and the other girls hate me because I'm getting preferential treatment. They all want me out and honestly… I'm not going to dance forever. Shouldn't you be protecting the girls that want to stick with you?"

He stares at me for so long I try not to squirm in my seat.

Finally, he shuts his laptop and then leans forward to shut mine too.

"I'm not protecting you because of the club. Yes, you are our best dancer and the biggest money maker out of all of the girls here for the club but I'm a selfish dick. I'm protecting you because I want to."

I swallow again, a lump forming in the back of my throat.

This feels too… real for me. I feel like he's actually trying to open up to me. I mean, I'm not sure what I was expecting him to say but it wasn't this.

I kind of thought he'd be telling me how much he hates me again.

"Who is your boyfriend, Angel? The one you're afraid of. Is he making you dance here and taking your money? Tell me his name and he'll be gone before the sun comes up."

I glance down at my computer.

I could tell him.

Except then whatever progress we've managed would be gone, he'd never trust me again, I'd lose everything.

Better to keep that secret close to my chest.

"I don't have a boyfriend. I… I've been knocked around some but there's no one now. I'm just trying to finish college, get a job, live a normal life. There's no big secret, Tomi."

He looks me over, his eyes too intense for me. "There is a secret. I don't know what it is but you're too fucking scared for there to be nothing. If you tell me what it is, I'll sort it out."

I sigh and lean back in my chair, fussing with the hem of his hoodie, picking at the threads there. "You want me to be honest with you Tomi, but you've given me no reason to be. Why should I trust you? I mean, the sex is good but there's nothing else going on between us… right? You don't want to be my friend."

He scowls at me, ignoring his phone when it starts to ring. "Angel, I don't want to be your fucking friend. I want you naked in my goddamn bed every night. I want you outta this club. I want whoever the fuck is hurting you dead and rotting in a fucking hole somewhere, and I want you to stop jumping at the smallest fucking noises. It's pretty fucking simple. You want me to prove myself to you or some shit? Fine. Your ass is protected by me and my club. Anyone touches you, they die. You need something? You come to me."

My stomach roils with nerves.

I want that.

I want him and that protection so goddamn much, having him for myself… fuck, that's exactly what I want. The stabbing feeling in my chest when he rolled away from me the other night, that was the worst fucking pain I've felt since I ran away from home.

Could I survive this if he's not being real with me?

"I've got four days until I'm going on a run for the club. You'll stay with me until then. When I get back, we'll talk. You'll tell me your secrets and I'll fix anything you need me to. Answer me, Angel. Say yes."

I clear my throat. Four days… four days together nd then when he gets back I'll have to tell him.

He'll be gone for my birthday.

It's probably for the best.

I clear my throat. "Okay. Okay, I'll stay with you. If it… works out, I'll tell you… everything."

Chapter Twenty Four

Tomi

By the time Angel makes it out of the shower, there's no one left in the changing room. The relief is right there on her face, clear as a fucking bell, and I make a note to find out what the fuck the other women are doing to her when I'm not around. I thought I'd made it clear that shit wouldn't fly but her face tells me she's still having a shitty time here.

No more.

I'm fixing all of her fucking problems.

"Sorry for taking so long."

Her voice is different when she's out of the getup she wears on the stage. It's softer, more hesitant and full of ghosts, and it sets my teeth on edge.

I can't think about whatever demons she's hiding, whoever it is that she's running from. Whichever piece of shit beat on her and has her scared of her own shadow.

"You're good? Let's get out of here."

She falters a little, that big bag of hers that she drags around everywhere with her over her shoulder. It's as if she packs her whole life to come to work just in case she might need something.

It's fucking weird.

I check the security cams before pushing the back door open with a palm, gesturing for her to go ahead now I know there's no one out there waiting for us both. "What's going on in that head of yours? From here out, Angel, you need something, you come to me."

She hesitates for a second and then shrugs, walking ahead

of me and leaving me with that sweet honey smell of hers.

Makes a man fucking ravenous.

I get her bag strapped onto my hog all while she fusses with her helmet nervously. I switched out my spare to make sure it would fit her head properly. I'm a fucking sap for this woman who's wrapped in secrets, coated in broken armor and trip wires.

Once her arms are wrapped around me tight and I can feel every fucking inch of her pressed against my back I get us onto the road and I let the hog fly, the deep rumble of the engine loud in my ears and like a balm on my soul.

It's fucking perfect.

For a second I can forget all about the endless bullshit I've got going on in the club, with my brat of a sister, with my cousin fighting for life, and with the beauty on the back of the bike. I can just pretend everything is exactly the way I want it to be.

I can pretend I was lovestruck at the sight of her and she's mine for keeps.

I'm still not sure that's what's happening here but at least I can say I tried. It's fucking perfect while it lasts but, as always, we make it to the club way too fucking fast and I feel the tension start to fill her the second the gates of the compound come into view.

I fucking hate how uneasy this place makes her.

Was the guy who beat her a biker?

I'll fucking fill him with lead or, better yet, beat the life right out of him. I pull up into my usual spot and huff out a laugh at Rue's missing rig. Guess he really is off stalking his little flower child again. It's a good thing tonight, means there's another set of eyes on Trink too.

I still need to find out what the hell is going on with her too.

Fuck.

Angel takes a second before she climbs off, her arms squeezing me tighter right before she lets go like it's hard to separate from me.

Fuck, what the hell is going on with my head tonight?

Seeing her cry at the sight of Speck, knowing she'd rather sleep on the streets than tell me she needs help, the shaking, the broken phone… she doesn't want to be touched.

Fuck.

Who the hell has hurt my girl?

Is she still being hurt? Is she lying to me about it?

Nope, can't wander down that thought spiral. If I think about if someone is still hurting her or, fuck, how they're hurting her, I'll be dead by dawn.

Killing rampages don't go down well in Coldstone. It's too fucking small to get away with that shit.

She glances up at the clubhouse and wraps her arms around herself like she's cold but it's still warm enough out. "Is there a party going on? I'd rather not go in there. Is there… somewhere else we can stay?"

"Nope, this is home," I say, trying to keep my cool. Pushing her isn't going to help my case but it takes everything I have not to just shake the answers outta her.

She sighs and scuffs her foot on the ground. "Okay. I guess… I mean, Speck said—"

"Stop fucking talking about Speck. You're sleeping in my bed where I know you're fucking safe for the night and then I'll drive you into work. You don't have to party or talk to anyone."

She nods and glances around. I follow her gaze and I see all of the extra bikes hanging around. There's a party going on like there usually is on a Friday night but the fear is real in every inch of her as she counts up the vehicles.

I see it now.

And I don't like it, not one bit, so I do something fucking stupid. I strip my jacket off and sling it over her shoulders, marking her up as mine and definitely not available to any of my brothers and then I tuck her tiny hand in mine. Wearing my shirt with the patch was one thing but wearing my jacket in front of other charters?

No mistaking that move.

"Come on, I'm not in the mood for a party either. I'll get you to my room and then I'll grab us both something to eat."

She nods and hesitates for half a second before stepping in close to me, using my body as a shield as we move into the crowd of men and women spilling out of the packed bar.

I feel ten feet fucking tall.

Her bag is tucked in tight between our bodies like she's scared it'll get ripped away by the crowd. There's shouts and jeering as we make our way through but I ignore them all. I've got zero fucking time for any of their shit tonight. I'm stone-cold sober and the only thing on my mind is Angel.

"Who the fuck is that? Is she wearing your patch right now?"

I roll my eyes and pull Angel in closer to my side as Monroe steps into my path. Fucking dumb bitch, if her daddy wasn't a brother I'd take her down a fucking notch right here but I don't have time to deal with this bullshit.

Angel just wants to get to my room.

"It's none of your fucking business. Go find Diesel and suck him off, I've got nothing for you."

She smirks, trying to get a look at Angel but my girl is tucked in tight with her head down. "Oh really? You bringing a fucking stripper home? Your momma must be so proud, Tomi."

Angel's hand twitches in mine but for once I'm not angry at her for getting her tits out at the club.

I'm fucking livid at Monroe for talking down to her.

She sees it too, sees the look in my eye that says she's fucked up and there's no coming back from it.

"Get your ass the fuck out of my way before I decide to take it personal and tell Diesel about your little obsession with Rue. Does he know you're trying so fucking hard to bend over for his brother? Fuck, does Dave know you're trying to fuck us all?"

She finally gets the fuck out of our way and I get moving, weaving through the drunk and stumbling crowd until I get us to my room. I get it unlocked and gently push Angel in there first, breathing a little easier when she's in my space and away from all of the bullshit and debauchery.

If she saw the four-way happening on the pool table she says nothing about it, just pulls the jacket around herself a little tighter.

She looks fucking perfect in my leather.

I sling her bag down onto the couch. "Lemme grab us some food. I saw burgers, anything you don't like?"

She shakes her head and I head out.

It takes me way too long to grab the shit. King tries to catch my eye but I ignore him, making my way back through the crowd without pausing for fucking anything.

When I get back Angel is still standing in the middle of the room clutching at my jacket like it's a goddamn lifesaver and she's stuck out at sea.

"Angel, you're here for the next couple of nights. You can't be standing around feeling fucking awkward for days."

She startles and turns around to give me a half-smile. "Sorry. I just don't want to get in your way... I don't want to rock the boat."

Her voice is quiet still, like she really is afraid I'm about to kick her ass out. "Here. Eat this so we can go the fuck to bed. I'm gonna go shower first."

She nods and takes the plate, perching her ass down on the couch and then falling onto the burger like she's gone days without food.

Come to think of it... "When the fuck did you last eat?"

She pauses with the last bite of the damn thing halfway to her mouth. "I can't eat before I dance. I'm too... nervous, I guess."

Breakfast. We'd gone to the diner for breakfast and she'd barely poked around at some eggs and a little bacon. We didn't get dinner after she'd finished dancing the night before either, just went straight into the hospital to see Speck, so she's only eaten that breakfast in the last two days.

She must be fucking starving.

"Angel, listen to me and listen good because I'm only saying this once. You're going to start taking care of yourself right the fuck now. You're going to tell me you're hungry when you need food and you're going to stop taking the fucking high road. I'm not a fucking mind reader."

She half nods and shoves the last of the burger in her mouth, glancing at the one I made for myself.

"Eat it. I'll get another one when I'm done in the shower."

By the time I get out of the shower, Angel is asleep in my bed with nothing but my hoodie on. It's a fucking tempting sight and I have to force myself out to the kitchen to eat something. I've barely had an hour's sleep in the last two days and I'm running on fumes. Keely and Hawk have taken the night shift with Speck to give us the break because they both know how long and hard Rue and I have been working.

Here's hoping Rue is actually getting some sleep too and not just obsessively watching Poe breathe through her bedroom window like a psychopath.

I eat in the kitchen so I don't get dragged into having a drink with any of the guys here. They're all used to me drinking and partying and fucking my way through any situation the club is in so there's no doubt there'll be questions if I go straight to bed.

I couldn't care less.

At this point, I'm sure half the guys already know I've been 'struck. Axe sure does but he's been good about keeping his mouth shut, probably thanks to all of the death threats I sent him when I put him on Angel duty.

When I get back to my room, Angel is still asleep but thrashing around a bit. Fuck. I can't remember the last time I slept next to someone and that shit doesn't look comfortable. Her arms keep flailing about and her legs are kicking… looks like she's fighting some asshole off.

I don't like that.

Not one bit.

I climb in the other side and try to get comfortable, not touching her in any way because I'm proving to her that this isn't just about the good sex.

I'm just a little pissed she said the sex was just good.

She fucking gushed, the wet spot on my bed was a fucking lake, that's more than just good.

It takes me a good hour to fall asleep but when I finally do, her body calls to mine like a silent siren's song. I only know that I've reached out for her when a strangled scream lets out of her throat and she scrambles away from me, straight off of the bed and onto the floor.

My brain is still half-asleep but even dumb, deaf, and blind I'd know exactly what the fuck that reaction meant.

Someone's hurt her. Hurt her real bad.

My mind goes fuzzy as my rage tries to win out over the hazy sleep.

She's barely awake as she pulls herself up into a sitting position against the wall, her chest heaving and her hands clawing up her arms like she's trying to gouge my touch out of her skin. This high-pitch keening sound starts up but the wild and frantic look in her eyes makes me sure she has no control over it.

"Angel, it's me. I'm not going to hurt you, sweetness."

The nickname slips out.

This entire fucking thing has caught me off guard.

I've gone from wanting to hate fuck her right out from under my skin to wanting to break any man that's laid hands on her in anger before.

She's still freaking the fuck out so I carefully, and slowly, get up off of the bed and walk over to the bathroom to grab some pants and clear my head.

I get her cleaned up with a warm washcloth. Her fingernails are destroying the skin of her arms, gouging at her own flesh like she's trying to dig something out.

I'm done messing around.

I'm finding this motherfucker and I'm killing him.

Slowly, after I've cleaned her up and tucked her into my chest, her breathing evens out before turning into quiet sobs.

I can't handle that either.

"You're back then? I've been trying to get you to talk for over an hour."

Her voice comes out in a little whimper. "I'm—I'm sorry. I didn't mean to—"

I cut her off because the thought of hearing her lies right now has my gut churning with rage. "Yeah, I get that. You gonna tell me who the fuck I'm killing for this?"

She tenses in my arms but I don't let her go. I'm not going to either, not until I have some answers. "You told me we were going to wait. I just… I need more time."

"Angel, you've got to fucking answer me. Where was your old place, who did you live with there? Thorn said you told Alby it wasn't this one hurting you so who was it?"

She turns to press her face into my chest a little more and I have to focus on my anger at the claw marks up her arms not to just say, fuck it, and spread her out. "I told you I don't have a boyfriend."

Thank fuck. "Then who kicked you out?"
She shakes her head. "No one, Tomi, please. I'm so tired, I just want to get some sleep."
I try not to fucking yell because that'll only have us going backwards. When I stand up and tug her towards the bed she pulls away from me.
"It's the bed. I can't—I can't sleep in it. I'm sorry, I'll take the couch."
Fuck that.
I grab her hips pushing her towards the bathroom. "Just go get a glass of water."
When she's gone I pull everything off of the bed and onto the floor. I've slept in a lot of questionable places in my life, spending a night on the floor won't fucking kill me.
Hell, I probably won't even notice.
"What are you doing?" she whispers and I ignore her, lying down amongst the pillows.
"Get your ass down here. No, you're sleeping right here where I can hold you. Right. Close your eyes and stop fucking thinking."
It hasn't taken much to notice she does best when I give her firm instructions. Clear and to the point, it's like her brain switches off and she just gets her ass moving.
Her heart races when I get her bundled into my chest but it doesn't take long before she's asleep, her body finally relaxing fully and the thrashing over with.
I sleep like the dead.
So does Angel.
Maybe we were made for each other.

Chapter Twenty Five

Angel

It doesn't matter how many times I try to sleep in the bed with Tomi, we always end up on the floor.

He pointedly doesn't ever try to initiate sex and it's suddenly all I can think about around him. His shirts just get tighter and tighter as the nights go on until I feel like I can count every last one of his abs.

Yup, he has a six-pack and one of those Adonis belt 'V' things that look photoshopped in photos.

It's wildly unfair, especially now that sex seems to be the last thing on his mind.

I wonder what it would be like to be with him and then sleep together afterwards? What it would be like to finish and not feel… dirty afterwards.

Jesus.

The last night before he leaves for the run, I wake up on the floor again. Tomi's arm is under my head like a pillow and the thin blankets from the bed thrown over us both, my face is pressed into his chest and his chin resting on the top of my head as he tries to soothe me. I'm shaking so bad that his arms are the only thing keeping me from vibrating all the way out of the damn room.

This is getting fucking shameful.

"It's okay, sweetness. Everything is going to be okay."

His voice is a slow, soothing sound and the rasp of it speaks of a shitty night of sleep.

Fuck.

"I'm sorry," I mumble and his arms tighten around me.

"Don't start with that shit, Angel. The only thing I need you worrying about is telling me who the fuck did this to you. I'll fucking end the gutless cunt."

The trembling gets worse and a sob bursts out of my throat, no matter how hard I try to swallow it. His arms turn to stone around me, crushing me to him as I dissolve into sobs, tears sliding down his chest as I just break the fuck down.

I'm waiting for him to get angry and leave, just walk out and forget about the stripper that was hot enough but too much fucking work. I mean, he's gotten the notch in his belt from fucking me already. What else is he around for?

"Angel, sweetness, please stop crying. I can't fucking take it, I'm gonna fucking kill every man you've ever fucking met if you don't stop soon, baby."

I can't stop.

It's like the dam has broken and now all of the tears I refused to cry when I ran away are flooding out of me. I try to pull away but he doesn't let me, just pulls me into his body even tighter so we're as close as two people can get. Fuck, it's as if he wants to absorb me completely until we're one person.

My dad used to say my mom was the other half of his soul and being together was as close as a man came to feeling whole again.

I don't know why that popped into my head.

Fuck.

I can't handle him holding me like this on the off chance this doesn't work out because when he knows everything he's going to hate me. I need him to stop right the hell now. "I'm fine. I just—I need a second. Let me go clean up."

"Angel, you're shaking too fucking much to get up. Just go the fuck back to sleep and we can sort it out tomorrow."

I settle down a little but his words come back to me.

You're mine.

Maybe I am his, maybe I can trust him and when I tell him everything he'll be… okay. He'll still want me.

When my phone pings and wakes me a few hours later, I wriggle away from him to see who the hell would be messaging me.

Your truck is done! Tell Tomi to let you out from your tower for the night and come get her.

I let out a sigh and text her back, a smile on my face.

"Should I be fucking jealous over who's making you light up like that or what?" Tomi grumbles and when I glance down at him, he's frowning and scratching at the shadow of a beard that's starting up on his face.

"My Chevy is fixed. I can grab her on the way to work tonight, Poe's going to bring me the keys."

He huffs and sits up, his back popping and crunching. I wince, it's my fault he's gotta be feeling sore. It must be guilt because I say to him, "It was my dad's truck. It means a lot to me."

He tenses up a little but doesn't make any other reaction. "Oh yeah? It's a beauty, '69?"

I nod and pull my knees up to my chest. "Yup. It was his baby, I got it in his will. He died of cancer when I was nine."

He nods and stands up, holding out a hand to help me up. I take it and let him pull me up, pulling me into his chest. He's only got a pair of boxers on, all of his tattooed skin on display and I kind of feel like he's teasing me with his nakedness.

"Listen, Rue is staying home to keep an eye on things while we're gone. He'll be splitting time between the hospital and The Boulevard. Axe will be there for all of your shifts too, so you go to either of them if anything is up. Anything at all, Angel. Promise me."

I nod and when he swoops down to kiss me I push up on my tiptoes to meet the kiss. Jesus, the first time he's doing something and I'll be late to work if we do anything more than just this kiss.

He groans into the kiss and pulls away from me, grabbing a box from his desk and handing it over to me.

"What's this?" I say but the box is clearly holding an iPhone.

"I need to be able to get hold of you while I'm gone. Keep it charged and on you." He pulls away from me properly and grabs up the bedding from the floor and throws it all back on the bed.

"I can't afford this kind of phone, I can get a cheaper one," I mumble and walk into the bathroom for a shower.

He walks in behind me. "I added you to my plan, take it. We're talking about where the fuck all your money is going when I get back Angel, no excuses."

I shrug and fuss with the hem of my shirt before I lift it over my head. I'm a stripper for fuck's sake and yet here I am, blushing like a fucking virgin because his eyes drag over every inch of skin on show as I stand there in nothing but a pair of skimpy panties.

He grabs my hips and drags me in close to his body, his eyes focussed entirely on my nipples. "When I get back we're talking about it, Angel. We're talking about the money, your ex, who the fuck beat you, and where the hell you're living. Non-negotiable. I'm going to your new place and I'm setting up security there, I'm sleeping in your fucking bed, and we're going to figure this shit out."

I tilt my head up to meet his lips when he leans down to kiss me. He's gentler this time, still commanding and brutal but the sharp edge is missing. Like maybe this time he's not trying to punish me, only possess me.

My legs are shaking before he straightens up. He reaches up and cups my cheek, stroking a thumb across my skin and staring at me like he's trying to memorize every detail of my face before he goes.

It makes my heart thump in my chest in fear.

Where is he going that he thinks he might not make it home?

"You're coming back, right?" I croak, my voice all gravelly from his kiss.

He smirks at me and rubs a thumb over my bottom lip. "Course I am, sweetness. Can't get rid of me that easy."

I smile at him and then, on instinct alone because I have no real clue on how the fuck to flirt with him, I suck his thumb into my mouth and watch as his pupils blow out wide, swallowing the brilliant blue of his irises. He groans and shoves me back into the tiled wall, one hand grabbing at my face to keep my mouth locked around his thumb and the other sliding down to cup my pussy through my panties.

"We don't have time to finish this tonight, sweetness, but when I get home I'm gonna give you something to swallow. Fuck, this pussy is everything a man could ever want and it's mine, you hear me? If you've been lying to me about having an old man you better lose him before I get back. When I'm home, we're making this shit official."

I can't speak around his thumb so I nod slowly. I've never felt this way about a man before, I'd never had the chance, and maybe he hasn't been the kindest or the sweetest choice but he's the only one I've ever wanted.

Maybe I could be happy with him.

I get through my shower and getting ready for work at the clubhouse. Tomi waits until I've made it down to Pops' safely to grab the Chevy before he rides out with the others, the roar of the motorcycles loud on the quiet streets of Coldstone.

Pops hands over the keys and talks me through what Poe has fixed up and what else I might need to watch out for.

"You bring her here from now on, you hear? We take care of family."

I swallow roughly and smile at him. "I really appreciate everything you and Poe have done for me. Really, it means a lot."

He waves me off, dropping the hood back down with that respectful sort of care a man has when he's dealing with a classic like this. "I saw you comin' out of the compound. You get rid of that man of yours and found a biker?"

I startle and clutch at my bag a little tighter. "Oh— uh, yeah. I'm seeing Tomi. It's much… uh… better. Thanks."

I don't want to lie to him, especially when he's showing such a kind interest in my wellbeing, but I also don't want to explain what the hell is going on.

"Tomi's a good man. Hawk and Keely raised good kids, Rue's a good one too. Watches out for Posey, keeps her safe. You're in good hands, Keely wouldn't stand for any of 'em raising a hand at a woman."

I wring my hands a little and he huffs out a breath at me again. "Off you go, you're a busy girl. Drive carefully, call if you need anything."

I make it to my shift and spend the night with Axe, following his every direction and studying quietly in Tomi's office between dances. I finally feel as though I'm getting enough sleep and food, and it's much easier to focus on my classwork between dances than it ever was at the library.

After my last dance I take a shower like I always do and when I get out Axe walks me to my truck, waiting there in the parking lot until I'm out and on the road.

I drive out to the next town over to get a hotel for the night.

Even with my truck back I want to get a little more classwork done before I pass out and… I mean, it's my birthday.

I want to spend the day quietly doing nothing but relaxing and sleeping.

I might go find cake to eat by myself.

I check in and park up, getting my bag inside but when I go back out to the truck for my laptop I find Rue leaning against the door.

I freeze.

"Well, well. This doesn't look like a new apartment, Angel."

Fuck. "Why are you following me?"

He gives me a dark look. "Tomi wants to know you're getting home safe. He's about ready to throw down over you, Angel, and this? This is going to tip him over the edge."

I pull my jacket around myself tighter. "So you're going to tell him I slept here? Can you give me a couple of days to sort my life out first?"

He groans and lights up a cigarette. "I don't get mixed up in his 'struck shit, Angel. That's something for a man to figure out by himself, y'know?"

Struck?

I don't have time to figure out what the fuck that even means. I'm so close to being out of this life and in a new one.

My chest aches at the thought of Tomi finding out and being pissed at me though.

"Look, there was a delay in getting into my new place and so I lied to Tomi about it being ready because I know he's heading out on a run. I didn't want to mess with club business. I'll be in a place next week. I have three nights left of sleeping in a hotel, it's not that hard. I'm safe here and it's really none of your business."

He looks at me, his face completely unreadable, and then he pulls out his phone.

Fuck.

"I'm taking Angel back to the club. I'll give her the keys

to your room… she's had a problem with her new place, she needs to stay for another couple of nights. She called Poe while I was there, I sorted it out. I'll call you if she disappears."

I swallow as he hangs up, shifting around until he's fussing with his keys and handing one over to me. "Consider this a favor. I'll lie about tonight and you'll stay at the clubhouse without kicking up a fuss because if you do, I'll drag you there and call Tomi without thinking twice."

I look at the key for a second before I reach out and take it. "I don't want to stay there without him. I don't like… how many people are there."

Rue shrugs. "I'll take you around the back way, there's a courtyard between me and Tomi's rooms. Grab food on the way home and you don't ever have to come through the front."

Uhh what? Now I'm pissed. The amount of times I've been groped or stared at or had people just get too close to me.

What an asshole. "Well, why the hell has Tomi been walking me through the bar if we could go around the back?"

Rue shakes his head at me, rolling his shoulders back and slinging his helmet back on his head. "The two of you need to get your heads outta your asses because this shit is getting on my damn nerves. Grab your shit, we're leaving."

I have no choice but to do as he says.

I'm pissed about losing the money for the night but Rue doesn't leave any room for argument, just stands around until I grab all of my stuff back out and dump it all in my truck.

I head straight to the compound, too anxious now to eat, and when I park up Rue grabs my bag and laptop out for me. He grunts a little under the weight of the bag and I try not to get twitchy about him touching it.

Just so long as he doesn't look inside.

He walks me around the back and through a tiny, walled courtyard. He taps his boot at me until I huff and get the door unlocked and opened. I grab my stuff off of him and he waits for me to get it all inside before saying, "Lock up. Both doors, don't open it for anyone but me. I'll come get you for work tomorrow. If you need anything, call me."

He's too freaking scary to try to be stern or assertive with, so instead I keep my eyes on his shoes and say, "I'd really like to know why I couldn't be using this door the whole time. Walking through the bar isn't fun for me."

Rue grunts and rubs his face. "Angel, for fuck's sake. He walks you through so every brother in this club knows he has claim over you. No one is going to touch you and, better than that, if they see your boyfriend smacking you around on the street they'll fill him full of lead and bring you home to Tomi. That's why. He wants you fucking safe and someday soon you'll need to start trusting him a little. I get that he was a dick but he's trying. Either try along with him or cut him the fuck out. Plenty of other clubs you can dance at that won't be messing with his head."

I fumble over my words. "I don't have a boyfriend."

He huffs at me. "Nah, you have an old man now. A Callaghan who will own your shit so keep your ass in line and start trusting us to have your back."

He turns away and only manages a step before he glances back at me. He's a little scarier than Tomi, harder and grumpier than his cousin, but he obviously cares about him enough to protect me… keep an eye out for me the same as he does Poe.

"The day you wore his jacket in here they knew. They all knew what that meant so you just sleep easy and keep both the doors locked. Pretty thing like you, too fucking tempting to idiot men and I don't need a war breaking out over Tomi skinning these men. Hell, he wouldn't get the chance to, I'd have them dead before he made it home."

I don't get the chance to say anything back to him.

I sleep in Tomi's bed, my head buried in his pillow and his blankets wrapped around me so tight I can barely breathe.

Chapter Twenty Six

Tomi

We get the news as we ride out for the run that Speck has finally woken up.

Keely tells me they expect him to stay in intensive care for a full week, rehab after that because there's shit going on with his lungs.

It's like a weight has been lifted from my shoulders but also the rage in my gut has been stoked, knowing the kid who has always been like a brother to me is fighting for his life in there while the rats who've played a part are walking around in my clubhouse, drinking beer and having a good fucking time.

Makes a man ready to fucking throw down for his blood.

I tell her we'll be home in a few days, which she already knows but I need to remind her to keep herself safe and secure while we're gone. She's used to Hawk and I fussing over her, Rue too but in his own grumpy ass way. I send him one last text about keeping an eye on everyone before we leave.

We ride through town to meet up at the rendezvous point Jameson picked out. He called Axe for their weekly football and beers call, and gave him the code so we knew where to find the container. There's a lotta country dirt roads that barely get used out this way and the Unseen know every last one of them.

We pick up the cargo without a hitch.

Hellion drives the truck with Hawk out in front and Cole and I flanking it. King takes up the rear, all of us carrying enough firepower to light any fucker dumb enough to try and mess with us the fuck up.

That should all be a sign of a quick and easy night but I know there's no chance that this is going to be a routine drop.

There's something wrong in the air.

Call it intuition, call it the Callaghan curse, I can feel it sliding across my skin like oil, coating the back of my throat until I feel as though I might choke.

It's only made worse by the fact that Rue isn't here too, because I may trust every member of my blood and brotherhood who's riding here with me tonight but none of them know me like Rue. None of them can form a plan with me without so much as a word between us, barely a fucking look shared between us, and sometimes that is the difference between life and death.

I have someone to come home to now.

I have a woman who needs some fucking help. I might not know exactly how I can help her but I know deep in my fucking gut that she needs something only I can give her.

The roads are quiet as we weave through the town and it only makes the unease in my gut grow.

We get to the state lines and find Thorn waiting there to see us through safely. We've only had to use him once to run interference but it was fucking handy to have and the day that Thorn leaves the force and patches in, Coldstone PD ain't gonna know what's hit it. He raises one finger from the steering wheel in a salute and I nod my head as we pass through, the rest of the roads clear as we move.

We're on the road for a solid ten hours, only stopping for gas and food.

We sleep at a shitty motel on the side of the highway. I'm convinced I'll be walking outta here with fleas and Hellion refuses to get out of the truck. He just puts the seats back as far as they'll go and passes out half sitting up. I'm jealous of him but he pulls rank on me when I offer to swap out.

Asshole.

The first thing I do when I wake up is text Angel.

I no longer give a fuck if this makes me a cuntstruck idiot, I'm twitchy as all hell about leaving her when my skin is fucking crawling in warning.

Something is going to happen.

I just need to keep my fucking eyes open and my mind on

the fucking job.

I slept in your bed last night. I dreamt about you instead of the other stuff.

Hawk is snoring exactly half a foot away from where I'm laying on this shitty single bed so I will not be thinking about those words coming outta that magic mouth of hers, the one that can swallow every fucking inch of me right down to her throat and sucks down every drop of my cum like she needs it to fill her belly.

Fuck.

Take the night off. Stay in my bed and spend the day fucking yourself on my sheets. I want to come home to the smell of your pussy all over them.

King gets up and hits the bathroom first, grunting like he's fucking dying or something. Hawk is still snoring through everything and Diesel is out on the last shift of keeping watch.

I think for a minute she's going to ignore my demands but then my phone pings.

I can't take the night off but I hope this will do.

She's sent through a photo of her fingers buried in her pussy, her black panties pushed down to her knees and the black fabric of my hoodie pushed up her belly. Fuck, I want a video of her fingers pumping in and out of her sweet, honey lips and the soft fucking mewling sounds she makes right before she comes.

King stomps through the room, yelling out, "I'm going for a fucking coffee, get your asses moving. Hawk! Wake up, asshole, we're not at fucking Disney."

Well, if that doesn't chase the fantasy away nothing will.

Wear the black lace when I get home. Wrap that pussy of yours up like a present for me to open because it's all I fucking want.

Another full day of riding before we make it to the drop off point in Montana and I'm fucking convinced by the time we get there that something is going on back home. This feeling can't be for nothing but the roads are clear and there's nothing out of the ordinary the whole fucking way.

I mute my phone as we get into Monarch.

The drop is happening in the national park, lots of cover and remote enough for the buyers to be happy about it happening in a different spot. King picked it and only the men here tonight knew where we're heading.

We arrive first, that's all part of the plan, but the curse is screaming to me at this point. I almost wanna power my phone back on and start fucking calling, work my way through the list to know my family is fucking safe.

I'm sick to death of these fucking cunts.

When I swing off of my hog I glance over to Hawk and decide that tonight is going to fucking hell. His face gives away nothing but he only locks down that tight when his gut gives him the warnings that something is up.

It's not just my own frustration at leaving Coldstone.

It's gonna be a messy fucking night.

Hawk grunts at King and then takes off, checking the clearing out for any obvious signs of traps or something that screams Demon but there's nothing.

This whole fucking trip might be for nothing, a routine drop off that tells us fucking nothing about what's been going wrong.

"Why'd you pick this spot?" I murmur to King, keeping my eyes on Cole.

He was the best choice for this trip. We needed the extra person but with Speck down for the count and Rue being in charge we had to bring another brother. The only other person I trust is Axe but he's watching my girl while Rue is busy.

I would be truly fucking shocked if Cole was a rat.

He's another ex-military brother. A veteran who was left behind by the service when his PTSD got out of control, he and Axe joined the club at the same time and have always kept their heads down and answered any fucking call we've had for them. Cole went from barely being able to stay sober and keep a roof over his head to having a family, a house, and a fucking brotherhood thanks to the club.

He's a good man.

I'm sure of it.

Doesn't mean I want him overhearing us and knowing a goddamn thing about what's going on in our family with our fucking mission to find the rats.

"The trees are good cover. It's also the only spot we've never been to before."

I shrug and glance behind us right as we hear the sounds of approaching vehicles. "That might make it the obvious choice."

King turns around. "Good. No time I want these fucks coming after us more than when we're actually here to see it. Secondhand accounts only tell us so much, I need my blood here seeing it all. Keep 'em peeled, Tomi. Without Rue here, you're the best set of eyes we've got. The curse sings to you two better than us old assholes."

I scoff and mumble, "Yeah, and it's fucking screaming right now."

Hellion starts unhooking the trailer from the truck, prepping everything so we can hand the guns over and leave without hanging around, trying to mitigate the chances of this ending in a fucking shootout.

When the cars pull up a scowl creeps over my face.

I don't recognize them.

I make eye contact with Hawk and he starts walking over to me and King, ready to shield our Prez if that's where this shit is heading. Hellion starts cursing the second the first car stops and the doors are thrown open, but when I glance back at him, his eyes are on the cars.

It's not our buyers.

There's a pause and then Cole curses and throws himself at King, taking him down to the ground as bullets rain down on us all.

Hawk bypasses King and Cole altogether to shove me behind the truck, then he dives towards Hellion only to get pinned down behind the motorcycles.

The bullets are flying out of the first car, but it's clear when the second car joins the firing squad because the bullets come in thicker and at a different angle, one that is much more fucking likely to get King killed.

They really fucking want our Prez gone.

I can't see any of the shooters, to stick my head out is to catch some lead between my fucking eyes, but they don't seem to be fucking worried about running outta fire power.

There's no way we're getting out of this alive, not all of us.

From where he's crouched behind the motorcycles, Hawk sees it in my eyes before I make a move, shaking his head at me as I scowl but I've never been one to listen to what I should be doing.

Best way out is with a distraction.

I can make it down the side of the truck without being in the firing line but whatever I do, I'm doing it on my own. It's a fucking weird feeling, I'm never in these situations without one of my cousins backing me up. Maybe if Rue were here this would go down smoother but there's no fucking time to be having regrets.

I stay low, creeping my way forward and keeping my feet as silent on the ground as the dead leaves and twigs will let me. None of the bullets are flying at this end of the truck, they're all focussed on where Cole is using his own body as a shield for King, and I have one chance at getting some headshots in.

Take some fuckers out and draw their fire this way.

Deep breaths, make it count, clear your fucking mind of all of the bullshit and just take these fuckers out.

There are three guys in the second car.

Grimm Graves himself is in the first one.

I can't get him but I take out two of the three in the second car before all hell breaks loose.

A fucking third car rides up and I blow out its front tires, unfortunately that means all four of the guys in it see me and draw their guns.

Time to get outta Dodge.

The forest is dense on either side of the clearing and I'm near the downward slope of the fucking mountain we're on so I make a dive into the tree line, staying low and tumbling down the fucking slope. I feel the burning pain of a bullet grazing my arm but that doesn't stop me from rolling my way through the shrubs.

If I hit a tree I'll probably snap my fucking back so I stick my legs out to try to slow myself down. The slope is gradual enough that I manage to slow my descent and come to a halt, the sound of gunfire finally petering out.

Fuck, I hope that doesn't mean they've taken the others out.

Hawk's face as he shoved me behind the fucking truck

flashes into my head. He came for me before his Prez, his instincts as a father kicking well the fuck in apparently.

If he's dead I'm gutting every last Demon on this fucking Earth.

I mean, if any of them are dead and I make it outta here that's the fucking plan but, fuck, there'll be an extra fiery need if they've killed my pops.

I walk slowly down the rest of the slope until I reach the small creek at the bottom where the trees thin out a little. Until I'm sure the Demons have fucked off I gotta stay the hell here.

I check my phone but the screen is busted and I can barely use it. I could take a call but not make one, I can't risk that shit right now.

I've stopped for about a half-second when the snap of a twig tells me I'm not alone but I don't have any time to react.

The cold barrel of a gun presses against the base of my skull.

"We'll take him in, Cliff. Can't get a dead man to give us what we need."

The beast of a man grunts and lowers the gun, the sound of boots crunching on the dead leaves on the ground telling me there's movement somewhere close by. I try to scan the woods without moving my head too much but there's nowhere I can get cover.

I guess the curse was singing about my death.

Fuck, I hope Rue keeps Angel safe.

I hope Trink figures out her shit with that dumbass she's chasing. I hope Speck lives a long and happy life. I hope Hawk, King, and Hellion find and kill all of the fucking rats.

I hope this doesn't fucking kill my mom.

There's a lotta things a man about to die hopes for and every last one of them comes back down to my family so I know I've lived my life right.

My only regret is Angel and not fixing her shit a little faster.

I just gotta believe Rue and Speck will sort that shit out for me, same way I'd watch over Poe until my last fucking breath for my cousin if the roles were reversed.

Pop.

The sound is soft enough that with the shouting and gunfire around us I almost miss it but the crash of a man going down is unmistakable.

I assume Hawk or Hellion have found me.

I'm wrong.

I turn around to see 'Cliff' on the ground with a neat little bullet hole between his eyes. I'm sure the exit wound on the back of his head isn't that neat but it's too fucking dark to see much.

I look up to find a Demon twisting a silencer off of his gun, before throwing it at me.I catch it on reflex. It's still warm to the touch even through my gloves.

His cut has the Graves tag on it but it's the eyes that give him away.

Colt Graves, Poe's half-brother and the fucking heir to the Chaos Demons.

I look down again at the Enforcer of the Chaos Demons but he's still fucking dead at my feet, killed by one of his own men.

I glance back up at Colt like a fucking idiot but he's too busy looking around for his own men to give a shit about me gaping at him like a fucking dumbass.

The sounds of guys getting closer filters through the woods and finally Colt looks up at me.

He lifts a finger to his lips to tell me to keep quiet and then jerks his head at me for me to run.

What the fuck is happening here?

When I don't move he scowls at me, flinging his arm out in the direction of the river and then turning on his heel to stalk back up the hill.

"He's shooting from the east! That way, asshole, go!" he shouts and the footsteps start to fade out.

He's just led them away from finding me.

What the fuck is going on here?

I move slowly away from the creek and down towards where the road starts, keeping my ears peeled and trying not to fucking bleed everywhere.

I walk for at least an hour, feeling fucking useless except that my job here is to stay breathing and get my ass back up to the truck without getting my ass lit up. I'm no help fucking dead and now that I've met Colt Graves…

I need to speak to Rue about him.

Shit isn't fucking right in the Graves house and how that

affects Poe, I don't know, but he needs to know about it.

I also need to get home to Angel and Trink and Keely. I need to keep watch over Speck until the asshole is up and walking again. I need to find out what the fuck is going on with Law and Lyn. I need to fucking finish the job of burning the rats out.

I guess I have a lot to live for these days.

When I get to the road, I turn around and start my way back up to the clearing, keeping to the trees and trying not to get too fucking frustrated at how slow this shit is.

When I finally make it up there I find Cole being patched up by King, Hellion cussing out the entire fucking universe, and Hawk looking fucking fried until he gets an eyeful of me.

"Thank the fucking lord, kid, your mother woulda skinned me alive."

I scoff at him and clap him on the shoulder. "Good to know you care, old man. How the fuck did you lot get outta it alive?"

Hawk huffs and shrugs. "Cole went full fucking berserker and went after two of 'em with nothing but his fucking knife. I dragged King and Hellion into the woods after you but when we found the dead Demon we knew you were at least fighting back. Good shot, kid. Cliff was a fucking good kill."

I don't even think about it, I just lie. "It was a lucky shot. So Cole took them on and what, killed them all himself? You guys just went on a fucking stroll through the woods?"

Hawk's eyes narrow at me but at least he stops looking at me like I'm some fucking hero.

I can't tell them I didn't kill Cliff without telling them who did.

I'm covering for Rue so fucking hard right now, the asshole owes me.

Little does he fucking know it.

Chapter Twenty Seven

Angel

Rue escorts me into The Boulevard each night and stays with me there.

He's having to split his time between the hospital and the strip club and I can see just how fucking stressed out it's making him. He's always polite and courteous, even in his own gruff way, but as the days go on he's looking grumpier and grumpier.

Tomi messages me every day, right as he wakes up and when they stop to pass out. I don't know where they're going or what exactly it is that they're doing but I know something hasn't gone great when the general mood of the texts and the bikers at The Boulevard goes from tense to fucking malevolent.

I'm also not a dumbass.

I keep my mouth shut, follow all the rules, and work my ass off.

I spend way too much money on food now Rue is keeping tabs on my eating habits but when I wake up on the last night before Tomi comes home I finally take a minute to count every last dollar bill of my money.

I did it.

I hit the magic number I worked out, the amount I need to buy a house and pay for college with a healthy buffer.

I don't have to dance tonight if I don't want to.

There's the small problem of how the fuck to get the money into a bank so I can buy a house but, fuck, nothing can kill my high.

Nothing.

I'll be home in the morning, Angel. Don't forget to wrap that pussy up like a present for me.

Shivers run down my spine.

It almost freaking killed me, but I stopped in at the sex shop on the way into The Boulevard the night before. Rue had to tag along and it was easy enough to tell him I needed new stockings but really I had a plan.

I don't want to wear my dancing lingerie for Tomi.

I want to wear pieces that are only for him… things that only he gets to see on me. The minute I quit my job I'm throwing the rest out and being done with it but I want to have nice shit for him. God, every time I shut my eyes I can see the fire in his eyes the one and only time he came and sat to watch me dance on stage.

He'd done it to prove a point to that other biker that threatened me but I know for sure he likes what I can do on the pole. He sat there drinking his whiskey and watched me without once trying to hide how hard I was making him.

I miss the weight of his cock on my tongue and the tight grip of his fist in my hair when he shoves me further down the fat length of him.

Oh God.

I've learned how to touch myself since he's been gone. I'm glad he's not actually able to see me beyond the photos he asks for because I'm so embarrassed and ashamed of doing it but the messages he sends me light a fire in my blood.

Show me how wet I've made you.

Spread your lips for me, a man needs to see what he owns.

Three fingers, Angel, your pussy misses my cock so bad you're weeping all over my sheets.

So I consider spending the day in bed here and waiting up for him. I could work on my college shit all night and then grab a nap before he gets home… it would be perfect, except then Poe messages me.

Speck's trying to sign himself outta the hospital. Rue's pissed and he's taking me and the twins to The Boulevard to keep us all locked down while he goes to fight the fucker with Keely and Trink. You're working right? I'm bringing my homework, I need your help.

A night with Poe sounds like more fun than being locked

up and I can make the dances my last ones. A little extra cash never hurt anyone.

By the time Rue knocks on the door I'm dressed and ready to go and he's… looking fucking livid.

"Oh. Uh… are you… okay?"

He scowls at me as he grabs my bag to carry and jerks his head at me to follow him. "I'm fine, I just need my dumbass fucking cousins to stop tryna fucking die. Are we stopping for food? I need to grab Poe on the way so follow me out that way."

I shake my head and stumble to keep up with him. Law and Lyn are both waiting next to my truck, Law grins and says, "Is it cool if we ride over with you? Rue's gonna be a dick if he has to take his truck over."

I nod and try not to wince at the idea of the three of us squishing into the bench seat because they're not exactly small guys. Rue sees my reaction anyway and snaps at him, "Keep your hands to yourself, I'll cut 'em the fuck off even if Keely would come after me for it."

Lyn scoffs and shoves his phone into his pants. "Tomi already got to her first, you might wanna take that shit up with him."

I blush and get into my truck before I can hear the response to that but Rue smacks him in the back of the head as he walks around to the passenger side to stash my bag for me.

I try not to think about how much money is actually in it.

"Poe's and then The Boulevard. If Lyn keeps running his mouth, I'll beat the little fucker until he learns. Law, get in the middle and don't fucking touch her."

I'm sure the drive is hell for the twins but Law doesn't once touch me. He has to damn near sit in Lyn's lap to do so but he's laughing and joking the whole time about it.

I try not to feel bad about it.

Poe looks fucking thrilled to be coming with us to The Boulevard, dancing around Rue and laughing like pure sunshine. He doesn't smile at her but some of the shadows in his face clear a little and when he gets a helmet out of the pack on his hog for her it has flowers on it.

My heart clenches a little at the sight of it.

Rue walks us in and talks to Axe about his plans for

the night. Poe sets up all of her homework on Tomi's desk, ignoring the state of it because there's still paperwork everywhere, and Law ducks into the bar to grab beers before the place opens. Rue scowls at him but the smiling twin just talks his way out of trouble.

I'm dancing up first so Rue and Axe keep their debrief in the hallway where they can keep an eye on the office and the locker room. I get dressed into a corset and a thong, keeping one of Tomi's hoodies zipped over myself so I'm not walking around in front of his family and friends bare.

I'm so fucking glad this is my last night.

I think I'm going to quit tomorrow morning to Tomi so I don't ever have to speak to Diamond again. Fuck, it'd be amazing to just… never show up again and never tell the bitch but this place is Tomi's and Rue's responsibility so I can't get away with that shit.

But it would be fucking great.

I get my bag locked up and walk over to where the guys are.

Rue gives me a nod. "I'll be back around three to take you guys home. Are you gonna drink with them?"

I shake my head. "I don't want to leave my truck here and… I'd rather not drink without… Tomi around."

I don't want to admit that but I don't want to drink with guys around, even if they are family. I could drink with Poe but not the twins.

Lyn hates me too much.

Okay, maybe it's not hate exactly but he definitely doesn't trust me and that makes me fucking nervous.

"Good, I need one of you keeping your fucking head. Stay with Axe and call me if anything happens. Nod your head, Angel, I need to know you're gonna stick to the rules tonight. Too much fucking rogue shit going on this week."

Axe shares a look with him and my stomach drops. "Is everything… okay?"

He shrugs. "Speck's a dickhead and there's not much I can do about keeping his ass in a hospital bed without beating him and Keely will slit my throat if I so much as slap him right now."

I nod, but the unease in my stomach doesn't go anywhere.

"I'm not going anywhere. I'll keep an eye on Poe, I've got you on speed dial… I'll stick to the rules."

Rue nods and a smirk starts up. "I don't know what Tomi's problem is, you've been nothing but good since his bitch-ass left town."

I blush and duck my head when Axe cracks up laughing. "Yeah, well… maybe I just needed a minute. A girl can't just fall into line, y'know?"

Rue chuckles and heads out, ducking his head into the office to growl one last threat at the three high schoolers already getting rowdy in there.

Oh, to be young and loved enough to live that free.

Axe strips off his cut and leaves it in the office with them before locking the door on them. I jam my feet into the hellish pair of heels I'll be glad to burn the second this night is over and he walks me out to the back of the stage.

"Diamond only put you on this dance tonight, she sure does have her panties in a twist over you," Axe mumbles and I shrug.

"Can you keep a secret, Axe? You seem like the type of man who can."

He raises an eyebrow at me right as the doors open, the sounds muted but there's clearly a big crowd streaming in. "Is this the type of secret that will get me dead when Tomi gets home because you're a nice enough girl, but no thanks."

I chuckle and try to fight the giddy feeling in my stomach at saying it out loud. "Nah. Tomi is happy about this secret, he just doesn't know about it yet. If Diamond only has me up here once tonight then… this is my last dance. I'm done here, college is paid for."

Axe grins at me, his eyes only dropping away from me when I unzip the hoodie. "Well, look at you! Doing that hustle to pay your own shit, girlie, Tomi's gonna nut himself in joy over that news. Plus the rest of us might actually fucking live to tell this tale. He's been a fucking nightmare about you, I hope you know that."

Oh God.

I mean, I already know he has been. Law showed me the messages and Rue made it clear but… I guess all of the bikers know about it.

It's so fucking embarrassing.

"Yup. This is it and then I'm done so... wish me luck, I guess?"

Axe grins and waves me off, taking the hoodie from me and staying backstage as I go out there and finish my career as a fucking stripper. It's hard to keep the smile off of my face, men want sultry and seductive not a grinning psycho, but I work that pole like my life depends on it one last time.

When the song ends I grab my cash and walk out the back, slipping the heels back off and tossing them in the trash. Axe laughs at me and hands over the hoodie again.

I'm laughing and trying to stuff the cash into the pockets when the sound of gunfire breaks, so loud it completely drowns out the music playing over the speakers.

Axe grabs my arm and drags me down the hall, intent on getting me into the office and I thank my lucky fucking stars I've got the heels off already.

When we get to the open doorway to the bar we find the entire front of the building flooded with bikers, all of them armed and screaming at the girls and patrons, fights breaking out everywhere, some bodies already bleeding on the ground.

"Angel, get your ass into the office. Go, right now before they see you and stay there until I come get you," Axe says, his gun already in his hand.

I nod and start to move but then the back door bursts open and we're fucking trapped.

Axe instantly shifts to stand in front of me.

Just blocks me completely, no way any of the guys can see me let alone shoot me and I'm so fucking terrified that I could burst into grateful tears right now. He moves to discreetly hand me the gun, pressing it into my belly until I grab it.

My dad taught me to shoot but it's been nearly ten years since I last held a gun.

The lights cut on and there are bikers everywhere. All of them have cuts on, the Chaos Demons scrawled across their shoulders proudly.

My stomach drops.

There's shouting and gunshots and I try not to panic but when I see Law and Lyn both get shoved into the bar my heart starts to race. There's a small gap in the crowd and I can just make them out.

Poe is jammed in between them with her head down.

She's not shaking, no crying or screaming like the other girls are all doing, she's just keeping her face covered.

Our conversation comes back to me.

Her dad is the Prez of this club.

Christ.

Axe pushes me back into the wall when more of the guys come around.

They start pulling the Unseen around, getting the men who are wearing their cuts into the middle of the bar and securing them. Every last one of them fights back but they're outnumbered, five-to-one.

Axe is dressed in black, his cut still hanging in the office by some stroke of luck. He looks like a security guy, some hired muscle who will just take their shit without needing to bleed for the patch.

"Find the girl."

My eyes snap across the room and meet Law's.

It's Poe.

They're here for her.

My eyes drop back down but Poe already has her phone out, the screen lit up from where I can see it so she's got Rue on the line already. We just need to stay alive and safe until he gets here.

Then the Demons start hurting the girls.

I can't stand listening to it and neither can Poe, I see her hands begin to shake and I know exactly what's going through her head.

They're going through the girls to find her.

They're being hurt for her.

I know it's not her fault, I know it, but I also know how heavy that shit will weigh on her because my skin is crawling at the sounds of the other women being thrown around.

When the group of guys comes to grab Axe he throws a few good punches but the club is now teeming with Demons and there's no real chance of getting the hell out of here without people dying.

Or a sacrifice.

I figure that out at the same time as Poe does but when she

opens her mouth I step forward, discreetly stashing the gun on the bar and ignoring Axe's scowl at me from where he's bleeding on his knees.

My voice shakes but they hear me clear enough. "I'm Posey Graves. You're here for me right? I'll go with you, just stop hurting the girls."

I can't choke the word please out of my mouth.

Poe makes a squeaking noise and I glance back to find Lyn's hand wrapped around her mouth, stopping her from arguing with me or saying a goddamn word.

Good.

Rue will be here any freaking minute for her and at least I'll die knowing my death will keep her safe.

It's more than I thought I'd die with.

I wish so fucking badly that I had the chance to put pants on before the Demons got to The Boulevard, because the feel of their hands on me has bile creeping up the back of my throat.

The comments that they make about me make me choke on it.

"I'm fucking her first."

The guy holding my arm and dragging me wrenches me closer to his body. "No fucking way. Fastest way onto the Council is bagging this bitch so she's mine! It'll be fucking weird, imagine sticking your dick in some bitch that looks like Grimm."

The guy walking out in the front laughs. "She doesn't though, thank fuck. If she's dancing in the club she's gotta have a decent rack under the Unseen rags."

The night is cool and quiet outside and I freaking pray that Rue will arrive now and shoot these assholes in the fucking head.

He doesn't.

They walk me out to the farthest end of the parking lot and with none of the other businesses even open the entire block is quiet. No one would even be able to tell that there's an MC war happening in this sleepy little town tonight.

It all turns to shit when we get to the car waiting there.

The guy holding my arms spins me around and looks me

over, unzipping the hoodie and grunting at me.

"Well, fuck! I wasn't expecting much from the little lost Graves girl but that's a fucking great rack! I'm sure you bring the green in for the Unseen, do you fuck them all too? You'll have to show me how good you service your men."

Instinct kicks in and there's no fucking way I'm just going to just lie down and take it. No fucking way am I being raped here or back at some other location.

If I'm here to die then they can just fucking kill me.

My hand shoots out to punch him in the nose and it breaks just as well as Mav's had. When blood comes pouring out of his face he flings me around by my arm until my body slams into the car, my head snapping back and colliding with the glass. I feel just a little dazed when he kicks my legs out from under me, sending me down to the gravel where he can kick the shit out of me.

He really does enjoy kicking me.

He just doesn't do it long enough to take me out.

"Fucking whore, tie her the fuck up! Get her in the fucking trunk, if she's not going to play nice she can fucking rot in there. It's a long drive to Texas, little Graves!"

One of the other guys scoops me up and drops my body into the trunk like I weigh nothing. I feel my ribs crunch, knocking the wind out of me, and I can't even fight back when they tie my arms behind my back, slipping a blindfold over my eyes as well.

When they slam the hatch back down the air in the trunk goes hot and heavy, but maybe that's just my panic.

I try to remember what the hell I'm supposed to do in this kinda situation but it's been too fucking long since my dad taught me. All I remember is to kick out the tail lights. It's loud as fuck but the car doesn't stop. They wouldn't be able to hear a fucking thing over that terrible freaking music in the front anyway.

Can't account for taste.

We drive for a while. It's hard to get a good feel of time passing but I'd guess about an hour or so. They drive recklessly and I find myself being thrown around in the trunk so I barely notice when the brakes are slammed and the car comes to a screaming halt.

The music suddenly shuts off and I hear muffled talking from within the car, sounding a little like an argument.

Then the screaming starts.

Blood curdling, bone chilling screaming from fully grown men.

Even being in the trunk it sounds like a fucking horror movie, the kind of screams that come from the worst possible deaths. If there were literally anything in my bladder, I'd wet myself in terror but instead I lie there and tremble like a freaking leaf.

Is it Rue?

Hell, did Tomi come home to find me gone and go into some kind of fucking rage-fueled massacre?

When the screaming finally stops the silence is even worse. If it's not the Unseen here to rescue me then that means I might be the next victim of… whatever the hell is happening here.

The trunk pops open and a squeal rips out of my throat that I can't hold in.

I don't recognize the voice at all when the man speaks. "I found her… yeah, I know the one… she's beat up but breathing, bring your medic."

Okay.

Okay, that sounds positive I guess?

Then I'm lifted up, the arms around me like stone, and even if the voice didn't tip me off I know for sure that I don't know this guy because this just feels… wrong.

I'm in danger.

Even if this guy was sent by the MC there's something not fucking right about this situation and I'm really fucking scared.

The man places me into a car and cuts the ties off of my wrists but he doesn't take the blindfold off. I heard him talking to someone on the phone, I know he's here to rescue me so why the hell hasn't he taken it off?

"If I take it off you, I'll have to kill you."

Oh God.

Maybe the Unseen hadn't sent him.

My hands shake and I clasp them in my lap, not at all trying to hide how fucking terrified I am.

The drive is smooth and the engine is a loud roar. It's a

muscle car for sure but obviously well maintained and he drives it like it's on rails.

I sit there in silence and try not to weep, no idea how much time has passed before he speaks again.

"Why did you tell them to take you instead?"

I swallow and try to calm down a little, just enough so I can speak without stuttering and crying. "Posey is my friend… my only friend. She's a good person, she's kind and caring and she would always do anything to protect her friends but… she's also pure. She's innocent. Whatever those men were planning on doing to her… I couldn't let them hurt her like that."

The car is silent and I think that I've fucked up somehow.

Finally, he speaks again. "So you were going to die for her? Just let them gang rape you to death in her place?"

I gag on the bile in my throat, my heart racing and my entire body shaking. I manage to choke out, "Better me than her. I'm already fucking broken."

He doesn't answer that at all and the silence takes over the car again. I'm sure I've said something wrong, sure that I've fucked up and now I'm fucking dead.

At least he hasn't seemed interested in raping me like the last guys.

At least I'll die with Tomi being the last man to touch me.

There's something comforting in that.

It's Tomi and definitely not Paul.

The car pulls over and I take a deep breath. Either this is the end of the road or… it's the end of my life. Better to accept that death with some sort of dignity.

The blindfold is removed and I squeeze my eyes shut a little tighter. Death it is then.

My teeth start to chatter, the shaking taking over my entire body. "Can you please just make it quick? Does my sacrifice for Poe buy me that at least?"

His voice is still lifeless, cold and blunt. "Posey is my youngest sister. I've killed a lot of people to keep her safe and I'll kill you without even thinking about it if you endanger her life by telling people about me."

I keep my eyes shut. "I wouldn't ever do anything like that. I'm not ever going to betray her."

He's silent, no sounds except the flicking of a lighter and

then I smell the scent of his cigarette. "I wouldn't have taken the blindfold off if I thought you'd talk about me. Fuck, I would have just slit your throat with it still on if I wanted you dead. Open your eyes, Jazmin."

Fuck.

He knows my real name? I open my eyes and look over to find the Devil staring back at me.

The gas station attendant stares at the Devil like he's actually going to shit himself. The tattoos make it fairly obvious for anyone ever adjacent to the criminal world to know who he is. I remember the story of what he did to that MC in Indiana. My dad would talk about it all the time, talk about exactly what it is that could kill that many men and... shred them like that.

The going theory is a wood chipper.

I try not to think about it. My hands already have a tremble in them that won't freaking quit and I don't need a full blown case of the hysterics.

What if I piss him off and he decides to just kill me to get it to stop?

Christ.

Stop thinking about it, Angel, hell!

He walks back over to the car and it really is uncanny, the resemblance between him and Poe. His eyes are the exact same shade and shape. The dark eyelashes and his brow... God, it's freaking terrifying.

I will never look at that sunshine girl the same again.

He opens the car door and slides in, handing me a burrito and a bottle of water. "They'll be here soon."

I nod and then stupidly ask, "Sorry, who?"

He looks out over the empty fields. "My sister. She's on her way to come take you home. I can't drive into Coldstone... I'm too recognizable."

I nod and carefully bite into my food, extremely conscious of not making a mess in his pristine car. It's like a freaking show car, immaculate. I doubt he eats in it.

He speaks without looking at me. "Poe eats in here all the time. She got cheese on the seats last summer."

Oh.

Okay.

I still keep a careful watch on my crumbs and when I finish I open the car door to brush the crumbs off, right as another car pulls in.

It's a freaking Ferrari.

Okay, I know nothing about cars but I know a Ferrari when I see one and I'm sure Poe would pee herself in excitement over this car if she saw it with her own two eyes.

Then the passenger side door opens and I realize she's definitely seen it before.

Her sister gets out of the car.

Those exact same eyes, holy fucking shit.

Along with a hot blond guy and a hot dark-haired guy. Oh, and Blaise motherfucking Morrison.

"Holy fucking shit," I croak and the Devil tilts his head.

"I don't see the appeal but his music isn't my style."

Right.

Of course I'm sitting here discussing music preference with the Devil himself. Of course, because that's not completely fucking insane.

He gets out and stares over at the guys standing by the other car, silent and completely terrifying.

Poe's sister walks over to me to crouch down and check the battered state my body is in. "Jesus, they got in some good swings."

I shrug. "It's not the worst I've gotten."

Her lips purse and she nods. "You'll live. Arbour can take a look, make sure there's nothing that needs more attention."

She straightens up and speaks to the Devil over the roof of the car, "Thanks for grabbing her. We would've been too late."

"I'm always happy to gut some Demons. You know that."

She shrugs. "Still, I know you were on a job and it was my turn to keep an eye out. I'm tempted to move Poe a little closer to the Bay."

He moves around the car towards her and the guys she's with all shift like they're uncomfortable.

"Coldstone is where she wants to be. I've tried to move her but she's not interested, I warned you the biker would get in the way."

Oh shit.

Oh holy shit, that's Rue they're talking about for sure and I feel like I'm going to fucking puke at the dead tone in the Devil's voice. He could just... walk into Coldstone and kill the biker for fun. For daring to catch his sister's eye.

He could come kill Tomi too.

Speck.

Keely, Trink, Hawk, fuck, any of the Callaghans, he could just drive his ass into Coldstone and take out the entire fucking MC to get his sister back if he wanted.

"Hey... hey, Angel, breathe. Breathe, ignore Nate being grumpy. He's just twitchy about Poe being so far away from us while the Demons get fucking worse. No one is dying, kid. We've got a close eye on Coldstone."

My mind slowly comes back online to find my hands clutching at Poe's sister's arms like a crazed fucking lunatic. "Oh God. I'm sorry."

She shrugs. "It's fine. My name is Lips, by the way. Grumpy over there is Nate, the guys are Ash, Harley, and Blaise."

The Devil's name is Nate.

He doesn't look like a Nate, he looks like a fucking Lucifer.

Morningstar suits him perfectly.

The blond guy stalks over and gently moves Lips out of the way. His eyes are assessing as he looks me over. "Can you move to the Ferrari or do you need help? Morningstar is late for a job and we should let him get out of here."

I nod and get up slowly, my legs shaking a little but not so bad I can't walk. The guy stays close enough to catch me but doesn't try to touch me so that gets him some brownie points.

I feel like I shouldn't be rude and thank the Devil but talking to him is fucking terrifying and I don't want to piss him off.

So I keep my mouth shut.

I guess I can thank him through Poe later and pray I never have to stand in his presence again.

"She already knows the score. She speaks about us, I carve her up until there's nothing fucking left."

I trip over my own feet and the guy has to catch me.

"Nate, for fuck's sake, she's Poe's friend! If she's willing to sacrifice herself for her then I'm sure she'll keep her mouth shut," Lips says, scolding him which clearly makes her the fucking bravest woman to ever walk this Earth.

"I don't believe in hoping for shit. I mean what I say, better she knows to keep her mouth shut. Call me when you're home, there's too many Demons on the fucking road these days."

The guy holding my arm snaps, "Ash, get the fucking engine going on this thing. I want to get the hell out of this fucking town and get some miles between us and that fucking psycho."

Right.

So Blondie is Harley, the dark-haired one is Ash, and I'm very aware of which one Blaise Morrison is.

I have a bag back at The Boulevard full of shirts with his face on it.

Harley gets me sitting on the front seat to poke and prod at my cheek, looking for breaks I guess. I wince but the way he's handling me is so clinical that I don't have the chance to freak out.

When he gets out a stethoscope and starts listening to me breathe he explains where he's going to touch me each time, waiting for me to nod each time before moving.

I feel really safe now.

Which, after the Devil is a fucking miracle.

He gets out a penlight and says, "Follow the light for me."

I do what he says and when he finally clicks the penlight again he says, "You'll live. You need painkillers and sleep but that's about it."

I nod and he helps me swing my legs around to sit in the passenger seat properly. Two minutes later we're on the road, Ash driving and the other three squished into the backseat.

"The— uh, I mean… Nate has already told me not to tell anyone about him. My lips are definitely sealed."

Ash scoffs as he changes gears and gets us back on the highway to Coldstone.

I can't wait.

"Ash will drop us off somewhere before he takes you back to the clubhouse. It's safer that way."

Uh.

What?

Ash glances at my face and smirks at me. "I'm the least recognizable person in the car."

I glance back over my shoulder and Lips shrugs. "Blaise is obvious but everyone knows the lost O'Cronin heir belongs to me and I've been pretty fucking careful about making sure no one ever knows Poe and I are related. We're never in public together, I avoid the Coldstone charter when they show up in the Bay… it's hard work but it keeps her safe."

I still have no fucking clue what they're all talking about and Harley finally huffs and says, "Lips is the Wolf of Mounts Bay, the fabled fucking assassin and one of the founding members of the Family. You might not recognize her but there's a few members of the MC that would put shit together and we know all about their rat problem."

Oh God.

Holy fucking shit.

My stomach bottoms out. "So you're the Wolf of Mounts Bay. Your brother is the Devil, and Posey Graves is your sister. The smiling, cheerful, rainbow of a girl I'm friends with is the single most dangerous person in Coldstone, not because of who she is but because of whose blood she shares?"

Blaise cackles and Lips shrugs with a grin. "I dunno. I've taught her a lot about how to kill people. Nate also showed her how to skin a man alive last summer so she's not exactly helpless."

Holy Jesus.

Okay, Rue has definitely underestimated her. So has his entire family, fuck. I'm vaguely scared of her now.

Actually, you know what?

Fuck that.

I'm fucking terrified of her.

Lips scoffs and leans back in the seat. "Just go to sleep, Angel. We'll get you home safe. That's what family does."

Chapter Twenty Eight

Tomi

We ride back to Coldstone as fast as we can fucking manage.

We still have to stop over in a roadside hotel for a night but it's only really a five-hour stop. I can't fucking shake the need to get home. I've kept in touch with Angel the entire time we've been away and she might be fine but that doesn't stop the need to get home to her from clawing at my gut.

Rue gives me a running commentary of her days and she keeps to every last one of my rules while we're gone.

Fuck.

Maybe she is fucking perfect for me. At the very least she's trying and if that doesn't make me wanna step the fuck up, nothing will.

We get back to the clubhouse just before dawn, the parking lot overflowing with hogs and all fucking types of rigs.

Rue's bike is there.

Angel's truck is too, thank fuck, and my plan is to bypass the entire party and just fucking eat her the hell up for the night. Fuck her so long and hard that she can feel me for days and know that she's marked as mine. My mouth waters a little at the thought of her in those tiny scraps of black lace she's been teasing me with.

Fucking perfection.

The high of thinking about being in her lasts for as long as it takes me to swing off of my hog, the truck Hellion is parking catching and keeping my attention.

The fucking rats lost us another shipment and almost our

fucking lives.

I could set fire to this fucking building with the heat of the rage in my blood.

"Get that look off of your fucking face before it gets you and the rest of this club dead. We can't do a fucking thing until we know who the rat is," Hawk says, his voice pitched low so no one hears us.

I jerk my head in a half-nod and then I say the words that have been choking me for weeks. "They're further up than we thought. That mess we were just in proves it."

He grunts under his breath, just as fucking pissed off about it as I am especially since we can't just fucking deal with it. I hate the mind games, the fucking lies and deception, and knowing that your brothers are supposed to have your back and instead they're twisting a knife there instead?

Fucking guts me.

King shoots us both a look and jerks his head to get us all moving, get us back into the clubhouse that should be our solace and yet we'll all be walking on fucking eggshells, watching our mouths and doing everything we can to not say something that might get our family and brothers killed.

The bar is full of Unseen from both Coldstone and the Shreveport charter but way too quiet. Damn near fucking silence in the room. My blood turns to ice in my veins.

What the fuck has happened now?

Rue comes walking up, thank fuck, and I'm relieved to see that he's fine until I get an eyeful of his face.

Angel.

"What the fuck happened?"

He holds out a hand like he's trying to approach a fucking bear and not get his face ripped the hell off. "Demons came into town… they took her, been gone almost three hours."

"Three hours? Three fucking hours?! And what exactly have you fucking assholes been doing while she's been gone?"

Rue doesn't flinch but half the men around him start shifting on their feet, uneasy with being so close to my rage.

Good.

I'm about to start fucking shooting.

"They took over The Boulevard, more than fucking forty of them at once. I didn't even know she was gone until we got it back. Twenty-five of 'em made it out alive, ten are dead, and five are trussed up in the back waiting to get their teeth ripped out for information. Brother, we will get her back. I fucking swear to you, I won't sleep until she's back here."

Three motherfucking hours.

She might be dead already.

I can't think, my mind is a whirling fucking mess of rage and sorrow and, fuck it, panic.

She might be fucking dead.

King starts snarling out orders at the guys around me, mobilizing them and getting together an army to get out there and fucking find my girl.

Poe is over by the bar, hollering at Rue and trying to get his attention but there's no fucking time to fuss after her mood. I need to find my girl. I'm already armed to the teeth and fuck protocol, I'm going to fucking Texas.

I can't fucking lose her before she's even mine.

Lights hit the side of the clubhouse as a car pulls into the parking lot.

"Stop fucking freaking out, I told you I had it covered," Poe calls out but I barely register her words. What sort of drug dealer has just showed up here in a fucking Ferrari?

She shoves me out of the way to get to the door and snaps, "It's my sister's boyfriend. If any of you fucking assholes would listen to me, you'd know he has Angel. She's fucking safe."

That gets me moving, hightailing it the fuck out of the club and ignoring the fucking ruckus starting up behind me at Poe's words but the kid is practically flying down the stairs.

The car pulls up outside the front steps and Poe rips the door open before the engine cuts out, pulling Angel into her arms and sobbing all over her. I've never seen the kid cry like that before, the fear in her over her friend is fucking jarring.

Angel's beat the hell up.

Fuck, her lip is busted and her cheek is bruised all over, fingerprints down her throat and I'm going to lose my fucking mind.

A snarl tears out of my throat in time for the driver door to open and a guy to get out. He's tall, dark haired, and clean cut. When he steps around the car in time to catch Poe as she throws herself at him I catch sight of the holsters and the guns he's got tucked under that tailored jacket of his.

Definitely a drug dealer.

Rue steps up beside me, his eyes fucking full to the brim with loathing as the guy tucks Poe into his arms a little more securely, murmuring quietly to her so we can't hear a fucking thing. Angel struggles to get to her feet, wincing as she moves and I snap outta the fucking trance this whole mess has put me in. I ignore the asshole holding Poe and glaring at me, fuck him, and pull her into my body. She stiffens a little but it's not one of her flinches so I'll call it a goddamn win.

I'm so fucked.

"You been checked out yet? I'll call Mom to come have a look at you."

She shakes her head and clears her throat, pulling away from me a little goddammit. "I'm okay. I've already been looked at by a medic."

"Who the fuck is that?" Rue snarls and Angel jolts in my arms.

I don't like that reaction.

I'm leaving Rue the fuck out here to deal with that shit by himself. I don't know who the fuck Poe's sister is, who the fuck that drug dealer is either, but all I can smell on Angel is the blood that's trickling out of her lip and her legs are still fucking bare because she was obviously taken between dances.

I want my girl fucking resting and I don't give a fuck about this medic, I need to hear it from Keely that she's okay.

"Angel."

I turn around with her to look at the guy. The way he fucking dismisses me has my teeth clenching violently, I want to beat his stupid face in. The tone he uses with her has me seeing fucking red.

"You know where to find us if you need help."

Ex-fucking-cuse me?

"Aw hell," Poe says, and moves in front of the guy.

I shoot Rue a look that could strip paint. "Fucking deal with him before I do because I'll start a fucking war, brother."

I get an arm around Angel before she can argue with me, leading her up to the clubhouse and trying my best not to rush her and risk hurting her more. There isn't a patch of skin on her that isn't fucking bruised and now, now I'm fucking pissed. Enraged. Rage pumping through my blood until I'm vibrating with the need to bleed those gutless fucks out.

"I'm fine," she whispers, and I shake my head at her.

"Clearly you're fucking not."

A hushed silence falls over the bar as we walk through, only the sound of Monroe's giggling breaking it and my control isn't even fucking visible from where I'm at.

"I will rip your throat out with my bare hands, Monroe. Don't fucking push me."

No one tries to stop us or speak to us which, really, is for the best.

I get Angel into my room and lock the door behind us. She's trembling a little and I have to stop myself from crushing her against my chest to get her to quit. I don't know what's hurting her under the torn up hoodie.

"Can… is it okay if I have a shower? I'm… there's dirt all over my legs."

Deep breath. She's scared and she always reverts back to meek and fucking hesitant when she's scared but I hate her asking me like that. It makes me feel like she thinks I'm going to stop her from taking what she needs.

"I'm going to call Keely to come have a look at you as well but we'll get you cleaned up first. Have you taken anything for the pain yet?"

She nods and I walk her into the bathroom, shocked at how clean it is in here but then I realize she's been living here while I was gone.

I like that feeling way too much for this to be nothing but infatuation, she's mine and I'll do whatever it takes to fucking keep her.

I now fully understand why both my uncles tried locking the women who 'struck them down with a baby because that sounds like a fucking plan.

"You need help in there?"

She shakes her head and just stands there, clutching at the towel like it's gonna fix shit. "I just… need a minute."

Right.

She needs space and even if it fucking kills me I'll give it to her. I step out of the bathroom and wait there until I hear the water start running. Then I dump my shit onto my desk because I don't need to be walking around fully armed where some asshole might run his mouth about her and end up with my knife sticking through his fucking eyeball.

I think about heading to the kitchen for food so I don't have to leave her again any time soon but I can't. I can't walk outta here without her right now because the hesitancy in her voice just tore me to fucking shreds.

Instead, I take a half second to clean up the piles of my shit everywhere. There's guns and knives left out over every surface and my desk is a mess of computer parts and security cameras I've been fucking around with. She hasn't touched any of that shit at all since I've been gone but the piles of clothes are gone and my wardrobe is neatly organized like she's been fixing shit in all her spare time. I know her schedule, I know she hasn't got any real spare fucking time, she's done it because she fucking cares about me even though I've been fucking nothing but an asshole to her.

I still feel fucking… on edge.

I don't know what it is, whether Angel is going to walk out of that shower and finally tell me her story or if the building is about to be bombed but the jittery feeling in my gut has never been wrong.

Whatever it is, I need to lock Angel down hard.

The water finally cuts off and I wait about thirty seconds before I try the bathroom door.

It's locked.

"Angel, what's going on in there?"

Her voice is soft through the door but I hear her well enough. "Can I… have one of your shirts? I've been sleeping in them and… I mean, it's fine—"

"Open the door, sweetness. Let me get you in bed."

She shuffles around in the bathroom for a second and then she opens the door, standing there in one of my towels and looking like she's been beaten within an inch of her life.

All of the air leaves the fucking room.

She fidgets a little and looks like she's going to fucking cry. "Sorry. I should have grabbed something before I went in there but… I want one that smells like you. Fuck, I'm sorry."

I swear to fucking God, if she says sorry to me again I'm going to lose my fucking mind.

But first, "I'm going to hunt down whoever the fuck did this to you and I'm going to kill him in the worst fucking way."

Her lip trembles and a little giggle bursts outta her, one with a hysterical edge to it. "They're dead. They're already dead and I'm probably never going to sleep again without hearing them… die."

Well then.

Maybe the drug dealer ain't so fucking bad.

Except now we have a whole new set of fucking nightmares to contend with. "Here's my shirt, sweetness, let's get you comfortable."

I tug a clean shirt over her head gently and try not to look at the mess her ribs are in. There's gotta be some breaks in there, it must be fucking killing her to breathe.

I'm back to wanting to kill the drug dealer, I needed those deaths myself because where the fuck am I gonna put this rage now that's pumping through my fucking veins?

My phone buzzes as I help her between my sheets, the little gasps coming out of her make me wanna fucking die. There's a text from King, church is starting and my ass has to be there.

Non-negotiable.

I take a deep breath and I try to force some fucking gentle tones out of myself. "I've gotta get to church and deal with some club shit. I'm gonna grab Cole to be on the door to keep an eye out for you, we'll keep it locked but I trust him. Just lay down and rest until I get back. Then we can… talk about what the hell happened."

She bites her lip, looking like she's gonna fucking cry again.

I can't handle that shit. "Angel, what the hell is wrong? What do you need?"

She swallows and when she speaks her voice is thready. "I need my bag. It's in my locker back at The Boulevard. I just realized it's still there and… I really need it."

My eyes narrow at her. "Why? What's in there that's so fucking important?"

She swallows again. "My money."

Jesus fucking Christ. "Angel, it'll be fine there overnight. If anything fucking happens to it, I'll sort it out. Just lay down and rest."

She wraps her arms around herself and whispers, "There's almost two hundred thousand in the bag. I need it here, with me."

She very suddenly has my full fucking attention. She's a fucking pro at getting it. "What the fuck did you just say? You have two hundred g's in that busted ass fucking bag?"

She nods.

Well fuck me.

I stare down at her and try to find my fucking brain but… why the fuck does she have all that fucking money on her?

There's a thump at the door. "Church! King said hurry your ass up!"

I stand up and try to sound calm and not at all threatening when I say, "I'll get one of the boys to go get it for you now. I'll be back as soon as I can, Angel, and then we're talking about it. We're talking about everything, you hear?"

She nods again, the tears still brimming in her eyes and I duck down to kiss her before I go. It's barely a kiss thanks to her busted lip but she manages a smile when I straighten up.

Two. Hundred. Fucking. Grand.

Sitting in a shitty bag inside a locker at The Boulevard, fuck me. Fuck me, this girl just keeps throwing me fucking curve balls and I have no fucking clue what to make of it.

I text Cole to get him moving for the money and then when I get outside of my room I find Axe already waiting.

He looks even fucking worse than Angel.

"Man, is she okay?"

I nod and gently clap him on the shoulder. "She's alive. I'm gonna need to hear exactly what went down but it can wait. Has Keely got a look at you yet?"

He shakes his head. "I'll live, I'm more fucking worried about her. She's a fucking good woman, Tomi, you need to hold onto her. She just—she saw what the hell was happening and she just stood the hell up. I've seen grown fucking men with less backbone."

Fuck.

I clap him on the shoulder again and leave him there to watch the door until Cole gets back with the fucking bag.

Two hundred grand.

When I get to the chapel I'm the last Callaghan there, but it's only my blood and, fuck, Thorn waiting for me to arrive. Speck's sitting with Rue looking like death warmed up but he's alive so I'll count it as a fucking win.

King is looking fucking thunderous but he jerks his head at the door, signalling me to shut it as I walk in. "What do you need to tell us?"

Thorn runs a hand down his face and grunts like he's in pain. "I'm not here in an official capacity."

King shrugs, he'd obviously guessed as much but Thorn looks like he's getting ready to fall on his own sword and this week has been a fucking clusterfuck so I don't blame him.

"Look… I still can't tell you jack fucking shit about Posey and the rest of her family. But I can tell you that getting them involved… fuck, it was a bad move. They're looking into shit."

"Yeah, well, we've just had half the fucking Chaos Demons roll into our town so my guess is they're already looking into our shit," Hawk snaps, and Rue frowns. This'll be killing him, he can't take people questioning Posey. It gets him all twitchy and trigger happy.

Thorn shakes his head. "I don't share custody with that cunt Grimm. I'm not telling you who I do share her with but lemme just say that they've killed a lot of people to keep Grimm away from her. They take out any threats that show up on her doorstep. And this… wasn't a good fucking idea."

Rue manages to keep his cool but fuck knows how. "We didn't involve them. Poe called her sister, not us. Fuck, how exactly are we calling some bitch we don't know?"

Thorn's lip curls but I cut in because I don't want to sit around here fucking gossiping when I could be with Angel. "What's done is done. Is there any new intel or are you just here to fucking run your mouth about what went down?"

Thorn glares at me and then slides a folder over to King. "Yeah, I have a whole list of fucking sins against the club and against you, Tomi, thanks to that stripper that was taken."

I fucking knew it.

I fucking knew she'd be poison and yet hearing that from him makes me wanna fucking scream.

I ignore the stabbing feeling in my chest.

King starts flipping through the papers and groans. "Fuck me, Tomi. You need to go wipe the security cams and all the records with her on them. Any association the club has had with her needs to be destroyed, and it needs to be fucking now."

Rue scowls at them both and Speck looks like he's going to pass the hell out but I lock my shit down tight. "Easy, it'll be done in under an hour. Is she a fucking Serpent? Or a Demon?"

He pegs me with a glare. "Neither. She's a fucking kid. A runaway from a shitty home situation. We've had an underage runaway taking her clothes off and shaking her titties in our fucking club."

Fuck.

My stomach drops to the floor and, fuck me, I think I might be the one to pass out. "She showed ID to the girls at the club."

Thorn scoffs. "It was fake. She only turned eighteen last week. She's barely older than Poe and she's been sleeping on the streets, stripping to feed herself, and saving her tips to try to have enough money to put a roof over her head someday. I got a phone call from Poe's sister about her… personally. She picked up the phone and called me. That never fucking happens and it's bad fucking news for the club that she did. I don't care what the hell it takes, the club needs to fix this."

It just gets worse and worse the more he talks.

Chapter Twenty Nine

Angel

It hurts to breathe.

It hurts to lie there doing nothing, it hurts to sit up and drink some water that Tomi left behind for me, it hurts when Cole arrives back with my bag and I have to get up to grab it from him. I try to avoid his eye but Axe is sitting there outside the door on watch looking like he's had the shit beaten out of him too.

He gives me a nod and doesn't move, his gun in his hand like he's waiting for another Demon to show up so he can have a do-over.

I feel so fucking guilty but I'm clean, I'm safe, and I'm in Tomi's bed again.

I manage to relax for about a minute before my phone rings. I frown down at The Boulevard's number on the screen before picking it up.

It's Diamond, the smugness fucking radiating down the line. "I just unlocked your locker for Cole, I hope that's everything of yours because you're fired."

I swallow. "I was quitting anyway so no skin off my nose. Thanks for the courtesy call."

She scoffs at me. "You better pray you don't run into Tomi."

My breath catches in my throat and I sit up in his bed as my eyes land on the door. "What's that supposed to mean?"

Her laughter is like shards of glass down the line. "An underage whore shaking her titties in his club? Sucking him off in full view of the security cameras? Shit, he's ready to kill you with his bare hands. Cops catch wind of that with how bad they're gunning for the MC? You'd better stay the fuck away from the club and the rest of the MC-owned businesses if you wanna make it out of this alive because they're out for blood."

I hang up before she can say another thing to me, panic climbing up my throat.

I think my heart is fucking breaking in my chest and this, this feeling is the reason I didn't want to let anyone too close because I haven't felt pain like this since Paul.

The good news is the beating I just took must have knocked some sense into me because I definitely don't want to die anymore. I think dying at Tomi's hands… fuck, my soul would never find rest that way. I'd always be tortured knowing he was the one to do it.

I need to leave.

Every inch of my body hurts but I get off of the bed and rummage around in my bag until I find my phone and I dial Poe's number.

"Hey! I was just about to come fight Cole until he let me in to see you!"

My voice is all sorts of fucked up. "Poe, I'm in danger. I need to leave right now, can you just like… make sure Tomi doesn't make it back to his room for the next five minutes?"

She gasps a little. "What danger? I'll call my sister, hell or my brother again. What's happened?"

"It's—no, it's fine. I just need to get a hotel for the night. Tomi's… the club isn't going to be happy with me. They know… they know I lied about… something and—Poe, I have to get out of this place before they kill me."

She starts moving, the sounds of her shuffling around loud down the other end of the line. "Okay, we need to talk about this like now but I'll distract him if you promise not to disappear. Where are you going?"

I swallow. "I'll get a room for the night, in the next town over. I'll call you once I'm there and we can talk about it. Please just do this, Poe. Please."

I sound fucking desperate even to my own ears and she agrees, thank God. My ribs are screaming when I have to bend to pull some tights up my legs and the weight of my bag across my shoulders is like torture, pure fucking torture.

Thank fuck for the side door, thank fuck my truck is parked up close and no one even notices me creep over to it.

I get the Chevy started and out of the parking lot in no time at all, the weird noise gone completely thanks to Poe and I make it out of the suburbs and onto the highway before the tears start but they come in so fucking strong that I have to pull over, the sobs wracking my body like someone fucking died.

Oh.

Right.

The future I thought I might actually get to have just died.

The future I never let myself even hope for until Tomi stomped into my life and rearranged shit. All I ever wanted before was a quiet life, one where I lived alone and had friends but never let anyone close to me. I wanted a roof over my head that no one could take from me, a job, a boring life but now that just feels fucking… empty.

He's fucking ruined it.

I drive for hours until I'm calm enough to stop at a hotel. I find one that looks safe and clean, very aware of the exact amount of money I'm now carrying and I can't afford to sleep in my car right now.

I need some help.

I get set up there before I call Poe and tell her the whole story. I mean, not everything, but I tell her why I ran and then I swallow my pride and I ask for some goddamn help.

"Do you know anything about laundering money and offshore accounts?"

She hums down the line. "You met Lips right? Aves can do that shit easier than breathing, lemme get ahold of her. What are you gonna do with the money? If you need someplace to go I'll call Lips back to get you."

I clear my throat to shift some of the emotions choking me. "No, it's—I've found a house in Coldstone. It's a foreclosure on a good street, it's where I want to live. I think… I think as long as the MC doesn't know I live there, it'll be okay."

Poe grumbles under her breath. "The MC are fucking outlaws, they're not gonna be fucking worried about you stripping a little younger than the law. I mean… they probably care but not like you're thinking."

Oh, the sunshine beam of a girl is back. I have to remind myself that she's not as innocent as she seems. "I need to think about myself right now, Poe. I need to cover my own ass so I don't get myself killed. I want to live in Coldstone because… I mean, it's the first place that's felt like home. The house isn't anywhere near the usual Unseen haunts, I should be… safe there."

She mumbles unhappily at me but promises to call her sister for me. I promise to call her in the morning, feigning being tired to get off of the line.

Instead, I crawl into the shower and cry some more.

I cry until there's nothing left inside me left to cry out. I'm exhausted when I finally climb back out, my ribs screaming and my face is pulsing in pain. I just wanna take some drugs and pass the fuck out.

My phone pings.

Open the door and hand the cash to the man there. I'll sort everything out for you, Angel.

Right. The Wolf of Mounts Bay has my phone number.

I try not to panic but I stash all of my clothes and other belongings into some trash bags and then I just take a couple of hundred dollar bills out to use… until the money is laundered.

When I open the door the man standing there waiting patiently is freaking huge and definitely part of the MC.

I stumble over my words."The Wolf sent you?"

He grins and tucks his hip against the door but it's not in a threatening way. More… flirty. Oh lord, why does this always happen to me?

"Yeah, she did. We were in town anyway, for club shit. The name's Roxas. And what's yours, gorgeous?"

I frown at him. "The Wolf didn't tell you?"

He huffs out a chuckle. "Yeah, she sure did Angel. I'm just trying to make conversation. If you're not into it I'll just take the goods and head off. Are you safe here? If there's something else you need, tell me and it's done. The Wolf was crystal fucking clear about how important your safety is to her and I like that kid enough to play along."

My heart sort of spasms in my chest.

She really does love her sister.

"I'm perfectly safe. Here's the… uh, bag."

He grins and gives me a little salute on the way out, jogging down the stairs to where his motorcycle is waiting. There's another guy there as well, even freaking bigger, but he keeps his head down and I duck back into the hotel room before he can see me, just in case.

I'm too tired to feel… anything about not having my money anymore, so I fall into the bed and pass out.

The bank card arrives by a courier the next morning, right to my hotel door.

It has my real name on it and when I take it to an ATM I find all of my money just sitting there, waiting for me to use it. Laundered and fucking available.

Holy.

Shit.

I read the note that came with it three times, my hands shaking just a little.

I've put an offer in on the house you want on your behalf, requesting an immediate settlement. Call me if you need anything else.

The house is a fucking mess but hell if it isn't fucking perfect for me.

I go to meet the realtor over there the same morning my bank card shows up and Poe insists on coming with me even though I'm freaking terrified at having someone finding out where I am.

Tomi hasn't tried to contact me once.

It only proves to me that Diamond was right and now I'm on the club's shit list, which is fine. It's completely fine, I'll survive it. People get their hearts broken all the damn time, so what if I maybe thought that I was falling for this guy? So what if he showed me that there are some men out there that understand boundaries and always respected my consent?

So what if I feel hollow inside now?

I take enough painkillers to take the edge off of the pain in my ribs and I take my time in making sure I look good. My lip has sealed up but the swelling and the bruising is officially at its worst and I need a lot of makeup to not look fucking hideous. I pull on jeans and then one of my dad's sweaters. It looks as though I'm trying to look edgy and vintage but really I just… I need him with me today.

If I can't wear Tomi's hoodie then you can be fucking sure I need my dad's sweater.

I pick Poe up from the library, a little worried about her skipping school but she shrugs at me like it's nothing.

"Lips called Thorn. I've got free rein for a few days to hang out with you."

I cringe. "So Thorn knows about… all of this too? Isn't he supposed to come arrest me or whatever?"

Poe tips her head back and cackles. "No, dumbass! I told you, he's a cool cop. He was more pissed that he didn't talk to you a little more, find out what was going on with you a bit sooner. Forget about it! Forget about dumbass boys, let's buy a fucking house!"

She's cute as hell about it and starts talking about school and Law being a dick since his dad came to visit. She also talks about Trink but at the look on my face she shuts that down fast.

I don't want to think about Callaghans. None of them.

The realtor is unbelievably accommodating. She is the picture of politeness, talking to me like I'm some fucking superstar and I try not to freak out over it. I'm guessing she really needs the commission because any questions I have about the place she practically falls over herself to answer.

I fall in love with it instantly.

Poe… doesn't.

She pokes around like she's afraid of catching a disease. "I mean… it's not the worst house I've ever stood in but fuck, that bar is low."

I scoff at her. "The neighborhood is safe. It's well below my price cap and I could fix it up in a big way with the difference."

She nods. "It's a bit small though. Are you going to have enough room here?"

I peg her with a look. "It's bigger than my car, Poe. And I'm living here, alone, until I die. It's fucking perfect."

She nods again and shifts to look out the back door. "The deck is fucking perfect for drinks and if you get a fence up around the whole place you'd be even safer. Maybe get a dog too. The neighborhood is really good, quiet and close to the library and school. That shit is important."

The realtor nods along like this is all fucking fascinating to her and I try not to giggle at her.

It's not until I leave that I realize Lips has done a lot more than just arrange this viewing for me. No, the realtor is shitting herself over the entire thing because if I want the place, it's mine. There's paperwork for me to sign and the settlement is being taken care of for me but the moment I lift the pen away from the paper there's a set of keys being pressed into my palm.

I wait until she's driven off before I arch an eyebrow at Poe. "What the hell was that? I have the money for this place, I'm paying my own way."

Poe rolls her eyes. "I know! Lips said she'll sort it out with you later, she just wanted you somewhere safe like today, not in two months time. I kind of agree with her so like… humor me."

I could argue with her. I could, but I won't because I'm beyond fucking tired and the thought of dragging all of my shit here and sleeping in a house that's mine? Fucking blissful, so instead I smile at her. "Thanks. Thanks for being here and for being my friend."

She grins back at me. "Thanks for trying to die for me, that was real sweet of you."

Poe insists on helping me move my trash bags of clothing into the house. It's almost embarrassing but she does everything with a grin and a long stream of funny stories about everyone she's ever met and… I think she's relieved to have someone she can finally talk to about her sister.

She doesn't talk about her brother.

Thank fucking God, because I'd probably drop dead if she did.

But I find out all about the infamous Wolf of Mounts Bay, about her family and the three, yes three, boys she's dating.

"Oh my God, you look so fucking scandalized right now and I'm freaking dying over it. Look, at least you didn't spend a week on a tour bus with them! I heard way too much, I swear I could fucking puke thinking about it."

None of that registers except, "You went on tour with Vanth Falling? Are you fucking kidding me?"

She laughs and shrugs, putting the last bag down on the fucking disgusting carpet in the bedroom.

It needs to come up as soon as I can manage it.

"Only for like a week. We were in New Orleans, I got drunk with Blaise and then I got a tattoo. Don't fucking tell anyone that, Thorn would shit himself if he knew. He'd start in on me about joining a gang and then I'd have to remind him that technically I was born into one."

A gang tattoo.

Posey motherfucking Graves with a gang tattoo.

I can't even think about it.

When she finally heads back to school to get picked up, I take stock of exactly what I need to buy to get this place looking like a home instead of a shit heap.

The list is long.

Something to sleep on is priority number one if I'm sleeping here tonight so I lock everything up and head out to find a furniture store. I pick out everything that I think I can fit into the Chevy and the guys there are nice enough to load it all up for me.

I duck into the hardware store and grab a whole heap of supplies to keep me busy for the next few days, little shit that I can figure out while I'm healing, and then I hit up the grocery store.

I feel a little jumpy over leaving the shit on the truck but I need food so I can stay locked up in my house for a few days.

I grab a cart so I'm not lugging things around and I start filling it up with things that don't require a fridge or any sort of cooking. I mentally add a microwave to my list and, fuck, maybe some plates… pots, pans, cutlery, oh my God I forgot about how much shit a house really needs.

I'm so distracted that I don't see Tomi until he speaks and scares my soul straight out of my body.

"What are you doing in here?"

I startle and look up to find Tomi glaring down at me like I'm the scum of the Earth. He hasn't looked at me like I'm dirty in months and something breaks in my chest at the sight of it.

I knew it was too good to be true.

He didn't want me, he wanted my body, and on the slim chance he really did want more, my lies broke whatever we did have. Fuck, it doesn't matter that I had no choice.

"I'm just getting some groceries, I didn't think this place was on your radar. It definitely isn't somewhere I've seen you before."

He frowns and stalks forward like he's going to murder me right here in the grocery store and instinct kicks in. I flinch back into the shelves and knock some shit over as I duck my head.

Old habits never fucking die.

"Jesus fucking Christ, I'm not going to fucking hurt you. There's a reason you haven't seen me here, this isn't a great area. What are you doing here, Angel?"

I take a deep breath and crouch down to fix the boxes of cereal up and get my eyes away from him. I mean, turning my back on a man who wants me dead probably isn't the best idea but my heart is still bleeding over him and looking at him hurts so much more than death.

"Diamond told me. When she called to fire me, she told me about what I'd done to the MC. I'm doing my best to stay away from… you."

I see his lip curl from the corner of my eye and I can't look at it at all.

"So you're avoiding me on purpose? Running away?"

I swallow and grab the basket again, straightening up but keeping my eyes on the ground. "I'm trying not to get in your way. I'm trying to just keep my shit away from you. If you and the MC feel the need to… kill me for what I did then I guess that's the end of the line for me. It's fine."

His knuckles pop at the pressure of his clenched fists. "Diamond told you I wanted you dead? That's what's happening here?"

I glance up at the security cameras. "Yeah. This probably isn't the best place for it though."

My phone buzzes in my pocket and, God, I forgot that I even had it still. It's his phone, on his plan, and I ran away with it. I pull it out with a shaking hand and hold it out to him.

His eyes drop down to it and the glare gets even worse. "Put it away, Angel. You're keeping it."

He just stands there and stares at me until finally my arm drops and I slide the phone back into my pocket. "It's late. I have classes in the morning. Poe knows where to find me if you need to kill me."

I walk over to the cashier quickly, ringing my order up and paying for my food. I put the cart away but before I can grab the bags Tomi stalks over and grabs them off of me. I try not to shake so goddamn hard that my knees give out.

"Angel, listen to me. I'm getting you out to your car, then I'm following you home. I'll get your shit unloaded and then I'm going to go sort this fucking problem out. No one is killing you. No one is fucking touching you, just get out to your truck so I can get you home safe."

Chapter Thirty

Tomi

I have every trace of Angel wiped from the The Boulevard records in under an hour.

Thorn disappears the second he's finished giving his little debrief and I try not to focus on the weight of everyone's eyes on me. The chapel is loud the entire time I work, Rue talking through the entire fucking mess of the Demons rolling into Coldstone. Eventually they open the doors and let the rest of the brothers in to tell their side of this fucking mess.

I don't fucking react to any of it until Axe takes his turn.

"They were there for Poe. Angel took her place, pretended so they'd take her instead. She heard Poe's name and just fucking threw herself into the fucking fire."

My eyes snap up away from my laptop.

I didn't know that's how it went down. Fuck, more shit is leading to Poe and if there's a war starting she's gonna be in the fucking middle of it.

I glance at Rue but his face is locked down hard. No one but me and Speck would even guess he's probably raging inside his head right now.

Diesel grunts. "Doesn't fucking matter. She lied to the club, lied about her age and coulda been the reason for another brother to be locked up."

Speck groans and Hellion shoots him a look. He's not even supposed to be in here, but extenuating circumstances and all that shit.

None of that shit matters to me.

"Diesel, lemme tell you this before you talk your way into

a fucking bullet. I don't give a fuck about her lying about her age. Question her again and you'll lose more than your fucking patch."

Hawk shifts to stare at me like he's never seen me before but King nods at me like he approves so I guess I have the president's seal of approval. Not that I need it, I'd fucking gut Diesel whether they like it or not.

I'm more of an ask for forgiveness kind of guy.

Diesel opens his mouth and Axe cuts him off. "She's a good fucking woman. I don't know exactly what her deal is but, fuck, she's done nothing but strip. I get she lied about her age but she keeps her mouth shut, her head down, and the second trouble came knocking she manned the fuck up and protected her family. That's what Poe has become to her and this club swore an oath to protect that kid for Alby. Simple as that, shut your fucking mouth before running it gets you dead."

The topic moves the hell away from my girl after that, thank fuck, because I'm struggling to keep my cool. I'm fucking angry about the whole thing but… I'm not angry at her.

I'm angry at whatever the fuck happened to her that had her living on the fucking streets. I need that file that Thorn handed over to King and I need it the fuck now. I might be heading out to kill some cunt tonight before I can sleep.

The meeting goes on and on for another hour before King finally sends everyone away.

I keep my ass planted in my chair.

Rue does too, his eyes on me like he's getting ready to either back me up or put me down depending on how I react.

King looks between us both and then sighs at me. "You can have the fucking file but don't make me regret handing it over. Go get some whiskey in your belly first."

I shake my head and grab it from him, waiting until he leaves before I open it.

Then I slowly but surely lose my goddamn mind.

It's pages and pages of abuse. Physical. Mental. Sexual. She's run away from hell and she slept on the motherfucking streets to get away from her stepfather.

A cop.

He's on trial for raping another little girl after Angel left him.

I close the file and then slide it across the table to Rue. I wouldn't except I'm going to need backup when I go to find the fucking piece of shit and there's no better backup than your blood with the same exact need for vengeance.

"I know a guy in Maryland. Lemme get the ball moving on this, we'll get him. You just worry about getting her healed up and safe, brother."

I give him a nod and get my ass moving. I take two steps out of the chapel to have a hand clamp over the back of my neck and my body yanked towards the Callaghan booth by Hawk.

I feel about five years old when he does it.

"Is there something you've forgotten to tell me?"

Christ. "I didn't know I had to tell you everything that's going on in my life."

Hawk shoves me into the seat and jerks his head at Monroe to bring us both drinks. I really don't want to sit here while Angel is hurt and alone but Hawk pegs me with a dark look when I try to get back up.

"One drink and you'll tell me what the fuck has been going on so I have an answer when Keely asks me."

So I have one drink and I tell my pops about the girl who 'struck me. The girl I judged badly from day fucking one while she was trying to survive, coming straight outta hell into the big, cruel world of Coldstone.

I need a helluva lot more than one fucking drink.

But I leave as soon as the whiskey in my glass is finished and Hawk looks a little less pissed off. "Bring her home for family dinner on Sunday. No excuses, Keely is gonna get all fucking weepy over this and after this Demon bullshit she deserves some joy."

No truer words have ever been spoken, my mom is a fucking saint for dealing with all of us assholes and I know just how happy this shit will make her so it's as easy as breathing to agree to it.

I get back to my room to find the door open and Rue snarling at Poe but nothing fucking registers except that Angel is gone.

Fucking gone.

"Posey, where the fuck is she?"

She shrugs at me. "She's safe. She's making plans and getting her shit together."

I grab her and yank her around, ignoring the snarl Rue lets out at me because he might be pissed but she's still his little fucking flower. "What the fuck does that mean?"

She tips her head back so she can stare me down, unflinching in that way that she has. Hawk says it's a Graves' thing, those eyes of hers, and it makes her look fucking fierce. "I ain't telling you a goddamn thing. She's my friend and she's a good person, but something's happened to spook her and you'll only make shit worse if you go after her, guns blazing."

How much worse could shit get?

My girl is running away again, only this time, I'm not going to fucking let her go.

I manage to stay calm, only because Angel took her phone with her and I have a GPS tracker on it so I know exactly where she is.

She drives for hours before checking into a hotel and I drive over there to drag her home but Poe's words just keep fucking ringing in my ears.

I have time to feel her out before I drag her home with me.

So I get a hotel room too, and sleep in the room next to hers all night. Well, I don't fucking sleep. I lay there in the bed and listen out for any little thing that might tell me what's going through her head right now or any signs of something bad happening. I feel like a pile of shit when she finally gets up the next morning and I'm careful about tailing her.

She buys a house.

It's a shitty little thing but she buys it in cash, signs paperwork on the front lawn leaning against the Chevy and she looks so fucking happy, I've never seen her grin so wide.

I'm definitely fucking lovestruck and an idiot about it.

I follow her around Coldstone as she picks out furniture and paint supplies. I call Rue to come help me because there's no fucking way I'm going to stay back and watch her lift that shit down herself with her busted fucking ribs and when he meets me outside the grocery store on the other side of town he scowls at me.

"You told her you're here yet?"

I shake my head. "I'm going to now. You good?"

He shrugs and scowls up at the store again. "This place is about as far away from her new place as she could possibly fucking get."

When I get in there and see her fucking terrified of me something fucking snaps in my brain and I almost rage the fuck out in the grocery store like an asshole, right up until she says who the fuck told her I wanted her dead.

Fucking Diamond.

I've always known she was a scheming bitch but this? She fucking knows Angel is mine, I've made it fucking clear.

We get Angel back to her new place. She fumbles around with her words and shakes the whole damn time but we get everything unloaded into her house and where she wants it before I stalk back out to my hog.

Rue stays behind to watch over my girl which is good because she still looks like she's gonna have a fucking heart attack and that only riles me up more.

I get to The Boulevard ready to commit murder. Cold-blooded murder because I'm not coming down here in a rage. Nope, I feel fucking nothing right now except the need to bleed out every jealous fucking slut in this building.

Axe and Cole are both already here for the night and at the sight of my face Cole starts cursing up a storm. Axe doesn't utter a word, just rolls his shoulders back like he's about to jump into a fight which is good.

I'm going to fucking gut someone.

"Asses in the locker room right the fuck now!" I roar and every single body in the room freezes.

I never raise my voice like that.

Before Angel, I was the easygoing one. I was the party lover, the one who's always having a good time, the one who ruled fair and loose.

I'm not that man anymore.

"Holy shit, is everything okay? Tomi, what's happened?" Mel says, already fucking naked even though the place doesn't open for another hour.

"Put a fucking shirt on and get your ass moving, I'm not a

man to mess with tonight. Where the fuck is Diamond?"

"I'm here!" she calls out with a smile, all sorts of syrupy sweetness but the shit leaves a bad taste in your mouth.

Fake fucking slut.

The bouncers both walk in as well, good, and Axe gets the door shut behind them, leaning back on it and crossing his arms.

"Is there something you want to tell me, Diamond? Something you've done?"

She pouts at me, all fake and fucking manipulative. We've let her take care of shit down here too much, she's gotten too fucking comfortable.

"You know I tell you everything, Tomi! We've got this place running like a well-oiled machine, even after the Demons were here. Oh, is this a debrief? I've already told Rue everything that happened but I'd be happy to go over it again."

I stalk forward and Diamond is the only fucking one who doesn't see the danger she's in. Nah, all she sees is a patch she so desperately wants.

Everyone else is hugging the walls, trying to get the fuck away from my rage.

"How about we start with who called you and told you Angel was underage, hm? Which brother stepped the fuck outta line and told you?"

Her lips press together but I expected as much.

"How about you tell me who the fuck gave you permission to speak on the club's behalf? Rumor has it you told Angel I wanted her dead. Now, I'd think really fucking carefully about how you answer this one because I'm here for blood."

Her jaw drops and she dares to look fucking shocked. "For blood? Tomi, she lied to the club! She could've had all our asses thrown into fucking prison!"

I take the last step towards her until I'm standing over her, the need to kill her thrumming through my blood. "She risked her life for you, you miserable cunt. She stood up and stopped the Demons from hurting you."

She blinks back tears but I've got no fucking time for that shit. "She practically put herself on a platter! She's a biker slut. She saw a patch she liked the look of and threw herself at them—"

Her words are cut off by my hand around her throat. I've never laid hands on a woman before but fuck if I'm going to get the job done right. She didn't just fuck with my girl, she stepped out on the club.

"She stood in for her friend to save you all and your jealous fucking self didn't even stop to say thank you. Now that's enough to get your ass kicked out but to lie to her about me? To tell her I want her dead? Bitch, you fucked with the wrong man."

Her eyes start bugging out before I drop her back down to the ground and she collapses to her knees.

"Listen carefully. Angel is mine and if I find out one of you cunts so much as side-eye her you'll get the same as Diamond. You hear me?"

I ride out to the lake to clear my head.

Axe must have called Rue because I find him tailing me before I even hit the highway, riding like a reckless fucking idiot because clearly he's in one of those moods where he wants to flirt with death. He's spent his whole damn life trying to decide if he wants to live or die and something is going on in that grumpy fucking head of his that has him questioning if he needs to go out in a blaze of glory.

I wait until we park up by the lake before I take a deep breath and try to calm the fuck down.

Rue glances at the blood on my hands and says, "Diamond?"

"Dealt with. We're gonna need to spend more time at The Boulevard."

He shrugs. "Worth it. Angel is fucking worth it."

Damn fucking right she is. I glance around but the place is empty like it always is. There's a reason I headed up this way once I knew Rue was riding along.

"Look. We need to talk about your little flower."

It's like a thunderstorm rolling in, I see the darkness shutter across his face. "No we fucking don't. Have I said a single fucking thing about your woman? Nope, I kept my mouth shut."

Fuck, maybe I should have brought Speck out here just so

we'd have a referee but he's still hobbling around like he's on the brink of death. "Shut up, asshole, I'm trying to tell you we have a whole new fucking problem to deal with. I've risked my ass for her on the run so cut the shit."

He doesn't say a word not even when I pull the silencer out of my pocket, like I need to prove to him and myself that I'm not fucking losing it or something.

"I got separated from the others at the drop off. I ended up with a gun to the back of my head from the Demon Enforcer."

Rue frowns. "I thought you got him with a fucking headshot."

I shake my head slowly. "Rue, I didn't kill him. I was about to be taken the fuck out except then another Demon shows up, talks him outta killing me."

I hand him the silencer and he frowns down at it. "What the fuck is this?"

"That would be the silencer Colt Graves used to kill Cliff without being heard. He let me go, doesn't say a fucking word to me, just lets me leave with my skull still intact."

Rue scowls down at the silencer in his hand like it's some impossible thing. I know exactly how he feels, I've been staring at the fucking thing for days… trying to make sense of what the fuck it all means.

"Why didn't you tell King or Hawk?"

I blow out a breath. This is the hard bit. "I live and bleed Unseen… but I also know Posey like I know Trink. I've watched that kid grow up, I know exactly who she is, no matter how much shit I give you about her. If I tell King he's going to think she's in on this somehow… that she's some sort of sleeper cell in our club."

Rue curses under his breath, swipes a hand over his face. "She's not. She's really fucking not."

I nod. "Exactly but she's also full of fucking secrets. You need to get them outta her, give her your patch, get her safe in our club and away from that other family of hers. Pure and simple, she's yours and no one else's."

Rue scratches at the shadow on his cheek. "Did Angel tell you anything about them?"

"No. But I'll be asking her about them the second I'm sure she believes we don't want her dead."

Chapter Thirty One

Angel

I wake up on the couch after my first night in my own house and two things filter into my head as I lie there looking at the morning sun filtering through the cracked and broken blinds on the living room window.

I love my house more than any woman really should love such a thing, and I'm fairly certain my ribs were bruised and not broken because I can breathe with only discomfort and not agonizing pain.

I'm sure after the day I'm planning that shit will change but I'm glad to take a minute and just lie around, looking at all of the cracks I'll need to fill and the mud that's still on the floor.

Eventually, I get up and eat a candy bar for breakfast.

It's not a great choice but I chase it with an energy drink and suddenly I'm ready to get to work on… fuck, something. Anything. Any part of this house that I can get to without needing an extra set of hands.

I start caulking up all of the cracks in the walls and ceiling.

Raising my arms above my head does start to feel like I'm going to fucking die but it doesn't take too long to get every room done. One of the many advantages of such a tiny house.

While I wait for that to set I run to the store and grab paint. This place needs some fucking love. I'm living here, on my own, until I die. There's nowhere else I ever want to be now that I've found friends and a little house of my own, so I need it to look exactly how I want it to. Even if that means painting everything myself.

I want it all white.

I want it to look bright and clean. I want it to look as though I know what the hell I'm doing, eighteen and owning something like this. It's only a one bedroom, one bath little place, nothing to write home about, but fuck. I'm so goddamn proud of it, so proud that I have a tiny house on a street that isn't the worst in town, and I fucking own it.

I need a fence.

Someday, I'm going to get a dog to keep me company. I'm going to plant a vegetable garden, maybe put in some fruit trees, and I'll plant flowers everywhere. I'm going to get a real job at an accounting firm in the next town over and I'll live a fucking life.

I just need to paint the walls first.

I keep myself so fucking busy that I don't think about Tomi at all. Okay, that's a lie. I think about him a lot without actually trying. The confrontation at the grocery store was fucking weird and the fact that both him and Rue were just heading past and saw me.

I'm grateful as hell they were there though. No way was I getting the couch in by myself. It's a big one, it takes up most of the living room and there's a section that folds out into a bed. I knew I had to pick between a couch or a bed because I could only fit one in the Chevy and with Poe declaring she'd be here every day after school I needed somewhere for her to sit.

So I manage to get a layer of paint on the walls in the living room before she knocks on my door. I'm too busy trying to figure out how the fuck I'm going to paint the ceiling to realize she's not alone when I open the door.

I come face to face with Trink.

Oh God.

I must look shocked and maybe a little horrified standing there in my paint splattered shirt and jean shorts older than I am, thrifted from some shitty flea market a few states over.

Poe nudges Trink and Tomi's sister huffs just like he does. "Quit it, Graves, I'm getting there."

She clears her throat and sort of rolls her shoulders back and I'm a little shocked at what comes out of her mouth. "Angel, I just wanted to say that I'm sorry. I'm sorry I treated you like shit without ever trying to get to know you first. I'm so used to strippers being around my family and using me to fuck my brother that I just… I made a shitty assumption. That's on me and nothing to do with you, I should've listened to Poe and not been a fucking asshole to you."

I look at Poe but her eyes are clear and open, she's ready to accept whatever decision I come to. I guess I can give this girl a chance. I mean… I think maybe things with Tomi might sort themselves out? God, I don't want to get my fucking hopes up again.

I step out of my doorframe and usher them in. "I don't have much furniture yet and there's no TV, sorry."

Trink shrugs and stalks in without any reservation. Poe grins at me and slings an arm around my shoulders. "Like we give a shit about chairs. I brought beer and we can order pizza. Let's talk shit about dumbass boys and cars."

I scoff and roll my eyes at her but, damn, it feels so good to have friends and Poe is the best one a girl like me could ever ask for.

Even if her brother is the Devil himself.

Jesus.

I've got to stop thinking about that shit.

Poe pulls some beers out of her bag and I don't at all wanna question her on where she got them because her sources seem endless. Trink orders a pizza and I insist on paying for it even when they both fight me.

The first slice is like heaven. Cheesy, pepperoni goodness, nothing can beat the taste. Everything is perfect until Trink ruins it.

"So tell me about Tomi, he told Mom he's bringing you to family dinner on Sunday."

I startle and try not to freak the hell out. "What do you mean? What about him?"

Trink laughs and Poe nudges her even though she's grinning like a loony. "He told me he was 'struck. I know what that shit means so how do you feel about him?"

I squint a little at her. "What the hell does 'struck mean?"

The smiles slide off of both of their faces. Trink recovers first. "You don't know? That asshole didn't tell you?"

I shake my head, fiddling with the label on the beer. I'm trying not to be upset that he's been running his mouth about me, especially with his sister. I didn't know they were that close. Shit, I didn't know he did Sunday dinners at his parents' place either. They're closer than I would have ever thought. Jesus, no wonder Trink hated me. I'm the slut stripper who sucked her brother off in The Boulevard office.

"The Callaghan men are cursed," Trink whispers and Poe snorts at her.

"Blessed. Keely says they're blessed but sometimes blessings go… wrong."

I blush. Are they talking about dick sizes right now? Because that's just too fucking weird.

"They're 'struck by the hand of God, Pops says. They meet the woman of their dreams and they feel it like a bolt of lightning through their chests, and they know they belong to that woman."

I place the bottle down slowly onto the floor before I spill that shit everywhere with the shaking of my damn hand.

Trink goes on. "Hawk was lovestruck. Met Keely, knocked her up, happily ever after and all that. King and Hell were both cuntstruck. The women they felt that bolt of lightning for were terrible, gave 'em nothing but their boys and years of chaos to clean up."

Poe leans forward, her eyes all dreamy looking. "Someday, I'm fucking praying Rue feels that for me. I just need to grow up enough for him to see me as a woman and not a fucking kid."

I force a little smile on my face for her but my chest feels like it's been carved out, my heart and everything else just fucking scooped out until I'm an empty cavern.

"Tomi told Keely the other day that you 'struck him. He's been trying to figure out what the fuck to do ever since."

Christ.

That's why he hated me so much.

I'm the fuck up, the failure, the fucking stripper he's been cursed to want even though he'd rather anyone else but me. Oh my fucking God, this is worse than I thought.

Poe's eyes soften. "Angel, you're not a cunt. There's no way this'll be a bad thing. You're one of the kindest, strongest, most loyal people I've ever met."

I smile at her and I'm so freaking grateful for the empty

feeling inside me because it means I don't have to fight tears over knowing just how I've ruined Tomi's life. Fuck.

"So. Are you guys seeing each other or what?"

I sigh and shrug. "I don't know. I think he wanted to before—I mean, before he found out I'd lied to the club. Now I just… I don't know."

Trink frowns at me, downing the last of her beer before cracking open another one. Clearly they're not going anywhere soon. "Explain it to me. Explain the whole thing, start to finish, and I'll try to figure this out for you. I mean, it's a little gross with him being my brother but fuck it, I'd rather it be you than some other bitch."

I open my mouth and Poe interrupts me. "She doesn't mean the sex bits, leave those the hell out. I still can't believe Tomi bagged someone as hot as you, he's fucking blessed."

Trink fake gags and I open another beer before I start the story. I need the buzz to get me through it.

Because there's only the three of us, I feel comfortable enough to work my way through the beers, my buzz quickly turning into the room spinning and my words slurring. I'm fucking drunk, for the first time in my life I've pushed it past my limit.

It's fine until there are lights in the driveway and Trink groans from where she's dancing to some song playing on her phone. "Fuck me."

Poe scrambles up off of the floor. "What is it? Is it Demons? I'll call it in, fuck, where's my gun?"

Trink scoffs. "No, dumbass, it's our ride. I told Tomi I wouldn't drink too much and here I am… fucking wasted."

My heart clenches in my chest.

Lovestruck.

Oh God.

Oh fuck, I'm too far gone to deal with him like this.

Poe giggles at the look on my face. "You didn't promise him shit, Angel! You'll be fine. Fuck, tell him to go home! Tomi! Go home, Angel is too drunk for boy bullshit."

I can't move from where I'm lying on the couch so there's no stopping her, no trying to get her to shut her freaking mouth and quit embarrassing the life out of me. At least I'm incapable of blushing in my current state.

From where I'm sprawled out I can see Rue scowling down at Poe while she dances around excitedly, yammering on about painting this place but I can't even chime in because she's talking a mile a minute.

Eventually, he gets over her shit and slings her over his shoulder in one swoop. He ignores her squeals of outrage and just stomps out, cussing and muttering about idiot girls.

Tomi stares down at Trink like she's his number one problem and she glares back up at him like he's some evil brother she can't stand.

This whole night has proved to me how much they adore each other.

"This is taking it easy?"

She grins at him. "Hell yeah it is! I even managed to talk Poe outta lighting your hog on fire for being a dick to Angel. You're fucking welcome."

He scowls at her and then shoos her out the door, shutting it and locking it behind her.

Wait.

He's still in the house. In my house with me and not driving away with his family. Oh God. This can't end well.

He stalks over to me, looking around at all of the cracks and shitty holes I've just patched up.

"I get that it's a pile of shit but it's my pile of shit, you know?"

He frowns at me like I'm being an asshole but he's the one standing there staring at the peeling paint like it's so fucking fascinating.

"Angel, I'm trying to figure out how the fuck you got up there to caulk shit. Like I give a fuck what this place looks like, it's yours and I'm gonna make sure it's safe for you."

I frown at him, watching as he walks up to the back door and looks out at my backyard like he's expecting some Demon assholes to show up.

"What are you doing here, Tomi?"

He scowls at me and stalks over, grabbing a bottle of beer out of the bag Poe's left behind. He offers me one but I need to sober up a little.

"Wherever you are, that's where I'm staying. That's how this goes now, Angel."

My heart does this stupid flutter in my chest like that was the most romantic thing I've ever heard.

Wait.

It kind of is.

"And what if I don't want you here? Do I get a choice in the matter?"

I don't know why my mouth is running but I'm too fucking wasted to stop it.

He shrugs and sits down on the couch with me, moving me until I'm draped over his lap and his hands are tangled into my hair.

I try not to fucking purr.

"If you don't want me here then I'll go out and sit on my hog all night, watch the place and make sure you're safe. I'm not letting you outta my sight again, sweetness. If that means I'm outside watching the house while you sleep, then so be it."

He sips the beer and stares up at the cracks again.

I need a TV to distract him from that shit. "Is this because you're 'struck?"

He shrugs. "I don't care why, I'm just letting you know how it's gonna be."

I lie there while he finishes the beer, enjoying the feel of his hands in my hair and the hard muscle of his thigh under my head. "What if I want you to stay? What if I want you to sleep on this couch with me?"

He drains the last of the beer and sets it down on the floor. "You don't have to ask, Angel. I'm staying."

I don't feel all that drunk anymore, just really fucking horny. I never did get the promise of his homecoming, to be able to wear those pretty little panties for him, and when I sit up and climb into his lap I almost feel ashamed of the state I'm in.

He's only ever seen me dressed up… or beat up, I guess.

"I bought some new panties for you, and a corset to go with it. Lemme go get changed."

His hands clamp down over my hips and keep me still, his own hips surging up from the couch to grind against my pussy. "Next time. You're perfect where you are."

His eyes are hot when they take in my face, a scowl taking over him when he sees the busted lip. I lean forward to kiss him but he's gentle with me, treating me like I'm breakable.

It's jarring.

I want him desperate for me, the same way I am for him, and my brain is all types of messed up because I whimper into the kiss. "Please don't give me up. Please don't stop wanting me."

His hand reaches up to fist in my hair again, tugging tight and holding my lips to his. "I told you. You're mine, just because I'm not hurting you doesn't mean I don't want you just as fucking bad as I always have. Take your pants off, sweetness. Panties too, I want that pussy riding my cock like you ride the pole."

I scramble off of him, his hands never leaving my hips and keeping me steady as I shove my pants down my legs and climb back onto his lap, my pussy bare and already wet for him.

He kisses me as two of his fingers stroke over my pussy lovingly, slowly sinking inside me like he's savoring the feel of my body clenching around him.

I pull the sweatshirt over my head and tear my bra off, leaning over to kiss down his jaw to his neck. I've never explored someone's body like this, I've never wanted to, but there's something so fucking perfect about licking and sucking and biting my way down to where his shirt and cut cover the rest of his skin from me.

He's still fully clothed.

I pout and he chuckles at me, hooking his fingers inside me until my pussy weeps for his cock to fill me up. I reach down between our bodies to unzip his jeans and stroke his cock, already hard and pulsing for me. He shifts around a little and pulls a condom out of his pocket with his free hand, all while the other is still pumping inside me until my legs shake.

He tears the packet open with his teeth, his hand covering mine and together we roll the condom on. It has no business being that hot but, fuck, by the time he's covered I'm fucking panting for him.

No flinching here.

Tomi's fingers slip out and he pulls my hips closer. "Hurry

up, Angel, before I fuck you on the floor. I don't want to hurt you but a man has limits and you're pushing mine."

I raise up on my knees before sinking down on his cock, groaning at the stretch of taking him like this. It takes me a second to get the hang of how to do this but, like he said, I'm used to riding the pole and my hips can fucking move.

He's sweating in less than a minute.

I find myself so happy that I giggle and he gets pretty fucking serious about making me come after that, a hand on the nape of my neck to keep my body close to his as his fingers work their magic on my clit.

When I come and clench down hard like a vise around him he follows me over the edge with a grunt, pumping his hips up into me.

The shaking starts as soon as I come down from my orgasm, my whole body trembling for no reason. I start to panic a little bit, sure that Tomi is going to zip up and leave me because I'm such a fucking mess.

"Where's your sweatshirt, sweetness? Here, have this one," he says, slipping his cut off and then his shirt before helping me into it. He's still inside me but now he's focused entirely on easing my tremors.

"Hips up, good girl. Right, lie down there until I get cleaned up. Do you have blankets? Good, you stay there. I'll fix it."

The shaking doesn't stop but I fall asleep before he gets back to me.

I wake up in his arms on the fold-out bed, tucked into his chest and fucking happy.

Chapter Thirty Two

Tomi

Angel wasn't wrong when she said the house was a pile of shit.

It needs more work than just a quick paint job but I'll be goddamned if I don't do as much of it for her as I can. When I get her tucked up on the couch and sleeping I do a proper walk through the place and start running inventory on what she needs.

I've been working for years for the club, my only expenses being my hog and my bar tab, so I have more than enough cash to sort this place out for my girl.

Starting with a fucking fridge.

Her cupboards are full of chips and boxes of Mac'n'Cheese, she's gonna get fucking sick eating that shit and there's no fucking way I'm eating it.

The bathroom tiles are cracked and missing in places. The carpet in the bedroom is fucking terrible, stained and littered with burn marks. Every inch of the kitchen cupboards need to be cleaned and repainted too, if not completely ripped out and replaced.

She only has a couch and some bags of clothes.

I text Rue and Trink before I head back into the living room to make up the bed. I'll need some backup and I don't care how hungover my sister is, she can come help out. I fall asleep with Angel's legs tangled up in mine, her arms across my chest and her face pressed up into my neck like she needs to be surrounded by me to sleep.

I sleep like the dead.

When I wake up the early morning light is streaming in through the broken blinds and Angel is already awake, watching me with this soft little smile on her face that has my words drying up in my throat.

She looks exactly like the name she chose, a fucking angel lying there on my chest and stealing my fucking heart away from me.

I wouldn't have it any other way.

We get up for the day slowly, like dragging our asses off of the couch is the hardest fucking thing we've ever done. Her ass keeps peeking out from under my shirt and, fuck, maybe getting up is the hardest fucking thing because spreading her out on the cushions sounds like a much better use of the morning than painting shit.

She laughs at me like pure fucking joy.

I grab my shit from my bag on my hog and I drag her into the shower with me, soaping her up with my shit so she smells just like me. When I leave everything where it belongs she quirks an eyebrow at me from where she's leaning against the bathroom counter.

"You leaving your shit here? I have to make space for it all in this tiny bathroom?"

I huff at her even if I am enjoying the hell outta the flirty tone she's slinging my way. "I told you, sweetness, I'm not fucking leaving. You better make sure there's room in your closet for my shit because we both live here now."

She huffs out a breath like she's mocking me but there's that perfect fucking grin on her face again. "Oh really? Are you paying rent or just freeloading off of me? I gotta tell you, my ass isn't worth what it used to be."

My palm slides down her back until I reach the mouthwatering curve of her ass. It's worth so much more than she ever made on that stage but this moment isn't about that shit.

It's about manning the fuck up.

"Sweetness, this place is yours. You bought it, you worked for it, you sacrificed for it, no one can take that away from you. But you're my woman. I don't give a fuck about that 'struck shit, you were mine from the second I saw you with or without the curse chiming in."

I grab her hips and draw her in closer, watching as her pupils dilate just from being this close to me and my dick is all for that shit. "I'm not paying rent. I'm covering the bills so you can go to school without worrying about a fucking thing. I'm getting whatever you need, covering everything, because you're mine to take care of. You're fucking mine."

Her cheeks flush and her head ducks. "You don't have to. I… I made sure I had enough. I've got it covered, just so long as—"

"So long as nothing, Angel. You'll leave it to me."

Angel startles at the knock on the door, ducking out of my arms to answer it. I already know who's coming so I get to work laying sheets down over the sofa and the floors.

"I brought beer and a tall guy, I think we'll have the ceilings sorted in no time at all. Speck was gonna come but Keely caught wind and threatened to drug him to keep him home. He's still a little… broken, I guess." Poe shrugs, talking a mile a minute, and Rue steps up behind her, his hands wrapping around her hips to nudge her out of the way. I scoff at him and get a glare in return.

I might be smug.

I got my girl wrapped around me all night, I got her pussy gripping me like a fucking vise and her soft morning eyes.

He's got blue balls and a fucking brat on his hands.

"Thank you for helping. I've got everything prepped in here and Tomi is doing the living room."

Trink slumps into the room like she's dying but she shoots Angel a smile, a real one which makes her whole face light up. "Let's get this over with, I need a fucking nap and that couch is comfy as hell."

Angel cringes a little and says, "Sorry, I didn't mean to get you outta bed—"

I'm about to chew Trink out but Poe butts in, always reading the room with ease. "Trink has nothing better to do. Besides, we weren't gonna let the boys have all the fun. Just promise me you won't let them choose colors, Angel, because Rue's colorblind and couldn't pick paint to fucking save himself. Did he tell you about the Indian he fucking ruined last year? Disgraceful."

Rue huffs at her and stalks into the living room, ignoring

Trink's cackling. "Where's the paint? Are we doing all of the rooms? Flower, quit bitching and call for pizzas. I didn't get breakfast and I'm fucking starving."

She grins at him and starts calling.

We get to work on the ceilings and the girls head into the tiny bedroom. It's the only room in the house with carpet still on the floor and Angel's already made a call about getting it replaced.

Poe helps her with the carpet while Trink plays with the bluetooth speakers and dances around like a crazy woman. At first I think she's not really doing anything but when we make it to the ceilings in the kitchen we find her scrubbing out the cupboards there. I haven't seen that kid ever do real manual labor before because she's fucking spoiled so I'm impressed.

I pay for the pizza when it gets here, shooting Angel down hard when she attempts to argue with me, and we eat it on the tiny front porch to get away from the paint fumes. We all talk about nothing, just cars and gossip about people around town and it feels so fucking normal.

After lunch. Rue drives Trink and Poe back to the compound, leaving Angel and I to go shopping for shit to fill her house up with.

I drive the Chevy even though she fusses at me like I don't fucking know how just because I'd rather have her on the back of my hog, wrapped around me with her honey scent all over the leather of my cut. That just means I'm a man who knows what the fuck he wants and my woman is the hottest fucking thing on Earth.

We pick out a fridge and a whole pile of shit for her house.

I tell her about Sunday family dinners and she stares up at me like a deer caught in headlights. It's cute but it's also non-negotiable, Keely is a force of nature and Hawk made it clear that he's expecting us to go along with anything she wants.

She wants to meet Angel properly and she wants grandbabies.

I'm only bringing one of those things up with my girl today because I'm not a dumbass and I know Angel has a list of shit she wants to get done before I tie her down like that but fuck if it isn't tempting.

I buy anything Angel so much as looks at, every little appliance and piece of cutlery, and when she gets flustered at me I swat her on the ass and ignore her fumbling words.

When we get back to her place Angel is distracted as she puts away her new shit. I give her some space to work her own shit out while I get her fridge installed and the other kitchen appliances plugged in.

She's still not right when I go for a shower.

I try not to let it eat at me but when I walk back out she's stripped down to my shirt again and something eases off in my chest a little. She's all over the place tonight, none of the calm she had this morning and it sets my teeth on edge. I don't fucking want anything upsetting her.

She ducks into the bathroom to brush her teeth and it only takes me half a minute to get the fold-out set up and the pillows and blankets sorted out. I strip down to my boxers and lie down to wait for her, my mood getting fucking worse as the minutes drag on.

She's freaking out about something.

I hate it.

She finally comes out and turns all of the lights off on her way in. One of the perks of this place being so tiny, there's not very far to go in the dark once she's got everything turned off.

She climbs in and even though she tucks straight into my body there's this tenseness to her, like she can't fully relax and I'm not fucking standing for it. There's no way I'm sleeping like this.

"What's happened, sweetness? Didn't we agree that I fix your shit?" I murmur, aiming for hushed and gentle for her nerves.

"I'm trying to figure something out with the floor in the bedroom. I could polish the floorboards but there's a few spots that need to be patched. I've just got a lot of classwork going on and Rue mentioned you'll be at The Boulevard more often so I need to figure it out."

I shift her around a little so she's lying over my chest more securely. "What happened to Kyle and his boys laying the carpet? You change your mind?"

She fidgets like she's being interrogated and I have to force myself to stay calm and relaxed underneath her even though I feel anything but fucking relaxed. "They cancelled the job and gave me the money back. Apparently they don't like money from my type. It's—I mean, it's not a big deal. I've got other options. I just need to figure out what I can get done around school."

My arms turn to stone around her.

There's no fucking way that I'm letting that shit fly. This goes beyond her being my fucking girl. Nah, this is about a girl who has worked her ass off and sacrificed fucking everything to support herself and take care of her own shit and I'll be fucked if I let people think they can treat her like that.

There's no fucking way I'm letting it go without setting them straight on how my girl will be treated around here.

I have to grit the words out through my teeth. "I'll sort it out."

She cringes a little like she'd like to get away from me but my arms stop her from going far. "It's fine. Honestly, what can I expect from people? We're in the south and I—"

I'm too harsh but I'm also fucking livid. "Don't finish that fucking sentence. I said I'd sort it out so you'll trust me to get it sorted out, Angel. Forget about it, sweetness, and go to sleep."

Chapter Thirty Three

Angel

I completely forget about the family dinner until there's a knock at my door on Sunday while I'm scrubbing out the bathroom. I haven't decided on tiles yet so it's staying just a little gross until I do.

Every time I ask Tomi for opinions on shit he tells me as long as I'm happy he's happy which is sweet but not at all helpful.

So I open the door to find Trink and Keely standing there with big casserole dishes full of food. I stare at them both like an idiot.

"Did Tomi not call? Course he fucking didn't. We're here for family dinner," Trink says, pushing me gently out of the way and bouncing her way into the kitchen.

Keely smiles a little softer at me, tilting her head and shrugging like there's nothing she can do about her unruly children. Fully grown adult children who she raised better than this, I'm sure.

"It's fine! It's totally okay, I was just—oh."

The words die in my throat as I look past her to see Tomi out on the front lawn with the rest of his family lifting a giant wooden table from a trailer. King, Hawk, and Hellion are already drinking while their sons do all the heavy lifting, the sounds of their joking and laughter ringing through the quiet streets.

No one would dare come out to complain when it's the bikers.

"They're going to take the table around back, Tomi said

you have a porch out there big enough for us all," Keely says, stepping in and kissing my cheek like this is all very normal and not completely fucking insane.

What the hell is happening here?

"I've already cooked all the meats, we just need to do salads. Reece has the drinks already, don't you worry about a thing."

I glance over at Keely and find her still giving me that same smile. I'm just standing around like a dumbass. "I could've… come to you guys. No need to bring everything to me."

Trink snorts from where she's raiding my fridge for cheese. "The table is a housewarming present from Mom and Dad, so you get delivery and the pleasure of the lot of us for dinner. Mom's being nosy, Tomi has been all secretive and she's getting fucking twitchy about it."

Keely shoots her a look and says, "I didn't want you feeling overwhelmed at our place again. Besides, Tomi said he wanted Rue here in the morning to help out with the cladding. I hope you don't mind, Tomi said it would be okay?"

Now I feel like an asshole so I rush to say, "No, it's—I mean, thank you. That's very kind of you and the table is lovely."

Trink snorts at me and shoos me into the bathroom to clean up for dinner. When I walk back out they're all ferrying the dishes out to the porch and I find myself in the kitchen with Speck, alive and only a little worse for wear.

I try not to cry.

He grins at me and gives me a look before I dart in close to give him a hug. "Fuck, I'm glad you're alive."

He scoffs at me. "I'm harder to kill than that, give me some credit!"

Keely walks in to see us hugging and before I can get too awkward about it she smiles at me like I've done something right… so I scurry away to find Tomi, ignoring Speck laughing his ass off at me.

The table is round, thank God, because there's no freaking way I'd be okay with sitting at the head and being the center of attention.

It's bad enough they all keep trying to talk to me.

It takes me three times as long as normal to get my shit

together and fill my plate up with food. The roast meats smell freaking amazing, the kind of homestyle I haven't had since my dad died, and there's every type of vegetable you could think of on this table.

"How are your classes going, Angel?" Keely asks, and I try not to choke on my potatoes.

"They're good. I'm in my final year so it's a lot harder, takes a lot longer to study and do the classwork."

"Doubled her course load too so she should be busy," Tomi says, nudging my leg under the table. I don't know what exactly he's trying to tell me because I'm too busy sweating under his dad's keen gaze. Fuck, his uncles both look like they're trying to look through my skin and into my brain from the other side of the table.

Trink sighs and pokes at her own plate. "You just had to be a fucking genius, didn't ya? Couldn't be a dumbass like Reece and I."

Speck scoffs and flicks a pea at her. "Speak for yourself! I've got more fucking brains than you and Rue put together."

Rue picks up his knife a little threateningly and Keely starts scowling at them all. By some miracle, that settles them all down.

Hawk shuts their shit out and says to me, "What are you gonna do after college?"

I shrug. "Accounting and specializing in taxes. I enjoy a challenge."

Rue chuckles under his breath. "You mean like how you spent one night on The Boulevard's books and managed to fucking save our asses? That didn't seem like it challenged you. Tomi had been trying for fucking weeks and it took you, what, an hour?"

Hawk's eyebrows draw together. "What happened?"

Keely gets up and starts handing out more beers, kissing cheeks as she passes them out and when she gets to me she does the same. Just throws me for a loop by including me in her little family.

"Mav was doing a shitty job with the books. Skimming from the top," Rue says, taking his beer from Keely and lifting his chin for the cheek kiss obediently. Even he accepts her fussing.

It's kind of adorable.

Hawk shoots me a look and I rush to clarify, "I'm not sure it was skimming on purpose or if he's just really bad at bookkeeping but yeah... if you got audited you'd have been in trouble. Tax evasion levels of trouble and my professors have all been talking about how cash industries are being targeted this year so it's only a matter of time. Very messy."

Hawk's eyes finally shift away from me and I take a breath. Jesus, his scrutiny is terrifying. "Guess we have a new accountant then."

Uh.

What?

"I'm not certified yet. I can't do it until I'm finished."

King shrugs. "That's only six months away, right? Perfect timing, ready for you to lodge our taxes. You can keep the books until then."

I swallow roughly, ready to try to talk my way out of it but Tomi jumps in for me. "She has classes, she's focusing on that. If she has time she can do them but class first."

That's not quite what I was hoping for in my rescue but I'll take it. Rue groans and says, "The garage needs the books looked at too. Diesel can barely fucking read, let alone sort taxes. We were using Vic but he's... not available anymore."

Everyone shares a look and I decide not to ask about him.

"Not available on account of a bullet in the brain," Trink whispers at me, and Tomi reaches behind me to smack the back of her head.

"Shut your fucking mouth, dumbass. Who's been telling you shit, anyway?"

Right.

She was just trying to scare me then. I get back to my plate and keep my mouth shut. I'm still feeling all sorts of... off. They're all treating me too well. I'm sitting here and waiting for there to be some change in them, something to happen and suddenly it's a bullet in my brain.

"Diego was yakking it up about the whole thing. Talking about how the club is losing credibility over killing our own members. I told him he was a fucking dumbass and then Law had to take a swing at him. I fucking hate the asshole."

Law.

Why aren't the twins here? Tomi nudges my beer at me and says, "Harbin's in town still. They're deciding if they're staying in Coldstone or going home to Mounts Bay."

Right. I keep my face blank. Like, super fucking blank because Rue starts eyeballing me like I'm the most fucking interesting thing on the planet. Joke's on him though.

The Devil is terrifying and I'm certain he'd know if I gave anything away.

"Did you meet Poe's sister?" King asks, and I mentally cuss him out. Of course he'd ask.

"I did. She's nice."

He stares at me. "Nice? Thorn acts like she's a fucking nightmare waiting to swoop in and lay siege on my club."

I take a sip of my beer and try not to freak out. "She was very nice to me. She loves her sister, would do anything for her. Everyone was nice."

Tomi's arm turns to stone where it's draped over the back of my chair. "Who the fuck else did you meet?"

Fuck. "Her sister and the boyfriend."

Trink makes this little squealing noise. "Holy shit, you met Morrison too, didn't you? Poe said her sister knows him too."

I giggle. "Yeah, I did. He was really nice too."

Speck cackles and I look over to find Tomi looking pissed.

"He was nice! I mean… all of them were nice."

I think that if it were only Rue here he'd be asking me a lot more questions but as it is he quit that line of interrogation so I guess not all of his family knows about his soft spot for Poe.

The rest of dinner passes a little easier. Tomi and Speck field a lot of the questions that get thrown my way, probably because I'm sweating so much.

Keely packs all of the leftovers into a plastic container and pops it into my fridge. I try to stop her but she waves me off. "You've got classes all week, this should keep you going for a few days. I'll drop some more off just as soon as you need."

I blush. "I'm fine. I mean, I'll totally live on ramen and energy drinks for the next few months but that's not anything out of the ordinary."

She laughs at me and slings an arm around my shoulders, pulling me in tight for a hug. "Tomi will be on the phone to me in a heartbeat to come fill your fridge up. He eats like a freaking bear, you'll be spending half your life down at the grocery store for him."

Oh.

Right.

I guess he's already told me he's not going anywhere so that must mean that he's… moving in? I just kind of stand there and let her hug me while I'm just struck fucking dumb over it.

"You broke her again, Mom. You need to ease up a little, she's all scared and shit." Trink cackles and finishes up wiping the dishes. I try to help her put them away and she shoos me off into the living room. I'm so freaking pissed the carpet isn't done in my room when Keely starts poking around.

"It's coming along so well! Poe was telling me about how much you guys have gotten done, she was excited to come help you paint. You should be so proud, Angel. Really proud of all you've done."

Tears well in my eyes and I clear my throat to try and shift them. "Thanks. It was... it was hard but worth it."

She nods and pulls me into another hug. "You call me if you need anything, you hear? If you're busy with classes or you need someone to talk to, you call me and I'll be around here in a snap. You've been taking on too much by yourself, you can lean on us a little while you get your feet under you."

I nod and clear my throat again, grateful when she lets me go and nudges me into the living room. "I think Trink is planning on parking her ass on your couch for the rest of the night, Speck too. Rue will drink with Tomi and the others until I drag Hawk home. Get yourself settled in, the Callaghans have made themselves at home.

She's right and they really do park their asses.

Eventually Keely drags the older men home but Speck messes around on my TV until he finds some action flick to watch and the beers just keep flowing. Trink ends up with her head in Rue's lap, whining about some guy she hates in her classes while he listens stoically. He's so gruff and grumpy usually, it's strange to see him just relaxing back and hanging out with his family.

Tomi locks everything up, checking the front and back yards before he settles on the couch with me, dragging me into his side and passing a fresh beer to Rue.

It's so comfortable, I fall asleep there without even meaning to.

I wake up in my own bed to the sound of pained groaning.

I find Tomi on his back, passed out and snoring next to me, and the door to the bedroom open. Trink is standing in the kitchen rummaging through my cupboards like a crazed woman.

I creep out of the bed and over to her.

"I should never drink with these assholes. I have school in an hour and my head is fucking thumping."

I smile and grab the aspirin. "I'll cook you some breakfast. A greasy breakfast will soak some of the alcohol up. Grab a shower while I get it sorted."

She turns her bleary eyes to me. "I fucking love you."

I shrug and push her gently to the bathroom. I get everything started on the stove top and I'm getting my goddamn stupid fucking oven lit when Tomi slinks up behind me, cupping my ass through the yoga pants I threw on to cover up.

"As good as the view is, get outta the way and let me do it. Have you got classes this morning? We'll go get a new one."

I've already looked up how much they are and I have to be careful with my budget, I still have to redo the bathroom, the carpet, and get a fence put up.

I move aside and shrug. "I've got classes in an hour. It's fine, I just gotta learn how to do it as fast as you do."

He lights it in no time and stumbles outside to pee because Trink's still hogging the bathroom. I bite my lip at the thought of old Mrs. Farley getting an eyeful of him.

The old bitch'll have a heart attack.

Rue stumbles through to the kitchen, eyeing the piles of bacon like a caveman and mumbles, "You need a fucking fence."

Then disappears outside to take a piss as well.

Gross.

Speck is still snoring when we all finally sit down to eat. I ask about waking him but Rue shakes his head. "More bacon for me, the little fuck can eat back at the clubhouse. Trink, pass me a beer. I need the hair of the dog."

It's all so freakin domestic.
This is what being a Callaghan means.

The problem is that I relax.

Now I have a life and a man and everything I didn't even know that I needed I relax into it and I forget that I wasn't just keeping secrets.

I was running from them.

I spend the day at the library studying and attending lectures. Tomi checks in constantly like he said he would but I'm feeling better today. My ribs aren't hurting at all and my lip has finally sealed over so with a little makeup you can't see a thing.

Poe and Trink both message me about coming over to help pick out tiles so I know I have to stop in at the grocery store. It's shocking to me how much food they all go through but I'm so thrilled at having them all around me that I can't really complain. I stop in at the store down the block from the Mugshots bar.

My saving grace.

I grab a cart so I can make a proper shopping trip out of it. I know all of the shit that Tomi likes and now I have a deep freezer I can get to filling it up with shit for him. Otherwise, I really will be in here every other day.

Everyone in the store is polite to me, all smiles and kind words as I pass and I just enjoy the hell out of living in this town.

As I walk to the back of the store I glance out of the window and I see the car.

My breath dies in my chest, my heart stutters to a stop, my skin begins to crawl.

I know whose car that is, that car is etched into my fucking soul for all of eternity but it should not be in Coldstone. No, it should be far away from me, all the way in Maryland where my monsters are supposed to stay.

Paul has found me.

I dart out of the grocery store leaving my cart behind and I fumble around in my bag for my keys. I need to get to the clubhouse right now. I need to get on the road and call Tomi.

A hand clamps over my wrist, squeezing it until I feel a snap, the pain like blinding light through my skull. "Jazmin, there you are."

A year ago, I would have frozen.

Fuck, six months ago I would have burst into tears and slid back into the mindset of that little terrified girl I once was. Alone and scared and utterly fucking helpless.

I'm not her anymore.

My keys are already in my hand so it's easy enough to lift the pepper spray and aim it at his smirking face, pressing the trigger on it and unloading the can of liquid fire into his face.

He snarls at me and his hand tightens on my wrist even more but I jerk myself away from him, ignoring the pain as best I can. He taught me how to do that.

Then I run. I fucking run so hard my lungs try to jump out of my chest. He's faster than I am and pissed the hell off but I know where I'm going, I know exactly where I'll be safe just the second one of the Unseen see me.

I just have to make it to the bar at the end of the road. One of the guys there will recognize me and I'll call Tomi. Fuck, or maybe he'll be there. Or any of the Callaghans. Someone.

Anyone.

I veer down the back alley because I know it'll slow him down to have to turn without anticipating it and when I get to the back door I find a biker there. His badge says Diesel but I really don't care who I'm running into, only that he'll help me.

His lip curls at me, I'm not expecting that at all, and snaps,"Girl, I know exactly how old you are. There's no way I'm letting you in here."

My voice is shrill and panicked even to my own ears. "Please. Please, I need to speak to Tomi now."

The heavy footsteps behind me catch Diesel's attention and I throw all caution to the wind. I just fucking blurt out, "That man is my rapist and if Tomi finds out you didn't help me right now, he'll kill you with his bare hands. I know it."

Deisel has his phone out and pressed to his ear the second the word rapist comes out of my mouth, shoving me inside the building and blocking the doorway with his body.

"It's me. Get your ass to Mugshots right the fuck now. Your woman was chased down here on foot by some cop cunt trying to touch her."

I stumble into the back room of the bar, disoriented and staggering but now there's a biker and a wall between me and Paul so I can lose my shit.

I really do lose my fucking shit.

I scream and kick the first guy who approaches me, the adrenaline of the chase still riding me, and so they all just leave me be after that. I stand there shaking in the hallway until Speck comes to find me.

"Angel, do you want to come sit down? Lemme get you a drink, girlie."

I can't move. I can't move or think beyond the terror pumping through my blood. Speck doesn't try to touch me or comfort me, he just stands there for a minute and then pulls out his phone. He taps on it and then carefully holds it up to my ear.

"I'm here, I'll deal with him."

I swallow but my voice still comes out like a rasp. "Tomi?"

His tone changes instantly, from that pissed off snap to the low, smooth tones he uses when I'm a shaking fucking mess. "Sweetness, you stay inside and stick close to Speck. You hear me? Park your ass in my booth and wait until I come get you. I'll sort him out."

Him. He says it with purpose, like he knows exactly who it is out there. "I didn't—I didn't know that you knew about him. I'm... Tomi, I'm scared."

I can hear Paul yelling down the line as well as muffled through the wall so I know Tomi is as close as he says. "Sweetness, do as I say. Just park your ass and forget about it. I've got it all under control."

I take a step away and Speck lifts the phone to his own ear. "Are you close? He's drawn a gun on Diesel and I think all hell is about to break loose out there. I've got Angel though, no matter what… He got his hands on her before she got away. I think her wrist is broken."

When he hangs up Speck leads me through the bar, his body covering me completely the way he has done a hundred times before at The Boulevard. I might not want him touching me but I'm also so fucking grateful for him to be here for me again.

He brings me some water and then stands close-by. My wrist is throbbing but I'm not about to leave the booth to get it looked at. Nope.

I'll keep my ass here until Tomi comes back for me.

I lose time a little. I lose the ability to focus on anything that isn't the little burn mark on the table in the booth. That little spot is my entire focus until Tomi gets here for me.

"Angel. I need to get a look at the damage to that wrist, sweet girl."

I startle and find Keely crouched down next to me, careful to not touch me even as she tries to get a good look at the damaged and mangled mess my wrist is in.

"I can't move. Tomi told me not to move," I croak and my eyes come into focus a little more. I find half the MC here at the bar. King and Hawk are both standing with Keely and watching me with careful eyes. I don't know what I've done to get them looking at me like that.

"Don't worry about them, they're here to protect you while Tomi and Rue take care of… that disgusting man. Can I check your wrist, sweetheart? I need to touch you to do it. I think it's broken."

I open my mouth to answer her when the door swings open so hard it bangs into the wall and ricochets back. Tomi is covered in blood, enough on him that Paul must be in pieces. The relief I feel only lasts a second.

He's going to be locked up for killing him.

He's going to prison for me.

The frozen, aloof, empty shell finally breaks and a sob rips out of me. I slump forward, my forehead pressing against the table, broken wrist be fucking damned.

"Fuck! Ma, why isn't she at the fucking hospital yet? She needs painkillers and the bone reset, for fuck's sake!" Tomi snarls as he stalks forward, and Keely doesn't rise up to the bait.

She murmurs quietly to me instead, "It's okay, sweetheart. Everything is going to be okay. Paul is gone. You are safe. I'm going to splint your wrist enough to move you and then we'll go to the hospital."

I can't stop crying. It's like all the times I've held it together through the worst situations have slowly been adding up and now I'm a mess.

"I can't do this. I can't have him go to jail for me," I mumble, misery choking me.

Keely finally reaches over, slow enough that I could stop her if I need to, and rests a hand on my back. "He's not going to jail, sweetheart. Our men have it all taken care of so let's just worry about the mess this wrist is in."

I nod but I can't move. No matter how hard I try, my body is frozen to the chair. Keely murmurs under her breath to me as she splints my wrist, all sweet and calming words that don't make sense to me now but they soothe me nonetheless. Then she takes a step back and Tomi scoops me into his arms and lifts me out of the booth, fussing until my head is tucked under his chin.

"I've got you, Angel. Ain't nothing touching you ever again."

Chapter Thirty Four

Tomi

Monday morning brings with it a list of shit I need to get done for my girl before I can get to work at The Boulevard. Rue tags along to help out. It starts with sorting out the carpet problem which is a simple fix.

I put a tire iron through the front window of the shop.

Not exactly subtle but I'm not in the fucking best of moods about this.

Rue starts cursing up a storm behind me and gets on the phone but I'm now made of fucking rage and I need some judgmental asshole to bleed.

There's screaming and yelling coming out of the store but I ignore it as I step through the giant fucking hole I've just made in the glass.

The girl at the reception desk is frozen in fear but when I straighten up she squeals and bolts out the back, brushing past Kyle as he walks through to figure out what the fuck has happened to his store.

I'm a little more pissed about this than I thought because I have him pinned to the wall by his throat before he can blink.

Rue follows me through the hole and says, "Put the guy down, Tomi. You really wanna spend the night in lock-up because you can't control your temper?"

Without a fucking doubt, I'd do hard time right now if push comes to shove because I'm not fucking leaving without getting this fucking fixed.

"This ain't about my temper, this is about respect."

Kyle tries to speak but my hand is tight and he has no

fucking air for words right now.

Rue scowls and stomps over to us. "What about respect? What'd you do, asshole?"

"He's refusing to do Angel's carpets. Thinks he's too fucking good to do work for my girl, made her feel like shit in my fucking town. I think he deserves a helluva lot more than a broken fucking window."

Kyle forces some words outta his mouth, the stream of them like a wheeze, "Look man, my momma took over running the office because Georgia's been off with the baby. I didn't know she cancelled your girl's appointment, I'd never let that shit fly."

My hands loosen just enough around his throat so he can breathe a little easier and he takes some deep, gulping breaths.

"I'll look up what she was after and head over there right now with my boys, get the job done this morning. The club has always done right by us, I don't want no trouble."

That's the answer I'm looking for but I don't feel any fucking better about it, not without being able to really beat the fuck outta someone. I huff out a breath and let him go, watching as he collects himself.

"You tell your momma she so much as side eyes my girl on the street and she's dead, woman or not. I'm not fucking around."

Kyle gulps and nods, rubbing at his throat and scurrying off.

Rue huffs at me. "Are you gonna just beat the shit outta anyone who looks at Angel wrong from here on out?"

I shoot him a look as we both walk back through that hole. "You got a problem with that?"

He smirks back at me. "Nope. Guess you'll just have to quit bitching about me doing the same with Poe though, won't you?"

Asshole.

We go back to Angel's place to start the cladding on the exterior walls while the carpets are being laid. Another perk to the place being small, it doesn't take too much time to get the front done and when we stop for a beer it already looks a million times better.

A little home instead of a shit hole.

When we have one side done as well, we call it quits for the day and ride out to go find a new oven for the kitchen. I don't want Angel struggling with fucking anything anymore and even though he'd rather poke his own fucking eyeballs out than pick appliances, Rue tags along to help me move shit.

I'm walking through the store when the call comes through.

Who'd have thought there were so many options when it comes to fucking ovens. I want the biggest and best for her but the kitchen is too small for that shit. Kinda narrows my options.

Rue stares at the stickers on everything like this is all fucking beyond him. The man can rebuild an engine with his eyes fucking sealed shut but looking at appliances is just too much. "You need to look at renovating her place. Stick some more bedrooms on it, bigger kitchen and a dining room."

I give him a glare. "Her house is fucking fine."

He huffs at me. "Her house is fucking impressive. I'm not knocking it, I can't fucking believe what she did. I'm just saying, Sunday nights are going to be there on the regular. We're all going to crash there too, fucking often. That's just how this shit goes so you might wanna look into expanding a bit. If she's down for that. Have you talked to her about patching yet?"

I want to so fucking bad. "Not yet. She's only just got the house and we're getting settled in. I'm taking my time for now."

When my phone starts ringing I don't even think about what it could be, I just scoff at the caller ID and pick up. Before I get a chance to say a goddamn word he snaps, "It's me. Get your ass to Mugshots right the fuck now. Your woman was chased down here on foot by some cop cunt trying to touch her."

A cop?

I leave the store at a run, Rue cursing and bolting after me without question. I doubt he knows it's Angel, probably just thinks it's something to do with the rat but I'll take the fucking backup.

I push my hog so hard I practically fucking fly to the bar. It's a fucking good thing Coldstone is a tiny speck of a town because I'm there before my mind has even come online about what I'm gonna do to him.

I'm going to enjoy this death, replay it in my head every fucking night like a lullaby to get me to sleep.

Rue and I park on the street, just ditch our bikes and stalk down to the bar but there's no one at the front door. Rue jerks his head at me, signaling the back alley and I nod.

My phone rings again and I curse as I look at the damn thing. Speck. His bike is here though so he must be calling for backup. "I'm here, I'll deal with him."

"Tomi?"

My heart stops in my chest at the sound of her voice. The broken, desperate, scared fucking edges to it. "Sweetness, you stay inside and stick close to Speck. You hear me? Park your ass in my booth and wait until I come get you. I'll sort him out."

"I didn't—I didn't know that you knew about him. I'm... Tomi, I'm scared."

The death I'm going to give this man… fucking biblical. "Sweetness, do as I say. Just park your ass and forget about it. I've got it all under control."

There's noises down the line and then Speck speaks. "Are you close? He's drawn a gun on Diesel and I think all hell is about to break loose out there. I've got Angel though, no matter what."

I owe him. "I'm here. Keep her safe."

He grunts and then says, "He got his hands on her before she got away. I think her wrist is broken."

I drop my phone and I move, too fucking pissed now to think clearly or form a plan beyond blood and pain and fucking rage.

I see him standing there, raging out and holding up a badge like it means something.

"I'm an officer and she's a fugitive, if you don't move I'll open fire."

"Fuck, is that him? Is that Angel's step-cunt?" Rue snarls, and I nod, way beyond the point of forming words.

This man.

This man broke her, gave her those screaming nightmares, made her flinch at my touch, scared her so bad she slept on the fucking streets for years. Put her in the types of situations that destroy little kids' entire fucking lives and I'm going to do more than fucking kill him.

Nah. I'm going to wipe him from the face of the planet. They aren't even going to find a fucking fingernail from this cunt when I'm done.

I start towards him but he's too swept up in his own little fucking fantasy to realize I'm there until I take him to the ground. He's a cop, or he was one, so the asshole knows how to fight but there's no chance he could get away from me or my club right now. No fucking way.

Rue stands there and watches as I beat the fuck outta the step-cunt.

There's a lotta anger issues in me about this man, a lotta rage I need to fucking pulverize into his face and I'm fairly certain he's already brain-dead by the time I get my knife out and slit his throat because there's nothing left of his face.

I've caved his skull in with nothing but my fists and pure fucking fury.

Rue grunts at me, "We need him in pieces, brother. Hard to move him otherwise."

Pieces. I can fucking do that.

I'm covered in blood by the time the rage clears a little and my mind comes back online. I glance up from the bloody corpse to see the alleyway blocked with a couple of dumpsters and Hellion's truck.

"I called for backup. I've got Keely in there with Angel, just focus on cleaning this mess up because it's broad fucking daylight, brother," Rue murmurs, and Hellion stalks over to us, a cigarette hanging out of his mouth.

"Cecee is gonna fucking love this shit. You did good work. He got what he deserves, the sick fuck."

I nod along but I'm too fucking pissed to comment.

We get the pieces of Paul loaded up into trash bags and into the tubs on the back of the truck. Rue grabs a hose and cleans down the side of the building, doing what he can to get rid of the blood.

I wait until this place doesn't look like a crime scene before I go find my girl.

Angel's wrist is broken and needs a cast.

Keely watches over her through the whole process, directing people so they don't touch her any more than they have to, and I keep a hold of Angel's other hand the whole time, scowling at everyone.

I changed clothes before we came in.

I'm too fucking twitchy after the step-cunt shows up to let her outta my sight so once she's fixed up I take her home for a shower and then we both head into The Boulevard so I can work while she naps in my office.

Diamond left the place in a fucking mess and when I work my way through the inventory I start to wish I could kill the fucking bitch all over again. Rue actually comes down to help me out and Speck shows up with him, looking just a little more alive.

Angel lights up when he slumps into the chair next to hers in my office.

"Miss me? Fuck, I didn't think I'd be seeing you down here so soon. Though I gotta say, I'm glad I'm not in danger of having my balls ripped off around you anymore."

She giggles at him and I give him a glare. "Think twice, asshole, because if you keep sweet talking her I'll risk Keely's wrath to knock your front teeth out."

Angel shoots me a glare and I leave them to it, focusing on the pile of work I have to deal with instead of them both gossiping about which strippers Speck is chasing after now.

Rue runs inventory on the bar stock and then interviews the new bouncers, scowling and being a fucking nightmare to everyone who crosses his path. It's a good thing, every last one of the girls is tiptoeing around us all now they've seen what happens when you overstep the Unseen line.

Rue's attitude just reinforces that shit.

We leave together after the sun comes up, Angel yawning and looking fucking edible even with the cast on her wrist.

We make it out to the motorcycles out back, laughing and joking around, and even keeping an eye out for shit we miss the slight woman hiding in the shadows.

"Jazmin?"

Angel stumbles a little, tucking into my side. Speck turns to look at the woman and startles. I know who she is before I turn to get a look at her but when I do there's no hiding she's Angel's mom.

"I know it's you, baby, I've had everyone looking for you."

Angel glances up at me but I'm too busy frowning at her mom like she's a fucking demon. I read that fucking file. I read it, I know exactly what this woman has done.

Angel doesn't exactly know that though.

"Can we leave? Can we get out of here?" she whispers, and I finally look away from her mom and back down at her.

Her mom steps forward and I move in front of Angel on instinct. "Jazmin, please. I kicked Paul out. I kicked him out so you'd come home. I didn't know! I didn't know what was going on."

Angel's hand slips into mine. "Tomi, I really need to leave."

I'd rather kill this woman but instead I nod and sling an arm over her shoulders, pulling her into my body as we walk. Speck takes up Angel's other side like a shield but Rue stays behind, meeting my eyes with a nod.

I swing onto my hog and Angel gets on behind me with ease now she's had enough practice, her arms tight around me as Speck grins at her from his own hog.

"You don't look like a Jazmin. Angel, through and through."

Her giggle is a little choked but it still sounds better than the thready tone she had before. "Words like that'll get you killed, Reece."

I huff like I'm pissed but really I'm happy Speck can get her laughing. "Stop fucking calling him that or he really will get fucking buried."

Rue stalks up behind us all and gets onto his bike. He meets my eye with a scowl.

Angel's arms tighten and I ask, "Anything important?"

He shrugs. "Just a whole lotta regret that's too fucking late and a warning about Paul so she doesn't know we have that covered. C'mon, it's late and I'm fucking beat."

Regrets.

It's too fucking late for regrets.

When we get back to the clubhouse the guys all wait around until Angel is off of the bike and then Rue hesitates for half a second before pulling Angel into a quick hug. He's slow enough that she can stop him if she wants to but she is so shocked that she lets him. Then he stalks up the stairs, the clubhouse quiet this early in the morning even with some stragglers still drinking from the night before.

"Jesus Christ, are you going to cry over a fucking hug? Angel, you're killing me here," Speck says, and I glance down to see that Angel's lip is trembling just a little as she shoves at Speck when he goes in for a hug too.

He clutches at his chest like he's wounded, cutting a little too close to home with that one action, and then jogs up the stairs after Rue.

Angel turns to me and I lean back against the seat of my hog, watching her carefully.

"I'm fine."

I scoff. "Sweetness, you're never fucking fine. I need to start tanning that sweet ass of yours every time it comes outta your mouth."

She sighs and tips her head back to look up at the early morning sky, the colors of the sunrise still bright. I wait her out. I've learned enough about this fierce and fragile girl of mine to know that's exactly what she needs.

"She knew. She knew what was going on long before I ran away. She didn't want to give up her grief for my dad for long enough to help me… to leave Paul and figure this shit out on our own."

I blow out a breath and tug her into my arms until she's staring up at the sky again with me wrapped around her like a shield.

I decide that life is too fucking short to keep shit from her. "Listen to me, Angel. I love you and I'd die for you. I've given you my patch so that if I do have to lay down my life for you, my club will protect you too. She's fucking nothing to you now. You have me and my family, my mom is yours now too. Forget about some weak bitch who never deserved you in the first place."

She moves to bury her tears into my chest, her hands clutching at my cut. "Tomi, I didn't know I could love someone like I love you. I'm not sad about my life anymore. I'm not happy about that shit and there's a lot of shit I'd go back and change but I'm not sad about it anymore either. I had to get through it to get to you so… I can live with that."

I hold her tight enough that her demons can't come to play until she's ready to move.

It's the least I can do.

Chapter Thirty Five

Angel

When we finally get into Tomi's room at the clubhouse I feel fucking fried.

I'm not sure why we're here instead of my house but when I ask he shrugs at me, "I had to move the bed for the carpets and I just wanna pass out. Plus, there's food already here and I just want you to fucking relax for a bit."

Seems reasonable enough, I can't argue with that.

The room is much cleaner than it usually is, no dirty clothes anywhere and all of the computer stuff is piled neatly on his desk. When he notices me looking he grins at me.

"I've gotta start packing. Keely came and saw the mess it was in and chewed me out."

Oh.

Right, he's moving in with me because we're a couple and he loves me. Jesus, it still sounds so fucking strange to me. I sit down on his bed and fall back on the pillows. The nap at The Boulevard barely took the edge off of my exhaustion.

"Angel, I need you to tell me about why you ran away. I wanna hear it from you."

Oh God.

My eyes immediately well up and I almost choke on my tears because it's been a long time since I tried to tell someone, and that had gone so fucking badly I swore never to speak of it again.

His eyes are piercing and true on mine as he sits on the bed with me, clearly there's no getting out of this. "My dad died. He had cancer, he was a cop for fifteen years back in Maryland.

The good type too, everyone respected him and he did what he could for people."

Tomi nods and pours me a drink. This time, I don't choke on the taste as I down it in one go, handing it back to him for a refill. I need the courage. "Paul was his partner. His best friend, my so-called uncle, and when my dad got the terminal diagnosis he asked Paul to take care of me and my mom."

My fingers fuss with the the edge the the blanket on the bed, my mind a fucking mess as I try to distract myself from not only the horror of my words but the very real chance that he'll leave me the second I've poured the story out.

"He stayed at the house and I loved him being there. He always called me princess and would do my hair for me with ribbons before school. My mom was a shell of herself after my dad and she wouldn't get out of the bed. Eventually, Paul stopped going home and just moved his stuff into the house. My mom started doing better and they fell in love. Got married, the whole deal. I was happy about it. I missed my dad like nothing else but at least I had Paul right?"

Tomi's face hasn't changed once and that gives me just a little courage. Like maybe if this is just ancient history, a sad story he wants to know, then maybe we can just fucking forget about it. I mean, I'm not stupid. I know it's going to change things but if I think about it too much I'll fucking run.

"So after the wedding, Paul sends my mom on a nice holiday with her friends. He tells her that he'll take care of me so she can just let her hair down. After the year she's had she deserves some time to herself. She's so fucking grateful to him, doesn't think twice about it."

I can't say the words, I can't describe any of it, but I'm well-versed on talking about it without mentioning the details. "Two years later, I got what I thought was my period and passed out at school. Woke up in hospital with police officers and a social worker. Turns out I was pregnant without even knowing about it and the bleeding was a miscarriage. There's a lot of questions when that shit goes down with an eleven-year-old. I tell them everything, every little fucking detail of it, and you know what they did?"

Tomi shakes his head and I take one last mouthful of the whiskey and push the glass away from myself. Anymore and

I'll spend the rest of the night puking my guts up.

"Nothing. They did fucking nothing about it. Paul told them I was a willful, disobedient whore of a child. Acting out about my dead daddy. A disappointment to the family. My mom backed him up."

I see it.

I see the moment the cracks start to form in Tomi and his entire opinion of me changes. I try not to let him see just as clearly my heart breaking.

I have to finish it now. "He started beating me after that. He didn't just… yeah, it was a lot worse. So I learned to keep my mouth shut, keep my head down, and the moment I could, I ran."

Silence falls between us and I can't be the one to break it this time. I can't give him anything else, I've run dry.

"Who did the fake ID for you? It was fucking good."

I rub at my neck. "I met a guy at my school. He wanted me but everyone knew I was the baby killing whore… yeah, rumor was I threw myself down a flight of stairs to kill the baby and make sure no one found out about my secret boyfriend. Middle school was a fucking lovely place. Anyway, the guy wanted me but not enough to deal with being the guy with the whore so he would invite me around after hours and try to fuck me. Well, his older brother was a forger and I somehow managed to convince him to give me the ID to get into clubs and then I ran. I'm not sure he even knew how good his fakes were."

Tomi nods and opens the bottle of whiskey, drinking it straight and as though he needs to forget the whole thing.

"I'll head home. I mean, it's probably best if I do," I mumble and his eyes narrow at me.

"You walk out that door and I'll be on your ass, dragging you back. You're here for the night and then in the morning we'll go home and finish the cladding on the house. We'll get the bed set back up and go pick out a new oven. We'll pick the fucking tiles too. You can have a shower and I'll go get us food. I think it's pizza night. Pick a movie, I just wanna lie around for a few hours before we sleep so you don't have your nightmares. Go on, go get clean."

It makes no sense.

I shower and scrub every inch of myself that I can, struggling with the cast that I've had to wrap in plastic. Next time I'll have to ask Tomi for help but he's being very… careful with me.

I can't argue with the fact that I need it.

Tomi yells through the door that the pizza is cold but I like it best that way. When I step out of the bathroom, clean and ready for bed, he's stripped down to his boxers and lounges back on his bed like some sort of cover model, a fucking living god, and I feel so freaking unworthy in my dad's old sweatshirt and a pair of his boxers that I've rolled the waist on until they fit.

He glances up from his phone at me and looks at me like I'm wearing lingerie, his eyes hot as they drag over me. I feel self-conscious but not uncomfortable.

I know exactly what to expect from him.

"Get your ass over here, I'm hungry and I don't know which type you want."

I shrug and stumble a little over my own feet as I make my way over to him and I pick up a piece of the pepperoni. He grunts and shoves half a slice in his face at once. "Pick a movie, I'll text Rue and make sure he's coming tomorrow to help out."

I nod and mess around on Netflix until I put something on. Jurassic Park is an old favorite of mine, something my dad used to watch with me because he loved it and he'd make me swear not to tell my mom about it. I haven't been able to watch it since he died but… sitting around at the clubhouse with Tomi, eating takeout and drinking a little whiskey, this is kind of my safe place now.

I can't believe that is even possible but here I am.

"Stop with that face, Angel."

I smile at him and kneel on the bed to fix the pillows, to make a nice little cocoon for us both. He watches me carefully and when we're finally tucked up together I pull off the last plaster from my heart.

"My name isn't Angel. Not really. My dad used to call me that so when Derrick made the ID I asked him to use that name."

Tomi's chest rumbles under my ear and he moves the

empty plate to the floor, flicking the lamp off and leaving us in the dark. "It suits you."

I think it's precisely because he doesn't ask me what my name is that I tell him, even though he heard my mom call out to me I want him to hear it from me.. "It's Jazmin. Jazmin Vaughn. I… don't want to go back to being called that."

He nods and strokes back my hair, his fingers trailing over my shoulder. "Nothing has to change, sweetness."

I fall asleep on him before the movie ends and I don't have my nightmares, as if the steady thump of his heart beneath my ear is enough to keep my demons at bay.

I never want anything to change.

When we leave that night, the bikers all tip their heads at me or clap Tomi on the back as we pass but none of the girls try to talk to me. It's not exactly a bad thing but they all stare at me with hatred. I ignore it.

It's not like it's new.

"I'm about to gouge some eyeballs the fuck out," Tomi growls and I squeeze his hand a little.

"Please don't. I'm fine."

There's a scrape of boots on the carpet behind us and then Rue says, "Fine never means fine. Tomi, you better lay down the law before it bites you in the ass. Shoulda done it months ago."

I glance back at him with a smile and he smirks back, the type he gives Tomi and Trink all the time.

The type he gives his family.

"Fuck them. We'll meet you back at the house tomorrow morning. We have something to do tonight."

The tattoo shop is sleek and clean, lots of black marble surfaces and gothic art on the walls. I feel extremely uncomfortable even walking in but Tomi is as relaxed as ever. I guess with all of his tattoos he's spent a lot of time here before, and when I thread my fingers through his he gives them a squeeze.

"What the fuck are you doing here? I didn't think there was an inch of you left to tattoo."

I peer around Tomi to look at where the voice has come

from only to find the tattoo artist standing a few feet away from us and snapping off a pair of black gloves.

I gulp.

He's huge. Like, freaking huge and his body is even more densely covered than Tomi's. His eyes are... weird, too intense for his face and the smile on his face makes me feel super uncomfortable.

"My old lady needs a patch and I need her name on me. Clear your evening."

The tattoo guy laughs and when Tomi doesn't join him he finally notices me standing behind him. "You're serious? Fuck. I didn't think I'd see the day. 'Struck or just the regular sort of romance."

Am I the only one who didn't know about this curse?

Doesn't matter, Tomi answers, "'Struck. Just know that if you try your usual brand of shit I'll happily deal with the club's consequences to put a bullet in you."

Okay.

Now I'm scared.

The tattoo guy chuckles and motions us into the back room. Tomi leads but he keeps a firm hold of my hand.

"How big is this patch gonna be and where am I putting it? Pretty little thing like her shouldn't be tramp stamped."

I hear Tomi's teeth grind together. "Shut your fucking face up and just do the job, Onyx."

He explains the whole thing, where it's going and how big, but I still don't know what this tattoo entails. Onyx obviously does because he has it all drawn up and the stencil on me in under a minute. When he directs me to lay down on the chair Tomi sits close enough to choke him out if he needs to and then he holds my hand the whole way through it.

It doesn't hurt all that much but I would do just about anything to get the guy to stop touching me. Just because I can take it from Tomi and his family now doesn't mean I like other people touching me. Nope, I'd still rather stick pins in my eyeballs.

"Speck wants to learn how to tattoo. Maybe I should vouch for him when he finishes up prospecting, just in case you want something else," Tomi mumbles, bringing my hand up to his lips to kiss my knuckles when Onyx finally finishes. He offers to show it to me with a mirror and I shake my head.

I don't want to spend any extra time here and to be honest, it doesn't really matter to me what the tattoo looks like. It matters to me that Tomi's eyes flare when he looks at it, that he loves it, and that it'll mark me as someone the Unseen protect.

That's what I care about.

"Right. What do you want then?" Onyx says as he cleans up his station and starts pulling out sterilized equipment.

"I want Angel tattooed on my throat. And I want Jazmin tattooed in the patch on my back. Put it in the skull."

My heart kind of stops beating a little, just skips along a little before it recovers.

"Two names? Your old lady is fine with that?" Onyx says, scoffing and inking up the gun.

Tomi doesn't explain it. He just strips off his cut and his shirt, handing them both over to me, and then sits through both of the tattoos. The one on his throat stands out, stark against the patterns he has there already, and the one on his back blends in a little more.

When we leave together, hand in hand, he huffs at my curious look. "Jazmin is still your name. It's what you signed for your house as. If you wanna change your name again I'll get that too. Whatever you need, sweetness."

I blush. "I'm sticking with Angel."

He pulls his jacket off and slings it over my shoulders before we climb back onto his bike, marking me as his and protected by the Unseen. He waits until my arms are tight around him before we speed back down the highway towards Coldstone, one of his hands holding my cast steady now I can't get as good a grip on him.

When he stops and pulls his motorcycle up alongside my old Chevy everything just feels fucking… right in my life now.

Mrs. Farley is on her porch, glaring at us both and I wave at her with a bright smile, channeling Poe just a little because I know it'll piss the old bitch off. She's already made her displeasure at having bikers living on her street well-known.

I'm killing her with kindness.

Tomi just wants to plain kill her.

"Angel, you need to stop playing with her and get inside before I bend you over your porch railing and fuck you out here in front of the old bitch."

My mouth snaps shut at his command and my legs get moving even as a giggle bursts out of me. Tomi chuckles and stalks up behind me, flipping the bird at my neighbor and laughing at her gasps of horror.

I get the front door unlocked and throw my keys down onto the countertop in the kitchen. When I move to turn around Tomi grabs my hips, kicking the door shut behind himself and pulling my hips back into the heat of his body before sliding a palm down my stomach to my pussy. "Did you wear something pretty for your old man, sweetness?"

My legs start to shake.

He leans down to bite me where the soft skin of my neck and shoulder meets and grinds up on my ass like he can get off on that alone.

Fuck maybe he can.

I turn into jello in his arms, my whole body melting back into him as a moan rips out of my throat. I feel desperate, achy and needy to have him, like there's no other way to relieve the pressure building up inside of me.

When I'm sure there's a nice big hickey on my neck he finally lets me go, spinning me around and slamming his lips down on mine like he wants to eat me whole, as if the taste of my lips on his is a drug he can't get enough of.

Everything feels different this time.

I don't know if it's because he's told me I belong to him or if it's something to do with him, like he's changed his mind about me and so now he's treating me like I'm his everything, but I choke on a sob.

I never expected to feel this way.

"Fuck. The bed's still in pieces," he says, his voice a low rasp over my lips as he breathes the words into our kiss.

I groan at the thought of stopping but he doesn't hesitate to hike me up into his arms and walk us both over to the living room. I wriggle to get down, both because I think I'm too heavy and because I need to make up the fold-out bed before we can fit together, but his arms tighten around me.

"Don't fucking move. I don't care about where we fuck, Angel."

I bite his lip in retaliation but it backfires on me, a low

groan rumbling out of his chest as his hands drop down to squeeze my ass, pushing me further into his body like he's trying to fuse us together.

"Can I at least set up the bed? This can't be comfortable for you and I don't want to get a rug burn on the floor."

He grunts at me like I'm insulting him and he lowers me to the couch, his lips never leaving mine as he kisses me so deep I'm not sure where I end and he starts.

Then he drops to his knees, his hands steady and sure as he undoes my jeans, tugging them down my legs and groaning at the sight of the tiny black silk triangle between my thighs as he pulls away from me to get a good look.

There's already a wet spot there, his kisses and rough handling of me like a drug I'm hooked on.

"Take your shirt off. Leave your bra on though, that's mine to take care of when I'm ready."

He catches my eyes with his own and holds my gaze, the fire there for me already burning hot. I bite my lip, squirming at the intensity, but he doesn't blink or look away. It's like he knows just how devastating this is to my entire being, that his eyes looking into my soul like this could destroy me and he's forcing me to be so open to him because nothing on this Earth could get me to look away right now.

It's even more intense when he hooks his arms under my thighs, pulling my body closer to him and spreading me open, all without breaking the eye contact.

My heart begins to pound.

This doesn't feel like all of the times before, like all of the times we've fucked desperately. This is too soft, too slow, too perfectly addicting for such a dirty word.

It feels like he wants to make love to me.

Do bikers even know how to do that? Fuck, do I? I've only ever been fucked, by force or with hate and the look he's giving me now is riding the edge of too much, too soon.

But he forces my eyes to follow his as he leans down and our eye contact only breaks when he buries his face into the apex of my thighs, breathing me in as he tugs my legs again to pull me in. It's as though he's desperate to be as close to me and the wet heat hidden behind that thin layer of silk as he can be.

He uses his teeth to move my panties aside, licking a stripe up the center of me and then dipping his tongue inside me. Fuck, his tongue drags along the most sensitive parts of me and when he finally circles my clit with it my thighs clench and tremble with the effort it takes to keep them open.

He licks and sucks my pussy until his chin is dripping, my orgasms shaking my body apart until I think I might fucking die, and when he finally gets up to undress me fully I slide off of the couch and onto my knees.

"Fuck my face? It's been too long."

He grunts at me like he's been shot, grabbing a fistful of my hair and shoving me down the length of him until he hits the back of my throat and I have to swallow around him to get him further down.

"Fuck, sweetness, you're too fucking good to me. I wanna come down your throat but I miss your sweet pussy gripping me so tight. Fuck, I'm never gonna get enough of you."

I can't help but touch myself, my hand slipping down into the mess he's already made and my pussy is so ready for him that three fingers slip in as easy as breathing. He doesn't notice at first, not until I groan and come all over my own hand, and he jerks my head back so he can see.

"Fuck, get up. Get up so I can fuck you properly, you can swallow for me later."

I groan and stand up, pulling at his shirt until he's naked and he's quick about getting my bra and panties off too.

Then he picks me up again like I weigh nothing and fucks me against the wall in our living room.

I barely have time to figure out where the hell to put my cast so I don't knock him out with it by accident but he doesn't give a fuck, just slams me into the wall and pounds my pussy like he'll die if he doesn't come soon.

His desperation pushes me over the edge with him and it's only once he sets me down that I realize we didn't use a condom, his cum slipping down my legs.

I stare at him in shock and he shrugs. "I'm not worried if you're not worried, sweetness."

Chapter Thirty Six

Tomi

"Why the hell does one man need forty black t-shirts? What in God's name would you need that many fucking shirts for, Tomi?" Rue growls, spitting mad about moving my shit in this heat and Angel starts giggling when Trink piles on.

"He's on the never-ending hunt for one that's tight enough to show off all his abs and shit. Fuck, now he's got Angel he might let himself go so it's a good thing he's got some spares."

I ignore the lot of them from where I'm moving all of my tech into our bedroom. Angel is sitting on the brand-new carpet trying to stuff my shit into the tiny closet space we have left but without tossing some of the stripper outfits it's just not going to work.

I won't let her ditch any of them.

Look, I hated her working there for sure but I also spent a lotta time picking out favorites and there's no way we're ditching them before I get my own private dances in them. I've started talking about putting a pole up in the living room but Angel keeps looking at me like I'm trying to kill her and pointing out that my parents come over for dinner every other week and she might actually die at seeing Keely's reaction to it.

I could handle it.

"You know the real reason he has so many is because he's fucking shit at keeping up with his laundry, right? You're going to spend your whole life washing up after that man," Speck says, setting down another box in the bedroom and wiping his brow off on his sleeve.

Angel shrugs and mutters, "I'll be too fucking busy cleaning up his goddamn books. He'll have to figure it out."

Trink jumps on my bed like a dramatic teenager and sighs, "He'll just call Mom to come sort it out and she'll come running because he's her favorite."

I shoot her a glare but Angel just laughs at her. "I saw your birthday present, don't fucking start that shit."

She giggles and sticks out her tongue to me. "Did you see what Poe's sister sent her? Fuck me, I've never seen a Shelby in the flesh before. Fucking pretty as hell."

Rue starts grunting and huffing in his bad mood and I share a look with Speck over it.

"Fucking millionaires. Makes you wonder where the hell they're getting all that money from."

I share a look with him. Gotta be drug dealers, between that and the Ferrari? The suit on the guy that showed up here? Definite drug dealer.

I get Speck and Rue busy hanging some shit on the walls while I get my desk together in the bedroom. Trink helps Angel rearrange all of my shit in the closet until it fits. It's bursting out and a definite hazard, but it fits.

Angel stretches like a cat and murmurs, "I'm ordering pizza. I just want to veg out tonight after getting all of your shit sorted out."

I tilt her head back and kiss her, slow and sweet. Trink snaps at us, "Can you two keep your fucking hands off of each other long enough for me to finish my goddamn drink? It's fucking sickening."

I huff and turn to snap at Trink, "Shut up or fuck off, they're your only options."

"You need more fucking rooms in this house, I'm sick of sleeping between dipshit one and dipshit two when we're here."

I actually don't mind her whining about this because I want to remodel the place a bit. Angel sighs and pulls me down to her lips again. "Maybe we will need to build another room for them."

I smile and grunt, "Three more rooms. An office, a spare room and a nursery"

Angel freezes and glares up at me. "What the fuck would

we need one of those for?"

A slow smirk stretches across my lips. "If you don't think the next thing on my list isn't filling this house up with kids then, sweetness, you got me all wrong."

She looks like a deer in fucking headlights for a second then she snaps, "I'm kicking you out. Rue! Grab the boxes, he's out."

Rue laughs like I'm joking around with her, I'm not, and I grab a fistful of her hair to tug her head back and expose her throat.

"You're not kicking me out. You're staying here with me forever while we build extra rooms on for all the fucking family that's going to be here all the damn time and for all of the kids we're having. I'm getting old, we gotta start soon."

She tries to shake her head at me, "I thought you were joking! I thought you were being like 'oh lets not panic' not 'lets have a fucking baby'! Tomi, I'm still in fucking college. Did you forget I'm barely fucking eighteen? Jesus, what will your mom think? Absolutely not."

Trink fake gags and stalks back out into the kitchen, slamming the bedroom door as she goes. Perfect. I haul Angel up and into my arms before walking her to the bed. "It'll be awkward for you to eat pizza with my cum dripping down your legs but I guess I'll have to show you now how serious I am."

Everything in my life is fucking perfect.

Except for the problem that there are still fucking rats in my club.

Our next shipment arrives untouched without any extra cargo, and the one after that is the same. You'd think we'd be happy about it but all that says is that the rats are digging deeper. We might have found a few and taken them out but there's no way we're out of the fucking woods.

When I arrive at the clubhouse for church I scan the bar area and find Angel giggling with Trink and Poe in a booth, bottles of beer around the three of them as they talk shit. I know for fucking sure it's shit because Trink is waving her arms around like crazy, Poe's laugh is like an evil fucking cackle, and Angel's cheeks look rosy red as she giggles along with them.

Fucking perfection.

"We gotta find this fucking rat. Gotta keep those girls safe and happy, it's the whole damn reason we started this club. Live outside the law and keep the family together. Safe. Fucking happy." Hell is fucking wasted, drunker than I've seen him in a long time.

I guess King's homecoming means his load has been lightened and with less on his plate he can let his hair down a little more.

I shrug and take a beer from him. "Nothing is touching them while we're around. Fucking nothing. Those three and Keely are top priority, as long as they're okay then we can sort the rest out."

The back door to the supplies closet opens and Speck comes out with a keg, laughing and calling out to Law like a fucking clown. I frown at him and when he gets an eyeful the grin slips from his face.

"Fuck. What have I done now?" he groans and I point my beer at him.

"Open motherfucking heart surgery, dickhead. Stop lifting shit until you're cleared, I ruined my best shirt keeping you alive, have some respect."

He rubs the back of his neck and shoots a look at Hellion. "Pops asked me to grab it. What am I supposed to do, say nah?"

I shoot my uncle a look but he's fucking wasted. "You get Law or Lyn to do it. They're around here to fucking help until you're cleared, don't be a dumbass. Keely will have a fucking heart attack of her own if anything happens to you again and I'll fucking gut you for stressing her out."

Law slaps him on the back as he passes to grab more beer and Speck stares up at me like a fucking kicked puppy. I smell the sweet honey scent of Angel before his face changes to the friendly grin he's given her from day one.

There's a reason I told him I was 'struck, makes him someone I could trust around her one hundred percent.

Her hand is soft as it slips into mine and I swear to fucking God my head grows three sizes at that tiny touch. She trusts me, trusts us, enough to do that here and in front of the entire clubhouse.

I want to sling her over my shoulder and carry her the fuck to bed.

"It's my turn to get beers, sorry. Do you want me to grab my own, Reece?"

Hell scoffs and walks off, too drunk to talk to Angel without sounding like an asshole and bowing out, thank fuck. I pull her into my side and jerk my head at my dumbass cousin. "A few bottles won't kill him to lift, deliver them with a smile, Reece."

He groans and walks off, shooting a grin at Angel as he moves. She sighs and tilts her head back, pouting those lips of hers at me until I wanna bite them. "Why are you being an asshole to him? He helped me clean out your room today, he drove me over to Southern Miss and walked around with me. He's been very helpful."

My eyes narrow as I look down at her. "You went in? What the hell did you have to do on campus?"

She bites her lip and I snap, swinging her around until she's in my arms and staring up at me with her pupils blown out, all soft and liquid with lust for her old man.

Her voice is breathy and fucking intoxicating. "I was changing my course load, I had to sign some papers. I've doubled what I'm doing now that I'm not working. I hope you weren't lying about covering the electricity and gas because shit's about to get fucking rough if you were."

Trink calls out to us like a fucking brat when I swoop down and kiss her, long and deep like she deserves, ignoring the jeering and fucking idiocy around us. That's what being in this club feels like, grinding on my girl in the middle of the fucking clubhouse so everyone knows for fucking sure who she belongs to.

"Get the hell off of her before I fucking puke, dickhead," Trink snarls at me, and Angel pulls away from me. I level my asshole of a sister with a savage look but she just grins back at me.

"Friday nights are church and ladies night, right? So get on, we're busy talking about important shit."

Angel huffs and squeezes my hand before she pulls away.

"How exactly is forcing me to listen to your conquest stories important shit? Posey looks ready to puke and I'm about there myself."

I give Trink another glare and she bounces off, her shorts too fucking short and Angel follows her, a little more comfortable around here now no one is watching her.

Well, Monroe is still watching her but we all know to just ignore that cunt.

King stalks out of his office and yells out, "Church!"

I shoot Speck a look to keep an eye on the girls and then I take my beer with me to the chapel. Rue is already in there, scowling at some paperwork and I park my ass next to him.

"What's happened?" I murmur, and he scowls up at me.

"The Demons went into Shreveport last night. Took out thirty men while they slept. Someone let them in, got them past security, and unlocked the brothers' bedroom fucking doors so they could be slaughtered in their sleep."

Jesus fucking Christ.

I take the papers from him and see the schematic of the Shreveport clubhouse, all of the security the Demons would have to get through to pull something like that off.

Motherfucking rats.

King shuts the door and walks back around to his chair but he doesn't sit down. Nah, his face says he means fucking business.

"I'm done playing around and keeping fucking quiet about this shit, so I'm saying it like it is. There's rats in our club. Not just this one but the whole of the Unseen MC and all its charters have been infiltrated by Demon scum. Now I was hoping to work my way through every last member until I could clear you but Shreveport just got hit hard. Luis just lost thirty good men while they fucking slept because the Demons are too fucking scared to face us like men. That being said, I'm not standing for that shit happening here under my roof so I want every man in this room to know if you're not my blood, consider yourself on notice."

Dead fucking silence.

No one wants to say a fucking thing to that and King nods like that's the right answer. "If you're a rat, you'll die. Simple as that, we will find out and you will fucking die. If you're not, you better start pulling your fucking weight to prove yourself and your loyalty to your patch. Better yet, find me the fucking traitors. This club is my fucking life and I'll be damned if I let Grimm fucking Graves take it from me."

When I leave the chapel I get to the girls before anyone else can, Rue hot on my heels. I want my girl safe but there's more than that getting me fucking moving.

"Are we just gonna fucking forget that there's a fucking Graves in this building? Are we just gonna let the obvious fucking rat sit there in our clubhouse?" Diesel snarls as he walks up behind us and I turn on my heel as I block him from getting any fucking closer to Poe.

Rue turns with me and I think Diesel is breathing his last fucking air.

Except King stalks out and saves us from the murder. "This club swore an oath to protect Alby's granddaughter, you lay a hand on her and I'll assume you're a fucking rat for disobeying my orders like that. Unseen don't break oaths, that's Demon shit."

I don't move an inch until Diesel huffs and stalks off. Rue is practically fucking shaking when I finally turn around to find Trink and Angel covering Poe like they were expecting someone to try to shoot her.

Makes my blood fucking boil.

"Get her home, brother. This place isn't safe for our girls right now," I mutter and he nods sharply. Poe and Trink both follow after him, quiet for once.

Angel tucks into my side as we leave together.

Shit's about to get a lot worse before it gets better.

Epilogue

Tomi

Months later

We're woken by my phone, the ringtone cutting through the quiet night air like a knife. I pull away from my woman, rolling to sit up and grab the phone to find King's number flashing at me

Fuck.

"What's happened?"

Angel sits up in bed next to me looking like a wet fucking dream, all naked and perfect and fucking bitable.

"You need to get your ass to the clubhouse. Law's dead, Diego's been shot, and Rue's about to go off the fucking rails."

Jesus.

I lurch out of the bed and start cursing up a storm. No way I want the type of hell that's just showed up on our doorsteps, not with my Angel blinking up at me like I'm her fucking savior and instead I'll be dragging her into a life of death and destruction.

Lawson is dead.

"What the fuck happened? Demons?"

There's shouting in the background and then King heaves out a sigh. "Has to be. I need you here right the fuck now, Tomi, someone needs to talk Rue down and he's already knocked two guys out."

Fuck.

"I'm on my way." I prop the phone up on my shoulder as I pull on my jeans and start rummaging for a shirt. Angel sits up in bed and starts looking for her phone in the sheets.

"Bring Angel. We're going into lockdown until we can get a handle on this shit. And Tomi?"

I pause with my cut halfway on at the tone of his voice. "Yeah?"

"You need to be ready for what you're walking into."

Fuck. "I've seen plenty of blood and death, King. I'm solid."

The shouting gets worse down the line and I hear him walking away.

"No, Tomi. It's worse than that."

What could be worse than a dead brother, another full of lead, and my cousin losing his fucking mind over it?

"Posey is gone."

Also by J Bree

The Mounts Bay Saga

The Butcher Duet

The Butcher of the Bay: Part I
The Butcher of the Bay: Part II

Hannaford Prep

Just Drop Out: Hannaford Prep Year One
Make Your Move: Hannaford Prep Year Two
Play the Game: Hannaford Prep Year Three
To the End: Hannaford Prep Year Four

The Queen Crow Trilogy

All Hail
The Ruthless
Queen Crow

Standalone Novels

Angel Unseen: An Unseen MC Novel

J Bree is a dreamer, writer, mother, farmer, and cat-wrangler. The order of priorities changes daily.

She lives on a small farm in a tiny rural town in Australia that no one has ever heard of. She spends her days dreaming about all of her book boyfriends, listening to her partner moan about how the wine grapes are growing, and being a snack bitch to her two kids.

For updates about upcoming releases, please visit her website at http://www.jbreeauthor.com, and sign up for the newsletter or join her group on Facebook at #mountygirlforlife: A J Bree Reading Group

Printed in Great Britain
by Amazon

40172163R00223